A NEW
DARK AGE

Published under licence by Brown Dog Books and
The Self-Publishing Partnership Ltd, 10b Greenway Farm, Bath Rd,
Wick, nr. Bath BS30 5RL

www.selfpublishingpartnership.co.uk

ISBN printed book: 978-1-83952-382-3
ISBN e-book: 978-1-83952-383-0

Cover design by Kevin Rylands
Internal design by Andrew Easton

Printed and bound in the UK
This book is printed on FSC certified paper

THIS IS REBEL FICTION

A NEW DARK AGE

A RECKONING

ROSS PATRICK

BROWN DOG BOOKS

They hang the man and flog the woman
That steal the goose from off the common
But let the greater villain loose
That steals the common from the goose

The law demands that we atone
When we take what we do not own
But leaves the lords and ladies fine
Who take things that are yours and mine.

1764 poem of unknown origin opposing the Enclosure Acts that took common land into private ownership. The Enclosure Acts between the sixteenth and nineteenth centuries, historian E.P. Thompson described as 'a plain enough case of class robbery.'

I

Rain lashed the quartered panes of Esme Sedgebrook's bedroom window. It provided a lighter counterpoint to the repeated thuds of her dad's bed banging against the wall in the next room. Esme squeezed her eyes shut to block out the invasive images coming to mind of her dad humping his young second wife, Lizzie. At least he'll be in a better mood tomorrow, Esme hoped.

Lizzie had been named after the old great queen apparently. Her mam must have been sentimental for a time before the fall. Esme wondered how like the old queen she felt, in the quiet, listening to Esme's dad snoring next to her. And how like the old queen did she feel when she was cleaning out the chicken coops, gutting and feathering the birds, or cleaning out the chitlins of the pig after the butcher had been to slaughter it, or when her hands wore the stain of being dipped deep into buckets of blood to catch and remove the veins before the blood puddings could be made. And Esme stretched to think of other images of Lizzie's not-so-regal life as the second wife of Esme's dad to distract from the creaking bedsprings in the next room.

Lizzie arrived three years after Esme's mam had run off to London with her lover, the bailiff. Dad said London would suit her. Esme understood the inference, because folk around the Fens didn't like London people. 'They ain't like us in the city.' Her dad said one time, when the vicar had been around. 'They don't look out for one another. They in't a community.'

Canon Braithwaite, the vicar, smiled at the comment, his views communicated through slight movements of the corners of his lips. Dad said shaking Canon Braithwaite's hand was like gripping a fish. Esme's dad added to his comment on London folk, 'They're only interested in money and pleasure.' When Canon Braithwaite was gone, Esme's dad would repeat his view that the vicar only came by himself for silver. He made Esme sit with them and take tea; Esme suspected he did this to avoid being left on his own with Canon Braithwaite.

The vicar was important in the community; his grace and approval could bring favours and Dad said they couldn't be too careful, what with Lizzie's youthful misadventures still colouring the community's view of her to some extent. Dad smiled as he said this and looked at Lizzie long enough for eye contact. Recognition demurred Lizzie's eyes in an uncomfortable combination of guilt and gratitude. The community had viewed Esme's dad favourably for putting his own miscreant wife's abandonment of Esme behind him and being willing to rescue Lizzie from desperate penury or worse.

When Esme's dad brought Lizzie home to live with them as his second wife, she brought an infant daughter with her. Tilly followed Esme around, tiny hands clutching skirts, such that Esme sometimes felt inclined to push her in one of the canals or bogs just for some peace.

When Lizzie came of age she eloped with a water-boy called Michael and the stolen petty cash from the dredging company he worked for. A year turned before Lizzie returned home penniless, with child but without Michael. A tale was told that folk chose to believe to temper disapproval, in which Michael had died protecting Lizzie and their infant child from Roamers.

Roamers were drawn from those that the Collapse had left with nothing. They drifted along by-ways between towns that had forbad them from staying. To survive they would ambush isolated travellers. They'd stalk the Great North Road, but as the more affluent brought more security, they were attacking simple folk more and more and drifting deeper into the Fens. 'They're never more than four or five.' Esme's dad boasted how he and a couple of other men had ran a group off who were harassing some unfortunately naïve travellers who'd been complacent about the quality of Fenland roads. 'Filthy buggers in rags, they were,' Esme's dad said and laughed how it was 'tough to tell which were men and which women; all hair and quick, nervy eyes.'

Esme's father had announced his intention to take another wife to Esme one evening, with the statement, 'It's time,' as though appropriate timing should be the guiding concern. 'We didn't have you to be our ewe baby.' Ewe baby was what locals called young daughters who stayed with aging parents rather than married, because the daughter never grew up, always a little lamb traipsing around with her parents. It would not be Esme's fate for she was fair of face, if a little shy, and it was assumed she'd make someone a bride.

Esme turned sixteen the previous year and was relieved to avoid what would have been her debutante season the summer that followed. 'Another summer ripened,' Esme heard her Aunt Jackie tell her dad, passing an eye over Esme, stood to one side feeling gormless, like a piece of livestock. Esme's dad smiled and winked at Esme, which left her unsure whether it should be treated as a joke or whether plans might quietly be in process.

Esme heard talk of how girls that pass their eighteenth summer feel the hurry-on that each year the choice reduces, and so each year the choice becomes less your own. Esme's Aunt Jackie said as much when she had been over last. Her eldest was only sixteen when she married, and she was with child inside a year. Then there was the mayor's boy, a year Esme's senior and said to have an eye for her, though they'd barely spoken. Aunt Jackie told Esme's dad, 'That would be a propitious union.' Esme barely knew Tom, the mayor's son. Sometimes she slipped into thinking these conversations weren't about her, or not in any real sense, only for remembrance to quicken her blood. The horizons in the Fens were distant; there was no need for prison walls. She couldn't just go to London like her mam.

The Fens stretched from Cambridge in the south ninety miles north to Lincoln, where the cathedral rises high and on clear days can be seen from thirty miles or more. The flooded marshes were sixty miles at their widest, from Peterborough in the west to the other side of Downham Market, where hills appearing as islets gradually step clear of the bogs and pull the land with them as they move east towards Norwich, on the other side of which the land once again falls away into arpeggios of East Anglian fjords and islets.

When Esme's dad left for work, the house breathed easier. Esme heard his bicycle on the gravel yard before rising.

In the corner at the end of the upstairs corridor, suspended from a coat-hanger on the old coat stand, Esme's wedding dress waited for her to step into like a new life measured by others to fit her.

Esme remembered Lizzie taking her to the haberdashers so that she could buy the material that she would make the dress from. It hadn't seemed to Esme real then, watching Lizzie and the shopkeeper roll out lengths of fabric, spools of thread and boxes of pins and needles. The shopkeeper, Mrs Fitch, was a middle-aged woman with pink spectacles carried on a chain around her neck and resting on a proud bust. Mrs Fitch carried a tape measure she used to measure sections of air out between her hands. She would then draw her hands together, only to repeat the action as she talked to Lizzie. Esme had been stood to one side with Tilly, so as not to get in the way. Eventually, she had been called over to be turned around, the tape measure stretched across her shoulders, down the length of her side and around her waist. With the dress on, Esme felt like a hand wearing a shoe.

At the kitchen table, smiling, Lizzie bounced Tilly on her knee singing a nursery rhyme...

This is the way that ladies ride,
Trit trot, trit trot, trit trot.
This is the way that gentlemen ride,
Clipperty-clop, clipperty-clop, clipperty-clop
And this is the way the farmer's boy rides,
Gallopy, gallopy, gallopy-clop
And drop down into the ditch.

She pretended to drop Tilly between her legs, only to sweep her up again, laughing. 'The rains have broken. The weather might be good this Whitsun.'

Esme shivered in thought of the day, little more than a week hence. Her choice to not think of it had made it arrive no slower.

Esme had a journal, a notebook she kept in a box beneath her bed. Her dad didn't know about it. She didn't attend to it daily, but when something needed expressing. The journal listened without question or criticism. The journal alone seemed to be on her side. In it, she wrote of the forthcoming Whitsun marriage season. 'There are kites anchored on the horizon, waiting. They are like bobbing goblins, grinning and boasting in wind-carried whispers something fearful yet tempting; an exotic pleasure only hinted at. If given lightly, its sweetness could stain.'

Esme had been reading Rosetti. Her mam had worked at the library in Fenby before it closed – when it closed, she acquired boxes of books that would otherwise have been landfill. When Mam left, her dad packed away most of Esme's mam's belongings. He didn't pack the books up; they were left in the bookcase in the parlour. When her mam left, Esme decided that she would read every book and that before she reached the last her mam would have returned. It wasn't that she believed in it but that she could distract herself with the notion. She no longer sought distraction from Mam's abandonment of her; she now sought distraction from her own forthcoming wedding. For Esme, acceptance was supposed to be the first stage of excitement, when acquiescence was all that was really required of her. She blew out her cheeks.

Lizzie was right, the rains had broken. The kitchen's stable-style door Lizzie had left the top half open, yawning, sucking light into the room like oxygen for lungs. Esme yawned; Tilly smiled at her. Esme was still wearing her white nightshirt but bare legged sunk her feet into her boots by the back door and stepped outside. They lived south of Fenby in an old pumping station that used to dredge the overflow water. Esme's dad used to be a navigator, leading a group maintaining canals, brooks and lodes, pumping and draining water from fields. Later he set up as a contractor with agricultural machinery, he said the house was perfect and it was cheap because it had been left unused and unoccupied since the dredging company went bankrupt.

Esme's mam had still been around then. Esme remembered her mam watching Esme play in the yard, or out back when her mam was working in the garden or pegging out the line. After she had gone, Esme would walk around the yard as though waiting for her mam to return. She'd gaze at the entrance, but Mam never showed. 'You were still just a child.' Her dad said to her. 'It was the first time I ever saw you sad, proper sad like. It broke my heart.' He sniffed and turned his gaze away. Esme looked where he looked but saw nothing. Maybe he looked for Mam's return as well.

It was five years since Mam left. Esme replied to her longing, 'I must learn to be happy living without also. After all, it is self-pity when I can see, even if there is little I wish to look upon.'

From the old pump house, Esme could see the slow-moving river, lily pads and branches of willow and sycamore decorated, drifting along by the causeway for a mile or two and leading the way to the Three Sisters Lake. The sisters in question were the sisters of Wendreda, the patron saint of Fenby whose bones and relics had only in recent times been rediscovered and reinterred in the crypt of the church that bore her name. Wendreda followed the spiritual path. Those who don't follow the path of the three sisters, who all married kings, are encouraged, like Wendreda, to follow the spiritual path. When Esme's severe grandmother recounted this story, Esme commented it would be hard for every girl to find a king to marry. Her grandma pinched her cheek in what Esme supposed must've been affection. 'It meant marrying someone who'd treat you as a queen.' That, though, could only be known after she married, and her fate was set.

So, it was in the Three Sisters Lake, behind the church on the edge of Fenby, where the rite of Neptune took place. She'd seen them, walking into the water in their white, cotton muslin dresses. A boy is sent in after the girl. She is to keep walking, though, without looking back, with the water rising higher around her, as if drawn down by Neptune himself to his kingdom of chasms, fathoms deep. It is bad luck for the girl to look back. The couple returns to the shore married by a priest, wading in the water, cassock soaked. He then binds the couple's wrists with a ribbon the girl will have worn in her hair, a shawl is wrapped around their shoulders and the couple return to their families and friends to be the centre of attention and celebrated.

On the morning of Whit Monday, it was tradition for the newly consecrated young bridegrooms to hang the bedsheets of their newly deflowered brides from their matrimonial windows to prove the virtue of the girl and signify good fortune and fruitfulness for the ensuing marriage.

When Esme's dad married Lizzie, these rituals were passed over, with it being their second marriages. Esme wondered if second marriages would be more successful than first marriages because at least there should be no delusions. Then Esme remembered the previous night's sounds from her dad's bedroom and wondered if Lizzie had known what she was letting herself in for.

Esme was distracted from her daydreaming by Sarah-May cycling into the yard. She part-fell, part-jumped from the bicycle she discarded, back wheel still spinning. She threw her arms around Esme, because that was the sort of person Sarah-May was, and announced, 'There's something I need to talk to you about and there's not much time.'

Esme knew a ridge across part of the fen only wide enough to walk single file to a small, elevated clearing and three trees. Sarah-May followed, she spoke, and Esme listened. A murmuring of birds rose away over the fen. There may have been the shotgun crack of hunters in the far, unseen distance. 'So, we're leaving, Esme, next weekend, after Whitsun.'

'What'll happen to the cottage, the geese and everything?' Esme asked.

'That old Mrs Quickfall, you know, she'll sort everything after we're gone,' Sarah-May replied, taking care with her footsteps along the narrow track.

Mrs Quickfall had asked Esme's father if his daughter would visit when Esme was young, soon after her mam's departure. Mrs Quickfall was old but dyed her hair red, sometimes there was a ring of grey visible at the roots when she was overdue a 'touch-up'. She'd married but her husband had died young when their house burnt down. They'd had no children and Mrs Quickfall never remarried. She described herself as 'old school' and said she found it harder and harder to understand the way the world had become. She lived in a grand old house stood well back from the main road on the way into Fenby. Mrs Quickfall would give Esme cake, ask her about herself and read her sad stories from a large hardback book she kept in the sideboard that would cause them both to end up crying. Mrs Quickfall said, 'The sky is so big in these parts, sometimes it seems to ache. When the sky is so big, time is slow to move. Sometimes, painfully slow.' Esme reflected the first audience for Mrs Quickfall's comments might've been Mrs Quickfall herself.

At the raised clearing, Esme and Sarah-May sat between trees with the flooded fen mere around them. 'Why now?' Esme asked. She knew she should've been pleased and excited, for she knew they had talked about moving on many times with comment the world was so much bigger than the Fens. Esme wondered if it was envy that caused her words to taste metallic and bitter in her mouth.

'There is a meeting this week in the cellar at the Seven Stars. You mustn't say anything as it's a secret meeting for dissenters.'

'Dissenters?' Esme asked.

'Mum says we shall meet people who can help us arrange passage. There is a march, a great rally being planned in London.' London, Esme thought. Everyone goes to London if they can; everyone except me.

Sarah-May's mam wasn't like the other women. Esme was quietly in awe of Sarah-May's mam. She was in her forties, she had dark hair with rainbows of thread twisted and twirled around loose tresses. She had a smoked laugh and a smile that suggested her thoughts were already way ahead of whatever devilry Esme may have thought of. She grew strange herbs and made curious potions and balms and some of the local people called her a witch, but when they were ill, and they couldn't afford medicine, they'd make the journey along the narrow Fen Road, past the lavender where bees clustered in summer. Their cottage was old with small windows and a large yard wrapped around where geese wandered as security and protection for Sarah-May and her mam, squawking and shrieking if disturbed and batting their wings. Their kitchen had a well beneath the table, which Esme thought neat, as they just pulled the table aside to draw water. An old dyke had been developed intó a canal that crawled along the side of the narrow track across the fen towards where a windbreak of poplars screened their cottage.

The grey sky pressed heavy and low over the shivering fen water. Esme sat and leant against a poplar tree. Sarah-May sat against a neighbouring tree. Esme gazed out over the wind-rippled sedge and the yawning, pale sky. Two teal ducks took to air and flew low over the fen, the flapping of their wings when taking flight caused ripples to hurry out behind them and across the still water. 'You should come with us,' Sarah-May suggested to Esme, though she didn't look at her as she said it. Sarah-May added, as absent-minded sounding as a breeze, 'You wouldn't have to marry then. There's nothing for you here, Esme. You say so yourself.'

It would only make Esme sad to wish for impossible things. Water that passes along the river doesn't return, her dad would say, and too much water has passed now.

Esme looked out again over the sedge and reed and fen. Closer to, she saw two white butterflies rise, spinning and dancing around each other in an unravelling double-helix. However much Esme wanted a life greater than Fenby and the old pump house, this was her home. It was all she had.

II

'We've been invited up to the mayor's house,' Esme's dad announced at dinner, like he'd been saving it up since getting in. 'Mayor asked me personal like.' He sniffed; it was his poker tell that he had a hand he liked. 'It's a chance for you to get to know the son.' The invitation had of course been accepted on Esme's behalf.

Esme studied the roots in the thin gravy she was pushing around her plate. There was some meat, but when Esme's dad noticed her ignoring it, he reached over with his fork, stabbed it, and moved it to his own plate, commenting to Lizzie, 'If Esme don't want it. Decent bit o' mutton.'

'There was a maggot in it,' Esme said. Her dad's eyes burnt, and she noticed his jaw tighten in clench, just for a moment, but she saw it, and he saw that Esme saw it before she returned her eyes to her plate. The mutton that wasn't smoked or salted as macon to preserve it for the winter was kept in a cold box outside the backdoor. The mesh nailed over the hinged front was supposed to stop the blowflies and other insects getting in – it didn't.

'There's note up wi' the odd maggot, girl. It's extra protein.' Esme's dad laughed without smiling. 'Do you good.' He then informed her they'd be going up to the mayor's house the following evening, after which, chomping through the stewed mutton, he told them about some members of the clergy who were attacked on the Lincoln Road. 'Most probably headed 'tween Crowland and Ramsey. Party included a couple of young novice nuns, apparently.'

'Were they hurt bad?' Lizzie asked.

'Killed, half a dozen, the nuns raped first.'

'And them brides of Christ,' Lizzie exclaimed. 'Mother of God! Whatever next?' Lizzie wasn't religious, and Esme imagined, with a contemptuous curl of her top lip, that Lizzie leapt at that expression because it conveyed an appropriate horror; how empty and ridiculous. Esme wanted to challenge her dad's account, as she'd heard a different tale from Sarah-May.

'Do they know who did it? Were it the Roamers again?' Lizzie asked, still shaking her head. Esme thought it was hard to imagine Lizzie, young and in love, skipping between villages, trying to stay one step ahead of trouble with her lover, Michael. Esme imagined she might have liked Lizzie more then.

'No, it weren't the Roamers, it was Hereward's people.' Words twitched inside Esme's mouth wanting to respond. Her dad looked between Lizzie and Esme's faces, chewing and smacking his lips. 'Bloody troublemakers, well I tell you: they'll have gone too far this time.'

'That's not right,' Esme said. The room paused. Even the oil lamp by the door, which hung from the ceiling with the slight sway from a draft, stilled. Esme's knee started to jitter under the table but only the cat could see. 'Sarah-May says those stories aren't true.'

'Oh, and your Sarah-May knows better, does she?' Esme's dad slurped his tea. 'What about Hereward's crossbow bolts then?' Hereward was an outlaw who came from the Norfolk Islands, feeding the Fenland rumour mill. He led a militia, the Woke. They were said to use crossbows more than guns for their guerrilla attacks, and so when sorrowful bodies were found pricked like voodoo dolls the accompanying black magic was said to be of Hereward.

'It wasn't Hereward.' Esme felt angry, far angrier than she should, for what difference did it make which of them was right?

'Sarah-May says if it's not the Roamers then they always blame Hereward around these parts.' Esme's dad snorted derision, but Esme persisted. 'I mean, if you wanted to blame it on them, you'd use crossbows, right?' Esme glanced in appeal at Lizzie, who shrugged.

'I'll tell you.' Esme's dad pointed his knife vaguely, gravy dripping. 'It'll be their fault when the state agents come to carry out the census. They're drawing attention when folks around here just want to be left to get on with their lives. They'll not be forgiven for bringing trouble to the Fens.'

Esme's dad looked at her, knife and fork paused in his hands. If there was no reaction, then he would take her silence as defeat and agreement.

'Before the census comes, they send out spies, often church people.' Esme didn't look up from her plate as she spoke; she wouldn't be able to contest what he said if she looked at him. 'There's a preacher called Joan Ball.'

Esme's dad studied her; the name had travelled with a cloud over it, even if Esme's dad couldn't prove it was from where the rain fell.

'Sarah-May says she's the people's preacher. Joan Ball says some in the clergy are too impressed by princes to care as much as they should for paupers. Apparently, some act as spies and informants for the state because people trust them.'

Esme lifted her eyes and found her dad's studying her. 'Sarah-May says it was the spies they attacked, and she says there were no nuns raped, that was just put about to scare people.'

'Why would they want to scare people?' Lizzie asked.

'Good point,' Esme's dad agreed, presenting Lizzie with an approving smile.

Esme withdrew her hands beneath the table, where her

fingertips tapped the tops of her thighs. 'In rural parts the church has information on virtually everyone, so Sarah-May's mam says.'

'Oh, it's the mother now.' Esme's dad laughed, laughed at Esme, who lowered her burning face yet further.

'Sarah-May says you know who the spies are because they'll drift around the markets and sit quietly in the corners of pubs, listening. After a couple of weeks, they move on and soon after the agents come to carry out the census and collect their tax. They already know where to go and who's doing what before they arrive.'

'Rubbish!' Esme's dad said, laughed, shook his head and laughed again. Esme suspected that there was no conviction to his laughter and folded a smile behind her lips. 'What rubbish,' he repeated. 'Whatever next? You girls do dream up some stories.' He took a big mouthful of his stew and, still chewing added, 'Best keep quiet with such silliness when we're with the mayor tomorrow, hey?'

* * *

The mayor lived on a long tree-lined avenue in a house set back and standing over three stories. Esme wore a blue dress with a pattern of white flowers, her hair braided into a French plait. Esme's dad had an old car he rarely used that ran on ethanol. 'We can hardly cycle around,' he joked. He looked Esme over and smiled.

Outside the mayor's house, Esme lifted and dropped on the balls of her feet.

Their heavy-set housekeeper answered the door. She invited them through to the drawing room, plush with deep, patterned rugs, heavy curtains and a piano in a corner, ornaments and figurines dotted around. There were shelves of books and great, heavy dark furniture. The south-facing bay windows had their curtains fully drawn back, so sunlight flooded through in bright bands lighting whatever they struck, and if they struck nothing they would light up the air they passed through.

Esme looked into the room from behind her dad's shoulder for a moment before she followed him in. There was Thomas Baker, the mayor, his wife, Mrs Mayor, and Thomas Junior, the son. The mayor was a large man wearing a dark formal suit. He had a big face, smiling, with an outstretched hand for Esme's dad to shake. Esme noticed he wore a gold signet ring on his little finger. Esme had seen him before only at civic events in his mayoral robes and sash and necklace. She mentioned this to her dad on the way over; he laughed and told her it wasn't a necklace, but he didn't know what it was called.

'Ah ha!' the mayor laughed. His voice furred up with the strong accent of his less august origins; loud so even his laughter, however hearty, was intimidating. 'Come in, come in. Greetings, Keith.' He smiled, using Esme's dad's first name, and Esme's dad beamed as he accepted the mayor's hand. 'And this must be young Esme.' He didn't shake her hand.

The mayor's wife stood perfectly still with her hands held before her, halfway between her husband and the settee that her son stood in front of, the way someone might if told to stand. The mayor's wife was more refined than her husband. She waved her right hand in a low arc before her and said, 'Please sit, there's no need to stand on attention.' Esme's father laughed, a little awkwardly Esme thought. 'Hello, Esme.' The mayor's wife addressed her.

'Hello.'

Esme and her father sat next to each other on a settee that didn't sink as they sat. The mayor's wife and the re-seated son sat across a gilded coffee table. The mayor stood behind his wife. 'This is our son, Tom,' the mayor's wife said, indicating Tom Jr, adding with parental faux chiding, 'Well then, Tom, say hello.'

'Hello,' he said, then looked to Esme's dad. 'I'm very pleased to meet you, sir.' He tried to sound polite and confident, but Esme noted his knee jittered. It was barely noticeable, but Esme saw.

Esme noticed how her own knee was jittery also. She felt sympathetic for Tom Jr, trapped like her in this awkward situation, until it occurred to her that Tom had asked for this ordeal, she had not. Esme wondered whether she was supposed to feel flattered that Tom enquired about her. 'Somebody has to do something, or nothing will happen.'

Esme felt a quiet, impotent despair at the prospect of marriage to Tom Jr, however nice and well-mannered he may have been. She wondered if afterwards they would both live there, in that grand house with the mayor. They wouldn't live back at the pump house with Dad and Lizzie and Tilly, after all. Esme would be expected to have children. What would their children be like? Esme looked at Tom; he was tall with broad shoulders and fair hair. She realised he was looking back at her. 'Esme,' the mayor's wife said, 'your father says you've finished your schooling now. Do you go out to business?'

Esme looked to her dad, unsure what the mayor's wife meant. On the way home Esme's dad would tell her that 'business' was what people of their class called work. At the time he answered for her. 'Esme helps out around the house and garden.' Esme's dad looked between the mayor and his wife hopefully. 'She's great with the infant. Dotes on you, doesn't she, Esme?'

Esme confirmed this to her feet, blushing and biting her bottom lip. The mayor and his wife smiled. The mayor's wife asked Esme if she liked children. Esme wasn't sure, so answered, 'I guess.' She failed to convey to the mayor's wife the unease and suspicion she felt having to answer these questions.

The mayor's wife asked Esme, 'It must have been hard losing your mother when you did?'

'She's not dead,' Esme said, and glanced at her dad as the expression the mayor's wife used she only knew in reference to the death of a family member. There was an awkward moment while the penny dropped for Esme. 'Oh, I'm sorry. I see what you mean.' And she thought again about Mam's flight. 'I guess it used to upset me. It's been a long time.'

They shared an awkward afternoon tea where limp sandwiches were served on prettily patterned plates with small cups of weak tea. Esme and her dad both studied the behaviours of the people they were with and tried to make the necessary adjustments in their own behaviour. The mayor's wife suggested she and her husband could show Keith their garden. 'Give the youngsters a chance to get to get to know each other.'

The mayor and his wife duly led Esme's dad from the room and left Esme alone with the son, sitting either side of the coffee table with nothing to say to each other. Esme wondered whether if she and the mayor's son said nothing people would decide it wouldn't work, and to everyone's relief they'd call it all off. Eventually, though, Tom Jr said, 'Thank you for coming. I wasn't sure you would.'

'It's okay,' Esme said and thought of how she had no choice.

'You look very nice,' Tom said.

'Thank you,' Esme acknowledged his compliment. He looked

hopefully at her to relieve his doubt and fear of failure.

She looked around the drawing room, distracting her nerves by fomenting fascination in the objects and fittings. 'You have a piano.' Tom glanced at the instrument in the corner with framed photographs on top. 'Do you play?'

'No.' Tom Jr explained, 'It's a family heirloom, mother's family.' He seemed to consider this before asking Esme more brightly, 'Do you play?'

'Me? No.' Esme was surprised by the idea she would be able to.

'Oh,' Tom Jr said, sounding slightly deflated. 'It doesn't much matter, it's flat and out of tune apparently, but Dad can't get hold of anyone to tune it up.'

Some more time passed before Tom Jr asked, lit by a sudden new thought of how he might impress Esme, 'You know what a computer is?' Of course, Esme did. 'Have you ever seen one?'

Tom led Esme out of the drawing room across the hall into his father's study behind a heavy panel door, which to gain access through he first had to disappear to find a key. He left Esme alone turning and looking around the grand hallway of the house. There were framed photographs along the walls of the hall and climbing the wall alongside the staircase. Some of the photographs seemed old, and as Esme studied one or two of the photographs while she waited for Tom to return she noticed numerous features that leapt out from their incidental context as bright, shiny indicators of a lost age. Streets lined with parked cars, restaurants bustling with life. Esme looked toward the locked door with the computer behind like the secrets of Tutankhamun's tomb.

Tom Jr reappeared, brandishing a key in his right hand with a wide smile. There was a desk below a window that exposed the side of the house, where a cherry tree centred a swathe of lawn.

Tom Jr swept a dust sheet away like a magician and revealed a white box with a dark blank screen and before it a keyboard set in a smaller thin rectangular box. 'Shall I turn it on?' Tom asked, and Esme just looked at him, unable to say 'yes', unsure whether they should.

Tom pressed a button, a tiny green light and nothing more. They waited gazing at the dark screen. 'Where does the electricity come from?' Esme asked.

'Dad has a generator in the cellar.' The screen flickered, followed by a bunch of words and numbers in white, at the end of which was a single phrase they understood: PRESS ANY KEY TO CONTINUE. So, Tom Jr did and through fractured, broken shapes and colours that took time to organise themselves, a pale blue screen emerged with a bunch of mysterious symbols. Tom Jr ran his finger over a square area of the keyboard that controlled a tiny arrow repeating the movement of Tom Jr's finger across the screen. Esme laughed, and Tom Jr said she could have a go moving the arrow about the screen. Esme played with the moving arrow also, but the amusement of watching the moving arrow soon became limited and Tom Jr admitted he didn't know much else.

'Does your dad know how it works?'

'He says he does,' Tom said. 'He used to use it to write letters but his printer broke, and it became impossible to repair, so, he got his secretary to write his letters on a mechanical typewriter instead. He says he's still looking for someone who can get it working properly again. He says the Horton brothers might have found someone in Cambridge who'll come up.'

With nothing more to do with the computer, Tom Jr turned it off, re-covered it with the dust sheet and they returned to the drawing room. Back either side of the coffee table, Tom Jr said,

'You know about the internet?'

'Yes,' Esme answered quickly, not wishing to seem ignorant. 'Could your dad's computer connect to it?'

Tom Jr smiled, short of laughing 'No,' but seeing in Esme's face the beginnings of a hurt formed in the powerlessness of ignorance, he explained: 'You need infrastructure, electric cables and things; in Cambridge maybe but not way out here.' Tom Jr shrugged, and Esme listened and recognised something likable about Tom Jr. Most of the lads bragged and liked to appear bigger than they were. Tom Jr, who some might say had reason to brag, didn't.

Esme's father was still being shown the garden; Tom Jr's mother carried a parasol with Chinese designs on it. Esme looked at the sky. It was warm, but it had clouded over again, and Esme wondered what the purpose of Tom Jr's mother carrying a parasol was. Maybe it's not to hide the sun but to hide the absence of a sun.

Tom Jr suddenly asked Esme, 'Have you heard the agents have arrived in town with bailiffs to carry out the census?' Esme had, of course, and Tom Jr continued. 'Father said they were bloody vexatious.'

'Why?'

'Father says they're already causing trouble and disquiet, and once they're done they'll bugger off and leave him to sort out their mess. Last night, at dinner, he said he had half a mind to gather a group of locals and drive the buggers out.'

'Do you think he will?' Esme asked, quickly, noticing their parents ambling back across the lawn toward the house, Mrs Mayor pausing to indicate some purple-headed flowers stood tall on long thick stems.

'Nah, I asked him,' Tom Jr answered. 'Said he'd like to, but it'd probably bring a whole load more up from London. He said some of the locals had complained to him and he had to tell them the best way was to suck it up and let it pass. That's what he said anyway.'

'What did the locals say?' Esme asked.

'When he said they'd be best to go along with it this time, one of them said, "This time and every other bloody time."' And when Tom Jr said this, he adopted a local's accent, which Esme thought strange as he hadn't adopted an accent for his father.

Mrs Mayor entered smiling; everything seemed loaded with significance for Esme. She was followed by Esme's father agreeing with something one of Tom Jr's parents had said on the other side of the French doors. Mr Mayor jovially proclaimed, 'Ha! It's excellent to see them getting on, hey, Keith?' And he nudged Esme's dad's elbow and laughed, 'Courtly but not compromised.'

Tom Jr's parents agreed to come to the pump house one afternoon and the mayor's wife agreed also, announcing Esme 'Really is lovely.' She took Esme's shoulders, leant forward and kissed her on both cheeks.

On the way home, Esme's dad listed the things that impressed him about Mayor Thomas Baker, his family and his home. His musings concluded with the worry, 'We'll have to clean the house up well before they come.' He paused amidst some other crowding thoughts about their visit before stating. 'They'll have to take us as they find us, won't they, girl?'

'Yes,' Esme agreed and knew her dad didn't mean it.

Esme's dad's excitement continued after he arrived home, maybe it was the two small glasses of red wine, as he claimed when Lizzie struck his arm, after he'd swept her up amidst talk of 'moving with a better set of people'. Lizzie glanced at Esme as her dad described the house to her and stated with a wink at his daughter that the mayor's boy 'seems very smitten with our Es.'

He called her Es or Essie when he was pleased with her. She begrudged it and yet couldn't resist a warm feeling of belonging that swelled within at her dad's approval.

III

On the evening of the dissenters' meeting at the Seven Stars, Esme's dad and Lizzie were in the back parlour. Esme had withdrawn upstairs to her room, reading by chamber lamp and waiting until the house was sufficiently quiet.

It was a habit of her childhood to keep the light of her lamp low at night. Mam would notice when the time was late. She would open the door a crack and whisper, 'Don't you think it's time to blow it out now, love?' Esme didn't seek to remember Mam; it was her memories that would sneak up and catch her.

Esme crossed to sit by her window in the dark. She searched for the shapes of constellations. At Sunday School she'd been told the stars were God's map. She used to sit with Davey Clay in class because they'd been friends since before they even went to school, and before anyone had a chance to put her off Davey on account of him being slow-witted and embarrassing. Davey's parents died when he was an infant, first his mother, then three years later his father died from a stroke, just dropped down dead one day. Davey lived with his grandparents, at their small farmstead on Gold Hill. It was hardly a hill at all, just a slow gradual gradient, rising barely ten feet above the level. A bump of raised land that was Davey's legacy, only Davey wasn't smart, and Esme's dad said his grandparents were worried what Davey would be able to make of it, if they died. So, Esme's dad helped them and assured them he would keep an eye out for Davey's good and care for the land. Or an alternative interpretation would be that Esme's dad gave Davey work in the hope that when the time came, he would be remembered in the will of Davey's grandparents. Gold Hill Farm was so called because when the late summer sun set slowly behind the farmhouse and scattering of trees, it bathed them in a golden glow.

Davey told Esme his mammy and daddy lived in the stars with God. Esme and Davey would lie on the grassy banks and gaze up at the night sky. 'Whereabouts?' Esme would ask him.

Davey would point at some distant, twinkling star and claim, 'There.'

'What do you think it's like there?' Esme asked.

'A bit like here,' Davey replied and the accompanying smile faded into thought, and he added, 'but …'

'But …?'

'But everyone's happy there and nobody dies or goes away or is mean.' Esme would smile and indulge him however ridiculous it was because his need was also hers, and they would talk about this happy place beyond the stars and what it was like there. Davey would list the things he could remember about his parents, as though by listing them he saved them from slipping away and being lost, leaving him with even less to cling to. Esme would listen to him and think of her own mam. She was not dead, but she might as well have been.

Davey daydreamed he and Esme would one day marry and live together on Gold Farm and 'be happy', as he put it. It was only a daydream, though, and Esme laughed and assumed that, deep down, Davey knew.

Esme had a plan to sneak out to the dissenter's meeting at the Seven Stars, which she'd not even told Davey in case he blabbed. She heaved up the sash bedroom window, sat on her window ledge, her legs dangling almost to the shallow roof of the small porch below. She'd brought a rolled-up sack she had found in one of the outbuildings and kept squeezed in the gap between wardrobe and wall. She dropped it on to the roof of the porch. She then took a roll of gummed tape and, using her teeth to grip and help tear a square, she tossed the roll back into her room and fixed the torn section over the window catch, so when she pulled the sash window down it wouldn't secure, and she would be able to climb back in later. She pulled the sash most of the way down and, with her boots finding the grey rendered wall beneath her window, she lowered herself the rest of the way down onto the roof of the porch. She then reached up and with stretching fingertips pulled the sash window down.

From the porch there was a close-by tree with a wide-reaching bough branch she could climb onto. Before doing so, she tossed the sack over the branch. The rain left the bark wet and the sack was to protect her jeans as she shuffled along the branch, wrapped her arms around the trunk and lowered herself as carefully she could. She knew to soften all her limbs and joints and prepare to slip when she hit the ground. Landing, she smiled. She had not needed to use her hand to steady herself.

She stood for a moment listening, but there were no new sounds from inside. She patted her duffle coat and pulled the hood up. She walked her bicycle out the gravel yard, glancing back towards the house when she heard the crunch of gravel beneath wheels and feet.

Along the road toward Fenby, Esme's hood fell back so the wind and last drops of rain in the air rushed against her face. The dynamo-powered lights of her bicycle flickered with her peddling though little was illuminated.

With its sign depicting the pattern of the Pleiades, skulking at the far end of the high street, on the corner of Bridge Street, was the Seven Stars. Esme leant her bicycle against a wall of an alley behind the pub. Head bowed beneath her black hair, Esme followed a couple down narrow, mean steps and past a fat bald man sat on a stool by the cellar door. Blocked, waiting for a clot to thin in front of her, she searched for Sarah-May amidst the shifting shoulders and shadows of the dimly lit cellar. An arched, brick ceiling closed low over the gathered crowd in the cellar of the Seven Stars, any fresh air had been sucked out, and the cellar was oppressive with smells of man-sweat, beer and hippy-weed. Upstairs, a band were playing to distract attention from the downstairs meeting, and so tub-thumping and throbbing bass notes tumbled over their heads.

The first speaker was an absurdly tall, thin man. Esme smiled watching his regular upward glances, fearful of cracking his head with its long thin strands of golden grey hair on the ceiling. He had a face the shape of an arrowhead with a long, Roman nose, prominent upper teeth, sloping forehead and receding chin. 'In the city or in the suburbs,' he said, 'security Agents might come and arrest everyone here for sedition. Most crimes these days are property crimes, even murder and rape are considered as crimes against property.' Esme picked her way between people at the back of the room, so to find a space to see. The tall speaker continued, 'Sedition is one of the few exceptions, but since almost anything can be considered sedition, there's a lot of it about.' His words seemed to bob around on the mumbled and murmured conversations going on beneath, and he didn't seem to command the full interest of those gathered.

To English ears such as Esme's, the second speaker that evening introduced himself as Owain Gruffith. He was a smaller man with salt and pepper hair; an historian from Wales touring the provinces with tales of the decline of the west in a beautiful lilting accent like Esme had never heard before. When he stopped to cough, he'd take a sip of water and apologise. 'My tight throat cracks in this airless room, like my ancestors, who croaked and coughed beneath ground, coal dust suffocating their lungs.'

High shoulders obscured from Esme much of the platform where the speakers were, and so Esme skirted further around the back of the crowd to where ancient stone steps climbed to a closed access hatch where the draymen brought the beer barrels in. Nobody bothered when she climbed a few steps and sat, knees drawn up with her arms wrapped around. Esme listened, dazzled by ideas she only half grasped and references beyond her reach.

Owain Gruffydd recalled the wise people at the end of the last century who spoke about an end of history. He said: 'People believed in an unbreakable line from Plato to NATO, but there never was a manifest destiny.' He explained the reason why nobody had computers and cell phones anymore. 'There were wars in faraway countries where the rare, special metals needed for computers and phones had been harvested. Following the wars, the trade networks broke down, one by one, countries connected by mutual reliance started to fall. It was just as it had been with the earlier oil wars,' Owain Gruffydd said. 'So, no more precious metals, no more technology, no more phones and computers as your grandparents relied. The internet is now a marvel of antiquity for most.'

Esme looked around, although in the dark she couldn't guess at what the other people were thinking, their hushed quiet suggested they had become as captivated as she was. 'We are encouraged to believe in eternal truths, like the placements of the stars as ordered by God.' Owain Gruffydd stretched his arms out wide. 'At one end of this grand scheme are the vulnerable, the other end are the powerful. To the vulnerable the powerful can offer protection, but protection comes at a price and that price is the deference of those less powerful to those more powerful. The child is made to learn to obey rules. Rule and order become as natural as mother's milk.'

When Owain Gruffydd described power, Esme thought of her dad and felt like the Welshman was describing her home. 'Heads bowed in deference,' Owain Gruffydd continued, 'are unable to look up and often don't see how those rules that keep order always cascade down. The master mocks the apprentice but rarely the reverse. They will make demands of people below them they wouldn't accept themselves, just as husbands can talk to wives in ways that wouldn't be tolerated if reversed.

'Everything is transactional, and everything is owned by somebody, even people.' Owain Gruffydd asserted that, 'Beginning in the sixteenth and seventeenth centuries, reaching its culmination with the Inclosure Acts of the eighteenth and nineteenth centuries, most common land became privately owned by fewer and fewer people – this consolidation of material property would become a feature of our great free market era, the invisible hand that frees a fellow to starve to death.' Owain Gruffydd's comments pushed a ripple of wry laughter through the audience. He waited for the laugh to pass with a hand held in front, a mild indication he wanted their attention, a stop sign softened by fingers wilting from the perpendicular. Esme's mind drifted as she gazed around; the cellar was fetid as a stagnant marsh pool. She'd expected to feel a tap on a shoulder and an older voice of one who'd identify her and ask what she was doing there. Nobody noticed her though, yet in that anonymity her identity had never felt more her own.

A NEW DARK AGE

The Welsh historian smiled as one who knows his secrets will glint and enthral in the dim light of the cellar. He didn't have a voice that commanded, Esme couldn't imagine him shouting. There was a photograph of Esme's dad taken when he ran a team of river navigators. It was a rare photograph and so cherished was it by Esme's dad, it was in a frame atop the mantel piece in the parlour. Esme had often gazed at it and wondered what her dad would have been like when he was young. In the picture, Esme's dad was standing on a bank over a long ditch half-a-dozen men were digging out. Her dad had one hand on his hip, the other on a shovel, his shoulders were back, his chest proud, and Esme could well imagine him shouting instructions or chiding some poor, young worker with his sarcasm. The audience in the Seven Stars were listening to the Welshman though, and as they listened they nodded to the things the Welshman said which they recognised from their own lives. Esme was fascinated watching these people. Many in full light Esme felt sure she would know and few people she knew from around Fenby would she have imagined as dissenters.

'Decades ago, when the collapsing had already begun, in a system where scarcity was a commodity there was always a need for the unemployed, the homeless and the hungry. After each economic crisis arising from falling demands and dizzying private debt, the rulers would leverage the people with further private debt to re-finance the financiers. When most people could no longer afford consumer goods, there were riots. Rulers called them an attack on democracy.'

Owain Gruffydd described a world that justified the anger Esme felt, and she thought she detected in some of the watching faces that they too felt Esme's fury, and she felt more kinship for them as a consequence. Owain Gruffydd's accent was soft but persisted like a nagging tune. 'Future riots were met with highly militarised, armoured police. With falling tax revenues companies took over financing the police, so the police increasingly function as capitalism's own Praetorian Guard, sometimes supporting rival business leaders, sometimes bringing about their demise and all the while living standards fall. The state's very structure begins to crumble. The resentments metastasise, and rival factions compete where the state withdraws. Because governments don't function, roads and bridges don't get fixed and built.' People in the crowd nodded and Esme thought of the potholed roads running banks and ridges between flooded fields that would never be fixed. 'And when there were outbreaks of the Falling Sickness, there was no state to provide hospitals for the infected.' There hadn't been a wave of Falling Sickness for some years, but Esme knew the words frightened people with the fears of those who remembered. The cities were worst affected; the slums were breeding grounds for infection, and there were plenty enough gravestones to remind the young, lest any should forget. Esme's dad told her they called it the Falling Sickness because one of the first symptoms was dizziness. At school, the kids played games imitating the falling, pretending to sneeze and touch their classmates to indicate contagion. Those that thought it bad taste were far fewer than those who thought the games and the nursery rhymes served to remind.

A round of applause met Owain Gruffydd's conclusion. He bashfully, gestured toward a woman sat at the side of the stage, seeming to suggest he thought the applause was in expectancy for her. 'Joan Ball,' he announced to further cheers, and Esme followed his gesture, along his arm, beyond his hand to where Joan Ball was.

Joan Ball stayed sat in a deep well of a great green cheaply upholstered throne of an armchair, a hand flat on each green, upholstered armrest, as the cheers quietened. Low at first, she began humming a single note like a Buddhist mantra. The audience started humming with her and as the noise of the humming grew Esme saw the tall first speaker look upward and smile, relieved to hear the band on the floor above, still beating the ceiling. Esme began humming and an excited, expectant smile spread across her face watching Joan Ball rise from her throne.

Joan Ball stood big and black and beautiful; her bright coloured clothes contrasted the muted, tertiary shades most in her audience wore. There seemed to Esme something bold and defiant in those colours and in the way spirals and coils of dark hair would shake and dance around her as she spoke. While Esme and the rest of the local folks' colour was drained by the wind and the rain, the rain seemed only to make Joan Ball see the colours more brightly iridescent. She lifted her hands high, hands shaking, left-right. Slowing, she brought them down and the humming quietened as if conducted. 'Sisters and Brothers,' she announced. 'Take the hands of the people next to you. Our strength comes from the unbreakable bonds between us.'

A man to Esme's left said to her, 'Good to see you sister, I'm Joe.' He took her hand and shook it. Then the woman to her right with a sweet smile beneath spectacles and pageboy bob extended a hand to shake also.

'Hello, I'm Angharad.' She briefly laid a second hand over their shaking hands and patted.

'It's always good to see a young sister like you getting active.' Her voice carried the accent of the Welsh second speaker. Esme beamed at the idea of being active and involved even after the woman had let her hand go and turned to the person on her other side to shake his hand. Angharad was a strange name; people around the Fens didn't have such names. To Esme, it sounded romantic and hinted at far away adventure.

Joan Ball spoke, 'Our Mother God, from whose infinite womb we came, the blossoming seeds of stardust. Care for us, your dirty faced children. Teach us to temper the energy that burns life ephemeral. Give us the strength to lift the weakest among us up and cut down any who'd set 'emselves above their sisters and brothers as gods themselves. And with humility return us to the peace an' harmony of your eternal love, Amen.'

It reminded Esme of her dad mocking the growing religious cults. He would imitate the fervent hedge preachers. 'Hmmm ...' Joan Ball growled her pleasure, 'Such sweet, sweet, swee-eet love!'

Esme wondered what kind of cult this was. She'd heard of some called Penitents who self-harmed to carry the punishment for us all and marked themselves with the wounds of the stigmata. There were some who danced and sang with tambourines and spread love through folk music and free pepper soup for the poor, and some said they practiced free sex in all sorts of strange and ungodly ways. Then there were the radicals; she'd heard stories they attacked the wealthy and Esme's dad reckoned them troublemakers. Esme liked the sound of them more, she liked their anger, their fury, and why not? Everything was ruined.

Joan Ball gave her thanks to the two previous speakers and to the audience. She stated, 'The twenty-first century has become one of the shittiest in history to live through, right down there with the fourteenth. It is a time when property has more right in law than life itself, and if you have no property, you have no rights ...'

The crowd responded with loud applause to Joan Ball's opening. Esme never knew there were so many people, people she lived amongst, who felt as passionately as she did. The bogs are sticky, people's feet well rooted, and fen people make the best of what they're given rather than challenge their world. Yet, here they were, some calling out with a naked rage that excited Esme. The politics for Esme were secondary; they were reasons to justify the passion.

'You know you can always tell when you're gettin' screwed by politicians 'cause you'll get told the issue in't political, like its part o' nature or an act o' God or the stars or some shit.' Joan Ball rocked back and forth in a peel of her own laughter. Esme applauded then quietened to hear Joan Ball continue. 'Famine and poverty are always a choice while some 'ave big fat bellies clothed in gold. And they bend their knees in plastic churches and when they leave, they pass the shivering cold without seeing 'em, 'cause they think if they don't look at 'em then their spectre is less real.'

Joan Ball had this way of starting quiet with a deliberate intensity, gradually growing in pace, in tone, and volume. 'You know what they call places like this in the city, they call it *the Dark Country*, 'cause they say the lights have gone off here and they ain't coming back on. Shit, the only time people around here see slick folks from the city is when they come to loot some more.' She mimicked these rich folks, touching her clothes to indicate their fine threads. She held her arms close and laughed at the way they were always flanked by security and flunkies. 'Oooh, you can see 'em comin', with their carpet bags, and gun dogs and hungry eyes. There's new taxes to pay for services we don't get, wars we don't want our kids dying in, and to pay debt we didn't create.'

There was a crash of applause. Esme clapped. She had forgotten herself as the daughter of Keith Sedgebrook from the old pump house, she, who it was said, would be marrying the mayor's son. She felt like someone quite different, cheering Joan Ball like the followers of Fra Dolcino of Novara. Higher up the access steps, head inches from the hatch, she could feel the cold street air on the back of her neck. Esme looked over the heads of the crowd, where Joan Ball stood imperious, her face panning from side to side with chin and cheekbones high and defiant. She seemed to look straight at Esme and hold eye contact for a few seconds before moving on. And between words, as she looked at her, Esme thought she saw Joan Ball smile all the wider and brighter as they reflected each other across the dimly lit cellar. 'While we're drinking water, friends, those bastards are quaffing fine wine.' Joan Ball laughed, and her laughter was infectious. 'While we feed off o' crumbs, the rich are sniffing Sowf American party powder through roles of our money.'

Somebody in the crowd shouted, 'Burn the rich!' so loud it cut across the cellar and even Joan Ball paused before bringing the noise of revolutionary zeal back down with pacifying calm palms, saying, 'Friends, friends, there's a time for all things, but to climb steep hills requires a slow pace at first.' The crowd settled and Joan Ball concluded by saying, 'This is May in the year 2061, and a more shitty time to be alive I can't imagine. Still, poor wretch I may be, petulant and debauched.' Hitting the word 'debauched' Joan Ball folded half over, laughing so hard the laughter broke down into coughing before she gathered herself up again and was able to finish, hoarser than before but all-conquering to Esme. 'Yes, a poor, debauched wretch I may be, but I'll tell you all what I'd tell them.' She paused dramatically and turned her face, her elegant cheek bones held high, and announced, 'There's a reckoning coming!' She nodded as people cheered and roared again. 'Lemme tell you all! There. Will. Be. A. Reckoning!'

Joan Ball then collapsed back into the green armchair, with a hand swept across her forehead. Amidst cheers and applause some started leaving the cellar of the Seven Stars, and so, with no reason to stay, Esme too slipped out, to make it home without her dad noticing she'd been out. As Esme walked her bicycle back across the yard of the old pump house, the gate of the out-house was swinging, regular quiet bangs beneath the growing sound of the wind and whipping rain. The lights of the house were off. She grabbed the bough branch with both hands where the sack still hung, slightly askew and damp. Only on the third attempt was she able to swing her legs up and around the branch, so for a few perilous seconds that ached at her arms she hung like a sloth. Once upright again, she shuffled back along the branch onto the porch roof. Stretching, she pushed up her bedroom window and scrambled up and over, falling into her bedroom on the other side. She paused for a moment, fearing her crashing entrance would rouse her dad, but nothing stirred. She pulled the window closed.

Esme assumed it would be the first and last time she would set eyes on the mad preacher, Joan Ball.

IV

When Esme escaped her chores, she followed the narrow fen path, beneath clouds breaking up after the morning rain across to Sarah-May's cottage, where her mam, Bella made them all tea with sunlight bursting through the raindrop-dashed windows and spangling across their kitchen. There were shelves in Bella's kitchen with rows of glass jars and small bottles, some emerald green or cranberry pink, all glinting from the shafts of sunlight. There were some jars where the glass was clear but the contents inside were a strange colour, and then there were a couple of jars where both glass and liquid within were clear but where there was something else in the liquid, what looked to Esme like a piece of bark. On other shelves were small clay pots containing other spices and balms. By the door to the store cupboard in the corner, suspended from the ceiling was a strange artefact constructed from chicken wire and netting with feathers attached. Bella told Esme it carried powers from the spirit world that protected the house.

Esme watched the geese in their yard wandering about. There were shallow puddles from the previous night's rain. 'So, you are going to do it?' Sarah-May asked. Esme shrugged. If one doesn't choose, then at least one is spared the responsibility for the choice. She had imagined telling her dad she didn't want to marry, but she felt as though her father's love was dependent upon it. She'd lied in bed experimenting with ways to construct the confession.

The mayor's son was involved now also. And the mayor and his wife, and most people in town knew Esme was betrothed to the mayor's son. She wouldn't be able to get out of it without being the centre of town gossip and judgement even if dad did agree – and there was little chance of that. And there was Tom Jr, the mayor's son. He would have people's sympathy. Anyway, at some point she would have to marry someone, and there were many who would be less appealing than Tom Jr.

Esme failed to impress Sarah-May and Bella as much as she'd hoped when telling them she had attended the meeting in the cellar of the Seven Stars, and Sarah-May dampened Esme's moment in the sun by informing her that she and her mam had been there also, and, unlike Esme, they'd waited around for the secret meeting after.

'I thought I was at the secret meeting,' Esme admitted, deflated.

'Oh, it was secret,' Sarah-May said, and touched Esme's forearm. 'It was just there was a private, secret meeting after. Mum was tipped off.'

Esme glanced at Bella. She mixed herbs and other ingredients in a mortar to be ground, and listened, allowing Sarah-May to describe the meeting. 'There were a group of about a dozen of us, all sat around a table in the cellar. The band upstairs had stopped so it was quiet, as though everyone there was waiting on something. Sat beside me was a Scottish woman, I think she was there to listen and report back to the rebels in Scotland. She didn't say much. What was her name?' Sarah-May asked her mam.

'Geddes.' Bella answered, grinding her pestle without looking up. 'Jenny Geddes. They say she's one of the leaders north of the border.'

'Apparently,' Sarah-May took over again. 'She started a riot in Edinburgh when she threw a stool at some government official, and it led to the London authorities being driven out of Edinburgh and most of Scotland.'

'It must have been a good throw,' Esme commented. Sarah-

May and Bella laughed. Esme found people laughed at her wry asides, and so she would use them as an object between herself and others. It had become habit. She had learnt that to enthuse was to leave herself open to the judgement or the ridicule of others, much better to deflect and keep her dreams buried deep inside.

'Jenny Geddes had travelled down with a man called Lilburne. Mum thought he was a bit of alright, didn't you Mum?' Sarah-May joked.

Esme laughed and asked Bella what he was like. Bella smiled, resting her pestle to say, 'He was fair with pale blue eyes like sunlit spring water.'

Sarah-May enjoyed recounting the event. Beginning with her mum, she went around who was there, sat around the table in the cellar of the Seven Stars as if they were seated around the kitchen table at Bella and Sarah-May's cottage. She pointed at empty spaces and told Esme about each of the people she remembered from the night. 'Some there were local. Big Mick Brown, the landlord of the Seven Stars was sat next to Mum, and there was Dr Hansford.'

'Dr Hansford?' Esme was surprised, and further surprised by the reported presence of Mrs Dingle, the postmistress, and Mrs Honeyman, the apothecary's wife, who had started a petition about the ploughing up of the village greens.

'And there was this old guy who wore a cape and great big, wide-brimmed hat who mum knew.' Sarah-May went on.

'William Grindecobbe,' Bella said. She was pouring the crushed contents of her mortar into a small jar. 'Nice old guy. Not the same since the death of his wife. Some folks say he's lost it. He thinks he's found something though.' She twisted a threaded lid fast to the jar and set it aside. Esme asked Bella what was in the jar. 'Oh, that's something for melancholia.'

'For melancholia?' Esme asked. 'I didn't know things were made for melancholia. I assumed it was like the weather.'

Bella laughed, but kindly, not at Esme but as one who enjoyed the comparison. 'Well, this contains Valerian root, St John's Wart, chamomile, rosemary and a little lavender oil.'

'Does it work?' Esme asked.

'So those who benefit claim,' Bella answered.

'I was telling you about the meeting,' Sarah-May cut in, and continued to recall people there, most of whom Esme didn't know.

When Sarah-May mentioned Joan Ball, Esme felt connected to the people being cited and assumed her to be central to the meeting, but Bella said, 'I got the sense that Joan Ball may have drawn the crowd to the evening's event, but she wasn't one of the important people trading secrets and making plans.'

'Who was making plans?' Esme asked.

'Hereward!' Sarah-May burst in. 'I didn't tell you Hereward was there. Mum and I didn't know who he was until we were leaving at the end and the old guy tells us.'

'What was he like?'

'Scruffy,' Sarah-May answered.

'By design,' Bella added. 'He sat smoking his pipe, taciturn and watchful.'

Esme sipped her tea, Bella made her own and it didn't taste like the tea she had at home. Its smell was quite queer, woody and floral. Esme only pretended to like it in small sips. 'And was it Hereward making plans?'

'Ye-es.' Bella considered. 'We'd decamped upstairs by then. It was late, so the main bar was clear.'

'Yes,' Sarah-May interrupted. 'That was after Luca's story.'

'Luca?' Esme asked of the unfamiliar name.

'He's this American on the run. He was looking for help in return for secret documents he'd smuggled out of America.' Sarah-May, with coy flush in the cheek, elaborated, 'Luca's young, not much older than us. He's really nice. I kind of befriended him. I shall be meeting him later, will you come?' Of course Esme would, curiosity compelled her; America had come to Fenby.

'Once his accent is heard by a few people in town,' Bella said. 'There shall be many who will be curious about Luca.'

'Honestly, Es. You'll melt into his eyes.' Esme smiled at Bella shaking her head.

'Looks can be deceiving.' She teased her daughter.

'Here we go.' Sarah-May laughed.

'I'm just saying.' Bella coughed as she joked, still clearing winter from her throat. She said to Sarah-May and Esme, 'If you see a snowball in the Sahara, I don't care how convinced you are it's a snowball. I'm telling you, if it's in the Sahara then it ain't no snowball.' Sarah-May groaned. Esme laughed.

'You said you liked him,' Sarah-May countered her mam's apparent scepticism.

'I did. I do,' Bella said. 'But remember, it's the cracks that let the light through. Seems and is are two different words for a reason. And,' addressing both Sarah-May and Esme, 'if you want to know who was running the meeting, it wasn't Joan Ball, Hereward, my Lilburne, or your Luca. You want to know who it was?'

'Who was it then?' Sarah-May asked.

'It was that ordinary looking Welsh couple.' Sarah-May drew a dubious furrowed brow. 'And I'd suspect her, with the owlish appearance, more than him,' Bella added.

V

Angharad, suffering the discomfort of reflux, was relieved when Michael Pollard tapped the side of his glass with a pen and suggested they take a break. From the blown-out cheeks and swift acceptance of his suggestion by most around the trestle table in the cellar of the Seven Stars, it was welcome. Upstairs, the band in the main bar had ceased. Indeed it was quiet and vacated but for a pair of aging stragglers who would most probably pass out in the corner warmed by the embers of a fire and return to their homes with morning.

Angharad slipped out the back, where the toilet was across a back yard in some outbuildings. 'It's howlin', alright,' Mick Brown said, holding the door open for Angharad and handing her an oil lamp. 'It's all bluster, more noise than force I should say.' Angharad smiled appreciation and wrapped her scarf around her neck. 'Blow itself out by morning.'

Having sifted through her layers and sat on the composting toilet, a necessary luxury in places where the sewage systems had broken down, Angharad allowed a moment with the gale full of sound and fury. The wind wasn't the only thing that was mainly bluster and noise, she feared.

Nevertheless, Owain's talk went well. He'd given it so many times now, Angharad reflected, remembering the way he would tremble and even make himself sick when she first persuaded him to stand before crowds he didn't know. The piece of coal he'd hold aloft with reference to their heritage was Angharad's idea. 'People like something to look at,' she'd told him. 'Besides, its physical evidence of your bona fides. People will recognise you as one of their own rather than the swotty kid who went to college in Cardiff.' He'd laughed and accepted what she said with a smile of self-effacing humility, dimples in his cheeks, such was his temperament. That was years ago now, when they first wandered the by-ways of their despair and righteous anger.

In those days they followed Emlyn's lead. He'd been with Rhodri's Ghosts years appearing and disappearing throughout Wales and Western England. There was still only a little black in his hair then, but the grey was strong like Port Talbot steel rather than the snowier white it had become. He was leaner then also, strong across the shoulders. They got hold of pictures one time that the authorities in Cardiff and Bristol were circulating; in it, she and Owain looked dopey, Emlyn looked tough as a slab of Preseli bluestone. Even then, he carried himself with resolute determination rather than anger. Soon after they'd joined the rebel militia, together with Emlyn, his partner at the time, Ruth Jones, and Dai Young, they were holed up in a barn near Monkswood in the Usk river valley. It was after the disastrous Battle of Pwll Melyn, when they were on the run. Somebody had betrayed them, the English had been ready and waiting; it was an ambush, a rout, nineteen of their militia cut down as they scattered. They were harried across Wales. Eventually, most of the few who survived headed back north to Rhodri's stronghold in Gwynedd.

When Angharad and Owain returned to the barn, Dai Young had bound two troopers back-to-back. Emlyn was in another part of the barn, biting his fist and swigging anaesthetising gulps of moonshine distilled from grain and rainwater, while Ruth pulled two English bullets from his leg.

It was after the murder of Owain's brother Hywel, Ceridwen and Rebecca. She and Owain had stood over their bodies, felt them still warm but lifeless, their spirit already departed.

Rebecca was just a child.

Angharad remembered.

She'd had the sweetest smile. Angharad had joked her smile had been cast by the same hand that cast Mary's smile. After Owain and Angharad buried them, they sobbed over the silence of God until their tears dried to a stain and a dull ache. It was such a small coffin. Emlyn made it, they all wanted to do something, even when there was nothing they could do. She was too small to be swallowed by the earth. For Christ's sake, she was seven years old. There was a small scab on her knee where she had fallen in play. Hywel and Ceridwen had nothing to do with Rhodri, not like them, not like her and Owain.

Angharad and Owain made an oath as they stood over the grave marked by a simple wooden cross, lost over the years so even she and Owain might have trouble finding it now. Truth and justice are lost to the layers of time, but Angharad and Owain would no longer cling to a past of trembling memories. They were at war from that time forward, and they were going to burn everything to the ground: everything! And salt the cursed earth after. Their enemies would come to know Angharad and Owain's fire.

Dai Young was circling the two troopers, taunting them, waiting for Emlyn and Ruth to join him to decide what to do. 'Softening 'em up, like,' Dai said upon Angharad and Owain's arrival. The troopers hadn't told Dai anything because, irrespective of the gags he'd bound around their faces, they didn't know anything. Angharad picked up a rifle leant against the wall of the barn, strode up to one of the two troopers and smashed the butt into his face. Due to the gag, the crunch of his cheekbone smashing was only responded to with an anguished grunt. Angharad held the rifle above her head, ready to smash down again, but Emlyn appeared behind her and while leaning on a crutch seized the weapon with his free hand.

'This isn't you,' he said to Angharad. 'It isn't us,' Emlyn continued as Angharad, after a brief struggle, ceded control of the rifle to him. 'Make your anger useful, not just cathartic.'

Rain dripped from guttering outside the wind-rattled outbuilding of the Seven Stars, where Angharad sat, easing release with a sighed out-breath.

Angharad then smiled to herself thinking of Joan Ball's rabble-rousing rhetoric. 'Good turn out,' Michael Pollard remarked as they'd sat around the trestle table. He was local and had set up the meeting. He was pleased not to have disappointed. It did surprise Angharad that there was this energy way out in the Fens, though perhaps she should be becoming less surprised.

John Wrawe confidently asserted things were changing. He'd been stirring dissent all over East Anglia. Wrawe wasn't overly tall, but thick-set in the shoulders. He spoke in sandpaper whispers; his character had grown in stubble that covered the acne scars of his adolescence. 'No notes. Nuffinks to be written down,' he'd stated at the start of the meeting, 'Just in case.' Some found his manner intimidating, Angharad didn't, just unnecessary. She had suggested taking minutes merely for her devilish hands to have something to do. Meetings like these were always full of hot air, men especially, who seemed to believe that the volume and certainty of tone in their voices carried more weight and meaning than the content of any well-chosen words. Commitments to unity often collapsed into factions of competing egos.

As they all made their way upstairs, Angharad had been stuck behind John Wrawe when he stopped to have a word in Chris

Cobbe's shell-like, a hand on his shoulder. 'Just listen, Chris. All smells a bit like bullshit to me. And what with the Taffies' plans and some rabbit I'm hearing about an Arab and a bird.' Angharad and Owain were the planning Taffies, and so noticing Angharad immediately after saying this to Chris Cobbe, he smiled, as one caught in the half-moment their eyes held.

'Nothing's quite on the level, is it?' Chris Cobbe replied. He truly was John Wrawe's man. Wrawe stepped aside to allow Angharad through, his smile starting to strain.

When Luca had been telling his story, Angharad looked around the faces of those listening. She watched John Wrawe, crumbs of pork pie gathered at the corners of his lips, he adjusted his seating position, an understated mannerism that suggested to Angharad his sceptical forbearance.

Holding the fractious factions together was already proving difficult. To the extent it had fallen upon Angharad and Owain to do so betrayed more the inability of anyone else as it did proffer any leadership qualities on them.

Luca had already been drawn upstairs and out of earshot when Wrawe asked, 'Well, that was some strange old shit, wa'nt it? What's to be made then of our American raconteur?'

Hereward slowly blew out three thick smoke rings before offering, 'Too much story. The truth don't need to be clothed in so much story-telling.'

'He did bring those documents and computer files with him,' Owain said. 'And experts say they check out.'

'Do they?' John Wrawe asked with a cynical raised eyebrow.

'That's my understanding.' Lilburne looked up from his drink to address Wrawe's scepticism.

'Experts, hey?' Wrawe laughed sardonically. Angharad

thought his was a scepticism of character. By reserving judgement, he could appear discerning rather than what he was, ignorant and distrusting. 'I suppose it could be true.' Wrawe shrugged. 'It don't much matter as I see it. Only makes things more urgent. People are like dry tinder anyway; all they need is a spark.'

'Really?' Hereward smirked. 'I'm struck more by their willing indifference and their cowardice.'

Wrawe had been piqued by Hereward's comments, which he took personal slight from due to his own role in building support amongst ordinary people. 'We've got contacts across the south.' He took a swig of his beer and from his pocket pulled a pouch of tobacco and papers and began rolling a cigarette while expanding. 'Tyler, south of the river, moving big numbers. In the city, Jacqui Straw, Shelley Ryman and their sagacious guru, Tom London, are seeing rising numbers wherever they speak. Rachel over in Swindon and Cornish Damo says the same.' Angharad knew there was truth to Wrawe's boasting. Even she and Owain had commented to each other they detected a shift. 'We's been going town to town and every town we go to we gets the same. Edmundsbury, Ely, Thetford and others have followed the example of Norwich. The corporate-state near enough need to ask permission of Bob Kett before entering Norwich these days.'

Whatever else might've been true of John Wrawe, Angharad would commend his commitment over anyone there. He'd twice been arrested, at least once tortured, even if he did brush references to it aside with, 'I were lucky. It wa'nt that bad for me. I think they must have been tired or bored.' He laughed hoarsely. 'But yeah, if I were to take me shirt off, you'd see the burn marks across me back. Branded like fuckin' cattle. All the same, I seen some who never recover, forever a-tremblin' and shaking.'

'And when the time comes,' Angharad pressed, 'all of this will only work if all the parts are ready, and the ducks rowed up.'

'When the time comes, there will be such numbers descend and gather on Hackney Marshes and from there down to Victoria Park,' Wrawe smarted. 'A decade back we was speaking in market squares to handfuls o' people who would either pause in passing out o' curiosity, or they were there to mock. These days, there are crowds waiting for us and they already know some o' the lines and chant 'em as we is saying 'em.'

John Wrawe thought Luca and his tale a distraction. Lilburne had admitted to Angharad his fears that if the documents were kosher and the Americans were preparing to come, and what with the French revival on the continent, Lilburne urged, 'If we don't move soon, the chance may well be lost.'

Angharad was pleased and slightly amused to see Jenny Geddes' wry detachment drain from her face when Michael Pollard quoted from the documents Luca brought with him, claiming to be in the president's own words they intended to 'Bring the Celts to heel also.' Geddes bristled but Angharad was sure she would take the warning back north of the border with her. When Angharad asked Lilburne how things were in Scotland, he replied, 'They're only waiting for something to kick off south of the border to declare independence.' He glanced across at Geddes, in conversation with Michael Pollard and Emlyn, clutching paper copies of some of the documents.

Leant in close, Lilburne spoke with Angharad, his words shielded behind cupped palm. 'They're confident, and it's not just bravado. For several years they've been playing games with the government in London, pushing them and backing off, seeing how far they can push before London threats become serious. Law north of the border is Scottish law and the London government can't raise taxes there 'cause the Scottish are only raising taxes now for their own affairs. When this started London would send people north; they don't bother now. When London officials cross the border, Scottish officers on the border will take hours checking all their papers and belongings before letting them through. They're making a point. All the navy posts on the Clyde are controlled by the Scots themselves. And all the while, they've been building a militia in the border country. If England rises, Scotland breaks.'

John Lilburne was a slender young man from the northeast and his voice carried the cadences of that area. He had fair skin, light brown hair and pale blue eyes. He'd attended the last great university of the north, at Durham, paid for through an inheritance from his father, Richard, who'd died a decade before, defending his property during the time of the riots. At Durham, the young Lilburne made the acquaintance of Jordan Hewson and Marcie Bastwick and the three ran an underground group using the university as a hub for dissent. Their clandestine association with militias in the area brought heat from the local authorities. It was low-level stuff, attacks on the infrastructure of corporate-state oppression, administration centres, and occasional hits on small patrol units. Then one of the local militia units discovered a huge cache of explosives and when they heard there were corporate-state representatives staying at the exclusive Columbia Hotel in Newcastle, they took the whole fucking building out. The attacks were significant enough for news of them to reach Angharad and Owain, who were doing runs between South Wales and the West Country around that time.

John Lilburne had commented to Angharad that his mam

told him they could hear the explosions in Sunderland. London sent troops north to make an example. There were raids all over the northeast. If suspects weren't given up, patrols would call in bulldozers and start demolishing houses and other buildings until they were given up. Lilburne, Bastwick and Hewson knew it was only time. When Bastwick was picked off the street, promptly prosecuted and imprisoned pending execution for pamphleteering and sedition, Hewson went to Scotland where he joined Geddes' movement. It was he that suggested Lilburne to Geddes as a contact with rebels south of the border.

John Lilburne wasn't drinking heavily though he held a jar while they discussed plans and the lay of things. Neither did he smoke. His eyes were always clear and sharp. Of the rest of the north, he said, 'You know when a glass screen shatters but holds together for as long as no pressure is exerted, but, at the slightest pressure, its delicate and brittle structure collapses into hundreds of tiny, sharp edged fragments. Well, that's the north.'

The sign hanging from the front of the haberdashers across the street creaked as it heaved with the wind. Angharad joined Owain stood at the window. 'Are you ready?' Owain asked, nodding toward the table where John Lilburne, Hereward, John Wrawe and Joan Ball sat, waiting for them. They had separated themselves from the rest of the plotting rebels of the secret meeting in the cellar. Some would already have been let surreptitiously out, were it not for a rising gale outside of the warm seclusion of the Seven Stars.

Angharad adjusted her spectacles and the lay of her clothing. She sat up with her weight pressed on her forearms. She glanced at Owain; she too was apprehensive. 'Well then, Mr Hereward,' Owain asked, 'do you have the bird?'

Hereward drummed the fingers of his free left hand on the edge of the table, drawing his pipe from his mouth. 'I do.' He reached to the floor by his chair and lifted a black bag onto the table. ''t's in there.' He nodded at the bag, pipe back in place, gripped between his lips.

Angharad pulled the bag to her, glancing at Owain as she realised its weight. She looked up; Hereward watched her with a smile, Wrawe also. She unzipped the bag and peered inside, and when she was satisfied with what she saw, she slid the bag over to Owain. He looked inside, then zipped the bag back up and with a strain Hereward had not betrayed in lifting it, heaved the bag to the floor next to his own chair.

'And will everything be arranged with this bin Salah as you said it would?' Hereward asked. 'We're gonna need cover when we make our move.'

'Yes,' Owain rushed to confirm. 'Don't worry. It's in hand.'

'But I do worry.' And looking between Angharad and Owain, he added, 'I'm risking more than I should on your plan. To be plain, Leo thinks it too much of a risk. I'm still inclined, perhaps because I'm a bit of a risk-taker myself – but I do worry.' Leo, or Leo Fric, for his full name, was Hereward's lover and the man he entrusted to run his base in the Isle of Ely when Hereward was not there, which was much of the time as Hereward preferred to be on the move, campaigning, claiming he grew restless. Hereward continued, 'I worry for my fellow travellers. People who place their trust in me want to know I can place my trust in you, and that appears to mean placing all our trust in this bin Salah, and many of my fellow travellers certainly distrust that name.'

'On that,' John Wrawe spoke, 'Mr Hereward and I do find agreement.'

Lilburne, turning his glass with fingertips around the rim, interjected, his voice soft, the tone as certain as diamond. 'Ismail bin Salah can shut East London down if he chooses; bring it to a total standstill.' Lilburne glanced across at Angharad and Owain before returning to the challenge of Hereward and John Wrawe. 'And mind you, he can do a whole lot more besides.'

'So, you will be ready won't you, Mr Hereward?' Wrawe asked with a smirk – not so much because his own doubts had been resolved, but in the knowledge he and the people he brought with him could be counted in regardless, and so his smirking question was just another of those merry moments for him to extract a moment's cheap joy from people he considered took too much of the sun.

Hereward leant forward and tapped the ashes from his pipe into a tin bucket filled with sand next to the table. 'Mr Wrawe, nor Mr and Mrs Gruffydd, nor young Mr Lilburne here, nor I, nor even Joan Ball are of this town, but only one of us could raze it to the ground this very night on a word. And those responsible would melt back into nothingness.' Hereward raised his closed fist to his pursed lips, blew his fingers fluttering away. 'As I say, Mr Wrawe, our role is understood.' And to all around the table he added, 'The nerves seem to be yours, not mine. When the time comes, our role is understood.'

Joan Ball, who had hitherto been silent as they talked, now spoke up. 'There are devils at play in the world, squalor and serfdom, and tales of plans of dark princes. These all herald return to our skies of the star called Worm-wood.'

'Jesus Fucking Christ.' John Wrawe coughed on his beer, laughing. 'What you been smoking, woman?'

Joan Ball glared at him. 'You can blaspheme, boy, but you'll see. We all will. There's to be a reckoning.'

VI

Sarah-May and Esme met Luca walking towards them along the Fenby Road. He was wearing local clothes of woollen trousers and jacket with a white linen shirt. Luca swung a reed idly by his left side. He wasn't big and he walked loose-limbed and relaxed like he had more time than he needed. There was a trim of jet-black hair around the flat cap he wore to blend in; Esme would be unsure whether it was because he feared being identified or whether he merely enjoyed the roleplay. 'He's been staying in one of the rooms above the Seven Stars.' Esme noticed the flush rise again in Sarah-May's countenance. 'Mick Brown doesn't charge him for the room, provided Luca helps out a little around the pub. It's a nice room.' And Sarah-May added coquettish: 'It gets the sun in the afternoon.'

'How do you know?' Esme asked, obliged as Sarah-May's friend to tease out her coy excitement.

With Luca approaching, Sarah-May waved and from behind the waving hand added, 'We were perfectly proper, I assure you, Miss Sedgebrook.'

'Hey. How're you doing?' Luca called out to them. His voice came from far away and later, when she and Sarah-May were alone together, they would imitate his accent, quoting in quixotic delight expressions he used.

Across the marshes there were three types of settlement: the towns strung around the edge of the great levels where the land becomes more permanent, the long thin villages strung out along causeway roads and the towns linked by the banked causeway roads, like where they were, in Fenby, an old market town on an island surrounded by flood plain. Where there was the smallest undulation of land, and drainage could be purposeful, there were outcrops of cultivated fields, spots surrounded by lake and marsh, accessible by narrow, banked tracks, the water rippling out either side. Trees from the old days would occasionally rise, still submerged, half their trunk with birds perched, sometimes in rows along their branches. The lodes and dykes that connected these lakes would bring eels and fish, and sometimes the perching birds, such as gulls or the odd kingfisher, would dive down to the water to tickle and wrestle for their dinner.

Esme and Sarah-May walked Luca up to Gold Hill Farm, where Davey Clay lived. He wouldn't be there; he'd be working with Esme's dad. Esme assumed this with some guilty relief, for he tended to traipse around after her. Sometimes, even with Davey, Esme felt her feet stuck deep in the mud.

Gold Hill was a feature in a fairly featureless landscape. It was little more than a pimple on the flat fen face, crowned with an old farmhouse approached via a long, straight road through a spinney, a dozen trees deep. Esme's dad had towed an old wreck of an abandoned car to where it since rested, nestled in amongst those trees but with a clear view out across the land and water, and toward Fenby beyond. After the Collapse, when fuel prices became prohibitive, it became common to find cars abandoned by the side of roads, suggesting they'd been run right up to the point the fuel ran dry.

The car was where Esme and Davey would hang out when the rain came, which was frequent, and when there was nowhere else to be, which was also frequent. One of the back windows was missing, so it could be cold when the wind blew though they had taped some cardboard over the hole. When they were younger, and the car was more exciting to them, they'd pretend to drive it or even imagine it were a plane and fly it, leaning in their seats as they banked. They'd talk about the places they'd visit, Esme's fascinating and real, Davey's imaginary and absurd. One time it was a place where all sorts of animals lived in their own houses, birds in tree houses and rabbits in labyrinthine underground complexes, and all the animals and people would regularly get together for a sort of council to decide what they should do, and the big meeting would be run by a wise, old barn owl. Another time Davey imagined a place where nobody grew old or died and everyone lived together across all generations and just sort of wandered around smiling at each other. Esme understood that place to be Davey's idea of heaven. Esme didn't think she believed in heaven, but she didn't tell Davey.

On the way to the car, Sarah-May pressed Luca to tell Esme his story. 'So, I'm from New York, well New Jersey, but that means pretty much the same if you don't know either?' Esme listened to his story, looking out over her grey canvass to the colours and exotic shapes of Luca's faraway tale.

'I got some temp work at a hotel, a huge upstate resort. I didn't know it was one of the president's places until later. There were marble tiled hallways, velvet drapes, paintings, gold mirrors, our president loves gold, gold everywhere, gold staircases, even some of the johns were gold. Out back were terraced gardens festooned with stone statues of roaring lions and grizzlies.' Luca shook his head at the memory. 'There were all these big guns and heads of families. They'd meet in conference during the day, and you were just supposed to be there, ready, if they needed anything from a drink to a light, whatever. We knew to see, hear and speak what the wise monkey sees, hears and speaks. In the evenings they'd relax, and some would party and play poker with Havanas, coke and girls all provided.'

'Girls provided?' Esme asked, surprised by the implication.

Luca shrugged. 'It is what it is. It's not just you don't say anything, you don't notice anything. And there was plenty not to notice even before what happened.'

The causeway was trimmed either side by grass banks that sloped away to sedge then reed and water rippling, stretching out either side of the track. It was quiet enough that distant sounds drifted across the water unobstructed from some unseen location where the land heaved itself above the level again. Esme could hear the chatter of Sedge Warblers; her dad had explained to her, 'Whereas the reed warblers have a slower, rhythmic song that sounds like conversation, the sedge warbler sounds excited, constantly chopping and changing, with a faster patter.'

Luca commented that there was so much water and Esme smiled and recalled her dad telling her there are some starting to build their houses on stilts above the water. 'He says he saw a place up near Lynn with half a dozen of them built over one of the big meres, made of wood, with walkways between the houses. He says you can only get to them by boat.'

'Sounds like a good place to hide out.' Luca smiled.

'Are you in hiding?' Esme asked him, then reflected herself, 'I guess anyone could lose themselves around here and never be found.' Sarah-May draped an arm around Esme, recognising the longing in her comments.

'Oh, I dunno,' Luca said. 'Isn't everyone hiding from someone or something?'

'I'm not,' Sarah-May said.

'Nor me,' Esme agreed.

'You?' Sarah-May teased Esme. 'You're hiding from yourself.'

'I'm not,' Esme snapped back with the trailing thought that maybe she was.

'Okay.' Sarah-May laughed. 'But you're hiding from your dad.'

'No, I'm not,' Esme said but added, 'Well not right now.' And glanced at her wristwatch. 'I got a couple more hours at least.' Sarah-May laughed, rather more than was natural for her, her arm wrapped around Esme's waist while her eyes were for Luca. Rare spring sun sparkled on the water. They looked out across the mere where, some way distant, a windmill was submerged deep enough that the downward sail trimmed the surface of the water. A rowboat tethered to another of the sails hung, suspended over the mere.

'It's peaceful here at least,' Luca said.

'Sarah-May said you saw a murder. Oh, sorry.' Esme immediately checked herself, but, committed, she went on. 'Is that why you're on the run?'

'Yes, that and the documents I stole.'

'What documents?'

Luca shrugged again. 'I don't really know. It was to bargain with, only it seems to have made my situation worse. Your friends in the underground were interested though.'

'My friends in the underground?' Esme repeated back as a question, only to settle back and enjoy the reference, however ridiculous, used to describe her attendance at one meeting. She looked at Sarah-May, but Sarah-May wasn't thinking about exaggerated references to an underground, she was eyes wide, ears agog, hanging on Luca.

They turned away from the mere and continued to trek up to the spinney with the abandoned car. 'I'm sorry for mentioning the murder,' Esme said. 'It must have been upsetting.'

'At the time,' Luca said. 'Wrong place, wrong time, I guess.' He blew out his cheeks. 'I didn't so much see it as hear it, from a balcony outside the room.'

'Still, it must have been awful,' Sarah-May said.

'Your imagination fills in the gaps. We, that's my pal Ricky and me, were crouched at the other end of this balcony, partly obscured by a large potted shrub, praying to God for a chance to escape unseen. We were only there for a few hash-pipe hits.'

They walked on, Luca telling his story. 'So, this couple come, and I remember a champagne cork pop and their talking and laughing and she's giggling like he's kissing her neck. Then the phone rings and we can hear the guy's mood change. He's getting his date to do lines with him but the phone call sure must've bust his vibe and so she's trying to seduce his body to temper his mind, if you get me? And when they start, you know, getting down to it, we hear the guy ask the girl to put her hands around his throat and she starts strangling him, you know, as they're doing it.'

'No!' Esme said.

'Straight up.' And Luca looked to Sarah-May as though to confirm, regardless that she would only be confirming she heard the same story. 'Then there's a pause as they swap around, she's hesitant but he persuades her. And we, my pal, Ricky and me, hear 'em going again, and we hear him groan long and for a few seconds nothing.' Luca illustrates the pause, and his voice lowers slightly, feigning discretion while drawing interest closer. 'The dude starts getting panicky, sounds like he's slapping her face to try to get her to come around, but she doesn't and now he's freaking, pacing about, talking to himself. Eventually he makes a phone call. We heard him say, "She's not breathing. I can't get her to start breathing again."'

'What then?' Esme asked. The story was from a different world, the tragedy distant.

'The guy makes a call and is just pacing around the suite kinda talking to himself, mumbling like. Me and Ricky are still on the balcony just trying to stay as silent as mice. Then this new guy comes, and he's brought a couple o' fellars with him. This dude says he'll sort it and next thing we hear a chainsaw rip and they've taken the girl's body to the bathroom. They're cutting off her arms and they're cutting off her legs, so they can dispose of her easier.' Luca paused, sighed, and gazed out over the mere.

Esme watched him, waiting. There was no part of Esme's universe that she could relate his tale to.

'It's funny but you don't take it all in at first. It was hours later when I was crouched between trees vomiting and crying.' Sarah-May took Luca's hand in her own. 'I remember Ricky pulling at my shoulder, saying we got to move but none of it seemed real, and it's like, the more real you take it, the more real it becomes.'

'How did you get out?' Esme asked.

'We walked.' Luca laughed and the laugh caught in his throat. 'Seriously, that was it. There were a few moments when the coast was clear, Ricky grabbed the man's computer on the way, said it could be useful insurance, and we walked. The retreat was in the middle of nowhere so there weren't fences to keep you in because there was no need.'

'Bit like round here,' Esme said and was glad nobody paid her comment attention because she immediately recognised it wasn't the same.

'We just kept running, we couldn't stop. Between the dead girl and what we'd taken, everything would be going super-fucking-ballistic.' Luca described running through forests and tumbling down hillsides, his lungs bursting but onward running until he and Ricky were far enough away.

Esme looked out across her drowned landscape, a landscape where nothing marked the horizon, it was just beyond where the eyes could reach and so the eyes melted the sky and land and sea altogether – the earth curves more than it rises and between the birds in the sky and whatever lurks beneath the rising water, there was little left 'man' truly has dominion over.

Esme's dad wouldn't believe Luca's story. She knew he wouldn't because he didn't believe anything for which he didn't know the veracity of the claim for himself. Unless he could take possession of the news and make it his own, he didn't accept it. Even if Esme's dad did accept the story, Esme could imagine him reminding her it only proved all that glistens isn't gold and the grass is no greener elsewhere.

They came upon the car before the end of Luca's story. He seemed relieved to be distracted. 'S-weet auto.' He laughed. 'One wheel missing, one with shredded tyre, many areas of rust.'

'Hey!' Esme laughed, watching him circle the car, identifying its problems.

'Do you know about cars as well?' Sarah-May asked him.

'I had an uncle who was an enthusiast. Pop the hood and I'll take a look at the engine,' Luca said, reaching the front of the vehicle. 'It's okay.' He looked up and smiled at them. 'The hood's not fixed down anyway.' Esme stood smiling back at him with her arms crossed. Luca lifted the bonnet. 'Ah, I see,' and he laughed again, 'no engine.' He let the bonnet fall and it bounced on the frame before settling.

Luca leant back against the bonnet of the car. Esme and Sarah-May joined him, gazing over the flat landscape. 'In the Fens, they don't even bother with hedgerows and fences, dykes and drainage ditches separate the fields,' Esme said. They were facing west, Esme pointed away over to the north at a line of trees. 'They plant them in lines like that as wind breaks. They're poplars mostly. With no hills, when the wind blows, they're all that halts it from ripping across the fields, tearing up fencing and stripping tiles from roofs. When it blows hard, you can see them bend and strain in the wind and after people have to go 'round clearing the broken branches and other wreckage.'

Prompted to return to his story, Luca explained how he and Ricky, on the run in the middle of nowhere, somewhere in upstate New York, were eventually picked up by some renegade militiamen, who bundled them into the back of a van and took them to a lock-up in Boston. 'It sounded like somewhere near the harbour, I could hear gulls. We got shown to this priest, Father Doonan. He says to us,' and Luca imitated the priest's voice, growly and gravelly to Sarah-May and Esme's amusement. '"Do you know what you got your grubby thieves' hands on then?" Father Doonan tells us we're going to get the documents out of the States, and he says we was going to take them as both Ricky and I would have more heat on us than we would be able to deal with. So, he sent Ricky north to Canada, and arranged me passage on a boat to Cork, Ireland where a traveller family who'd been contacted by Doonan's people escorted me across Ireland to the coast and from there on to Britain.'

'What was that like?' Esme asked.

'The Moore family I travelled with were a world unto themselves. And to be fair, it was a world that made me welcome, a world I didn't know existed. There are many worlds I didn't know existed before.'

'What do you mean?'

Esme scanned her world from sat atop the bonnet of her wrecked old car. People are supposed to move while the landscape stay still, she thought, but here the landscape shifts in seasons of water and earth, but the people remain fixed, like reeds in the stream. She asked Luca about the travellers.

'The Moores? Well, there was Francie Moore, a bear of a man. He had dark hair and an accent that were both thick and curly. Sometimes they'd talk to each other in a language I didn't understand. Francie told me it was Shelta, a mixture of English, Irish and slang that made as much sense to outsiders as they wanted it to. They had half-a-dozen piebald ponies and four caravans. There was an old whiskery woman called Nanna Moore, who was the matriarch of the family. She was curious about me and would make me ride in her vardo with her. And there was Morna.' Luca glanced again at Sarah-May.

'It's okay,' she replied. 'Different worlds, right.'

'Morna was Francie's cousin with coils of fair hair and green eyes,' Luca said. 'In the evening the family would gather between their caravans with food cooked over a fire. They fed me a stew of rabbit they trapped, mushrooms foraged from the woods and seaweed from beaches. One of the travellers played a fevered fiddle, another banged a bodhran, and Francie played an accordion, smiling at everyone as he did. And Morna would sing.'

The stillness brooded in the Fens, waiting. With so much space thoughts can travel far. Esme asked Luca, 'How did you end up here, in Fenby?'

'Everywhere is at war these days, and Francie informed me Ireland was no different. I remember Nanna Moore became solemn and serious. I suspect she was concentrating hard due to be being slightly drunk from lacing her orange cordial with moonshine. She stared into my face and said, "Your folks have old wizardry; eyes everywhere, so we'll ride the silent ships."' Again, Luca adopted the accent of the character of his tale to the amusement of Esme and Sarah-May, furnishing her with a thick, old Irish accent.

'There was a fishing village, but fishing didn't pay so it became a smugglers village. Tramore climbed a slope to a headland at the northwest corner of Tramore Bay, where three tall columns stand, one with a statue at the top called the Metal Man that points out to sea. Morna claimed there was a custom if a woman hopped on one-leg, all the way around the Metal Man, she would marry within a year.' Luca smiled at the memory and recalled with a flat, faraway voice his last evening spent in Ireland with Morna. 'There were Japanese gardens where wisteria had overgrown a wooden pergola, and shrubs, ferns and bamboo everywhere. A stream meandered through stones and little blue flowers, through three ponds covered in cherry blossom, where I sat quietly with Morna, before crossing the next morning when the tide was high. Japanese Zelkova trees reminded me of New York, where they're common in the streets.

'There was a crescent five-kilometre beach, where I first saw our silent ships banked up. Past a relic of an amusement park, a crow perched on the perimeter fence watched us through the twilight. A rusted Ferris wheel rose behind. Beyond the beach were some former boating lakes where crows and gulls gathered. The boats banked on the beach were rudimentary, wooden, with creaking masts and oar berths along each flank of their shallow hulls. I was told to help a sailor named Damo load up with sacks of grain, other produce and, to one boat, a commodity I'd not expected: slaves, maybe as many as twenty. They were branded with a tattoo on their shoulder or hip of the ouroboros, the snake that eats its own tail. It symbolised the inescapable cycle of life, death and rebirth, each slave a link in an eternal chain.

'At sea, a sou'wester helped us clear the Irish coast. Waves buffeted the boat and wind tore at the sales, not just the masts but the hull frame itself ached.' Esme wondered how someone could adapt to change and loss as quickly as Luca seemed to. It suggested to her an unsettling lack of permanence. What was the value of anything that could be abandoned so quickly and with such apparent ease?

'The crossing from Ireland was rough,' Luca recalled. 'For a few hours in the afternoon, with the Welsh coast growing more certain, the wind quieted, and the sun was warm. There were a couple of birds in the crow's nest at the top of the mast and Francie laughed and explained they were cormorants, sea crows, and still laughing asked me if I'd heard the expression "as the crow flies" and then he asked me if I knew what a Venus pool was.'

'What is a Venus Pool?' Esme asked.

'A Venus pool is the secret of how the cormorants navigate the silent ships safe of rocks and to the coves where the smugglers land. We headed for a great crescent of beach where Francie told me the ancients banked their boats. At the one end of the bay, blanketed in pink thrift and sea campion, was Ynys Lanwol, Welsh for "tidal island". There was the ruin of a long abandoned medieval monastery there, built on the site of an Iron Age hill fort. At the other end of the bay was Worm's Head; two islands, the Outer and Inner Worm's Head, each over fifty-feet high above the sea and connected by a dolerite rock formation called the Devil's Bridge. A channel of sea water passes under the bridge and between these two islands to the Venus pool, formed from great slabs of this bluestone in a horseshoe shape where gathered cormorants perch and dive for fish, brought in on high tide and trapped there for the cormorants to feast on. Out at sea, the cormorants identify the Venus pools from afar and guide the boats in.'

'The boats banked high into the sand and shingle of the beach, beyond which high rock faces climbed with caves hollowed out. Campfires flickered in the mouths of caves. We drank and rested. Sailors with ukuleles and one with a fiddle filled the starlit beach with song.' And Luca quietly sang the song he remembered the travellers and the sailors singing that night.

> *We're sailing on a strange boat*
> *Heading for a strange shore*
> *Carrying the strangest cargo*
> *That was ever hauled aboard*
>
> *We're sailing on a strange sea*
> *Blown by a strange wind*
> *Carrying the strangest crew*
> *That ever sinned.*

'The following day, everything was hectic. Francie introduced me to Emlyn.' Luca turned to Sarah-May. 'You remember Emlyn, the guy I was sat next to with the grey ponytail.'

'Oh, yeah,' Sarah-May confirmed. 'He wore a cable-knit sweater with a hole the size of a heel in the middle.'

Luca laughed at her description of Emlyn and with hand cradling her shoulder close, he continued. 'He took me away from the beach to meet two other people who he said would be interested in the documents I had.'

'Who were they?' Esme asked.

'They were Angharad and Owain Gruffydd,' Luca said. 'The four of us then travelled across Britain, always avoiding main routes. I was unknown and couldn't believe I'd be recognised so I assumed the people I travelled with preferred not to be noticed. I don't know why we ended up in Fenby, they kept changing our destination while we travelled, but there was always talk of a meeting with other rebels.'

'Speaking of travellers, it looks like we got company.' Away on the road Luca caught sight of a figure.

It was Davey, with hand shielding his eyes, looking back at them from the track. 'I'd better go. He'll wonder.' Esme lifted herself from the bonnet of the car. 'I'll be back in a minute.'

Davey had paused to look at who was there on the car. His brown hair was woolly from being blown through by a day's working wind. 'Hey, Davey,' Esme said. She paused a few metres shy and waited for him to come to her.

'Who's on the car?' Davey asked.

'Sarah-May,' Esme said. 'You know Sarah-May.'

'They're kissing,' Davey said.

Esme looked. 'Yes, Davey. They're kissing, people do.'

'Who is he?' Davey then asked, stood side by side now staring across a field at the two figures, turned toward each other, silhouetted to Davey and Esme by the position of the sun.

'His name's Luca. He's Sarah-May's friend,' Esme said. 'The name's Italian; he's American.'

'American?' Davey rubbed his chin, still staring toward them. 'Did you say it's okay for them to sit on the car bonnet?'

'Yes.' Esme gazed at Davey's face; his eyes were fixed on the interlopers at their car. 'They've not been inside, only outside.'

Esme added and clicked her fingers in front of his face to break his attention.

'If you says it's alright, Essie, but I don't think they should be sitting on the bonnet like that. They might break it.'

'The car doesn't work anyway, Davey.' Esme tugged at the sleeve of his sweater. 'There's no engine, remember. Come, I'll take you to meet him. You'll like him.' And as they walked, Esme added, 'We've been waiting for you to come.' It pleased her how he smiled to think she would've brought them to meet him and that they waited there for him. And Esme thought, there are surely times when to lie is not a sin.

VII

There was a skeletal lattice of causeway roads that criss-crossed the flooded Fens, connecting the scattered ridge villages and islet towns. Approaching Cambridge by these roads would have meant dealing with the uncertainty of the condition of these roads followed by the certainty of having to produce papers at Cambridge's northern gatehouse, where bored or officious security guards could go through their belongings. To avoid that, Angharad and Owain, Emlyn Lewis, Joan Ball and John Lilburne shared water transport to Cambridge; a Norfolk-style fen wherry piloted by two traders, the Horton brothers, who were returning to Cambridge where they would buy goods they could trade throughout the Fens. It was mainly commodities such as tea, coffee, chocolate, some silks and fabrics less coarse and provincial than much of what would be usual across the Fens. Otherwise, electrical goods that were near impossible to source in the Fens without a contact were much sought after.

The Horton brothers were not originally traders, their father and his father had been mechanics running a garage halfway out to Norwich. As petrol and gasoline became rarer commodities and the machines fuelled by them became more expensive to buy and run through the age of austerity, the Horton brothers diversified and reinvented themselves. Although their roughly hewn manner would feign no such thing, they were becoming part of the new rich of the area – though wealth was relative and theirs certainly modest.

Luca had told Emlyn that he'd decided he'd like to stay in Fenby. Tired of travelling, he saw no reason to be in Cambridge;

his files and documents they had, and there was nowhere in England lower to lie than the Fens.

At Waterbeach, at the southern edge of the flooded fen-plain, barracks could be seen with sentry towers that had spotlights sweeping across the black water searching where superstitious folks said ghosts whisper at night amongst the reeds and pull people down. 'Neptune's tithe' some across the Fens called it. They were amidst a flurry of half-a-dozen small vessels waved through the sentry post at Waterbeach with a cursory nod by disinterested sentries.

They continued their approach to Cambridge via a maze of canals and lodes, relieved by levees. Across these levees, standing above the water line like flamingos, were regiments of wind turbines. Between raised embankments, safe above even unseasonably high water-levels, fields of reflective solar panels glared in the summer sun, and sluiced streams of water were channelled through turbines producing electricity for the city. Cambridge still functioned as an imitation of what it once was, sufficiently redolent of its dazzlingly brilliant halcyon past that those still burrowed deep into its musty grandeur retained hope. Beneath Cambridge's bridges they lowered their sail and the mast which folded down over the length of the wherry. They drifted, Arcadian, past the river traffic of punts and toward those august temples of academia.

A large fare was humming with activity on Midsummer Common. Joan Ball asked to disembark. Recovering her poise on the bank, she turned to those in the wherry, 'Right, I'll see you all again soon enough, I shouldn't wonder.' Then she was gone, off into the hubbub of the crowd.

They continued past Magdalene College on their right, under the covered Bridge of Sighs at St John's College and past lawns where young students sat at ease, young lovers courted on the grass, and occasional academics came and went as the wherry drifted past. They were like images from Keats' 'Grecian Urn'. For those on board the wherry, it stirred both sentimentality and resentment.

They passed Trinity College on their right and moored on the left, where steps approached a narrow, cobbled street shaded by the high brick walls of warehouses. At the end they turned right and along another narrow street that snaked through to the grand front façade of Trinity Hall. It was there the Gruffydds' party were to meet with Professor Priestley and colleagues, to whom the information provided by Luca had been entrusted.

For some in the corporate-state in London, Cambridge had been too long indulged as much for its fading prestige as for the possibilities they provided the government. They were considered hotbeds of dissent more than hotbeds of innovation, which was only ever partly true as its dissent tended to be over-nourished in discussion and under-nourished in willingness to action.

A college porter with more hair beneath his nose than atop his head, knock-kneed and slow but with a valet's courtesy, greeted them at the Porter's Lodge. John Lilburne he knew, and greeted as such. He fastened his top button and straightened his tie, the unnecessary habits of a bygone era. In the arcane and insulated cloisters of Cambridge, there were many who sought reassurance in delusion. The porter led them across Avery Court with its geometrically designed hedges, passed the stained-glass windows of the college chapel and along corridors patterned with black and white tiles, to a panelled, heavy oak door. Emlyn Lewis and John Lilburne were instructed to remain outside. Only the Gruffydds were wanted beyond.

Three people sat behind a row of desks awaiting Angharad's

party with apologies for a fourth academic yet to arrive. Behind them were a pair of leaded, mullioned windows through which early evening sun poured through like syrup.

Professor Priestley chaired the meeting. His white shirt ached as it stretched over his vast, domed belly with a sliding, red patterned tie that had to be repeatedly centred.

Owain pulled at the knees of his trousers before sitting, and when sat he pulled at cuffs and even collar of his shirt in settling himself. The academic to Priestley's right glanced at her watch and to kill time asked, 'And how are things in Wales? With the struggles and such.'

Owain answered, 'The Welsh are freer and more chaotic than ever they were. Some might describe it as a study in entropy.' The woman studied him as he said this. Owain smiled and added, 'Mae'n dir hardd fy nhadau, mae eu straeon yn galw ar draws amser.' The academic to the other side of Priestley tapped a pen repeatedly against her hand.

There was bustle behind them, the door opened and closed and a flustered man entered with piles of papers clutched across his chest. 'Hello, sorry about being late. Tardy mark in Professor Priestley's big book for me, I'm afraid.'

Professor Priestley had already introduced himself as professor of physics and time and his two colleagues he introduced as an historian, Anne Farron, and Ariel Du Terre, who was a mathematician and musician working 'to compose a symphony literally written in the stars and conducted by their movements.' Angharad tensed not from nerves but a thought that cast these people in contempt for how little of life outside of Cambridge they knew and how insulated they still were.

Priestley introduced the latecomer as Rupert Reddy. He spent some moments untangling his gown from his chair as his eyes skipped around the waiting faces. Professor Priestley rolled his eyes. 'We've all had a chance to review the materials, so maybe we should go along the line and set out where our current thinking is. Anne?'

Anne Farron had long grey hair she swept behind her ear from the side of her face. She looked up from her notes, over her glasses, and asked, 'The information your American contact brought is interesting and concerning.' Farron glanced along the line to suggest consensus from the other panellists. 'The American is not with you though.'

'No,' Owain confirmed. 'He was a reluctant courier who knew nothing more than anyone else who could read.'

Farron considered this. 'Can you be sure this isn't disinformation?'

'No,' Owain stated; matter of fact. 'We just present it to your interest.'

Farron nodded, removed her spectacles and bit the end of one of the earpieces of the frame, an unconscious act, which she paused from to comment, 'Like you, Owain, I'm a historian. I view things through that lens. You do know how revolutions usually end?'

Angharad watched Owain fold his right leg over his left to combat a jittering impulse. 'Is history not driven forward through the successive combustive effects of revolutions?' Angharad thought Owain sounded too meek. 'Previous failures shouldn't be a reason not to try.' Angharad smiled at him, supportive.

'That seems a little dispassionate,' Professor Farron suggested.

'We won't fail,' Angharad interjected, words bursting past the restraint she gripped on her lap in fiercely interlocked fingers.

Professor Farron turned to Angharad. 'But should you?' In the lingering pause that followed her question, she considered further Angharad over her spectacles. 'I don't doubt your commitment, but what of the risk for those who follow you?'

'Most are committed by circumstances, not by us,' Angharad replied. Professor Farron leant back, laid her spectacles down on top of her papers. It was a signal for Priestley to move on to Professor Reddy.

'I'm interested in the universal mind, telepathy and intuition, ways to explore what we understand without knowing,' Professor Reddy endeavoured to explain. 'I'm exploring how the whole of history is the process of something Hegelians call weltgeist. That is, history as directed by a common unconscious spirit we are all a part of.' Dr Reddy accepted the incredulity of others to his work with the good nature of one used to such sceptical responses.

'What interests me is whether you represent an expression of the manifestation of the weltgeist.' Dr Reddy, his hair shorter, thinner and a little greyer than it once was when he'd been based in Bristol and Owain had known him a little. He was pale of skin but flushed of cheek with eyes dreamily adding to the impression he was perpetually herbalised, though some claimed it was the effect of fasting. He looked across Owain and Angharad with an ethereal detachment rendering him almost as abstract as his thoughts. Whether just or not, Professor Reddy's manner irritated Angharad. She regarded his philosophical daydreaming as fiddling while Rome burns.

'I suppose my question is, are your peasants with pitchforks the weltgeist with pitchforks, or just an angry, largely directionless mob that will be put down and subsequently melt away under fear of punishment?' He smiled. 'I'm not, of course, saying that is the case, just asking.'

'This will be a feature, not footnote, to history, Professor,' Angharad stated.

Dr Reddy gazed at Angharad for some moments, finally resolving, 'Fine.'

'Fine, Dr Reddy?' queried Professor Priestley.

'Yes, fine,' Dr Reddy confirmed, nodding. 'That's enough for me.'

'Fine,' Professor Priestley repeated back. 'Dr Du Terre, you're next.'

'Thank you, Professor.' Dr Du Terre held Angharad with a fixed gaze. 'There is a high probability, whether your uprising is successful or not, the state won't cope with further instability.' Dr Du Terre was a thin woman with short dark hair and a nose which, while not being large, came to a perfect point. She spoke with hands of long fingers, well suited to a musician. 'Richard King and his government are strongly allied with the Americans, but there is still much support for the Europeans, keen to block the Americans.'

Dr Du Terre continued, whether others followed or not. She was not a woman to be restrained by the bovine limitations of those people plodding after her. 'The Scotch will break of course – the Geddes woman only confirmed what I'd already surmised. With such instability in England, it is also conceivable Rhodri will be successful in Wales. Although,' and here she paused, held her fingers extended in a line over her lips beneath her nose, relishing her moment as though its scent was painted on the tips of her fingers, 'a collapse in England will be like a black hole; the gravity will suck any nascent Scottish or Welsh state down with it. There will be chaos as vested interests compete to pick over the ruins. London will still have value, much diminished, but the rest of the country that is already moribund will be left to die.' She paused again. Heard through the windows, a bell tolled somewhere in Cambridge's dreaming skies. 'The speed with which the inhabitants of the cities and large towns of the north and the Midlands spill into the countryside will increase. Disease and mortality rates will increase concomitantly with the decline of medical care and research, common illnesses like colds and flus will become more epidemic. However,' Dr Du Terre paused again for dramatic effect, 'Cambridge can protect itself. It'll need to raise a militia but there are sufficient unemployed and idle even in Cambridge for that.'

'Especially in Cambridge, I'd say,' Professor Priestley commented, only to receive a sharp glance from Dr Du Terre that suggested his interventions were neither useful nor wanted distraction. Angharad developed in the short time spent listening to Dr Du Terre a dislike for her that far exceeded the antipathy she had felt toward her dopey colleague.

Priestley asked, 'Do you have a question for them, Dr Du Terre?'

'No,' Dr Du Terre answered, briefly regarding her notes before fully addressing Professor Priestley's question. 'No, I've run through all the possible scenarios, the various questions. I've factored for discrepancies due to dishonesty. I've cross-referenced all of it with stellar and planetary positions. I have all I need.'

'Well, that being the case,' Professor Priestley brought the meeting to order. 'Our lives, like the life of Albion, are defined by events, by individual moments that direct the course of the flow. We may barely notice these events piling up until a point when the future suddenly calls us to account. I remember with hindsight the different points that measured our decline, and the architecture and machinery of our lives that broke down. Here in this oasis of Cambridge, there have been times when it has felt as though the darkness has been closing in around us. And in that darkness the waters rose and the rivers swelled.' He paused and smiled with a proud chin over his oration. 'Psychologists tell me progress can only be found by first recognising the patterns that entrap us.'

With a background in psychology, Professor Reddy commented, 'That's true enough.'

'But what if by recognising those patterns, we can step beyond them?' Professor Priestley picked up his theme. 'I have heard psychologists say too often in life we adhere to patterns that fail us for fear of risking the unknown, and so we're trapped to forever repeat these patterns.'

Professor Reddy commented, 'That's true enough.'

'Consumerism consumes itself. The ouroboros eats its own tail. There is only so long water can be drawn before the well is exhausted and the land fails. The state totters, governments fall until to avoid becoming an irrelevance they remove the electoral traps that kept tripping them. Tax revenue seeps out through the pores of corruption and the state infrastructure crumbles, atrophying. Soon, the people return to nebulous groups scavenging a survival. Through these experiences the people recognise only through collective effort for collective reward can they survive and prosper. Their ambition is not to renew but to build anew. Now,' Professor Priestley paused, thumbs and forefingers pinching his lapels in Churchillian affectation, 'if you'd wait outside for a few minutes, we shall discuss your proposal and decide the measure of assistance affordable.'

Owain and Angharad stood, but before leaving Angharad addressed them with Joan Ball's foreboding words. She wasn't sure why, perhaps they were all that cut through the noise in her head. 'There will soon come a time when worm-wood will fall from the sky and even you in Cambridge, you precious few, as elsewhere, will have to decide where you will stand. There is a reckoning coming that none shall be able to avoid.'

VIII

Outside, waiting on Professor Priestley's deliberations, two women approached along the corridor. Their shoes squeaked on the parquet flooring, one of them wrung her hands as they approached.

'State agents are on their way. I'd better tell the professors.' The older of the pair passed between Angharad's group, knocked and entered the room with the academics. When she re-emerged she handed a package to Angharad, a stuffed manilla envelope. 'This is for you. Dr Du Terre said you'd understand.'

The other newcomer was a contact of Lilburne's she introduced as Grace. She said, 'We need to buy you some time if you're to get away from here and up to Wandlebury. Come, we have a punt ready to launch.' Grace had a model's lines to her face and the crystal vowels of a debutante's accent. She was on her toes with alert eyes but Angharad, admiring her shiny chestnut hair, wondered how much she'd suffered, how much close-to involvement she'd actually faced. *She will.*

'I'm going to play the part of Angharad...' She turned to the voice of the older woman and mention of her own name. She knew Angharad's name; Angharad didn't know hers, and yet this woman would take Angharad's place in the firing line. It prompted an uncomfortable feeling that Angharad couldn't describe but which would linger with her long after they had departed. 'I'll need someone to sit in for Owain. It's not got to be convincing, just something to delay them.'

'I'll do it,' John Lilburne said.

'No.' Emlyn cut across him. 'I'll do it. They know Owain is Welsh and besides, you're too young.'

Owain was uneasy leaving Emlyn. 'Come, it's best,' Angharad said. 'They'll buy us time.'

Emlyn nodded. 'It'll be tidy, butt. I'll see you ahead.'

Owain hesitated still and time dilated. 'Now Owain!' Angharad urged him out of his reverie. 'They're on their way. We've got to leave now!'

On the far side of Latham Lawn, they walked quicker and quicker but checking themselves so not to stumble into running and betray their inconspicuous exit. Lilburne and Grace danced around them like electrons, possessing energy that alluded to their youth and idealism and, Angharad thought, their lack of experience. Troopers on the bridge could only watch as they made their escape. Grace pushed the launch clear but kept the punt close to the bank. Angharad looked back at two shrinking figures, uncertain like memories, looking along the river after them.

* * *

Back in the room with the professors, Emlyn and the woman acting as Angharad, with grey hair threaded through black and string of pearls exchanged glances. A call had informed Professor Priestley they were on their way and in that pregnant moment there was nothing but the sound of rain peppering the windows and the heavy clunk of an old grandmother clock in the corner.

The door swung open. Two men in suits entered, a broad, thick-set man with thick, curly hair followed a leaner man, who wore a trilby. The one with curly hair stood with his back to the door he had closed behind him. His leaner associate directly approached Professor Priestley, took up his water glass and a pen and 'tinged' the side of it, unnecessarily ensuring he had the attention of all.

He smiled, lowered the glass and pen to the table, slowly removed his hat and dropped it on the table in front of Professor Priestley. The hat declared its owner's authority. His hair on top was gone, just a collar around the sides that had kept his hat secure. 'My name's Miller. My colleague is McCain. We're up from the London 'burbs. This is much nicer, isn't it, McCain?'

'Much nicer,' McCain agreed. He had a Northern Irish accent that sounded like distant thunder.

'We're off into the Fens next week.' Miller was tall and stood with an imperious height. 'It's like another world there, isn't it, McCain?'

'Another world,' McCain confirmed, and embellished, 'Cambridge and its fineries would be like pearls to swine for them.'

'Thank you for that, McCain.' Miller took over again. 'You know you're very lucky. Now, here we are, a moment caught between yesterday in the 'burbs and tomorrow in the Fens.' Miller turned again to McCain.

'And today, we're here,' McCain said.

'We are,' Miller agreed. 'And tomorrow Monty arrives.'

'He won't be happy if this isn't sorted,' McCain announced.

'He won't,' Miller agreed.

Professor Priestley, with a nervy timbre to his voice, asked, 'Why are we being questioned?'

Dr Du Terre gave Priestley a look that called him an idiot.

Miller replied, 'Let's start with the doubts expressed about the nature and legality of this meeting and we'll take it from there.'

Professor Priestley stammered, 'But, but this isn't political; it's an academic meeting.'

'Oh, do behave, Professor.' Miller chided him. 'Everything is politics.' Adding, 'That's Thomas Mann, by the way.' Professor Priestley looked up and his lips considered speaking but thought better and he lowered his eyes back to the table. Miller asked, 'You are Professor Priestley?'

Professor Priestley stammered further, failing to find his voice to answer.

Miller mocked his stammering before laying a hand kindly on the professor's shoulder and saying, 'Don't worry, sir. I know who you are.' And looking around the room added, 'I know who you all are.' Miller turned his attention to Emlyn. 'So, who are you then, sir?'

'Owain Gruffydd,' Emlyn said.

Miller looked around, but nobody contradicted Emlyn.

'Oh, you're Owain Grufud,' Miller said with intentional mispronunciation. 'We're going to need to speak then, you and I, aren't we?' Emlyn didn't answer.

'And who are you?' Miller said to the woman sat beside Emlyn.

'His wife,' The woman answered.

Miller drew a handgun from inside his jacket, a revolver, pointed it at the woman and shot her point blank in the forehead – he didn't wait for the expression to turn from surprise to horror and fear as she recognised the gun pointed at her, and Miller didn't wait for begging and explanations. The force of the impact of the shot snapped the woman's head back and mocked her with a third eye punctured through the centre of her forehead. She sat upright for a tottering moment, all three eyes wide with surprise, before slumping from her chair and crumpling to the floor.

'You shot her,' Professor Priestley stammered. 'She's ... she's dead.'

Miller put the gun back under his jacket. 'So, are you still going to persist that you're Owain Gruffydd?' Emlyn didn't answer. 'McCain, I'll keep Professor Priestley and our whiskery wizard here. Have the agents take the others in. Then you come back and join me.'

Miller watched McCain lead the three academics out by the nose of his revolver and only when the closed door blocked his view of them did he return to Emlyn and Priestley. 'I can tell immediately if someone's lying. It's a gift,' Miller explained to Emlyn. 'What did you say your name was, sir?'

'Owain Gruffydd,' Emlyn answered without delay.

'Tck-tck-tck.' Miller pulled a switchblade knife from his pocket and toyed with it. 'You heard what McCain said, didn't you? Monty comes tomorrow.'

'Who's Monty?' Emlyn asked.

'Have you met Monty?' Miller replied to Emlyn's question with a question. He turned the switchblade on its point on the tabletop.

'How do I know if I've met him if I don't know who he is?'

'You'd know Monty if you'd met him.' Miller idly waved the switchblade at Emlyn.

'It's all been so long. There's been so many people ...' Emlyn began.

'You'd know Monty even if you'd not met him,' Miller added.

'So, I must know him.'

'You must,' Miller confirmed. 'Monty's kosher, the real deal, believe me. I know him. I knew him from way back. He's the mensch. You're a fraud though, aren't you, Welshman?' Miller changed his grip on the handle of the knife, so that it was carried with the impression of greater intent to harm.

'I'm no fraud,' Emlyn Lewis stated and held Miller's eyes even after Miller accused him of having fool's pride.

' ... And you know what pride comes before, don't you?'

Through gritted teeth Miller asked Emlyn. 'Are you a Welsh rebel? Do you answer Rhodri's fiery call with the spirit of Glyndŵr in your blood? Do you speak the old tongue?'

'No,' Emlyn answered, 'That language has been banned since the blue books.'

'Ah,' Miller said. 'The treachery of the blue books.' Alighting on Emlyn's reference, Miller turned to Priestley, 'You know the Welsh are savage people. A report was commissioned by the king and the prince of Wales.' Miller glanced back toward Emlyn to read his expression at reference to the reviled prince of Wales, George, that fat philanderer who had to make a moonlit escape last he was in Cardiff. A crowd had gathered at the hotel where he was laid up, drunk, mauling a pair of local girls.

'The report found it didn't matter how much money the crown wasted.' He turned again to watch Emlyn as he spoke. 'They found it was a waste pouring more and more money into tumbledown townships where the people were ignorant and lazy and backward believing. Isn't that true, Welshman?' Emlyn didn't speak, and Miller smiled at the fury burning in his eyes. 'For nearly a thousand years the English have tried to civilise the Welsh, but it's always the same; they drink and fight, they're morally base, just see this fellow with his grey ponytail. He thinks he's Merlin.' Emlyn still said nothing. 'Who are you, Welshman? I know you're not Owain Gruffydd. I want to meet your Owain Gruffydd. Monty wants to meet your Owain Gruffydd. Owain Gruffydd has something that should belong to Monty. But you, sir, you are no more Owain Gruffydd than she was your wife.' Miller nodded casually toward the dead woman with the hole in her forehead slumped on the floor.

'I'm Owain Gruffydd. I came here to lecture on history. I

don't know what you're talking about.'

'Do you sing?' Miller asked.

'What?'

'I heard it said the Welsh are great singers. So, do you sing, sir?'

'No,' Emlyn said. 'I don't sing.'

'Oh, but you will sing. When we're done with you, sir, you'll be singing so much you'll be fit for one of your all-male voice choirs.' Miller lifted his hand high for a split second, and then drove the knife down through Emlyn's hand that was laid flat on a small table to his side. The knife burst through skin, powered through bones and sinew to nail his hand to the tabletop. Emlyn screamed and bit his lip, the scream continuing in his eyes and across his face.

'Stay there,' Miller quipped.

McCain returned, shaking his right hand and rubbing the knuckles with his left. 'Everything okay?' Miller asked him.

'Aye,' McCain answered. 'A moment's disagreement with the philosopher, but it's all sorted.'

Miller watched Emlyn crouching with his hand nailed to the table; black-red blobs of blood falling from his hand.

'The philosopher claimed to be something called a Hegelian,' McCain explained. 'He says we're all part of God and the universe. So, I'm thinking, could be a cult or could be terrorists. Either way it sounds like sedition.'

Miller turned to Professor Priestley, 'Do you see the problem, Professor?' The professor shook his head. Miller turned back to McCain. 'The Professor doesn't see the problem, McCain. Perhaps, you should further elucidate for the professor?'

Emlyn let go of the handle of the blade skewering his right hand to the table when McCain approached and took the handle himself and yanked the blade free. Emlyn clutched his wounded hand with his free hand and slumped back down between his chair and the panel of desks. McCain then handed the knife back to Miller. 'He was polite,' McCain conceded.

'Good,' Miller remarked. 'Politeness is important – it goes to the very essence of the core of the heart of the character of a person.' Miller then casually slapped Emlyn across the cheeks.

A thin trickle of dark, yellow urine issued from the professor, stained his trousers, gathered at the hem, and trickled to a tiny puddle that splashed the side of his right brogue. 'Look what you've made our professor do?' McCain laughed and pointed at Priestley, before continuing his own account. 'He was polite enough, the philosopher, I'll give him that. But I had this feeling he was laughing at me, like I'm just some rustic peasant, you know?'

'Condescending, you mean,' Miller interjected, 'supercilious.'

'Aye,' McCain agreed. 'Condescending, supercilious, as you say.'

Miller turned to Emlyn slumped on the floor, 'I hate that sort of thing, don't you, Welshman?' Emlyn didn't answer. Blood from his wounded hand leaked over the clasping hand.

'Polite though,' Miller heard McCain again say.

Miller was gazing down at Emlyn and drawing a pristine, clean and folded handkerchief from his trouser pocket, which he unfolded and tossed down to Emlyn. 'You look a little pale, Welshman. Tie that around your hand. You can sort the cost with me later. Not now, not now. You're bleeding, man.' He stood over Emlyn while watching him bind his hand. 'Ooh, it does look nasty. Make sure you bind it tightly. It'll be of little use if it's not tight.'

Emlyn said nothing but used his teeth to help grip the handkerchief that he pulled tight with his free hand.

Miller returned to McCain, 'So what of the polite but supercilious Hegelian then?'

'He tells me, this fellar Hegel says we are all part of God and the universe, and we all share this world spirit.'

'Oh,' Miller said. 'So, it's worse than sedition then. It's socialism.'

'I brought this problem to his attention,' McCain said. 'He protested he was an academic speaking academically ...'

Miller cut in laughing. 'They always say that it was all academic, just theoretical, or I was just speaking in the abstract. One minute it's this Hegel, the next it's Marx. The abstract becomes concrete if the flower isn't nipped in the bud. What did you do?'

McCain explained, 'The man was working himself up, quite hysterical, so I was duty bound to pacify him.'

'How did you pacify him?'

'I punched him in the face.'

'Ooh,' Miller grimaced, then grinned and asked, 'Did it work?'

'Knocked him clean out,' McCain replied, sheepish but pleased.

'Ha!' Miller laughed and clasped a hand over his mouth. When he slid his hand away, he revealed lips more seriously set. 'What then?'

'Two security agents carried him off to a detention centre.' McCain looked over Professor Priestley and Emlyn with a sigh in his voice. 'Are we finishing this all up yet?'

'Sure, sure,' Miller said. 'After all, Monty comes tomorrow.' He smiled at Professor Priestley sympathetically, as one might a tongue-tied child, and turned back to McCain. 'This one's a nebbish fellow.' Miller then pulled up a chair to sit beside

Professor Priestley. McCain sat himself on Priestley's other side. 'The professor looks a little nervous. Hold his hand while I ask him a few questions.'

'Hold his hand?' McCain asked.

'Yeah, hold his hand,' Miller repeated. 'Be like his friend. Confessing is tough, sometimes a person needs a little friendly support.'

'You're wanting me to hold his hand?'

'Hold his hand,' Miller repeated. Priestley looked between them. McCain shrugged. 'Okay, I'll hold his hand.' And McCain did, gently stroking the top side and smiling with sweet reassurance at Professor Priestley.

'Do you recognise this as Owain Gruffydd?' Miller asked Priestley, indicating Emlyn slumped with eyes imploring Priestley to confirm he was indeed Owain Gruffydd, as he had claimed. Priestley hesitated before confirming. 'Are you sure? Are you sure that this ... this ...' Miller searched for an expression that would successfully convey his contempt, ' ... this delusional hobo and wannabe wizard with no magic, this is Owain Gruffydd?'

'Yes,' Priestley whispered, meek and unconvincing. McCain held Priestley's right hand between his own. Miller blew his cheeks out. 'You know, you're really starting to get on my breasts, Professor. You're just not trying to help, are you?' Miller swept his fingers across his mouth and chin and tried again. 'Owain Gruffydd has something. Did you see it?'

Priestley looked around for a way to avoid the inevitable betrayal. 'Help him, McCain.' McCain looked up at Miller not fully understanding. 'Digital extraction.' Miller added.

McCain adjusted his hold of Professor Priestley's hand, tightened his lips, and pulled on Professor Priestley's little finger, dislocating it. Professor Priestley whimpered rather than screamed. Miller asked again, 'Is this man Owain Gruffydd?' McCain took the professor's fourth finger. Priestley looked sadly at Emlyn and shook his head.

'Good,' Miller said and kindly stroked the top of Priestley's head and briefly kissed it before standing to continue. Priestley glanced at McCain still holding his fourth finger. Miller asked, 'He was here though, wasn't he?' Priestley nodded. 'Good, good. And did he have it with him?' Professor Priestley sadly and resignedly nodded. 'You're doing very well. He is doing well, isn't he McCain?'

'Very well,' McCain replied. Professor Priestley's little finger hanging loosely at a tangent. 'Very well indeed.'

'And you know where Owain Gruffydd went, don't you?'

IX

'Is that you Davey Clay?' Esme felt like she was being watched as she looked out over the fen. In the distance, dark black clouds were banking up in the direction of Peterborough. A blustery wind had gathered and grown more insistent, sufficiently that some of the clothes and linen Esme pegged to the line across the back garden had blown free and scattered across the vegetable patch and beyond the hedge and out over the fen. Esme wondered whether this could be different if she married Tom, the mayor's son. She looked around, pulling her hair away from her face. 'If you are there, Davey Clay, show yourself and help me retrieve this washing.'

Esme waited but there was nothing. She walked to the gap in the hedge where the wind-blown picket gate stood open, wobbling and threatening to swing back and forth again. She paused. It was as though something she hadn't seen had nevertheless caught her eye. 'Don't be silly, Esme,' she whispered to herself, shaking her head. 'Everyone says you've got a fanciful imagination.'

She was bent, picking free one of Tilly's dresses, which had caught up in the hedge, when she heard the definite crackle of breaking twigs and of movement. She snapped to attention, looking around. There was nothing but the rumble of a motorcar's engine. The motorcar circled slowly to a stop in the gravel yard. Two men got out the car wearing dark suits and hats with brims that shaded their faces.

'They must be agents.'

She watched them approach the front door. One stood slightly behind the other, he glanced around as he waited. For a long moment he seemed to be looking directly in Esme's direction. She didn't move. 'He's not seen you. It's not you he's looking at.' Having spoken with Lizzie at the door, they turned and left. Esme watched their car leave the yard and listened to its engine trailing along the road before she returned to the house herself.

Lizzie confirmed they were state agents. 'What did they want?'

'They asked who lived here,' Lizzie answered. 'And who the head of the house was. I said he's out and they says they'd come back when he was in. They ask, when will he be back, so I says, he's working up at Moscow Farm, it's a fair trek, so he's been leaving early and getting back late.' Lizzie gazed into space, recalling the conversation as if it were playing out in front of her. 'They ask where Moscow Farm was and commented it was an unusual name. So, I told 'em where it was an' 'splained what yer dad tells, that it climbs the first high ground 'tween here and Russia, so when the cold weather blows from the east the folks 'round here'd say the weather comes straight from Moscow. The agent fellars smile but I can see they ain't interested and they ask me if your old man's a farmer and I says no he's an agricultural engineer, an' he'll be up at Moscow all week, an' I know that 'cus he's taken his machines up there and Davey Clay to help.' Then Lizzie stopped talking like thoughts had gotten hold of her words and she gazed at a point in space as if there was something she was wary of, and she eventually added, 'Hope your dad won't be raw.'

'Why would he?' Esme responded.

'Telling them fellars he's got machinery and such. It'll all go in the census. Your dad says taxes are bleedin' us and these taxes ain't fair. Your dad says loads o' people are up in arms 'bout it all.'

'Why aren't they fair?' Esme asked.

'Your dad says it ain't fair 'cause it don't matter if you're a beggarman or a banker, you pays the same. An' he says folks away from London are even rawer, 'cause they say we don't get nought for it.' Esme didn't know what to say. She didn't really know much about taxes and such like, and though she knew her dad could get raw, she had no idea if he would for what Lizzie had said. She and Lizzie both sat, gazing out into the yard at the space where the agents' car had been.

The afternoon drifted. Esme finished bringing the washing in from the line while Lizzie pushed and turned the posser inside the dolly tub. The sun came around the house and was lower in the sky when they heard the car tyres on the gravel yard.

They both looked at each other.

They heard footsteps but didn't see the agent until a face appeared in the aperture created by the open upper half of the stable door. His face was huge with a great dome of thinning hair, and it was staring straight at Esme.

'Hello!' He grinned at Esme. 'You weren't here when we called earlier, were you?' The face noticed Lizzie sat in the corner and again to Esme, he said, 'Maybe your sister told you.' Beyond the face, Esme could see his accomplice strolling around the yard.

'Oh, she's not my sister.' The second man approached behind the first; he was thick-set and looked younger.

'Oh,' the face said. The face rose, its body straightened.

'It was easier than explaining,' Lizzie spoke.

'Maybe we could come in for a conversation with you both.' As he said this, he took a small, black notebook from the inside pocket of his jacket and made a note. He noticed Tilly and smiled at her as he returned the notebook to his pocket. He turned his expression into a strange grimace, then back to a smile. Tilly giggled back at him. 'What d'you say? Would that be okay?'

'Can we say no?' Lizzie said. Esme was surprised at her protest.

'Of course, you can, Mrs Sedgebrook.'

He already knows our names, Esme thought.

'We're here to ask just a few questions for the census. The great census covers all of us. It's the first step in re-building our nation. Who couldn't want that, hey?' Lizzie assented, and the first man reached over the stable door, pulled back the bolt and let himself in. 'Good afternoon, ladies. My name is Miller, my colleague is McCain.' His colleague nodded only to acknowledge his name. 'We won't take long, though we may at some point need to see your husband, Mrs Sedgebrook, at some separate point.' Tilly joined her mother and clutched her leg. 'So, just a few questions. Maybe we could take tea?'

'I'll get it,' Esme announced, as surprised by her sudden voice as anyone else in the room such that she repeated, 'I'll get it. I'll get the tea.'

Miller sat, pulling at the knees of his suit trousers as he did. He wore a waistcoat, his associate, McCain, did not. 'So, shall we start by confirming you are Lizzie Sedgebrook, married to a Keith Sedgebrook.' Lizzie nodded. 'The little girl ...' he referred to his notebook, flicking back a few pages from where it opened, 'Tilly.' Hearing her name, the infant looked up at Miller. 'She is ...' He read. 'Not your present husband's child.'

Lizzie nodded and beneath the line of his eyes, said, 'Tilly was from my first marriage.'

Miller made a note in his little book. Esme placed mugs of tea down in front of each man. 'That was very quick.'

'The water was on.' Esme fetched the milk from the pantry.

Lizzie said, 'We were preparing the supper.'

Miller addressed Esme, 'So, you aren't Mrs Sedgebrook's sister, but you do live here.'

'Yes.'

Flicking through pages of his notebook, Miller asked, 'So, tell me about yourself?'

'Lizzie's married to my dad.' Esme looked uncertain, glancing at Lizzie.

'O-kay.' Miller made another note. 'And your name is ...?'

'Esme.'

'Esme Sedgebrook.' Miller repeated back. Esme nodded. 'And how old are you, Esme?'

'Seventeen,' Esme said. Miller glanced at McCain and tapped his pen against his notebook. 'There are really two things we need to do now, then we can leave you in peace.'

'We'll still need to talk to Mr Sedgebrook,' McCain spoke for the first time.

'Yes,' Miller agreed. 'Aside from catching up with Mr Keith Sedgebrook. But even then, I think we can get most of what we need now.' Miller turned back to Lizzie, assuming she was the senior. He said, 'We need to ask some questions about what you have here and such like, and we'll need to have a little poke around the house. Nothing major, just popping a head around all the doors really. Make sure you've got nobody else hiding out up there, hey.' He laughed. McCain laughed also. 'So, why don't I talk with you, Mrs Sedgebrook, we'll knock off these questions while Esme quickly shows McCain around the rest of the interior of your fine home.'

So, Miller began asking questions that Lizzie's voice in responding suggested she feared were set to trip her. Esme introduced the parlour to McCain with a banal comment of its use for 'sitting and relaxing in the evenings'. She was unsure what he was looking for and therefore what she should be guarded about and what she should say to satisfy him in the hope of them leaving the more quickly. McCain glanced around but inferred disinterest in the parlour.

Upstairs, the same pattern continued, she'd introduce McCain to each of the upstairs rooms, the small bathroom, Tilly's box room, the other bedrooms. McCain would ask whose room each bedroom was occupied by, make a cursory glance under the bed and inside any wardrobes and then turn away from the room with Esme following him out again. In the landing between upstairs rooms McCain said, 'We do have something of a problem, Miss Esme.'

Esme stopped in the landing, but McCain instructed her to show him the next bedroom and as she started to move again, he explained his problem. 'The new tax rules charge every man and woman with the responsibility to pay a fee, only children are exempt. It's the same for everyone under God.' Esme was listening and willing to help mainly because, as she didn't really understand what he was talking about, she assumed there would be no way she could help him. 'Our job, you understand, is to complete the census accurately. If we don't, the trouble we can get in would make the trouble anyone faces for not paying seem like a child's punishment, do you follow, Miss Esme?'

'I er, I think so,' Esme replied, she opened a door to another bedroom, this was her bedroom.

'To be honest, Ms Esme, you are the problem.'

For the first time since their arrival, Esme was individually fearful, rather than merely the unease of one sharing the problem of others.

'Are you married, Miss Sedgebrook?'

'No,' she answered.

'You're of marrying age though.'

Esme nodded.

McCain waited, observing her.

Esme explained, 'My dad remarried. I didn't feel ready.' Esme felt her face flush to speak about these things with a total stranger. It got worse.

'Do you earn an income?'

'Sorry?' Esme asked.

'I need to determine whether you should be paying the tax, Ms Esme.'

'Oh,' she smiled with briefly passing relief. 'No. I don't go out to work.'

'Still,' McCain said, 'That is no longer excuse enough, especially as so much work is not declared these days.' He rubbed his fingertips briefly against his temple. 'Especially in these parts. Especially for a young woman, hey?' Esme sensed an inference in his tone but not what was being inferred.

He quietly closed the door behind him, so he was turned away from Esme when he added. 'There is a method for checking your status, Ms Esme, which the state has licenced me to perform.' Turning back toward her, Esme waited for him to explain his meaning. McCain glanced at the desk behind Esme, stationed on the far wall, under the window. 'Would you turn around and lay your hands flat on the desktop there, please.'

'Sorry?' Esme heard what McCain said but his words collapsed into piles of letters.

'If you just turn around and lay your hands on the desk, I'll quickly examine you, and, provided you're the maiden you say you are, we can be done here.' Esme turned around, she didn't understand what was happening sufficiently to negotiate or even just protest. She laid each of her hands upon the desk, her elbows locked, she felt her arms tremble as McCain approached behind her. She felt his boot tap the inside of her right foot, with the quiet instruction, 'A little further apart please.' McCain spoke and handled her with a formal authority that made it seem inappropriate to question the instructions.

Esme felt him pinch the fabric at the sides of her dress and pull the dress high and clear of her legs, up and folded back over her hips. She stood petrified, the only moving parts of her body were her heart and her restless leg. She felt McCain's hand against her knee, straightening her leg and holding it still for a moment. She heard him behind her whisper, 'Shshsh. No need for nerves, sweetheart; soon be done.'

His fingertips went under the waistband at the front of her underpants. Esme squeezed her eyes tight shut. In her head, she started repeating, 'This isn't happening,' but it was. She wanted to squirm, but he held her steady with a hand flat on the small of her back. 'This isn't happening. This isn't real,' she repeated behind tight eyelids.

Eventually she felt the man remove his hand and pull her dress back down. Esme didn't move. She didn't say anything, she didn't open her eyes, she tried not to breathe until she felt sure it was over.

McCain stepped back from her. He said nothing as she opened her eyes, but she knew he was still stood behind her and she wanted to cry. 'Okay?' he said as she straightened and started to turn to face him, though her head was bowed, and her eyes lowered. Did he want her to confirm things were okay? Did he care? Or was he telling her she was okay, having 'examined' her?

She started to feel disassociated from the different parts of her body. On trembling legs, she slowly rotated her feet.

He towered over her; she thought McCain even bigger than her dad and wondered if even her dad would be able to save her from this man. She didn't process what she noticed at first, when McCain said, 'Give me your hand.' The belt and flies of his trousers were undone, and his penis hung freely over the top. McCain held her palm around his penis and made her stroke him. He said, 'Keep going, and we'll be all done.' He touched lightly her hair and the side of her face, as she continued to stroke him. She wondered when would be enough. She saw an expression of murderous ease pass across his face, a held moment he breathed out. 'Okay, that's fine.' He removed her hand from him. He took up her dress and cleaned himself even as she stood wearing it. She looked at her hand.

Downstairs, Miller glanced up at their descending footsteps on the staircase. 'All done?' He smiled at McCain. Esme followed behind, on jelly legs, watching only the footsteps in front of her and wishing them gone.

'Yes,' McCain said. 'Everything was fine and in order upstairs.'

Miller smiled at Lizzie, 'Well, we may need to catch up with your husband, but otherwise I think we're done here.' He stood. The men crunched across the gravel yard back to their car.

Lizzie looked at her. 'Esme?'

X

Sitting in a bath in the washroom filled with water heated in the copper, it occurred to Esme that her body didn't belong to her. It was just another thing, like a pen or a skirt to be used or worn, by her or by another. She was caged and bound by her bones and skin. She scratched at her arm. It felt good but didn't reach the itch. She reached to scratch the back of her shoulder and the side of her legs, but she couldn't get at the cause of the irritation there either. There was a thin film of reality between her and her body that she couldn't get through.

There were a large pair of scissors, they were dress-making shears. Lizzie was a useful seamstress and earned a little extra cash for the family making clothes for people around Fenby, as well as of course making the dreaded wedding dress for Esme. Esme held her long hair and the shears opened to cut across what would be the ponytail beneath her fist. She decided to start with her hair. She remembered that man, McCain, touching her hair as he made Esme touch him. And then she thought of her wedding to the mayor's son, and she wanted to cry and even though she didn't want the wedding, she didn't want any of it, she couldn't cut her hair, for what would her dad say? and there would be no way to grow her hair long again by the weekend. It was customary for young women to wear their hair long, indeed there was a suggestion that the act of a woman cutting her hair was symbolic of her change in circumstances. Some thought it not even appropriate for a young woman to cut her hair shorter. 'Maiden,' Esme said out loud to herself. That was the word Agent McCain used. Esme let her hair go. Instead, she squeezed her eyes shut and traced the edge of the shear's blade over her forearm. She looked with pleasure at the thin red tract that appeared on her arm. The cut wasn't deep, and it scabbed a paper-thin line immediately. It was a new sensation that cut through to a fundamental experience of being. Raw and immediate, and Esme had control over it.

After her bath, Esme went to bed, though she didn't sleep. Lizzie said she would tell Esme's dad what he needed to know. Summer meant the evenings stretched late and Esme's father worked until the light was too poor. With Moscow Farm being several miles away, it was late when Esme heard her father's bicycle on the gravel. She didn't hear their conversations that evening, not Lizzie's explanation nor her dad's reaction. She opened her bedroom window and sat beside it in her thin nightshirt. She felt the wind blow against her skin. She traced a finger lightly over the thin scab line from the cut she made with dress-making shears.

The dark was lonely.

The next morning, Esme woke to the sound of banging. From her bedroom window she could see her dad clearing up the yard. Esme glanced at the clock on the small table beside her bed and wondered why her dad wasn't up at Moscow Farm. She then worried, because she knew it would be because of what happened with the state agent.

Esme crept downstairs and into the kitchen. She asked Lizzie why her dad hadn't made his usual trip up to Moscow Farm. 'Your dad was up early and at Moscow even as dawn was still breaking. He said he went to fire up the engines, get the machines working, and then he came back here. He went into town to meet with some of the other fellars. There are others with complaints, Esme, it's not just you. They all reckoned your dad was best placed to go and talk to the mayor. I'm heating the water for him to have a bath; he'll need to be clean and smart if he's representing the locals.'

'Why's dad best placed?' Esme asked. She knew dad would have to tell the mayor what happened to her, and that meant the mayor's wife would know, and they might tell Tom, and even more people would know what the state agent did, and so it would never be unknown again.

When Esme's dad passed through the kitchen en route for his bath, he smiled at her and asked if she was alright. He asked without really looking at her though; it was a conversation he didn't want to have – he knew enough. Esme said she was okay because it wasn't a conversation that she wanted to have either. She and her dad wouldn't speak of it and yet unavoidably he would speak of it with others. Her burden he carried as his own. Esme would have to carry the guilt of her burden being his burden also. He would take action to deal with his burden, and Esme herself would be powerless to deal with hers. She was as powerless as she had been in her bedroom with the state agent.

Esme wasn't sure she could explain how it made her feel. Whenever she closed her eyes, it was that moment again, not like she was remembering what happened, but as if it was actually happening. Every part of it, experienced anew, seeing it and feeling it as though it were happening. His voice, his presence behind her, his breath so close, she could feel it on her skin and in her hair, and however long she soaked her skin and her hair, she couldn't wash him out. His touch left invisible slime behind, on her skin. She could feel it even if she couldn't see it, and no matter how she scrubbed at her skin the slime was still there, smelling of him. She felt as though her skin had exploded into an inflamed rash wherever he touched her, and she couldn't resist the need to scratch at her skin until red tracts emerged to mark the parts of her body where she needed to tear him off her. But she couldn't tear him off, and that was when she thought of the dress-making shears, and how much better they were at cutting through. When the washroom was free again, she lowered the toilet seat her dad must have left up, sat down, rolled her sleeve up, and an inch or two above the first line, across the top of her forearm, she traced the shears and scored a second paper-thin line. She put the shears down and looked at her arm. She'd done it, she smiled. She touched the line of blood, satisfied it was scabbing quickly. She rolled her sleeve back down.

Twice that day Esme's dad took the motorcar out and drove up to the mayor's house, but each time the mayor wasn't there. He drummed his fingertips on the table as he waited for Lizzie to bring him a sandwich of leftover gammon from the shoulder she'd boiled a couple of days prior between two thick wedges of bread, an apple he cut up with his pocket-knife and dark, stewed tea. 'I'll go up Moscow 'savo, you two be alright here on your own. I could fetch Davey down, have him earn a few pennies clearing up the yard.'

Lizzie looked at Esme and took the responsibility of thinking and answering from her. 'We'll be a'right, Keith.' They watched Esme's dad leave on his bicycle and sat in quiet expectancy all afternoon. They spoke little, the way people waiting for something to happen say little as at any moment they imagine interruption. The time seemed to be measured by the tick-tock drop of water hanging suspended from the rainwater pipe that fed the butt outside the kitchen. The state agents didn't come back that afternoon. Lizzie said they'd have no reason to, but it didn't stop them both, from time to time, glancing out of the kitchen window and across the gravel yard.

Time is like space; it doesn't disappear if a person is no longer there. When Esme missed her mam, she would still see her in the yard or around the house. When Lizzie came, Esme's mam became harder to see, not so much because of distance but because of the amount of life piled up between those times and where Esme was. There were no obstacles obscuring the presence of Agent McCain; he was wandering around the yard, he was poking around the house, he was in Esme's bedroom, standing behind her. The space was still his.

Late that evening, after Esme's father was settled in distracted thought with a cup of homebrew, with the women of the household in the back parlour, there was a rasp at the kitchen door that caused Keith to jump out of his skin and his heavy and unspoken ruminative thinking.

They were local men by their accents. They spoke with Esme's dad in whispers. Keith closed the door to the parlour where Esme and Lizzie were.

After the men left, when Esme's dad re-joined them in the parlour, he said nothing of what was discussed. When Lizzie voiced the single word 'Keith ...' in plaintive request not to be forsaken in ignorance, Esme's dad only replied it was business for men, and he wouldn't want them involved.

'Better that way,' he said and, 'safer.' Whatever that meant. Esme's dad wore an expression of impatient but restrained fury. He smoked a pipe, as was his tendency in the evening, which he chewed the end of thoughtfully.

Saturday was market day when traders came from the wider area to fill out the stalls in the marketplace, and with it being the Saturday before Whitsun, it was expected to be busy. The family walked as one into town for market day, as usual. Esme wore a blue dress and a white cardigan, Lizzie was wearing a green dress, Tilly a little red dress with each of her hands upstretched holding her mum's hand on one side and Esme's on the other. Keith walked a step or two ahead, he wore a cap and an old black jacket, but he wasn't dressed up with brill-creamed hair as he had been when they visited the mayor.

The road to town was straight, lined with dykes on either side but no hedgerows as the dykes performed the same function of marking out perimeters. There was a field with crows and blackbirds and piles of sugar beet being loaded on trailers. 'A'right there, Keith,' The labourers hailed as they passed.

Keith called back, 'Helloa!' As an agricultural engineer, Esme's dad's machines, and often his operation of them, was sought by most of the local farmers and land-workers, such that he was known better than most in the area despite owning barely any land himself. He'd begun as a navigator following the water's rise and the need to reinforce banked roads and develop more levees, dykes, canals, and waterways. Since the rivers' rise, he set up on his own and was making decent money for the time, not like the old days but better than many. He considered himself upwardly mobile and Esme's marriage to the mayor's son would represent the consolidation of their upward mobility. Nevertheless, he described himself with pride as 'a yeoman of England.'

Approaching Fenby, rain-spots of people gathered into streams that merged into a steady flow greater than usual for a Friday market. 'There's a lot of people.' Lizzie commented. 'Must be for the Whitsun festivities.'

'Rubbish,' Esme's dad said. 'I tell you, there's something else afoot here.' Turning down Broad Street, it was far busier than the usual Friday market. Crowds were gathering from the memorial water fountain, all the way down Broad Street. Although the shops were busy enough as usual, most people headed over the bridge that crossed the old course of the River Nene through the centre of Fenby, and onto the marketplace overlooked by the town hall. Its grand red-brick façade echoed the heyday during the eighteenth century, when Fenby was an agricultural centre, producing and trading wool, grain and vegetables connected by water and later rail. Upon arriving in the market square Esme's dad said, 'Have you money, such as you need for provisions, Lizzie?'

'I have,' Lizzie confirmed. The women, many with children in tow, hugged the market stalls, while most of the men folk gathered in groups around the marketplace. Normally the men folk who'd escorted the women to market would pursue other business while the women shopped. There was a hardware store with many of its wares out in front on trellis tables. Others might head for the auction rooms, while a few would have to meet such or such a person in the Griffin Hotel, whether the need to meet so-and-so was genuine or exculpatory to avoid accusations of drinking. This Friday though, most seemed to be gathered in clusters of serious and agitated conversation replete with curses loud enough to drift and be heard by passers-by. The speaker of one such curse was rebuked by a man he was talking with. 'Steady, son, there are ladies about.'

When the sun came back around from behind the back of the town hall, the square was lit up, a picture of market stalls with multi-coloured canvas covers. Esme drifted around the market, following Lizzie with Tilly's tiny hand in her own. She'd lost sight of her dad until just after the noon bell tolled when she saw him with two others, who she didn't know, approaching the entrance of the town hall. Esme nudged Lizzie's elbow, she was pressing fruit for ripeness. It took the voice of the stall holder to wrench Lizzie back to her purchases.

Lizzie was paying the baker. Esme held two large canvass bags Lizzie loaded while Tilly clutched at her dress. When Keith found them again, Lizzie turned to him and smiled. He looked past her and back toward the town hall. 'The mayor's not in. His assistant said he'd be in late afternoon. Won't do.'

'What won't do?' Lizzie asked.

'They asked me to speak to him, being close what with his boy and our Esme betrothed.' He looked around where clusters of men still stood apart from the general hubbub around the stalls, milling their stories into granular details of resentment. 'Esme's not the only one.'

Hearing her name, Esme shrank and yet became more conspicuous at once. The memory of Agent McCain returned to the forefront of her mind; she felt hot and oppressed by the people in the market square. She couldn't breathe.

Esme needed space to breathe.

She began to feel dizzy, and the people seemed to crowd around her more.

Her dad was still speaking. 'The mayor needs to be here.' He nodded across at the Griffin Hotel, 'They're staying there.' They gazed at the hotel front while Keith deliberated. 'Are you finished here?'

'Yes,' Lizzie confirmed.

'I think I should stick around here and join you back home later. Are you okay getting along home on your own?' Keith asked.

'Of course.' Lizzie looked at Esme. Esme begged with her eyes for leave. 'We can get on home fine.'

Keith was still looking around the marketplace. 'Good, good.' He left them to join some men across the square in serious discussion.

Three men, state agents by the cut of their suits, emerged from the Griffin. They walked through a collective gasp, across the market square and toward the town hall. Esme didn't recognise McCain amongst them, or his colleague Miller. They all wore the same suits though, and the same authority and purpose in how they walked.

Esme looked between her father and the men around him, and the three agents striding across the square. Then the situation changed. Everything became active and increasingly frenzied and unclear. One of the three men staggered and moved his hand to his temple while his hat fell to the floor. Another of the agents turned and demanded, 'What was that?'

'An apple,' a voice from the crowd shouted and a ripple of laughter ensued. An apple had bounced from the agent's forehead and burst open when it hit the cobblestone ground. As the agent who'd been struck rose, clutching his rescued hat, the agent who spoke up suddenly crumpled over holding his face. Another chorus of laughter but as this agent stood there was more than mere embarrassment and apple that coloured his countenance, this agent was bleeding. He held his hand in front of him so all could see the blood on his fingers. He reached for a white handkerchief to stem the blood. One of his associates reached for a revolver from a holster concealed inside his jacket.

The laughter stopped.

The eyes of the two unbloodied agents scanned the crowd. A second agent pulled his revolver out from beneath his jacket. One of the agents demanded somebody step forward from the crowd. The individual's reluctance was initially supported by others but the reality of two armed and drawn agents soon encouraged them to give up the miscreant amongst their number.

The figure who stepped forward was Davey Clay. One of the agents approached him, slapped his face, and ripped from his guarded hands a slingshot. The other uninjured agent joined him, spun Davey Clay around and snapped handcuffs around his wrists. When the three agents moved to take Davey into the town hall with them though, a crowd moved and surrounded them. There hadn't been any leadership up until this point, whatever resistance they were showing was haphazard and organic. One of the agents addressed the tense stand-off. 'With the power vested in us as crown and state agents we are arresting this young hooligan for assaulting a state official. He will be taken to the cells where he will stay until such a time that he may be tried by law, like any other person. Now, step aside to allow us through.'

One man stood forward and both Esme and Lizzie were horrified to see it was Esme's dad. 'Let the boy go,' he stated. 'He ain't bright but he means no harm.'

'The boy will face the law like any other. Carry on as you are, and you could join him.' None of the crowd moved but looked to Esme's dad to lead.

'Look around you,' Esme's dad stated. The crowd quietened to hear him. 'I'll tell you this for your own good. There's three o' you. You may be armed, you may shoot some folk, but if you try to take the boy anywhere you won't leave this market square but to be carried out as carrion for crows.'

A shiver passed through the crowd. Nobody knew how much of what Esme's dad was saying was desperate bluff, but they also noticed the doubtful pause on the part of the agents. Lizzie would later joke she could tell Esme's dad was 'building brick walls in his britches behind all his bravado.' That was later, by which time he was being toasted for his heroism.

A car pulled up at the edge of the square and the mayor bustled out and across the market with two assistants. Whether he had been alerted or his timing was opportune was unclear. He was eager to de-escalate the situation with pleading voice and plaintive, pacifying hands.

Esme's dad, he would claim so as not to upset the mayor, stood down, backed away to join the rest of the crowd in agreement the mayor would talk to the agents. The mayor persuaded the agents to re-holster their weapons and persuaded a woman stood at a nearby stand to bring 'a plaster, or bandage or a compress for the wounded agent's head.' People stood without sympathy as the mayor appealed to their better nature. 'Whatever else we may or may not be we have not, surely, become so impervious to a man bleeding in the street.' A dispatched woman returned with bowl of water, rag and compress that was taped to the wounded agent's left temple.

The mayor spoke to the other two agents while the first was treated and when he turned to the crowd, some said he looked a little pale and uncertain. He steadied himself under the observance of the crowd. They were his people. 'We shall take the boy in with us now for a statement, once completed, we shall discuss his release, as is our custom in such matters.' The mayor emphasised the word 'custom', distinguishing their local law from laws made in London and imposed by these state agents. The crowd were not satisfied until the mayor agreed to meet with some of them in an hour, 'privately, to discuss matters.'

Another local man challenged the mayor's use of the word, 'matters' and the mayor rushed to correct; 'Complaints. We'll discuss your complaints.' A flustered mayor finally got to escort the agents and the arrested Davey Clay inside the town hall and the crowd began to disperse, some muttering there would be 'another time'. Esme heard someone claim that the mayor better understand which side he needs to be on.

XI

Beyond the Mathematical Bridge, the flooded Coe Fen opened on the southwestern side of Cambridge where there were flooded meadows with spots and flurries of partially submerged trees. There were also abandoned boats, where the pilot had lost track of the channels and banked on the boggy earth beneath. So long had some of those boats been abandoned they provided rough markers for those crossing the fen. Algae gathered like water-moss that creeped out from where deeper recesses caused sitting pools to lurk.

John Lilburne's associate, Grace, commented, 'In summer, when the water is low, the wind whistles across the long grasses and sedge-bearded shallow water. In autumn, leaves quilt parts of the water. When the water is high, colonies of wading birds gather; oyster catchers in spring, you can tell them by their long red bill and pinkish legs. In winter, there are curlews, knots, redshanks and godwits, on passage to breed in Scandinavia.' As Grace described the fen, Angharad gazed back toward the retreating lights and towers of ancient Cambridge.

At the far side of the flooded fields of Coe Fen were two science-fiction-looking water mills of heaving and thumping machinery. They pumped water through channels and sluices, splashing over artificial waterfalls and through turbines that lit the south side of Cambridge. The water emptied into deltas across the old Grantchester Meadows. There, beyond the slow-moving wide channels of the Cam, geodesic biome domes rose like transparent mounds, so people of Cambridge could still consume bananas, coffee, cocoa for chocolate, guava and avocados from the tropical dome and from the Mediterranean dome harvests of olives, grapes, lemons, limes and oranges, all of which were lost to those who lived outside of Cambridge or the city of London. In the flooded fields beyond the domes, paddy fields for rice production, where peasants waded shin deep in water, with sacks over their backs, stripping rice from genetically modified grasses for a crop more resistant to intemperate and inclement weather. Much of the former grain fields had been lost to the changing conditions.

They left Coe Fen along Vicar's Brook, which crept out of Southern Cambridge toward Great Shelford and the low, chalk Gog Magog Hills that rolled south and away from the flood plains, amidst which was Wandlebury Hill where they'd meet other members of the resistance.

South of the city they passed the flickering fires of squatters' encampments along the west bank of Hobson's Brook. Lilburne switched the punt quant for oars, and they followed a narrow branch east. A crack willow leant over the brook. 'That's the one, John,' Grace said. A broken branch floated along the brook, made visible only by the slight disturbance it made to the black surface water as it passed. The crack willow cracked in the aching night; its split limbs tumbled down. Tied to it was a yellow scarf fluttering in and out of the moonlight.

Grace leapt onto the bank and crouched down on her haunches, steadied the boat as the rest disembarked and climbed away from the riverbank using exposed tree roots as footholds. 'We walk from here,' she said. 'After a mile or so, there's a small stone circle where two roads meet. On the other side is Wandlebury Hill. It tends to the boggy but hardens as you climb. It was a hill fort from before Roman times with a series of henges before the summit plateau.'

'Why there?' Angharad asked. Her tired feet picked over the heavy earth.

'Between Wormwood Hill and another hill called Telegraph Clump, you can see the Icknield Way,' Grace explained. 'The hermits move by way of the old routes. Better for avoiding state agents, and secrets confer trust between those who share them.' Angharad listened politely, smiling thinly, for she knew of the hermits' ways well enough without lesson; it was the proximity to the Icknield Way she was unfamiliar with. The hermits were an underground group who sprang up after the internet got fire-walled, before it simply went dead for most. Their purpose was to keep people connected and they operated a messenger service. Their name derived from what they claimed was the true origin of hermits, not as recluses but as servants of Hermes, the messenger of the gods.

John Lilburne gently took Angharad's elbow. 'Come; we're safe here but there's no advantage in slouching.' The small stone circle, to which Grace referred, was at the intersection where two roads crossed. The hermits built a mound, eight feet or so high, the top was level and around the perimeter the hermits constructed a ring of eight columns, four in the line of the approaches, four in between, of bricks recovered from abandoned house-wrecks in the area. In other areas, hermits used other markers, always physical and durable for an age where book-smarts were less assured. If these markers were ever damaged, they were swiftly reconstructed. From the summit of the mound, they had clear vision along the roads. The column in the southeastern corner was set slightly aside to indicate their route over the buried lines and markers of an ancient golf course and to the summit.

A large, waxing moon hung low over Wandlebury Hill. Mature

trees climbed the banks shading their approach with whispers in the undergrowth. John Lilburne led the party over a low rampart of chalk rubble that formed the inner ring of the summit. He called out, 'Knight to knight, come forth.'

An owl replied, unseen in a tree, and Lilburne called again. The others cautiously followed Lilburne into the centre of Wandlebury Ring; a large six-hectare area dotted with trees. The large former stable block, still standing but in some considerable state of disrepair was on the far side. Approaching the moon-washed middle, Lilburne called again, 'Knight to knight, come forth!'

Emerging from the shadows of the stables, in silhouette, was a mounted knight on a stallion with something resembling a jousting lance. Under watching trees, Angharad stood with Owain. The horse charged toward Lilburne. Angharad tilted her head watching the mounted knight sway uncertainly as the horse charged, the lance no longer held high, nor pointed toward John but sweeping wide to take out his legs. Lilburne jumped but the lance swung in a wild, wide arc and caught him on his shins, sending him falling and rolling, clasping his legs. The impact further unbalanced the knight though and he fell tumbling off the back of the horse still gripping the lance until his shuddering impact with the ground shook it from his grip.

Lilburne waited several yards from the knight watching him recover his bearings before charging at him. He pinned the knight down, pushing his shoulders toward the ground. The pair of men struggled in wrestling grips of head locks and pressure points on elbow and shoulder joints. Cheers and laughter could be heard from the stable block where two other figures emerged. Grace had walked toward where the horse had slowed his charge to a canter to a trot to a point where the horse was idling and Grace was able to pat the horse on the flank, stroke the side of his neck, take the reins and lead the horse back toward those gathered around Lilburne and the fallen knight. The fallen knight's insignia was a large Nike swish across his chest with the peeling white words, 'Just do it!'

Grace picked up the discarded lance from the ground. It was a stake otherwise used as part of a fence. The Knight of Nike charged and buried his shoulder into Lilburne's midriff with a grunt, winding him. Lilburne clung onto the knight, so they turned in circles, drifting as one strange creature with busy shuffling feet, an additional head emerging under the hook of an arm, with both Lilburne and the knight now reduced to slapping each other on the ass with a free hand and squealing as their own behind received the other's sharp smack.

Standing back from the fray, moonlight cast a hooded figure with a monkish cowl. 'Willow Walwyn,' Angharad whispered.

'Fuck this. I'm knackered.' The Knight of Nike's breath billowed in the night air, blowing hard with his hands clutched to his hips.

Lilburne extended him his hand. 'You cracked my bastard shins.' They embraced as old friends reacquainted and Lilburne introduced 'Gerrard Winstanley'.

The pair who'd followed Gerrard over from the stable block were associates from the northwest. It is unlikely Mary Smith's real name was Mary Smith, but like other radicals, especially in the north, she adopted the anonymity of a name that echoed the everyday person. Mary Smith grew up in Liverpool, on the Tocky estates, where they'd skip dive before they could read properly and, as Mary Smith boasted, 'could pick yer pockets before we could count what we'd grafted from yers.' Gerrard met her when both were hiding in sewers around the old Lime Street Station. There were riots and so London had sent troops up to reinforce the local garrisons.

Next to Mary, Gerrard introduced Red Nev, an organiser from Bury. He was a wiry man with short dark hair beneath a flat cap. Red Nev became a leader of the campaign of 2058 that brought Liverpool, Manchester and the northwest to a standstill. Mary Smith and Red Nev had both travelled with Gerrard Winstanley down from the northwest. There was an unspoken informality between them, where jokes were made with only the eyes.

Turning toward the old stable block, a monkish figure stood in their path like a statue, arms folded in front with hands veiled by the sleeves of a robe. Willow Walwyn had been a doctor willing to treat the poor without fee, but as medication became prohibitively expensive for many, Willow procured black-market medication, often unreliable synthetics from ghetto labs. She drew favour from bin Salah's Muslim quarter and often found their drugs more reliable and their pharmacists more expert. She had been instrumental in contact being made with Ismail bin Salah, though even then it was through a shadowy mutual contact, known to Lilburne and Willow only as 'the Doc'.

Willow Walwyn donned the robe and went underground following a betrayal that led to a cell in Battersea being rolled out. The original informant hadn't known of Willow's involvement but following the subsequent arrests, interrogations and torture, her name was brought up. So close was she to getting picked up that she saw four agents outside her house in Kentish Town from the end of her street. They would have gone through her things; she had no idea how many people she would have inadvertently compromised, or how many of them might now be dead. She only escaped by way of the River Fleet culverts. Since then, she operated under cover from the hermits.

Grace walked alongside Gerrard, handing the reins of the grey horse back to him. He said, 'You tamed the beast. You must be a horse whisperer.'

'She's a lamb.' Grace dismissively swished her hair like the mare might.

Willow Walwyn peeled back the cowl of her robe revealing an angular face, framed by dark hair. She looked across the faces of all those who approached her, but it was to Angharad she smiled, stepping forward with arms opened to embrace. 'Angharad Wyddeles – it's been so long.' Stepping back but retaining Angharad's left hand and with a glance at Owain, she said, 'Are you still getting each other in trouble?'

'As always, Willow,' Angharad replied.

'I'll take you over to meet the hermits,' Willow then said. 'They were keen to know when you arrived. We've much to discuss.' Willow led them toward the old stable block, flanked by Angharad and Owain, the others behind.

In its heyday it was the residence of the Godolphin family. In the eighteenth century they bred and raised racehorses there, one of the three thoroughbreds from which all thoroughbred lines descended was stabled at Wandlebury, but that was long ago. Through the centre of the once-grand and austere two-story limestone grey façade was a great arch. There was a roof veranda, its balustrade wounded and weary, and a sloping attic roof with a series of small round windows inset. Crowning this sloped roof, a four-sided cupola clock added in the nineteenth century, the hands of each face stuck at different times. Along the ground floor were windows and two sets of French doors to the left of the great arch that could have opened out onto the lawns, had they not, like the other ground-floor windows, been nailed shut from the inside with boards across them.

Inside the main building, the refurbishments of the twentieth century had curled and browned and flaked and begun life's inevitable return to dust. Plasterboard revealed broken walls beneath. The doors of rooms to the left and right of a broad entrance hall were closed but for one where a door no longer hung, and into that room Angharad could see floorboards in varied states of disrepair, toothy and gappy, and the flotsam and jetsam of decades washed up against once-grand wood panelling. Otherwise, there was just a blue sleeping bag scrunched up like a large, discarded sock awaiting the return of a familiar foot.

A staircase rose from the centre of the entrance hall, turning in two platformed landings. 'Mind your feet' Willow said as she led them up, the banister wobbling in Angharad's hand. 'Did you know the collective noun for hermits is an "observance of hermits", and this,' Willow Walwyn said, arriving at a small door at the top of the staircase, 'this is their observatory.'

Inside was a long room with a low, sloped attic ceiling, small round windows like portholes and at each end a larger window accompanying doors out onto the roof veranda. Along the centre of this attic space was a long table with five figures seated around in hooded cloaks. One, opposite the door, looked up as they entered; the other hermits didn't initially seem to notice their entrance, despite a wind that had pursued them up the stairs and blown into the room, disturbing papers on the long table that were chased and caught by a hand emerging from a robed sleeve. He, who looked up, immediately lowered again a cowled face to the papers being studied. It was night, the only light in the room came from four flickering candles, guttering with wax gathering around stumps.

The authorities knew about the hermits but there was little

will and no resources to harry them. Their numbers were assumed too few and too sparsely spread to pose much threat, and besides, the hermits operated under some degree of protection from the church. The church and religious groups generally were more powerful in these times when state and secular power was so diminished, and people were looking for permanence.

Following Willow in, the rest of her party filed along one of the low walls, some stooping beneath the sloped ceiling. One of the hermits laid down papers and looked up, pulling back a hood to reveal a woman, old by the colour of her hair, white with yellowy tinges due to the black-market drugs she took for her diabetes cocktailing with another set of black-market drugs she took for high blood pressure. 'We've been expecting you. Why are you so late?'

Willow answered, 'Trouble in Cambridge.' Adding for her companions, 'This is Mother Michael.'

'Problems? What problems?' Mother Michael asked.

'More agents and troops up from London.' Mother Michael looked around those gathered in the attic. She was passed a sheaf of papers scanned with her right index finger aloft to instruct the need for a pause. When done, she looked up again to scrutinize the phalanx of newcomers lined up in her observatory recluse. 'You're Owain Gruffydd.' She pointed the finger she'd been holding authoritatively aloft. Owain confirmed his identity. She then moved her finger along and identified Angharad. 'Sit, sit. You don't have to stand on ceremony here. We're all equal under God and the stars.' As she said this the other hermits all began gathering up papers, sliding them into folders and those folders into satchels they kept by their chairs.

Only Lilburne remained standing, listening to the following

conversations while gazing out of the window. The ground beneath the house was dark, the bushes in the distance darker still, but Lilburne looked out at a bright moon with clouds marbling the blackness, scrolling across the sky in lighter grey swirls. The window Lilburne looked through faced east towards Newmarket ridge beyond Telegraph Clump, where a hermit was stationed permanently operating a stage of a semaphore line running from London up into the Fens, East Anglia and beyond. From the veranda wrapped around the hermits' attic room, Cambridge could be viewed several miles to the north, and beyond to the northeast; on clear days, Ely Cathedral could be seen rising, a beacon over the island.

To the southwest was Wormwood Hill, where the hermits had a beacon stationed for the attention of travellers on the Icknield Way. When the time came, all towns under the control of the resistance would light their beacons, and Shelford to the west, Newmarket to the east, Cambridge to the north and even the Isle of Ely would be visible from Wandlebury with their beacons lit.

The hermits pulled back their hoods to reveal Debbie, a woman with jowls and a kindly smile. There was a little man called Ned, with a bald head but for strands that fluttered from the top like strings anchoring invisible balloons. Another pair of hermits sat either side of Mother Michael; a scrawny woman with lank fair hair and a hunched back and to her right, a young, strong-looking man with an open, square face and short hair, dyed blue.

'Mother Michael,' Angharad said. 'Are we able to speak freely?'

'You are.'

'There is change in the air. You must feel it?' Angharad said. 'John Wrawe's gone south of the river. There's movement there also.'

'I've heard,' Mother Michael harrumphed. 'And I heard you have a plan.'

'It's time,' Angharad urged.

'Time for what?' Mother Michael replied, and she looked toward a bare corner of the room as if there was something of distraction there.

'Time to move,' Angharad asserted.

'Move!?' Mother Michael laughed dryly and banged her hands down on the armrests of her wheelchair. 'That would be a fine thing.'

Willow had told Angharad about Mother Michael. A woman tortured by bitterness and resentments, and yet, for all her cynicism, severity of judgement and apparent dislike of people, she was also a woman who'd donated her life's efforts to the service of others. A duty she bore with ill-tempered pride.

'We've been travelling all over the country, Mother Michael.'

'What do you think the hermits are doing?'

Angharad persisted. 'There's a different mood, and not just at the meetings. Change is coming.'

The irritated old hermit shuffled items on the table. She turned to the hunchback hermit to her left. 'Ooh do rub some of that unction on my back, Karen. It's terrible itchy.'

'Yes, of course. Your back's the devil, init?' Karen replied without irony.

'Back, legs, feet; doctor said years ago I wouldn't make old bones.'

'You'll outlive us all, you ol' bugger,' Karen said as she rummaged in her bag until she found a clay pot with a cork stuffed in it, lined with a rag to fit the hole, as the cork and pot had not originally been partnered. Mother Michael dropped her robe from her shoulders so low that had her breasts been younger and prouder they would've been on display. There were a few brown spots over her chest and some more on her back that were apparently, like the yellowing hair and the peeling skin, a response to the medication she was taking. Karen began rubbing white gloop into the peeling skin of Mother Michael's back.

'I've got a plan, she says,' Mother Michael mocked Angharad. She moved items on the table imperceptibly small distances: her water glass, a small ornamental wooden box, the papers in front of her.

'I know,' Karen said. 'I heard.'

Mother Michael snapped at Angharad. 'You've been rumbled, girl, how else were state agents on you so quickly?' She studied Angharad's discomfort before continuing. 'You've made a bit of a pig's ear of this, haven't you, dear?'

She turned to Owain, 'You're no better, sitting there all sulky and pathetic. What's the matter? Cat got your tongue.'

Owain lowered his eyes. 'There was a traitor.'

'There usually is. Any idea who?' Mother Michael turned to Lilburne. 'What about you? Any ideas? Priestley?'

'No, not Priestley. If he were inclined, he wouldn't have the courage.'

'Well certainly not the epistemologist you made me meet. Man was an imbecile. He didn't know anything. How many of our people are at risk, John?'

'Don't know yet,' Lilburne replied. 'We'll see how many get out of Cambridge and re-group at Telegraph Clump by sundown tomorrow.'

'Will Telegraph Clump be safe, John?' Mother Michael asked. 'Will we be safe here?'

'Even if they've already got talkers,' Lilburne speculated. 'They'll not try to take Wandlebury at night.' Out through windows to the east, though there was no sun, the sky was starless and more blue than black.

Mother Michael drummed her fingers on the table. 'Right, this is how we're going to avoid a total shit-show.' She turned to the balding hermit. 'Neddie, you're going to have to load up and get over to Telegraph Clump.'

'Me?' the old hermit replied, more in surprise than protest.

'Yes, dear,' Mother Michael replied. 'You just need to hold fort there and gather what reinforcements we get out of Cambridge. Let's hope some come.' The last comments were addressed to Angharad and Owain, who dutifully lowered their guilty faces. 'Besides, Debbie's a crack-shot, I'll want her here, and Willow, we may need her medical skills. It makes most sense for John and Grace to take Owain and Angharad into Cambridge to meet with the Doc. Gerrard,' Mother Michael said. 'Are you listening, young Gerrard?'

'Of course.' Gerrard Winstanley turned his attention to Mother Michael.

'Good, you'll organise things here. How many have you got?'

'A dozen, maybe a few more,' Gerrard replied.

'It'll have to be enough. Debbie, have you got that ...?' She didn't finish the sentence before Debbie handed her a rolled-up map, which was un-scrolled across the table, weighted down at the corners by the candle holders, Mother Michael's wooden puzzle box and a snow-globe paperweight – inside the snow-globe tiny snow-trimmed fir trees gathered around a happy house, all calm. 'There's an access road as far as the outer ring on the west side of the hill, from there two approaches cross the henge ditch and climb to the summit emerging from the trees either side of the stable at the back of this building.' Mother Michael traced an index finger over each of these paths as she explained. 'Defend the inner ring, Gerrard. Debbie and I'll hold fort here, we'll provide you cover, and then there's the geese.' There was a knock at the door. 'Come!' Red Nev entered, followed by Mary Smith. Nev said, 'There are some vehicles on the road south from Cambridge, could be carrying a few dozen.'

Mother Michael scanned the gathered faces. 'John: There's a Jeep in the sheds that should be charged. You need to go now. I'm going to send the remarkably resourceful Mazcek down to blow up the main approach road.'

'Is it not a touch radical?' Neddie ventured. 'To blow up the only access road. You know, burning bridges and all that.'

'It's vital to take the initiative,' Mother Michael said. 'We'll take out the first of the vehicles they send up and make them approach on foot. Mary, I want you to go down and help Mazcek, try to set some traps if you can: Anything that can delay them.' She turned to Neddie with a smile surprisingly sweet. 'You need to get over to Telegraph Clump now as well. Make sure you don't leave the signal post, there.' Mother Michael watched Neddie organise some belongings and rise from his seat, looking around as of one checking he hadn't forgotten anything. Mother Michael smiled and said, 'Take care.' There was no response as Neddie's hearing wasn't the best.

Mother Michael turned her attention back to Owain and Angharad, she studied them for a moment. 'How was the American? As we expected?'

'More genuine,' Angharad said, 'or at least more genuinely charming.'

'His stuff's good though, isn't it?' Owain said.

'Appears so.' Mother Michael looked about her at the papers on the table, and smiled gratitude when Debbie handed her the relevant one. 'Yes, here it is. I knew I had it.' She scanned the paper then looked up at Angharad. 'You still have the goods, complete and intact, I presume.'

'It's as I told Willow,' Angharad replied.

'Good.' Mother Michael addressed those in the attic at Wandlebury. 'We need to hit them before they hit us and keep fucking hitting them.' Mother Michael was grim-faced. 'There will be people die on Wandlebury Hill this day. For the love of God and the stars, for fuck's sake, don't let it be you.'

XII

Esme froze when she first heard footsteps, Lizzie rushed to the window, turned, and smiled. 'It's him. It's your dad.' He was later than expected. Tilly was already tucked up. Esme's dad sat in an armchair in the parlour with a glass of replenishing Christmas whisky that he swilled as he spoke; Esme listened as Lizzie questioned him for details.

'Just three of us went in and it was agreed I'd speak, on account of taking a lead in the square, as you both saw, and on account of having a personal relationship with the mayor. When we got in though, we didn't get a private meeting. Two agents insisted on being present, and the mayor agrees, he says it's fair to hear both sides.

'The mayor made us discuss Davey first. He said that was more immediate with him being in a cell. So, we says the boy's not bright but he ain't bad. He's no danger to anyone. One of them agents contests this and says he proved he was a danger and must stand trial. So, I says, fine, but he can be released before trial, nobody in the community wants Davey locked up. The agent though says, "No." Just like that, even Mr Mayor looks at him with a face like a slapped arse.' Esme's dad drank some whisky, coughed, and continued. 'The agent says, while we're here, he stays in his cell. So, I says I want a word privately and the agents agree to step outside for a minute. Once they're out the room I tell the mayor what's been happening with our girls and womenfolk and asks him what he's going to do. He's standing but after I says this he sits. He looks at me like he's watching my face and he asks, "Esme?" Just that.'

'What did you say?' Esme couldn't look at her dad as she asked this.

'I said, "I'll take care o' my girl."' He nodded and was quiet for a bit.

Esme burnt.

Esme's dad continued, 'Mayor says to gi' him a few hours. Do nothing more now and he'll come by here and we'll work some-it out.' Esme's dad sipped his whisky and sighed. 'The other fellars weren't sure, but I persuaded 'em to give it a shot, so now it's on me 'n all.' Esme's dad then sank the rest of his glass of whisky he'd been swilling. 'I also swung by Moscow.'

'Were they a'right up there?' Lizzie asked.

'They'll be,' Keith replied.

* * *

Esme was still in bed the following morning when Lizzie called for her to rise. 'Esme!' Lizzie called up. 'Esme!' Footsteps tripped up the staircase. 'The mayor and his wife are here.'

And as waking stirred sense into Esme, she heard voices from downstairs. Lizzie burst into her bedroom, rushing and fussing and insisting on 'tidying' Esme up for the mayor and his wife, excitedly telling her, 'The mayor's around to talk wi' your dad. The mayor's wife's come to talk to you, Esme, about what'll be needed sorting for the wedding and after.'

'After?' Esme asked, lagging.

'Because you're going to marry her boy, so they'll be changes to arrangements. We'll all be one family, and it's like your dad says, "Families have to look out for each other."' Sometimes, Esme wondered about Lizzie. She had assumed Lizzie's marriage to Esme's dad had been entered in a spirit of resignation and defeat. There were times though, when she really seemed to like her role as Esme's stepmother despite there only being three years difference. Aunt Jackie said a girl learns to love; otherwise, it's just infatuation anyway.

Maybe it doesn't matter who you marry, Esme considered, smiling forbearance as Lizzie pulled a brush through her hair. Maybe it's all the same. Maybe you're just forever blowing oxygen into the embers of disappointment. Esme tried, but she couldn't imagine being married to the mayor's son. It was all desperately silly to Esme, and yet it was real, and it loomed like an ending.

Lizzie adjusted the lie of Esme's hair as though Esme were a doll for a schoolgirl's fantasy. Maybe that's all any of us do, Esme thought. We spend our lives reconciling the fading dreams and broken promises of our childhood until all we have left is to play out the roles that others have set for us and try to fool ourselves it's what we always wanted.

The mayor was bustling about full of nervous activity when Esme arrived in the kitchen. He saw her enter and stopped talking and the room stopped. His face visibly searched for the most suitable comment. 'I'm sorry for your experience, Esme.'

The thought of him knowing and that others would know caused Esme to feel bound tight and sick. She smiled as default and was unsure how long she could hold the smile for. She was swiftly ushered into the parlour to sit with Mrs Mayor, feeling once again under inspection, dependent on another's approval.

In the parlour, Lizzie set out tea and a jam sponge. Mrs Mayor was all compassionate questions, caring eyes and she held one of Esme's hands between her own. 'With all of this disruption,

I shouldn't think you've had a chance to think of Sunday's festivities, have you, Esme?'

Esme could only look back, big eyed, at the mayor's wife. Lizzie spoke, 'I think Esme has found everything a little overwhelming.' The mayor's wife smiled at Lizzie's comment but didn't seem much interested.

'These times are always rather hectic though, aren't they?' The mayor's wife said. 'I remember my wedding week. All butterflies in the belly, hey?' Mrs Mayor spoke in gentle questions that obliged Esme to agree. 'Tom's father, Tom senior, was more gregarious than his son is. Your Tom's quite shy really, isn't he?'

It wasn't that Tom Jr wasn't a nice person. Esme knew she should be flattered by such interest. It wasn't Esme's fault she didn't know Tom Jr to confirm the qualities Mrs Mayor attested, just as it was not Esme's fault that she desperately did not want to marry Mrs Mayor's son.

Esme thought it absurd of Mrs Mayor to describe her son as Esme's Tom. He wasn't her Tom. 'He'll be a caring and loving husband for you, Esme.' Esme wasn't sure if she was supposed to thank Mrs Mayor.

But what about me? Esme thought, where do I fit in all these tidy plans.

At school Tom hadn't been one of those lads who would tie the girls to trees on Oak Apple Day and sting them with nettles. Esme only got caught and stung one year, usually she was pretty good at avoiding the boys with stingers and besides, Davey Clay was always hanging around to rescue her. She wondered how Davey was, stuck in a cell. She wasn't sure he'd cope.

'Would you like a slice of cake?' Lizzie, looking ornamental, asked. 'Esme baked it.' The mayor's wife looked between the two women and the plate of cake on the coffee table and for the first time Esme felt some amusement, watching Mrs Mayor obliged to enjoy a piece of cake. The parlour curtains were only partially drawn and there was a band of sunlight cast across the middle of the room, severing Lizzie from Esme and the mayor's wife, bathing the jam sponge in warm light; its cream already starting to sweat.

When conversation lulled for want of anything meaningful to say, Mrs Mayor complimented the house and the room where they were sat. Esme glanced around the parlour. The curtains were heavy and long though somewhat weather worn. The furniture was also heavy and may once have been good quality, but the varnish on the Ercol had flaked along the armrests and edges, and the seats were comfy from being lived in like a favoured old pair of boots. 'Will you be moving straight into our house after Sunday?' Mrs Mayor asked. 'We have a housekeeper, Esme, so much of the housework you won't have to do.' Mrs Mayor went on with her pitch. Esme glanced at Lizzie, who was now listening from behind a slightly smarting teacup and saucer on account of Mrs Mayor's apparent lack of interest in her chatter.

Mrs Mayor took up Esme's hand again. 'In time, you and Tom will want your own place. Tom's only just starting in business and there's no hurry, although time does pass quickly, and before you know it there will be children and the need for more space.'

Esme waited for the afternoon to pass. The clock struck the hour, she heard the tap of China cup and saucer. Everything was still going ahead, and after, nothing would be the same. There was a knock at the parlour door, 'Are we ready, Mrs Mayor?' Mr Mayor appeared.

'Yes, though Esme and I were talking and there's still much

to do, Mr Mayor. But …' Mrs Mayor glanced around the room at nodding faces. 'What isn't achieved before will have to be finished after.'

After he'd returned the mayor and his wife not only to the door but all the way to their motorcar, Esme's dad said, 'I've much to tell you both.' And sat again in his favoured chair, upright and alert with his knees and feet well apart. 'First things first. Davey will be staying in the cell until after the weekend's festivities. The mayor felt, and I agree, we don't need problems that could ruin tomorrow. Davey will be fine.'

'He was looking forward to the day,' Esme said. 'He told me.'

Esme remembered talking to Davey a few days prior. He'd looked absurd wearing a suit with a periwinkle pinned to his lapel. 'Been sent to change the flowers on me Ma's grave.'

'I like your flower,' Esme had said with a smile.

'Thank you.' He'd blushed and asked, 'Are you at the Whitsun wingding?'

'Yes,' Esme told him.

'Are you with anyone?' He blushed and studied his feet in shiny Sunday shoes.

'None o' your beeswax,' Esme told him and pushed him playfully in the arm when he'd looked down at his feet, and he laughed from her push and smiled.

Davey lifted the daffodils he carried for his mother's grave, plucked one from it and handed it to Esme, 'I got to go, Essie, but when I see you Sunday I'll want a dance.' By the time he said this, he was hopping from foot to foot, like he wanted to turn to hide his face once the words had been said.

Esme's dad cut across her memories. 'He'll be a'right, Esme.'

'I want to visit him,' she announced.

'Would there be time?' Esme's dad asked and Esme thought he was going to find a reason why it wouldn't be possible.

'Maybe first thing tomorrow,' Lizzie suggested with a quick smile toward Esme as she did. 'Es doesn't need to be ready until the afternoon. It'd be quiet with most at church in the morning.'

Esme's dad folded his arms but agreed. 'Okay. Okay. I'll check with the mayor, but I should think that'll be a'right. Anyhow, here's what I wanted to tell you.' He stood again as indication that Esme and Lizzie needed to listen. 'So, you know I got that barrel o' home brew in the shed. I suggested to the mayor we could take a walk across the yard and chat over a cup o' beer. So, our mayor enthusiastically accepts. He was a'ready a man before his own father became mayor, and so he's not forgotten his roots, y'know. I mean no disrespect to your Tom, Es, but he's been brought up in gentleman class, like his ma's fam'ly, but the mayor, he's more like us. I know how to deal with the mayor.' Esme's dad nodded to himself. He approved of the mayor's roots. 'Anyhow, the mayor's a'right, you know. It's like I told a couple o' the other fellars. Yeah, he's mayor but he's one o' us. I said this to the mayor as well. I was clever see. I knew I needed to appeal to that man and not the guy in the robes and the chains. So, I remind him of how his old man made his name. When everything was in chaos and the flooding had started and the locals were fed up, 'cause nobody was doing owt. It was the mayor's father when he was in charge o' council that got rid of the Poles and the Lithuanians. You won't know this, Es; I can barely remember but these parts used to be full of Poles and Lithuanians and Latvians. Pa used to say there was a lot of tension back in those days and more men used to come over, and some would bring their womenfolk, and some not, and those who'd not brung their womenfolk were prone to drinking and fighting with the locals, and some claimed the reason was they'd been hassling the local girls.'

As he said this Keith realised what he said and remembered Esme and apologised, but Esme hadn't made the connection and instead asked 'Where'd they go after they got thrown out?'

Esme's dad wasn't sure. 'I think a lot were shipped out to Peterborough, beyond I guess, I'm not sure. Maybe London. I don't know, maybe they were sent back to where they came from.'

'Where did they come from?' Esme asked.

Her dad literally scratched his head before saying, 'Well, Poland, Lithuania and Latvia, I suppose.'

'Why did they come here?' Esme then asked.

Her dad was more confident on this point. 'Because governments let them in.'

'But why?' Esme persisted. Lizzie's head switched to and fro following their conversation and Esme's dad became exasperated with Esme's questions. He sighed at the distraction but soon warmed to opine on the theme of the distraction. 'The governments were paid to let 'em in. They were cheap labour so the rich could make more money. The English were abandoned.'

'No,' Esme persisted, and her dad groaned. 'I mean why did they want to come here?' The tone of her question implied amazement that anyone should.

Keith opened his mouth to speak but realised he couldn't think what to say and so closed it, and for some moments nobody said anything. Eventually Lizzie asked, 'So what did you and the mayor decide?'

Esme's dad was pleased to be back on solid ground. 'So, I told Mr Mayor this was his moment.' He laughed as one does as they know what they're about to say before they say it, and it amuses them. 'To be honest, I remembered when I used to captain the footie team, when I was young. It was like I had to motivate him. So, I told him in each man's life there will come a moment that defines him.' And as Esme's dad repeated his spiel, he stood and delivered it to the room rather than Lizzie and Esme. 'At that moment there's no choice to make. A man knows what must be done. There is no time, I told him, for doubts. To do nothing is worse than doing the wrong thing for doing nothing makes a man a hostage to fortune. This is your moment, Mr Mayor. As it was for your father when he expelled the foreign invaders and when he built up the banks to protect the island and ridge towns. Now is your moment to seize, Mr Mayor.'

Lizzie clapped. 'What did he say?'

Esme's dad slammed his glass down on the mantel piece, but he was laughing like he was imitating the mayor's newly discovered conviction. He said, attempting the mayor's contented growl, 'I will, I will. You know, I bloody well will.' Keith broke into laughter again. 'But he didn't know what to do, so he says, "We could 'ave a whip 'round." But as I tell him, that's a bloody tax then. Eventually he says, "Right, let tomorrow pass and get as many fellars together in the market square come Monday. We'll let the lad go and we'll send the agents on their way just as you say, the way dad did with the foreigners. We'll give 'em an ultimatum, we'll fill out their census the way we want, and they'll sign off on it, or ..." And here he paused 'cause neither o' us knew what our threat would be, so eventually he just says, or else we'll send 'em wi' nothing. In other words, take what we are willing to give or get nowt from us.' Keith looked at Lizzie and Esme and concluded with, 'So that's what we're going to do.' He blew out his cheeks and added, 'Lord knows what'll happen after.'

That night, as Esme lay in her dark bedroom, she could hear her dad's voice through from the next room. 'It's been a difficult few days, but I reckon we'll be a'right. Get our Es married, see these damned outsiders off, and you know I was thinking, maybe you and I should 'ave a little 'un, oursel's. Still need a boy in the pack.' Esme didn't hear what Lizzie said but she heard her dad add, 'We're a'right. Water finds a way through, they say, an' so'll we.'

Esme lay in the dark again with a strange feeling of drowning.

XIII

Owain and Angharad sat in the back of the Jeep with the bag between them. Lilburne was driving, Grace alongside. The canvass roof had perished so the wind blew cold through their hair as they tore up the arterial road to Cambridge. The road surface was cracked and in patches the earth beneath burst through. Either side, the flooded fen rippled away. The Jeep's headlamps highlighted early morning mizzle. Lilburne's fingers tapped the steering wheel.

They followed a tree-lined avenue back into Cambridge past bay-windowed houses from a bygone time. Lilburne had arranged for them to meet the Doc at the Colony, a ramshackle collection of nineteenth and twentieth century former university buildings close to Magdalene College. They parked the Jeep and cut through the Fellows' Garden of Magdalene. Monks' Walk, a raised footpath lined with black poplars, formed a flood bank for the Cam. The path led on to Chesterton Lane, opposite the entrance to the Colony.

The sun in the southeast burst bands of golden light across the fellows' garden with other areas still cast in shadow, shifting and shivering from drops of icy rain. A squirrel skittered between a quince tree and a plum tree. There was the tap-tap-tap-tapping sound of a woodpecker Angharad could hear, unseen, in the branches above them. Owain looked back over his shoulder. Angharad took his hand, without fuss. Every step they made; they were further committed. Tomorrow would avenge yesterday.

The Colony was a mishmash of different buildings, amongst which was Castlebrae, a mid-nineteenth century, Tudor-style residence built in red brick with stone dressing and decorated with blue brick. It had been student accommodation but when the university shrank a group of affluent bohemians bought it along with the rest of the Colony and turned it into a commune, though some said it was better described as a cult. Angharad looked over its distressed grandeur, another study in atrophy.

Castlebrae had attempted a kind of experiment in self-sufficiency, but it died in arguments and acrimony due to underlying tensions between dominant members and their emerging factions. The Colony declined once the original belief in its purpose waned and gradually it became a squat without pretentions. Signs would be erected declaring its imminent sale or demolition, but nothing would happen. The signs would weather and work free of whatever fixed them, if they'd not already been removed by squatters, wreckers or bored kids. Sometimes officials would come with security agents and clear the Colony out, but nothing else would happen, the newly erected signs would once again pass like winter snow and squatters would inevitably return.

The weather-distressed front door was solid, heavy, and unlocked. Inside the wide foyer two kids with shadows bruising beneath glazed eyes melted through a doorway into a room, the door closing behind them. Angharad could hear a cello drifting down from an upper floor in lachrymose strains.

'Come on,' Lilburne said. 'Let's see if there's anyone about.'

Entering a room, three huddled faces snapped to attention and there was the click of a revolver cocked. 'Tut, tut, tut, John Lilburne. You know to take more care than to aimlessly wander into closed rooms.'

The three huddled faces turned their attention to the figure to Lilburne's right with the gun. They were sat around a fold-down card table with green baize top, upon which were bags of marijuana, a two-foot bong, playing cards and matchsticks acting as chips. 'And you bring friends.' A rich band of sunlight flooded in through those huge, mullion windows, illuminating a tall man at least six-four and broad like a bull, with salt and pepper hair and short beard. He was sat in an enormous high, wing-backed armchair of worn and tired red velvet. 'I got to get my vitamin D fix when I can.' He un-cocked and lowered the revolver he was holding. 'This is a grey, grey country. Come in, come one, come all.' One of the huddled faces sniggered. 'And close the door behind, would you.'

'Alright, Eben.' Lilburne nodded at the man with the revolver. Owain heaved the heavy, panelled door closed behind them as instructed. There was a fireplace with a Victorian feature mantle; the pine surround may have been scratched and scuffed but the tiled, cast iron insert survived with much of its elegance intact. A fire burnt there built of a broken old coffee table bolstered by whatever burnable rubbish could be gathered. The singed remaining leg of a Queen Anne chair leant against the side of the mantle next to a poker and a set of bellows. The flames licked high, reflecting in the pale faces of the trio gathered around the card table; two men and one woman, she in a bobble hat. All three were in rags of long worn jeans and holey sweaters.

'So, any of you want anything from Santa's little helpers, here?' Eben casually waved his hand, holding the revolver toward the three witches of weed clustered around the smoke issuing from their cauldron-like bong.

'Nah, you're alright.' Lilburne laughed.

'We're here to see the Doc,' Grace said.

Eben smiled at Grace, amused at her naïve self-confidence.

'You're in a rush are you with your bagful of secrets?' He narrowed his eyes and looked between them and at the bag Owain carried.

One of the witches mocked Grace in repetition, mimicking her educated accent. 'We're in rather a hurry to see the Doc.'

Eben laughed then coughed and pointed his revolver at the mimicking witch. 'Shut the fuck up, if you're just going to be rude to our guests.' He turned to Grace with gun lowered in plaintive outstretched hand. 'Miss Grindecobbe, forgive the guttersnipe here. However.' He waved the gun about again; it was an extension of his hand. 'Remember, the Doc has squirrels in the trees, owls at night to see and larks in the morning to sing.' He turned his attention to Angharad and Owain. 'You're the Welsh fugitives.'

The female witch asked what they wanted. Eben turned to her. 'They're rebels. They want to help the poor like Robin Hood.'

'We're poor,' the witch replied, and another added, 'Dirt poor.'

Eben laughed. 'Do you want to rise up to take on the powerful?'

One of the witches replied, 'Nah' to muttered agreement from the others.

Eben laughed. 'The smart ones say nothing. Keep their heads down and hope not to get too battered by the wankers rushing past them.' He smiled. 'I met this old Irish guy once, up in Liverpool, I'm half Scouse.' He shrugged at their disinterest and continued. 'The old guy made pennies outside Lanigan's, pretending to play a cardboard cut-out mandolin, and hollering old folk songs. People paid him to shut up. He told me this rhyme. The ending went ...

The moral of this story is: this land's a victim-farm.

Don't you ever feed a beggar here, he'll eat your fucking arm.

And don't blaspheme the strong ones, if you want to stay alive,

Now smile and give them thanks when they say, here's a pack of lies.

Impatient, Lilburne asked, 'Do you know where the Doc is or not?' Eben coolly observed him. Disturbed by this cool observance, Lilburne snapped, 'You know what. You're full o' shite, you? Sittin' in here wi' your teenage fuckin' acolytes running around after you. You're a fuckin' parasite, mate. Burrowed in here like a fucking tick.'

'What's his beef?' Eben asked Grace but didn't wait for her reply. 'Pax omnibus, John Lilburne, pax omnibus.' Eben raised both hands to indicate truce though the right hand was still holding the cocked revolver. 'Cool your boots, man. You need to see the Doc, you say.'

'Where is he?' Lilburne asked.

Eben looked upward. 'Dude, just follow the sound of the cello. You'll find him.' Adding, 'I'm only a gatekeeper, Mr Lilburne, not the wizard. You expect too much of me.' He reached into a pocket and removed a big, old metal mortice key and held it aloft. 'You'll need to take this. The guards upstairs will only let you pass with this.' Lilburne stepped toward Eben to take the key, but as he reached for it, Eben held on. 'Piece of free advice, Mr Lilburne. In the long run, charm will get you further than belligerence.' He let go of the key. 'And grab a torch off o' one o' me elves, here. Lights don't always work upstairs.'

Eben called after them as they exited his room. 'Good luck, Taffies. Oh, and swing by on your way out if you want anything.' Behind the closing door Angharad could hear Eben softly singing. 'Hey kids, rock n' roll, nobody tells you where to go, baby.' To which, one of the witches cackled.

At the top of the stairs the light did dim, but it was still perfectly visible. Grace carried the torch by her side, untested. Cello drifted along the landing from a staircase leading up to a door to the attic. At the foot of this staircase, two painted goons with shaved heads and wearing cheap denim and tight, white t-shirts were stood. Grace brandished the key and the two goons looked at each other. One, the taller but slightly less bulky bullet-headed goon, with uncertain bravado, took a lead. 'I'd better take you up and check this out.'

When the door to the attic room opened, the cello could be heard clearer; low and mellifluous. The goon told them to wait. Past the door, left ajar, Angharad saw flames reflected in a large, free-standing mirror. The goon reappeared and allowed them entry with a finger pressed against his pursed lips.

The Doc was in his seventies, his hair was grey, pulled into a ponytail and fronted by a neatly trimmed beard. His face was creased with many years, but he was otherwise notably spry. To the Doc's left was an occasional table, tall standing on three elegantly carved, polished legs. Atop was a small silver tray with a bottle of sherry and two cut crystal glasses, a cardboard box containing icing-sugar dusted cubes of Turkish delight and a chessboard with finely carved pieces of Chinese origin, which stood four inches high and were made of white jade and malachite. They were distributed across the board as though midway through a game. To the right, and blind-sighted from the Doc's position by a five-panel tapestry screen, a beautiful, black-haired woman played the cello. She wore a black evening dress, and the firelight bouncing around the room's many mirrors found screen on her pale skin and glittered in the earrings she wore. She also wore a collar around her neck with a ring and a lead attached, the other end of which was secured to a heavy music stand. Playing the cello, she seemed to Angharad to look neither happy nor sad, detached from the moment, lost in the sounds her bow made sliding across those thick cello wires and the fierce concentration of her finger work, those achingly mournful finger vibratos.

The Doc listened, sometimes watching her play in reflection in the mirror he'd set for just such purpose. He held his hand aloft, so they knew to remain quiet. The goon who'd shown them in closed the door behind his exit. The cellist's bow wept. The Doc waved his hand toward a chaise lounge upon which Angharad, and her companions perched in a row. Sitting opposite him they were able to see the actual cellist rather than just her reflection.

Angharad watched the woman playing cello, the easy grace of her movements, the stillness and acutely focused action, and the collar around her porcelain neck, framed by black hair, the silver ring and the chain.

The Doc observed his guests watching the cellist. 'You think it wrong that Natalia's here?' he asked. 'She was being trafficked when I discovered her. She finds this far more pleasant.'

Angharad felt strangely diminished listening to Natalia's playing, fearful of her inadequacies and that she over-reached herself.

Owain also watched the cellist, troubled by his own reaction to her caged beauty. Lilburne glanced at his colleagues and back to the Doc with the impatience of the easily bored young. The Doc had once again closed his eyes in sweet reverie, abandoned to his senses, thrilled by the piquant tension of the listeners' inevitable surrender to the troubling beauty of Natalia's song.

They waited.

'Ah.' The Doc eventually breathed. 'How it touches one and calls strangely to some lost ache that words can't describe – only music.' The Doc reached for his box of Turkish delight, spearing a cube with a tiny fork, and popping it into his mouth. 'It is a demanding piece but richly rewarding. A cello suite Britten wrote for Rostropovich.' He held the box out for his guests.

Lilburne stepped free from the chaise lounge, took the fork from the Doc, and spiked a piece of Turkish delight. 'And your friends?' the Doc offered, so Lilburne took the box and each person perched on the chaise lounge took a piece in an act Angharad thought denoted some ritual of complicity, not only for what they were there to negotiate with the Doc, but complicity in the whole scene, even in the chaining of Natalia. 'Sherry?' Doc asked, but each declined so he too, with a shrug, reset the bottle.

The cellist ceased, the movement complete, she set the cello in its stand, laid her bow down beside her chair and sat neatly, knees together. Her gaze floated in a moment not wholly her own but also a moment not wholly owned by another. Whatever thoughts and feelings she had were kept her own. She possessed a stillness that seemed to Angharad eternal. 'Is it in the bag?' Doc asked. Angharad nodded. 'May I see it?'

Lilburne took the bag from Angharad and crossed to where the Doc was sat. He crouched and unzipped the bag and peered in. Lilburne lifted from the bag an artefact wrapped in newspaper and masking tape and handed it to the Doc. With the wrapped artefact rested in his lap, the Doc took a pair of scissors from the table to his side and cut carefully away at the wrapping, sweeping it from his lap to the floor. Lilburne stood the unpeeled object on a table to his right. The Doc said to him, 'Would you turn on the lamp there so I can see it?'

The artefact was a black, carved bird, standing about a foot high. 'Well, what do you think?' the Doc addressed his guests.

'It certainly has some heft,' Lilburne commented.

The Doc smiled. 'It is the Falcon of Ándalus.' He shuffled forward in his chair and leant in toward the bird, aspects of which were lit by the lamp. The Doc tapped the bird and scratched its surface with a letter opener. 'This is black enamel.' The Doc shuffled back into his seat with a smile of sweet satisfaction. 'Thank you. Mr bin Salah would also wish me to pass on his gratitude.'

He reached for the sherry bottle and a small cut crystal glass. 'Are we sure nobody would care to share a small glass of sherry?' the Doc said. 'It is Sunday after all.' He sipped, holding the glass between the fingertips of both hands. He spoke with the deliberate pleasure of an expert imparting knowledge to a captive audience. 'The falcon was cast by the master craftsmen of the Abbasid Dynasty from finest gold and jewels. It was intended as a gift for the caliph of Córdoba but was captured en route by Berber pirates. The falcon was retrieved only to be lost again when the Ottomans captured Baghdad in 1517. Later the same century, the Knights of Malta planned to make it a gift for the king of Spain, the caliphate was gone, of course, by this time, and so again the bird was lost in transit. Since then, stories can be traced of how it passed from owner to owner and twice around the globe before reaching here today.'

'Gold and jewels?' Lilburne asked. 'The size it is, it must be worth a bloody fortune.'

'Mr bin Salah has a man named Fakhoury in the city for authentication. Assuming Mr Fakhoury confirms what we have here. The value is inestimable.' The Doc added with a wry smile, 'A king's ransom.'

'So,' Angharad found unpleasant such talk and devotion of beautiful objects in an ugly and desperate world. 'Do we have a deal with Mr bin Salah?'

'Natalia!' the Doc called. 'Natalia, would you play some Bach?' He smiled serene hearing Natalia shuffle papers on the stand and move to take up again the cello and bow and begin to play. His world was once more in order. 'ID and papers, as promised.' He passed a thick manila envelope to Lilburne.

From within, Lilburne distributed the relevant ID cards and supporting papers to Angharad and Owain. 'Will this get us in and out of the city, okay?' Angharad asked.

'Not just the city. This product is so good you could get in and out of the country,' The Doc claimed. 'You've all got highest level clearance, but it's nice and subtle, you know, nothing too flashy. Owain is a civil servant called Malcolm Morris working in the crypts beneath Whitehall. Angharad is a technician from the big data storage centre between the Tottenham Court Road and Shaftsbury Avenue.'

'Judith Baker,' Angharad read. She looked at the face in the picture, round with large spectacles, not the long hair of her twenties and thirties, now a pageboy style haircut with threads of grey. So, she thought, you're a Judith Baker these days. Even though the photograph was small she could still detect the creases of crow's feet around her eyes. Where did the young woman go? It didn't seem so long ago. She smiled, absent for a moment from the room she was in. The time, the days, they just run away. The shapes of her youth were not brightly lit and solid now, but the lengthening shadows cast by a sun sliding not slowly enough over the horizon. She looked at Owain, he was in the room though and listening as the Doc explained the different documents and bar-coded identification that would be needed to navigate the city. Angharad reached over and touched Owain's hand. He glanced, didn't look, but held her fingers in his own. Maybe she and Owain could've tried again for children. When they decided not to, they were still young, and the world seemed old. Now, they're old. It wasn't Owain, it was her decision more than his. She swallowed a breath back down, deep, deep down and returned to the room.

'John is military, special ops, off duty from a northern garrison, a security level that would mean reporting to the mandarins of ministers in Whitehall. The name's Nigel Cooper. All good, solid English names.' The Doc laughed. 'And Willow Walwyn, not here, I take it you've not taken her place?' The Doc asked Grace. Lilburne confirmed this wasn't the case and he would pass on Willow's papers before Grace caught chance to answer for herself. She looked like the only child not to get a present.

Lilburne read over Willow's papers and commented. 'Wendy Wilson. background as a military doctor, now servicing plutocrats in the city.'

'Yes,' the Doc commented. 'She'll be registered with a practice off Harley Street. They'll deny it of course if the authorities check too closely but it should do for a few more weeks.'

'Will we get the help we need?' Lilburne asked the Doc.

'You understand Mr bin Salah has no involvement in this political tribulation, and for what it's worth, I have even less inclination in that direction myself.' The Doc laid his glass of sherry down. The atmosphere of the room was softened by his languid sanguinity and strains of Bach accompanied by a quiet pop and crackle from the fireplace. The Doc drew a notebook, silver pen, and pair of half-moon, wire-frame spectacles from inside the blue velvet jacket he wore. He scratched some lines out, tore off the small page, folded it over, and looking up, asked if someone could fetch one of his 'boys from the stairs'.

When the goon arrived, he approached the Doc and leant in close for something to be whispered in his ear before taking the folded note.

With goon dispatched, Doc wrote them out an address, which he handed to Lilburne. 'You will meet representatives of Mr bin Salah here. I'm confident agreement can be reached for you to receive support in your endeavours.' Doc paused and over his spectacles added, 'There is one further issue however.'

Angharad had drifted to the sound of Bach's cello, the attic room was hot from the fire, and a fatigue she had resisted, and fought against, was finally breaking through her will and resolve. She noticed Lilburne sit forward, alert to the Doc's words, Grace also was like a meerkat with all the eagerness of youth. Owain listened, pretending to pick imaginary motes of fluff from the crossed knee of his trousers. Angharad turned her focus fully back on the Doc.

'It seems you're in possession of a little more than a bird in a bag.'

'I don't know what you mean,' Lilburne answered.

'Oh, I think you do.' The Doc turned his sherry glass between his fingers. 'Some transatlantic correspondence.' The Doc sipped his sherry. Nobody spoke to address his reference. 'Very well. We shall discuss Mr Luca Chimera and his goodies again at some point.' He held the note with the address out for Lilburne to take. How do they know the American's name? Angharad wondered. Since meeting him at the Welsh coast, they had kept their asset under wraps and out of sight.

'This is the address of a public house in Woodford called the Hanging Gate. They serve food there. You need to ask for a reservation. Representatives of Mr bin Salah will meet you there.'

They left the Doc to the strains of Bach's first cello suite.

XIV

Esme and her dad cycled into Fenby. There was a determined silence following him out of the house, only the sounds of their footsteps across the yard, the creak of the shed door, the slicing of their wheels through shallow puddles formed from light overnight rain seemed solid. The sky was grey, its thin light drained.

Before entering the town hall, Esme said to her dad, 'Thank you. It's just, you know how scared he must be.' Esme's dad nodded and Esme said, 'I saw how you stuck up for him. I was proud of you, Dad.'

'Come on then, girl.' Esme's dad led them into the town hall rather than meet the compliment. Esme was relieved to see no agents about. Esme's dad told Darren on the desk they were going to visit Davey. It wasn't a request. Darren wore a badge over his left breast, but it was a token from the mayor without practical meaning in the community, and with the mayor's son marrying Esme that afternoon he knew to oblige.

The cells were in an annexe at the back of the town hall. Their footsteps clattered the otherwise silent, tiled corridor that approached the three cells, where Davey was the only inmate. Darren unlocked the door. Davey was sat on a low bed on the opposite wall. He'd looked up upon hearing the door and Esme recognised fear in his face. 'Can I speak to Davey alone, Dad?'

Esme's dad glanced at Darren who shrugged, and both withdrew. Darren said, 'We'll wait outside, Miss Esme. Knock when you want letting out.'

'Okay,' Esme replied and turned to see the door close. She heard its heavy mechanisms and looked at it closed. Never had a door seemed so impassable. Davey stood trembling. Esme watched his mouth try to form words but not know the words he needed, and a tear welled over his right eye, burst, and slid down his cheek. He pressed it away beneath an embarrassed palm.

'Essie,' he said, his lips trembled, and he teared up again. She knew she should reach out to him, hold him, but the thought of the touch of another caused a chill to shiver through her.

Esme sat on the bed and asked him to sit next to her. He sat, grateful. She could hear the church bells through a high, small blue window. 'I shouldn't have done it, Essie.' Esme watched him rock back and forth, perched on the edge of the cell bed next to her. 'Jack Belton threw an apple.'

'So, you used your slingshot.' There was no judgement in Esme's tone.

'I'm good with it, everyone says. I got a good eye. I never meant to hurt the man. You know that, Essie.'

Esme knew. Davey would try to save wounded animals he found. He could hit the catch on a shed door, causing the door to open from across the yard, but she'd also seen him sit and weep over his old and dying dog, and she and Davey had both been present when Barney Rudkin's heifer first calved, and Esme had seen the excited joy in his face watching the calf, with uncertainty, stand and start to walk. 'I know, I know you wouldn't hurt anyone, Davey.' And as she said this Esme rubbed Davey's shoulder and his rocking steadied and he looked at Esme and smiled. But to his smile that reached out to her, Esme responded by whipping back her hand and folding it safely into her lap.

'I'm scared, Essie,' Davey said, with the round, brown eyes of a child.

'I know, these are scary times, but you'll be alright, Davey.'

When Esme watched his fear, she thought of the look in Davey's dog's eyes as Davey had cradled him dying. The dog felt the ache, on some level he knew the certain hopelessness, he just didn't understand any part of it. He couldn't understand the discomfort and pain that wouldn't cease, or why he couldn't lift himself from where he was laying. Davey stroked the dog's side and wept while the dog looked up at him, open eyed but fading and drifting beyond some horizon.

She leant over and whispered in Davey's ear, 'Don't worry, Davey. Be strong. I know you're getting out tomorrow. Trust me. I promise. I know this.'

Davey pulled back and looked at her to see if he could believe her. Davey was incapable of lying and thought Esme incapable also. 'You promise?'

Esme traced the points of a cross. 'I promise.'

Their smiles tripped into laughs before quiet as Davey thought again. Esme knew Davey needed more time than most to think. She remembered admonishing people who became impatient with him, 'For Christ's sake, give him a sec. He's getting there.' Afterwards Davey repeated 'for Christ's sake' back at her in an imitation of her voice and laughed.

Sat in the jail cell, at the back of the town hall, alongside Esme, Davey said, 'Are you off to the weddings this after?' Esme shrugged and Davey thought some more and asked. 'Will you be marrying, Essie?'

Esme shrugged again. 'I guess so. It's time.'

Davey watched Esme stare at her own hands in her lap and asked, 'Do you want to?' Esme shrugged so Davey asked, 'Will it be Tom?'

'Yes.' Esme stretched and then stood up unable to meet

Davey's eyes, not for the disappointment she knew that she would find there, but because she knew his eyes would ask her if she wanted to marry Tom, and she knew that she did not. She wanted to be a child again, playing in the barn or out on the fen with Davey until her mam's voice called them in.

Davey watched her as she rose on the balls of her feet and down again. He said, 'Will you still be my friend?'

'Of course!' Esme protested. 'I'll always be your friend.'

'Esme!' She heard her name called through the door.

'We'd better call it a day.'

The mechanism of the door started to clunk into activity.

'If I'd been there, Essie,' Davey began, 'I'd, I'd, I'd have asked you to marry me.' Esme smiled but the door started to open and draw their attention from each other. 'I'd have, I'd have asked you for a dance anyhoo.'

Esme smiled, the door opened, and Esme's dad said, 'Hello, young Davey. How're you doing there, lad?' Davey smiled but looked like he wanted to cry. 'Hey, cheer up, lad. I'll have you out and helping me with work in no time.' Davey knew Esme's dad was being kindly so he smiled but he turned to Esme and looked at her again with those same helpless, abandoned eyes.

Outside in the corridor, Esme watched the door close back around Davey.

XV

The morning of the festival of Neptune was a red-letter day for church observance – St Wendreda's was heaving. There were others though emerging from the Seven Stars Inn while the slow bells marking the end of the Sunday service preceding the wedding ceremonies were still ringing out.

Saint Wendreda's church was the most important in the Marshland diocese after Ely Cathedral. It was proud of its double hammer beam angel roof honouring God and Saint Wendreda, the peacemaker. Generally, those involved in the weddings would feel duty bound to attend the service before and Esme saw more girls milling around the grounds of Saint Wendreda's in variations of the white muslin dress Esme was wearing. There were teenage boys in suits pulling at the sleeves and collars of their shirts.

Due to the high bank and the slope of the meadow down to the lake, it was difficult to gauge the scale of the event until past Saint Wendreda's, after which waves of voices broke the bank and fell away into a rumbling, rolling sea. At the top of the bank Esme looked out over the meadow at hundreds, maybe a thousand people from all over the Fenby area. Parents and families proudly flanked children. This was the day their childhood would be left behind and, in that knowledge, faces were lit both by excited expectancy and still shaded in doubt and anxiety, shifting between feet with the restlessness and uncertainty of water.

Esme viewed a sea of figures mingling in movements of shape and colour, more people than she thought she had seen gathered in her entire life. People drifted about fanning themselves with folded cardboard programmes that detailed the forthcoming events. Before ceremonies commenced people drifted about with glasses of imported sparkling wine and local canapes; vol-au-vents stuffed with egg and mushroom, delicacies of eel on thin slivers of toast, fish roe and creamed cheese. At the far end of the bank was a raised platform with bunting where the mayor was. He was dressed in his full regalia of robes and chains as the occasion demanded. Esme thought he would become very hot and red and sweaty later – he was not a man who coped with heat well.

Walking out from beneath the shade of a pair of elm trees, Esme discovered Sarah-May with Luca. They stood together as the first cohort of girls was called to the water with mothers, sisters and aunts fussing around them. The mayor made a jolly, crowd-pleasingly short speech to start proceedings. Esme would be one of the last called down to the water's edge on account of marrying the mayor's son. 'Near the top of the bill,' Esme's dad joked before striding off toward the mayor's enclosure for a few words, a veritable delight in his galloping stride, Lizzie and Tilly trailing his shadow.

One of the priests rang a heavy brass bell.

Hush descended.

The matriarchs withdrew and the first four girls turned toward the water where the preacher and his assistants stood, submerged up to the knees in soaked vestments. The preacher's voice drifted over the meadow. 'We're gathered in solemnity but also in celebration, to bring Christ into our community and to bring the community further into the embrace of Christ.'

Esme noticed Mrs Quickfall at the top of the bank. Esme was glad she came. She was receiving support getting settled into a chair. The preacher's words drifted by on a zephyr. 'As is written in the book of Genesis, God said, "It is not good for man to be alone, so I will make a partner for him." And God blessed them and said to "be fruitful and multiply. Fill the earth and subdue it. Rule over the fish in the sea, the birds in the sky, and over every living creature that lives on the ground."' A curtain hush was drawn from the bank around the meadow and the lake. A line of four priests, two arms' lengths apart and maybe twenty feet into the water, in turns called the first line of girls by name: Amy, Edith, Genevieve and Marianne. The girls stepped tentatively into the water and when Amy slipped, nobody laughed or even commented, only the voice of the preacher she was approaching could be heard as she picked herself up to continue. 'Keep coming toward me, child. Don't look back.'

Each of the girls stood in a line, willowing in the water, and to each a preacher spoke and lay a hand on the forehead, in blessing, and the small of the girl's back to ease her into the water. This too, was a signal for the first line of four boys to make their way out to meet the girl, barefoot but still in suits as the tradition was. In turn, each of the four pastors said to the girl they were taking through the rites, 'When you are submerged in the water you may feel Neptune try to take you down. You may feel his arms around you. When you rise from the water, you will be blessed by the light of God and your husband will find you. Are you prepared to face Neptune?'

'I am,' each girl in turn replied. She was then lowered carefully back into the water, supported by the hands of the preacher, while behind them were the increased splashing of the boys struggling through the water, ankle high, shin high, knee high and eventually rising over their thighs toward their waists. When the girls were lifted back out of the water, gasping and standing shivering, the water running off them with the boys sounding nearer behind them, the preacher would touch the tip of his middle finger against the forehead of each girl and trace a cross from her forehead, along the length of her nose, touching her lips, her chin and along the breastbone, and from one shoulder across the girls' neckline to the other shoulder. 'Ad gloriam et ad lumen audite vocem Domini Dei.'

Esme felt herself tremble before the spectacle. She shivered as she watched the preachers touch each of the girls.

The preacher's palm pressed against the forehead, pushed the girl backwards, ideally to be caught by the boy. He replied with the only words of Latin he'd ever know, learnt by rote. 'Ego gloriam Dei et stellas.'

At the water's edge each couple had a white shawl tied around them and a ribbon from the girl's hair to bind their wrists. They then joined the groom's family for the remainder of the ceremony. Luca nudged Esme's shoulder with his own and asked her to show him who it was she would be marrying, and so she pointed out the mayor's son.

Tom Jr waved at Esme from the mayor's enclosure, a little shy but clear, he must have seen Esme and noticed her point him out. Sarah-May laughed as Esme waved back and said, 'So, you are going to marry him then?'

Esme shrugged. 'He's quite sweet really.' Esme watched another line of four girls walk into the water toward the preachers and trembled.

'It's not too late to come away with us,' Sarah-May said. Esme sighed. 'You could. It wouldn't have to be forever if you didn't want, but this does.' Four more boys trudged through shallow water to their partially submerged betrothed. 'If you don't now, you never will,' Sarah-May added and Esme began to want to walk away from her, join her dad and Lizzie, talk to other people, people who lived contentedly and didn't protest the way things were and had to be. Esme had never known a moment as heavy.

Then everything changed. Eight state agents approached the mayor's enclosure. A phalanx of locals flanked them, claiming offence at their presence.

A girl was let go of. She fell in the lake with a splash, her young suitor distracted by the disturbance at the mayor's enclosure. The preacher, distracted also, was slow to react to the girl's descent into Neptune's depths until finally called by the splashing of flailing arms. The preacher lifted the girl, coughing water, and conjoined her with her distracted betrothed, but by this time most people's attention was diverted.

One of the agents spoke to the mayor. It wasn't Miller or McCain. The crowd gathered closer around the mayor's enclosure. Those at the water drifted back away from the suspended rituals. A lead agent turned to address the crowd. He introduced himself as State Agent Mark Tait – a bully in a suit claiming violence protects decency and order. 'Due to events this afternoon we've decided to take the unusual course of action of speaking to the whole community. We understand most of the community are here, those that aren't will no doubt get to hear what I am to say. As some amongst you must be aware, we have been encountering increasing problems gathering the census data we need. This is not altogether unusual for us, however, this afternoon events did take an unusual twist. A young man called David Harold Clay, who was being held under arrest in cells at your town hall pending trial for a violent assault of a state agent, has disappeared.' A murmur passed around the crowd. Esme looked around the crowd also, searching for her dad and to understand. The speaking agent let the murmur pass before continuing. 'A Mr Darren Edward Ward, the only guard on duty,' the agent glanced at the mayor, 'was confronted by two masked men who gagged him and tied him up in a cell. The boy and the two men who broke him out should now be given up.'

The agent paused. A laugh tripped through a few people before someone called out, 'Get out!' and another shouted, 'Even if I knew, I wouldn't say.'

The state agent raised his hands and the crowd hushed to hear him. There were hotheads, but most people seemed anxious, perhaps the state agent suspected this when he announced. 'We will complete our census, you will pay your tax even if the state requires every spare penny you have, and the extra expenses we are having will be added to your taxes, and we will have the boy.'

'Mr Mayor,' Mick Brown, landlord of the Seven Stars, standing near the front called out, 'tell these hounds, there will be no more compliance with the agents.' There was a ripple of clapping. 'There will be no more poll tax.' This time there was a round of applause though still a great many people glanced around, uneasy. 'And we will not help them get Davey Clay. He's one of ours, he stays one of ours.' Another round of applause but some at the front noticed the agents were now reaching inside their jackets and pulling out revolvers.

Esme lost Sarah-May and Luca in the crowd but found Mrs Quickfall.

Mick Brown continued unconcerned by the firearms. 'Until we have satisfaction over the treatment of some of our womenfolk by these dogs …'

Mrs Quickfall greeted Esme. 'I thought I'd come down to watch this year. More eventful than normal, I see. Whatever else, you do look lovely, dear.'

State agent Mark Tait, with both hands gripping the rail at the front of the mayor's enclosure, addressed the whole community directly. 'If you have evidence of any of my agents involved in any kind of wrongdoing, present the evidence. Otherwise, you have twenty-four hours, after which we will send for units from Peterborough or Cambridge, meaning two-dozen heavily armed troops who'll take your backward little town apart to get what they want.'

There was a gasp as he said this, and an angry silence followed.

'Esme,' Mrs Quickfall said. 'You must go tonight. You will be missed but you will return.' Esme wanted her to be right. As she watched events unfold at the mayor's enclosure, there was a part of her hoping that the day would be cancelled and she saved, if only for a time.

Someone in the crowd shouted, 'What say you, Mr Mayor?'

Esme believed in Mrs Quickfall, but it was impossible. She clutched at her dress, 'I'm supposed to marry.'

'Yes, the mayor's son. He's a good lad, he'll understand.' She thought for a moment. 'He has potential, that one, but not yet.'

State Agent Tait at the front of the platform said with authority few would argue with, 'I can answer that. Your friendly town mayor is not in control.' He paused to pan his head across the crowd, 'You people need to understand the rules have changed. We can reach into your lives and turn them off like this.' and holding both hands aloft he clicked his fingers, an effect mostly lost on the farthest flung of the crowd. 'We are in control now.'

Puncturing the quiet deflation that followed the agent's assertion, what looked like an arrow but was a crossbow bolt whistled through the air, striking the boards beneath the rail Agent

Tait's hands gripped with an embedding thwang. There was a man, dressed in dirty rags, coming forward from the edge of the meadow, who a few knew as Hereward. Alongside Hereward walked Davey Clay. Hereward shouted, 'We have the boy!'

The crowd started to part. Davey hesitated but Hereward dragged him along by the wrist. 'But you ain't having him.' Davey looked terrified.

Some folks were leaving, others were transfixed. Sarah-May and Luca passed Esme talking with Mrs Quickfall. 'Hey Esme, you know where we'll be,' Sarah-May said as she passed.

Mrs Quickfall looked at Esme with an expression that didn't need words. 'I can't,' Esme said and clutched the sides of her dress again as explanation.

A voice roared from the edge of the meadow. 'You need to listen, Mr Agent Goon. You're not in control here. We are!' And as Hereward said this, a volley of crossbow bolts was fired, immediately four of the eight agents slumped to the ground or recoiled from the crossbow bolts. From the gullies, the dykes and beyond the banks walking in the opposite direction to much of the crowd and toward the fray were a dozen or more of Hereward's people, armed with crossbows and shouting, 'The Woke! The Woke! The Woke! The Woke!'

Esme saw Lizzie leaving and calling to her with a beckoning hand. 'I got to go,' she said to Mrs Quickfall.

'Precisely, Esme,' Mrs Quickfall replied, and Esme groaned forlornly. 'Go,' Mrs Quickfall whispered. 'I'll help smooth things over here.'

Hereward whispered something to Davey, slapped him on the shoulder and the boy went searching for someone he knew. Esme was too far away with Lizzie and Tilly on the far side of the crowded meadow. Hereward climbed up on to the platform to address the crowd. A groan came from Agent Tait, trying to pull the bolt from his chest, looking at his colleague next to him, blood leaking from the crossbow bolt torn through his neck. Hereward turned to Special Agent Mark Tait, aimed a smaller crossbow that had been slung over his shoulder, calmly attached a bolt from one of a pair tucked inside his boot, and said, 'Sive vivimus, sive morimur, Domini sumus.' He shot a crossbow bolt into Agent Tait's eye from a couple of feet, so when it exploded his brain gore squirted from the eye that Hereward needed to wipe from his sleeve.

Hereward turned to the mayor, who looked quite bilious. 'Mr Mayor,' he said, 'I return to you your town and your community.' And louder for all, he declared. 'You, and all good folk here, need to take heed. Your enemies will return. We must take the fight to them and so any amongst you who will come, we leave tonight. And for those who remain, to any who ask, tell them,' Hereward paused for impact, 'the Reckoning has begun.'

The crowd stayed silent while Hereward's words settled. Into that gaping quiet, led by members of Hereward's militia, a chant broke out that many in the crowd joined in chanting. 'The Woke! The Woke! The Woke! The Woke!'

XVI

A swallow scooped an arc of sky above the old stable on Wandlebury Hill.

Down at the roadside, Mary Smith and Mazcek had broken the surface with heaving swings of pickaxes. They scraped out a pothole in the track, filled it with dynamite, covered it with leaves and broken branches, and trailed a wire into the trees that clothed the hill slope.

'Where did y'say they were?' Karen said, back on the roof of the old stable. Mother Michael passed the binoculars to Debbie, Debbie subsequently passed them to Karen, who looked in the wrong place and so couldn't see the train of five vehicles heading along the road toward them.

Mother Michael took back the binoculars and scanned the situation. Down below Gerrard's people scurried about, most finding positions amongst the trees. He took more people to defend the path closer to the intersection, which left Red Nev and his best shot, Casey Tully, crouched behind an old horsebox they'd pulled across the opening at the top of the less-defended second approach. They were armed with the only rapid-fire machine gun the hermits had, raised on a tripod stand, slightly obscured, poking out around the horsebox's coupler. In the sheds to the side of the stable house, somebody was preparing the geese.

Mother Michael swung the focus of her binoculars back to the road, tracked along it until she reached the train of vehicles. 'They're at the hill.'

'Right,' Debbie acknowledged. She'd put her spectacles on. 'I'm pistol-primed and ready. Where do you want me?'

'I need you to keep mobile, for the mo,' Mother Michael said. A walkie-talkie on the balustrade crackled into life. 'Yes, Willow.'

'They're beginning their approach.'

'Are we set?'

'All set.' Willow would be Mother Michael's ears and eyes on the ground. Mazcek was amongst the trees crouched down low with the plunger box. Mary was higher up the bank, crouching between trees, low amongst bracken, mud smeared over her face, hood pulled up over her head. She had a crossbow slung over her back by a strap and a Molotov cocktail tucked inside the belt she had drawn around her jacket.

'And the P.A.?' Mother Michael asked.

'We ran a line down from the generator in the stable,' Willow said. 'We won't know if it works until its time. Its line is covered in gaffer tape repairs.'

Mother Michael looked grimly at Karen and Debbie. 'It's about to begin.'

There was an explosion so loud it might've cracked the hill open. Shrapnel and huge mounds of earth and debris whistled around, bouncing and crashing with sparks of fires and shattered glass. Mazcek let the first Jeep pass and caught the first of the converted, military-appropriated mini-buses that followed.

Through binoculars trained on the approach road, Mother Michael watched the first minibus explode when the fire caught the fuel tanks. It leapt, propelled by a blast beneath its chassis that cratered the road several feet deep and wide. The minibus turned over in the air, more graceless than a spin and crashed into trees. A thick elm branch smashed through the web of shattered glass of the minibus's windscreen. Whoever was inside was trapped when the fuel tank caught light and exploded.

The three vehicles behind the blast screeched to urgent stops. In front, the Jeep rocked by the blast stopped of its own volition. Behind them, a man crawled from the back of the burning, side-grounded minibus in desperate, forlorn groans; unable to stand, his legs trailed behind him, a bloody mess of smashed bone, blood and sinew.

Mary Smith emerged in front of the Jeep with a Molotov in one hand and zippo aflame in the other. She tossed the bottle with an ethanol-soaked and lit rag stuffed down its throat. Through her binoculars, Mother Michael watched it spin in the air, arc in a steep parabola, strike the windscreen and roll, fiery, into a groove between the bonnet and the windscreen wipers. The uniforms leapt in synchronicity from the Jeep. The fire reached the engine and blew the bonnet clear. It twisted and turned in the air, glinting in shafts of morning sun. Mother Michael lowered again her binoculars.

'We're ready ...' Willow's voice panted from running over rough terrain, ' ... if you want to broadcast.'

Mother Michael pressed a button on a microphone and emerging from crackling interference and over the sound of burning and rushed, unclear voices, she spoke. 'Ah, what this one? Are we already on? Oh, okay, right.'

'Where's that coming from?' a uniform called out.

'Visitors listen! It is in your interests to take heed.' Through snowy reproduction and diminished by her awkward beginning, Mother Michael persisted. 'If you continue up this hill, you will die. You are safe nowhere here, your shadow stalks you.' Mother Michael's voice echoed as it bounced around the trees. 'The woods, that even now some of you cower in, are booby trapped throughout. Every aspect of the hermitage's defence is already determined. Wandlebury Ring is sacred ground. You will be smote.'

Mother Michael's walkie-talkie crackled into life. Karen reached for it but was stopped by Mother Michael. 'No!' Karen's hand froze over the walkie-talkie. 'Willow will talk to us, we listen. If we reply, we could give away her position.'

Thus rebuked, Karen withdrew her hand and Willow's voice, quiet but clear enough, reported an unfolding scene and the futility of Mother Michael's threats. 'They've shot the speakers,' Willow said. 'Two units fanned out around the ring. They're beginning their ascent.'

'They're on the way.' Mother Michael turned to her companions on the roof. 'They're on their way.' Debbie kept bringing her rifle sight to eye only to lower it again. Amidst the squawking and flapping of wings, the geese boxes were wheeled into place. Usually, the geese roamed around the stable, already agitated by being boxed up behind gated walls of chicken wire, they were about to be sent hurtling down the slope, and they weren't happy about it. The moving trailer beneath them had already enraged their intemperate nature.

The trailer was launched from the top of the path. It was lost to Mother Michael's sight as the approach track disappeared amidst a canopy of trees. The trailer bumped and bounced with gaining speed down the track, slammed into a tree and toppled over in a cacophony of crashing boxes and angry birds. 'The geese are free,' Willow whispered from some observable distance, dug in deep beneath the line of bracken and fern; the coppicing and pollarding of the alder, elm and birch trees increasing the cover for the rebels. The furious geese attacked the troopers, harrying them back down the track or into the trees to be picked off by Gerrard's people submerged in the undergrowth.

Mother Michael closed her eyes and remembered some long-time distant but never forgotten wisdom. 'Know when to fight and when not to fight. Avoid what is strong and strike at what is weak. Know how to deceive the enemy: appear weak when you are strong, and strong when you are weak.' Tapping her fat fingers over the barrel of her binoculars, at eighty-eight, Mother Michael denied nerves. Many years earlier, during her travels in the east, when Mother Michael had been a young woman who went by the name of Rose Rowett and having found her irascible nature ill-fitted to an ashram in Uttarakhand, she headed further east, into China, where she was taught Eastern philosophy of ethics and strategy by the hermit Guiguzi Xiansheng, also known as the Sage of Ghost Valley. When, after twenty-one years, she returned to the west in hermit robe, she became known first as Dorothy, for the poor she helped revered her as a gift from God. Only much later did she become the Mother Michael of myth.

Two troopers had been unfortunate enough not to escape the geese unmolested. One slipped, turning, and lying face down a goose, by repeatedly striking the trooper's helmet with its wings, had dislodged it and further strikes removed it entirely. There were two other geese standing on another trooper's back, covering his head with his hands in futile attempt to block the geese from pecking at his head and abdomen, his nose already bloodied and broken from a goose wing strike. 'Fall back! Fall back!' another trooper screamed.

Mother Michael watched most of the geese take flight and they were gone. The troops winged one goose that banked and dived one last earth-bound time like a Second World War Spitfire going down, its one good wing flapping desperately as the goose spun and tumbled in its final descent.

Up each path, two groups of about ten troops walked, watchfully.

With visor fronted helmets, Kevlar body armour covering their torsos, thighs, buttocks and groin, and keen automatic rifles twitching, Mother Michael knew a straightforward battle would result in the troops swiftly sweeping them aside.

There was a series of explosions and new screams. Mother Michael's walkie-talkie crackled to life, Willow was on the move again, panting as she spoke. 'That's Mazcek and Mary up in trees with Karen's Molotov cocktails.' Another pair of explosions burst from the approach paths. The smell of the blasts rose in thick clouds of noxious smoke. Karen had made the bottle bombs with methanol and a small quantity of her damson jam so the flames would stick to whatever they hit and keep burning. She littered the solution with tiny metal fragments to create hot, flying shrapnel that could shred skin and flesh. Into each bottle a kerosene-soaked rag was stuffed and lit. Crossbow bolts were fired from shadows between trees. From close range they smashed through visors, could sometimes puncture Kevlar from short distance, and if not would usually floor a trooper from the kinetic energy discharged. Mother Michael heard a crash loud as though the ground cracked open. She glanced at the walkie-talkie but there was nothing. In the darkness, noises made shapes in the imagination.

'Mary's down,' Willow said. Mother Michael sighed. 'She was about to throw a Molotov when a trooper noticed her movement and fired. He blew apart her hip and raked a chain of fire up her torso, neck and face. She fell. Her head hit a branch on the way.' Willow paused. 'She was dead before she hit the ground.'

'Christ have Mercy,' Mother Michael said, but did not press the button on the walkie-talkie, so Willow continued her whispered explanation.

'Mary's bomb exploded in the crook of a limb of a tree, the

trunk cracked, the top half of the tree heaved and fell after Mary. It crashed down and blocked the path behind the troopers. Red Nev and Casey Tully have them trapped. Casey has the big gun and is shooting them like they're fish in a barrel.'

It was always the noise and smell of battle that struck Mother Michael. Everything happened so quickly. Survival became instinctive. It was as though all nature and reality were conscious and connected, and in that heightened animistic state, one could know without understanding and react before things happened, attuned to an unfolding that transcended reason.

Another explosion and a trooper thrown by the blast brought to a crunching halt against a tree. Casey Tully fired off what rounds she had left in her machine gun, its nose smoking. When Casey had spent all her rounds, the few troops left on that approach returned fire with a sustained assault on Casey and Red Nev. Rogue beams of splintered sunlight burst through the perforated horsebox. There was no more fire from Casey Tully or Red Nev behind the horsebox and the remaining troops began climbing the path without response.

Mother Michael sighed and lowered her binoculars. 'You're going to have to blow the horsebox from up here, Debbie.' She said.

'Red Nev and Casey?' Debbie knew the answer to her question. She straightened her spectacles and moved into position. She switched her rifle for a crossbow Karen passed her with bolt attached wrapped in a paraffin-soaked rag. 'Now, Karen,' Debbie said. The hunchback hermit leant forward with lit taper, moving swiftly clear as a flame leapt up and started licking back along the shaft of the crossbow. The sky was darkening as a band of rain moved south from Cambridge, a low sun lighting the underside of the cloud and the rain in the distance. Debbie fired the flaming bolt. The soaked rag created a bias the bolt turned erratically around, the whoosh of oxygen through the paraffin nose sent flames licking back along its shaft and streaming behind. A fiery comet racing in downward arcing trajectory into the belly of the horsebox, its side panel already stripped back, opened up like a crib with a bed of straw and several kegs of dynamite – the end of their cache.

The horsebox exploded, a perforated near-side panel blown away, flying down the hill, tumbling over itself. The roof of the horsebox shattered from the blast and sent jagged slats of steel stripped away like tin foil, burning hot, flying and bouncing, and pitching deep where they landed. A trooper was struck down by some flying debris, groggily shaking his wits back into his head before being killed by a crossbow bolt finding a gap in his body armour.

On the first path, three of the four remaining troops were pinned. Willow watched the man who'd shot Mary receive a volley of crossbow bolts. One missed, flying angrily by and striking a tree trunk with a mighty thud and twang. The other four crossbow bolts punctured the trooper like a voodoo doll. He dropped his gun and crumpled to the floor. The other three troopers threw down their weapons and threw up their hands.

'Gerrard's secured the first path.' Willow's voice leapt from Mother Michael's walkie-talkie. Out of the trees they stepped, five crossbows reloaded and ready. Willow joined them. A medic is precious little use to the dead. 'We're moving down the path toward the Jeeps,' she informed Mother Michael. 'Gerrard wants to know if we should double back to defend the house from those others.'

'No,' Mother Michael said. 'Secure the Jeeps and those with them first. They're on us here anyway. We'll do our best to hold them.'

Through the fire of the burning horsebox, the black smoke, the dust and debris thrown up into the air and the shimmering heat haze, gunshots and crossbow bolts were fired from a position high on the stable block. Karen and Debbie had already blocked all the doors from the inside, Karen struggling without complaint from the pain it caused her back to drag furniture and other obstacles in front of the doors. The stairs were doused in ethanol – if the troopers broke through, Mother Michael was prepared to torch the staircase, stay on the roof, and hope reinforcements came before the house was consumed.

Gerrard led Willow and three others into the clear sight of those troops around the vehicles at the foot of the approach road. They immediately opened fire, cutting three troopers down around the vehicles, another scrambling away behind a truck. The last trooper wouldn't be allowed to escape though. Willow would recount the conflicted feelings she felt hunting him down with Gerrard and the others. He held his handgun up in front of his face, gripping it with both hands, shaking. He blew out his cheeks, and peering around the vehicle, shot. Fear rushed the action and he missed. They didn't fire back immediately but trained their weapons more keenly and continued to approach. Once the trooper was in sight, they fired, shooting him multiple times in the back. He collapsed as he ran.

Back on the roof: 'We have another problem,' Karen said. Out across Wandlebury Ring and away from the fighting, half-a-dozen or more troops were running across the ring from top paddock on the far side. 'Some must have made their way around the back. Knocked out the pair Gerrard stationed there.'

Mother Michael tapped the side of her rickety chair as indication to Karen she needed moving. 'Lock and load, ladies, it's all we can do for now.' Mother Michael reacquainted herself with a crossbow and lined up targets jogging across the ring toward them. She felt her hands gripping the crossbow tremble. Adrenalin coursed through her ancient blood.

From their roof positions Debbie took down a couple of those charging across the ring toward the stables with her hunting rifle. Mother Michael winged one with a crossbow, but he'd only been winged, and there was still another half dozen who made it across the ring from the back entrance and joined the half dozen from the main group breaking into the stable house.

Mother Michael heard a crash and cheer as troops broke through the main doors on the ground floor, followed by the scraping of furniture being pulled aside. Soldiers' boots crashed through broken steps and upward. A table was pushed against the door to the attic and on top of it and around the table were piled chairs, boxes, anything they could find to add weight. Debbie sat in the attic room with a rifle trained on the gap that would shortly open. The obstacles behind the door heaved. A chair on top of a cargo box on top of the table started to totter.

Debbie adjusted her rifle and a red dot appeared midway up the door, just below the handle, it fidgeted on the spot and steadied.

The door shifted, the chair tumbled and fell from the side of the pile, and the door opened little more than three inches through which a shot cracked like a whip. A cry was heard as the door fell back. Debbie's shot had been for where the gap would appear. The target and the hit were unknown but soon pressure was exerted again to the door. The obstacles piled behind lost structure, so the door moved more easily. Another shot from Debbie. The door fell back again with a shout, but the door heaved again soon after.

Another shot but also one in reply. The door fell back but

Mother Michael turned at the sound of Debbie dropping her gun. She'd been hit high where her chest met her left shoulder.

Karen was crouched by the wall the door was on, Molotov cocktail in one hand, lighter in the other. The door moved again. Karen lit and tossed the Molotov cocktail through the gap and the door fell back with a scream of, 'Shit!'

Debbie slumped from her chair, crawled away and crouched against the back wall, sat under a porthole window on the east side of the vaulted roof.

The staircase was starting to burn, but not so it prevented the troops making another attempt. The door opened, a soldier, with his visor down obscuring most of his face, looked directly at Mother Michael but was unable to get his shot away before Mother Michael shot him. It was a shot of accidental good fortune. Despite the jerk of Mother Michael's arm from the kick of the weapon, it tore open the trooper's throat, his head snapped back and forward, his knees faltered. He crumpled and collapsed through the narrow gap of the door, blocking its closure.

With an adrenalin surge Mother Michael shot again, through the space vacated by the fallen soldier, hitting the soldier behind in the chest. His Kevlar armour saved him, but still the impact charged him back down the staircase.

Karen tossed another Molotov cocktail through the gap while Mother Michael reloaded. It bounced outside the door, exploded on the edge of a step and trailed a stream of fire down the already smouldering staircase.

Karen then lurched forward, and in great pain and discomfort grabbed at the fallen soldier and pulled him through so the door could be slammed shut and obstacles shoved hopefully against it. The strain on Karen's back tore through the expression on her face. Dead bodies are heavy, especially for a hunchback.

Blood from Debbie's shoulder was seeping through her blouse. She was pale and as she removed her glasses, every action fatigued her. Pearls of icy sweat appeared as condensation over her forehead.

Mother Michael secreted the American's documents beneath the seat of her chair, for her wheelchair also functioned as a commode and the documents fitted the basin. She pointed at Debbie and waved her toward the door to the roof veranda.

The man on the other side of the attic door shouted, 'I'll give you precisely sixty seconds. Then we're going to blow this door open. I'm saying this as an offer and as fair warning to you.' Mother Michael knew they were scared; hesitation is never born of sympathy, especially in the midst of a battle.

Karen had four remaining Molotov cocktails which were emptied out over the contents of boxes, chairs and table. She stripped back the lid of one box full of papers, dusted and discoloured. She lit the papers and backed away from the pile, slowly, somewhat hypnotised by the fire leaping from the box of papers, with great sails of flame gathering air. Debbie crawled onto the roof and slumped against the balustrade. Her blouse was discoloured by her loss of blood. Mother Michael managed to negotiate her wheelchair through the door also. Those flames soon caught the taste of kerosene and ethanol.

Karen backed away more quickly toward the door, still watching the entire pile become engulfed in flames. The door burnt through like a sheet of paper and the box of dynamite exploded, blowing away not only the doors but most of the wall, the floor surrounding the door and the top of the stairwell. Anyone standing close to the blast would've been disassembled, shredded and ripped asunder.

On the balcony they sheltered their heads from the noise. The shockwave from the explosion blew the windows out. Debbie had slipped and was lying on her side surrounded by fragments of smashed glass. The troops retreated from the attic staircase entirely and decided to torch the whole building instead.

Karen nudged Mother Michael and pointed beyond the balustrade to where figures, not in uniform, were appearing out of the back path and across top paddock. Neddie had returned with reinforcements, so too Mazcek and Gerrard and Willow and others. Mother Michael laughed, though the strain hurt.

The troops gathered around the building took up defensive positions, around corners and in the shadows of the great main arch. From the pond, halfway across the ring and still beyond the range for rifle or crossbow, Mazcek lead their advance, dashing between trees to cover their approach. A tired Mother Michael looked about her, not for want of something she'd lost but rather as an unconscious betrayal of her impotence and frustration.

Karen, armed with a crossbow, leant over the side of the roof and shot a trooper who crept along the side wall through the back of the neck, where the spinal cord meets the brain. Another soldier following looked up to see Karen fire her bolt and shot. Karen was hit in the shoulder. She dropped the crossbow, became unbalanced and tumbled over the side of the wall after.

Her bones crunched on the ground below.

Gerrard, Willow and three others broke free from the woods behind where the troops were positioned and attacked. Four troopers were immediately cut down in a rapid flurry of gunfire. With those crossing Wandlebury Ring charging also, the handful of remaining troops surrendered.

Inside, the main building still burnt and through the flames

Mazcek used a ladder. He grinned broadly at Mother Michael, sat grumpily on the roof. 'You took your time,' she snarked.

Mother Michael commented to Willow, as she and Mazcek helped her, 'I don't usually concede such thoughts because when I do, I want the words to carry their full weight.' She sniffed, with another glance at Debbie and the space at the balustrade where Karen had last been. 'I feel especially sad at this moment.'

Mazcek crouched down next to Mother Michael, put his arm around her and rubbed her shoulder. It's strange, Mother Michael thought, when you're old, people often manhandle you, but they rarely seem to touch you. Simple human contact meant far more at nearly ninety than it had at any time since she was nineteen and full of tremulous longing. Yes, even she knew those feelings once. Yet for all the passionate embraces she may have had between nineteen and ninety, fewer than many perhaps, nevertheless, even of those she might have had reason to remember with a thrill, in truth, it was the simplest touch of hands, or a shoulder being rubbed, which in sublime simplicity meant most. She touched Mazcek's hand on her shoulder. She had no children, but if she had … The thought didn't need finishing. She patted his hand.

Carefully conveyed by four people, Mother Michael was reunited with her chair, back on firm ground outside. A pyre was constructed with straw from the sheds, broken boards, furniture and whatever was around. Mother Michael watched people stood close to the fire, scarves over their mouths, lifting the sagging corpses, held loosely by limbs as they were hurled on top. She turned away, unable to watch the bodies of Debbie and Karen added.

The stench of the burning corpses was overwhelming. The smoke carried their spirits upward and their bodies far and wide.

The hermits had to vacate Wandlebury Hill. The authorities

would return. Mazcek led most back to Telegraph Clump to collect others who'd washed up since the raids in Cambridge. The next day they travelled onto the Isle of Ely, which Hereward had taken and established as his southern Fenland base.

They left in the dead troops' Jeeps. The sky was surprisingly blue over Ely Cathedral in the distance. 'They say there's a reckoning coming,' Neddie commented to Mother Michael.

'We'll see,' she replied.

XVII

Back at the old pump house, Esme had changed out of the wedding dress. It was alright for Sarah-May and Bella; they were not originally from the Fens. They were not as bound, their feet less stuck. She filled the teapot and fetched two mugs from the shelf. She could leave a note to explain – she knew if she faced her dad she would fold. She tapped her fingers on the side of the sink and waited for the kettle.

Esme's dad swept into the kitchen: 'Your wedding's been put back to next Sat'day.'

'Oh,' Esme replied. 'A week.'

'Yes, so, best keep that dress o' yours nice and clean, hey?'

'Yes,' Esme answered and repeated the words 'a week' in her head. Seven days, then it was over, and then she would have to be exactly what other people wanted her to be, and it would never change unless she ran away like mam. She didn't want to be like her mam.

Lizzie came through. 'What's happening in town?'

'Nothing for you ladies to worry about.' Esme's dad reached out and pulled Lizzie to him. Esme suspected he may have been drinking. 'A few of us are meeting at the mayor's house tomorrow, a few volunteered as runners to other marsh towns, they've gone tonight. So, we'll see tomorrow.'

'What about Davey?' Esme asked.

Her dad turned toward her, his arm around Lizzie's waist, he laughed. 'No, we've not sent Davey. Can you imagine?' Adding, 'Mind, it might make the need seem the greater.' And he laughed again and gave Lizzie's side a squeeze from which she squealed.

'No!' Esme pursued. 'I meant how is Davey now?'

'Oh.' Esme's dad laughed at his mistake and then said, 'I saw him helping old Mrs Quickfall back to her house. He'll be back with his grandparents by now.' He looked at Esme and smiled, sympathy in his slightly bleary eyes. 'I told him I got some work for him, so he'll bob back to the surface tomorrow, you'll see.'

Lizzie added, unhelpfully, 'He's sure to check up on you tomorrow.' And she laughed. 'You know how he trails around after you, Esme.'

'That sort of thing'll have to stop when you wed, Esme.' Her dad said. 'You'll have to stop encouraging it, 'n all.'

'I don't encourage it,' Esme protested. Her dad slapped Lizzie's behind playfully and said he needed to speak with her in the parlour.

'The mayor doesn't have a parlour. They have a drawing room.' And Esme thought of how she'd have to spend evenings in the drawing room with Tom Jr – what would they talk about? And in the evenings, they would go back to the same bed, and he would want to touch her. Tom wasn't Agent McCain, and Esme knew that, but he would want to touch her, and she wouldn't be able to say no. Not if Tom Jr was her husband.

She sat on her bed, unmade since the morning's rush. Her stomach was a tight grip on her worries. She straightened the quilt, clutched a pillow and sighed. There was an empty fabric bag hanging from the door by its shoulder strap that Esme began filling with clothes and a box from her top drawer where she kept her precious things: a brooch her mam had given her, a black and white photograph of a young Esme posing between her mam and dad; they had it taken on a daytrip to Cambridge. For a frozen moment she held the stuffed toy her mam had made from an old winter sweater of her dad's. It was part of what she couldn't take with her, part of what she had to leave behind. She laid it back down beside her pillow.

She lifted her bedroom window, as she had the night that she snuck out to the meeting at the Seven Stars. She held a square of gummed tape ready to fix over the catch, but she wouldn't be coming back that night, so she scrunched it into a little ball and tossed it inside her room before pulling her window down.

She heard the quiet clunk of the catch.

The moment got stuck in her throat and she noticed her hands tremble. She turned to the big bough branch she'd make her escape along.

Beyond the gravel yard, the lanes were silent, an owl's hoot and nothing more. The sedge and reeds whispered. A solitary eventide bell from St Wendreda's tolled, its solemn bong drifting from the town across the Fens. There was a T-junction where Esme would leave the main causeway road and follow a narrow track down alongside a river. Esme hurried and as she turned onto the narrow track, she stumbled and fell. Her bag skidded off the path and into the dyke alongside. A shadow crossed her. A fear leapt in her heart, but a familiar voice said. 'Essie, I'll help you up.'

Esme looked up. 'Davey! What the hell are you doing here?'

'Mrs Quickfall says I got to protect you.'

Esme looked up at him. 'What do you mean you've got to protect me?'

'Mrs Quickfall says I should keep you safe, do as you say and be a gentleman.' Esme laughed. 'Why are you laughing?'

Esme stopped laughing. 'Okay, could you get my bag and help me up?' Davey salvaged her bag from the dyke, swung it over his shoulder and pulled her to her feet. He pointed ahead and said he'd seen the boat 'by some trees there, not far.'

'Have you not brought anything with you?'

'No, I forgot.' Esme laughed and he added, 'didn't know what to bring anyhoo.' Their footsteps patterned a little out of sync beneath the moonlight due to Davey's long, lolloping stride.

The good thing about Davey was he didn't expect anything of her. Ahead, the boat was low and tucked in against the bank. It was their means of escape, something that could take Esme somewhere.

XVIII

The sign suspended from the wall of the Hanging Gate ached. Arcing over the image of the gate painted on the sign, were the words, 'This gate hangs well, and hinders none. Refresh and pay and travel on.' Its welcome suggested a cynicism about patrons' inclination to pay. It was a large, red-brick, three-story block in Woodford, in the borough of Redbridge, and so in an area under the de facto control of Ismail bin Salah. Bin Salah was a name attached to a shadow few had seen. Even Doc admitted he usually met with intermediaries.

The Hanging Gate was on the corner of an intersection of two wide roads, once filled with traffic and fumes, the few electric vehicles there were had to negotiate the intersection, avoiding drifting pedestrians and sometimes animals.

Angharad and Owain, Willow Walwyn and John Lilburne travelled down from Cambridge on the old M11, in a Jeep from the 2030s leant them by the hermits. Mazcek had re-serviced it and assured them it would hold its charge. He told them, 'These old batteries used lithium and cobalt. They're better but hard to come by since the cobalt wars.' They passed the squatter camps that sprang up at the service stations along the way where the disused and abandoned units were claimed by the homeless Roamers. Through the old Home Counties' commuter belt, they passed Saffron Walden, Bishop's Stortford and Harlow, once affluent dormitory settlements turned to waste ground dead towns since the Collapse. The Envy Riots and clearings that followed, when the new city walls of London were constructed, became the catalyst for the emptying of cities into the surrounding countryside. Why live on the streets when wayside verges in the country were more idyllic places to starve to death in? Equally, why squat in tumbledown tenements and old warehouses when the former Home Counties were strewn with leafy market towns and spillover new towns littered with properties to be appropriated? Some of these towns tried building walls of their own but they lacked the security and when the Roamers grew in numbers, infesting their towns, a trickle evacuating for the security of city walls became a torrent.

London, diffused, sprawled more than ever, and the demarcations between badlands, slums and safe areas were blurred. The borders were porous, so pockets of suburbia not so different from reminiscences would appear, surrounded by desperation, somehow clinging nervously to their existence while it lasted. Woodford was better than many because bin Salah provided some of what the state no longer did, but even here there could be stark differences between neighbourhoods in Woodford Bridge from those in South Woodford.

The Hanging Gate was the type of establishment where conversations paused when strangers entered. Willow Walwyn, Angharad, Owain and John Lilburne approached the bar, their measure taken, conversations resumed. A woman behind the counter, pink in the cheek and full of figure, greeted them. Willow asked, 'We have a reservation, I believe?'

'But of course,' the woman answered.

Angharad looked around the Hanging Gate Inn. A group sat around a table in one corner playing dominoes over copper bets, at the next table a sorry looking man, eating soup. Two other men played darts. A woman sat before an open fire in a green, crocheted cardigan nursed a small beer in hands clawed by arthritis. The man with her chewed his pipe, pausing to tap the fire grill. Along the bar, two men and a woman perched on stools studied Angharad's group.

'Here we are.' The woman looked up from the ledger with a smile.

'I'll take them through, Mabel.' It was a voice familiar between the figures at the bar: it was Eben, the Doc's man. Standing, he hitched up his jeans and led them along a corridor of faded promotional posters, chatting about a Mr Wolfenbarger, whom Eben had known years earlier and who had turned up in London, apparently much to Eben's surprise and interest.

'Small world,' John Lilburne commented with a wry glance at Willow.

Eben always had much to say and a story to tell. Approaching the corridor's end, he told them to remind him to tell them the full story of Mr Wolfenbarger before they left. He laughed a private laugh to himself, adding, 'Mr Wolfenbarger's like a dog with a bone when he has sniff of a scent. Know what I mean.' Eben turned to them all and made a noise like a dog with a bone in its jaw that it refuses to let go of, shaking his head in imitation and then laughing.

They entered a back room with half-a-dozen tables, set for meals, where in the corner two figures were sat. Eben melted back into a chair behind them, askew from a table and next to the door to the corridor.

They approached the table, recognising the Doc, his companion was introduced only as Samira. The Doc wore a dark suit, the top button of his white shirt undone and no tie. He was smart with his beard and ponytail neat, and a manner more formal than when they last met. Angharad remembered his attic in Cambridge; the fire, the cellist, the Doc's velvet smoking-jacket manner.

Samira wore a suit also: London City cuts, Angharad presumed by their obvious quality. She removed a pair of spectacles upon their arrival to reveal a heart-shaped face of subtle lines and geometrically precise and elegantly threaded eyebrows over disarming brown, almond eyes. Raindrops began dashing against the window behind the Doc and Samira. They had already taken tea, with lemon. They'd drunk little. There was also a carafe of water on the table and glasses.

Samira offered them tea. John Lilburne pulled a chair across from another table. Samira's offer of tea was just about the only comment she made through the entire meeting, and beyond her name no explanation was given. 'Mr bin Salah was very pleased with the falcon,' the Doc began, once all were settled. He glanced at Samira. She confirmed this with a tiny nod.

'Good,' Willow answered for them all.

'And the papers? The IDs and so on. I presume they satisfy?'

'Yes, we've been into the city. We have full access as you promised and, so far at least, the covers hold.' Angharad was replying to the Doc, her eyes drifted to Samira for confirmation and acknowledgement as she said this. Samira gave no facial indication Angharad's comments were relevant to her, and so Angharad returned her eyes to the Doc. 'So, next steps then.'

'Indeed.' Doc smiled as Willow Walwyn rolled a map of Greater London out over the table. Angharad removed the salt and pepper from the cruet set to weigh it down. What was unusual about the image on the map was that rather than roads, it marked the rivers and canals, many of which ran subterranean. A second map she laid out was of the underground sewage system of London with markers denoting points of access. Willow traced her finger along the line of the River Lea. 'They'll come into the outskirts through the marshes covered with squatters' encampments. The river passes through a series of reservoirs; little attention will be paid to them there.'

Willow Walwyn spent more time in the slums than most who weren't stuck there. Tuberculosis, infectious hepatitis and dysentery amongst other ailments had become rife. The poorest lived in shacks built from recovered bricks and stones with sheets of metal or corrugated iron for roofs. Sometimes the abodes were made from re-constituted vehicles; for years as the oil supplies dried up old wrecks were found and appropriated. Vans, lorries and buses were better than the ad-hoc shacks because they could be locked.

Willow had taken Angharad and Owain; she liked to show people what they were fighting for. There were increasing cases of rickets amongst the children of the slums and few mothers who'd not buried at least one of their own. The poor diet of the women caused some to stop menstruating, while both men and women seemed to prematurely age there, with hair loss, tooth decay and weakened immune systems leading to the re-emergence of diseases thought to be history. There were even children with the symptoms of kwashiorkor.

There were four families Willow knew that lived in a bus they'd appropriated, the windows of the lower deck boarded up for security. How the bus got moved there, Angharad couldn't guess. With an arm around the shoulder of a twelve-year-old mixed-race boy with the most piercing blue eyes, Willow led Angharad and Owain through a crowd of dwellings and maze of pathways. Channels of raw sewage crept in shallow disgust along the centre of some of these paths. The boy's father, a grandparent and a young brother, were ill. He described symptoms of fever and fatigue and the coughing up of blood. Willow knew the signs of tuberculosis, there were increasing outbreaks. She'd obtained some antibiotics, isoniazid and rifampicin, but they were unlikely to be enough.

'You see here,' Willow said, indicating a feature on the map. 'If they leave the Lea here, between the squatters' park and the ruin of the old London Stadium, the Hertford Union Canal links with the Hackney Brook, from there you can get through culverts to the underground waterways and the sewage system.' She tapped the centre of the map with her fingers. 'And then boom, you're amongst the palaces of mammon.'

Doc listened with arms folded across his chest. 'They'll pick up on movements and boats, there are drones criss-crossing overhead constantly.' He looked them all over. 'You're moving them in slowly, down beneath the city.'

'Exactly so,' Owain said.

Doc pulled at his bottom lip thoughtfully. Angharad said, 'They won't know what's happening until it's happened. They'll be distracted so much by the troubles in the north, and the rally on Hackney Marshes and Victoria Park.'

'And you four will be on the inside, preparing the ground,' Doc said.

'Angharad will get inside their systems, disable the communication feeds and computer-controlled operational systems,' Owain confirmed.

'So?' Willow asked.

'So,' Doc repeated, pulling at the cuffs beneath the sleeve of his jacket. He leant on his forearms. 'Mr bin Salah feels that the bird is doing a lot of work for you. The papers are one thing, but the protection and cover you're hoping for him to provide ...' He glanced again at the woman next to him. 'It doesn't come without a cost or a risk to Mr bin Salah and the people he ...'

'I thought we had a deal,' Willow Walwyn interjected.

'I would describe it as a relationship, Ms Walwyn,' Doc responded. 'And all relationships take work and no little compromise.'

'How do we know we can trust your Mr bin Salah?' Angharad asked. She knew bin Salah had them over a barrel.

'Mr bin Salah is an honourable man.' Doc smiled and sipped his lemon tea, dabbing his lips with a napkin. 'In a world where yesterday's commodity is tomorrow's luxury, a person's word of honour is of inestimable value.'

'What's the compromise you seek?' Willow asked.

'The American. Luca.' Doc awaited their response as glances were passed between Angharad's group. Doc leant back in his chair, picked an imaginary fleck from his sleeve and smiled.

Lilburne looked to Angharad, there was hesitancy, so he asked, 'Why should we give him up? He's our asset.' All knew Lilburne was stalling.

'Asset?' Doc stifled a laugh. 'This is the time to realise the value of your asset, I would say.' He paused as one who knows the limits of their opponent's hand. 'Where is he now?'

'Lying low in the Fens,' Owain admitted flatly.

'The Fens, you say?' Doc withdrew a notebook and silver pen from his inside jacket pocket. 'Where precisely?'

'Why do you want the American?' Angharad asked.

'That's Mr bin Salah's business,' Doc answered. 'But it's a red line.'

'And what can you guarantee?' Willow Walwyn asked. 'We need safe passage for the march when it passes through East

London.' Samira nodded. 'And we'll need cover for Hereward's people until they're subterranean.'

'Of course.' Doc smiled. 'But the American's a red line. No Luca, no pasaran.' Willow looked at Angharad and Owain.

'I can't give you an address,' Angharad said with a glance at Owain. He smiled at her, supportive, it had to be done. 'We last saw him in Fenby. It's a small place north of Cambridge, east of Peterborough. I can't tell you if he's still there, but that's where we left him.'

Only after they left did Willow inform Angharad and the others the woman with Doc was Ismail bin Salah's sister, Samira. Her involvement meant this business had moved up the food chain.

Following the meeting, Eben saw them through to the front door of the Hanging Gate. He asked if they would like to share a drink with him and hear the story of Mr Samuel P. Wolfenbarger. 'Has big ears, does ol' Sam P. And he has this thing he says.' Eben adopted the man's slow southern drawl. 'My, my, my, time may pass. Question is boy: Will you?'

Lilburne declined the story on behalf of them all with excuses about being in a rush. Eben, who'd been gazing past the group and into the night, shrugged, leaving them at the front door to the establishment. 'Another time then.' He closed the door behind them. 'I doubt Mr Sam P. Wolfenbarger will be going anywhere, anytime soon.'

XIX

Luca passed the oars to Davey. An inflatable dingy tied behind the rowboat carried supplies. There was a sheet of old plastic covering it and tied down fast. Occasionally, the towing rope would get caught in reeds or river detritus and need remedial attention but otherwise they drifted on. Esme's tired eyes drifted over the water, where the ripples snatched at the moonlight. She heard the quiet splash of the oar and yawned.

In her sleep, Esme was far away in space and time, a child, returned to an innocence distantly remembered. Her dad had strung a hammock between two trees; it still hung there, worn, frayed and ignored. She remembered balmy summer afternoons, a tiny garden windmill and a flurry of computer disks suspended from a clothesline on a thread of cotton running through their centres and twisting in the breeze. As they turned, they sent bursts of sunlight dashing about in different directions. Some of them struck where Esme lay as she gazed up into the blue. It was funny to Esme the ways useless treasure from the old world was reused.

Behind their house was a limestone path that cut across boggy meadows, where reeds and rushes grew amid the rippling tides that Esme could hear as she slept. The limestone path climbed a gentle incline to Dunham Wood, where, as a child, she was not supposed to go unaccompanied.

There were horse chestnut trees in Dunham Wood where Esme would gather conkers in autumn. Esme's mam skewered them and threaded them onto old boot laces. One day, a boy with a brute of a conker smashed hers so hard it came off the string and bounced across the schoolyard pursued by the stamping foot of the boy. Esme had complained, 'You'd won, you didn't need to smash it.' His response was to laugh at her.

After that Esme stopped participating in conker fights. Those she collected, her mam threaded on to frayed old shoelaces and suspended them in front of the window of Esme's bedroom. So, when the window was open and the breeze blew, they tapped each other as understated wind chimes.

There were the sounds of tiny splashes and the slow heaving of water by paddle drifting through the images of Esme's memory. She was gently rocked in the hammock between the trees, carried in mam's arms, wombing, dreaming.

The wind blew across the meadow. In her dreaming Esme walked between fields of rustling reed and rush. Into the woods, she sheltered from the wind whispering in the trees above. She rested beside a prone tree trunk in a small clearing, where light from a low sun accentuated the shadows of trees.

Between the trees Esme saw his face; his figure emerged, huge and looming. His was a silhouette recognisable by his menace.

She remembered the touch of him, and the woods were transformed into the muted shades of her bedroom, and she was again looking out of her quarter-pained bedroom window onto the front yard with Agent McCain standing behind her: searching in the yard for any features Esme could find to distract herself from his touch and his invasion.

He smelt. She remembered now how he smelt. Everyone has a smell, and she remembered his, like a stain burnt onto her. She remembered having to touch him. He told her to, so she did. Could she have refused? It wasn't her choice to touch him. It wasn't her choice.

Esme tried to escape from the woods. She turned in circles to find where memory suggested a path. Her right foot caught up in some undergrowth that bound around her ankle. The thought of giving up, of collapsing onto her haunches bullied her. The effort of freeing herself almost caused her to fall.

Light danced between the gaps in the covering of branches and leaves trimming the river, playing on Esme's eyelids. She yawned. Davey was sleeping. Esme smiled at the way he slept with his mouth open. The sedge was high either side of the river. Ahead there was a boat heading in the same direction. Behind, she saw another rowboat with four figures on board. 'Most everyone's running away from something,' Bella said.

Other boats bobbed around between them and the low horizon. Others picking their way through narrow tributaries and gliding along channels of fret-worked fen rivers. It would be evening before these different boats dotted about in their different channels merged into a few broad waterways, gathering them up into their caravan as they went. Along the riverbanks were wading birds, so used to the boats drifting by, they stayed where they were in the shallows and watched the caravan pass south toward the Isle of Ely.

In the west, the sun set reds and oranges casting birds in silhouette. Still some miles short of where the inland delta opened into the flooded planes around the Isle of Ely, boats began banking, fellow travellers established encampments, planning to cross to Ely the following morning.

Luca untied the dingy and with Sarah-May hauled it up between two trees where they built their tent and strung up wind sheets. They joined those gathered around a large fire, where food was cooked on hot stones or skewered on sticks, flasks of barley wine and pipes of hippy-weed were passed around.

Bella was one of the first to open her pouch of weed to share. Esme coughed and pretended to enjoy the effects that crept over her. She looked at Davey grinning. Next to him, Luca was telling Davey something, and it allowed Davey to feel like a real person even if Luca was only being kind. Luca wasn't teasing though. Davey knew when people teased him, even if he didn't understand the meaning.

Esme twitched to an imaginary sound.

Sarah-May laughed and took her hand. 'How are you? Are you glad you came?'

'Yes.' Esme smiled and felt strangely lonely and sad for no reason and so she smiled again. Bella asked Sarah-May something and so Esme, with only her thoughts, looked around at all the people. Everything was so temporary. Why are they all here? she wondered. Beyond the fire the river flowed. A pair of men sat away across the fire, one with a guitar, and they sang wistful harmonies.

Later, having drunk some barley wine as well as having smoked some of the hippy-weed, Esme snuck off away behind some trees and threw up. As she wretched, she wondered what her dad would do when he got hold of her. She'd held her hair clear as she threw up, and on her knees she looked out between trees to the river where she could still see wading birds by moonlight.

She froze at a sound. It couldn't be him. 'Who's there?' Esme called, on her knees but pulled upright, eyes wide staring forward, listening and alert.

'It's Bella.' Esme's shoulders relaxed an inch. 'Sarah-May's off with Luca, Davey's at the tent whittling some wood, says he's going to make a little flute.' Esme laughed. 'So, how are you doing?'

Esme stood up. 'I'm okay.' Bella touched her arm, it felt nice. 'Think I may have drunk a little much,' Esme added.

'Sometimes you got to, and sometimes you got to throw up after, it's like purging the shit out your life.' Bella laughed raspy and smiled and Esme could understand why Sarah-May was so close to her mam. She wished her mam ... She didn't finish the thought. She didn't know how. She struggled to imagine how things might have been if mam had stuck around because she hadn't; she'd left long ago. Bella asked: 'Are you missing your home?'

Esme shrugged. Her feelings conflicted such that she couldn't organise to express them.

'Anytime, if you want to go back, I know people up and down these rivers who'll make sure you get home safely. Just say.' Esme shook her head though. 'You'll be able to write to them from Ely through the hermits at the cathedral there.'

'Can I ask you something?' Esme said with Bella's arm around Esme's shoulder as they walked back to the camp. 'What happened to your husband?'

Bella laughed. 'Do you mean, did I do him in like the some of the Fenby gossip-mongers would have it?'

'Sorry, I shouldn't have asked,' Esme spluttered.

'You're alright, kid,' Bella said. 'There never was a husband. Sarah-May's father never stuck around. Then again, I never got around to telling him. I spared him the agony of that dilemma. Had boyfriends but after a while couldn't be doing with men. A while later found I couldn't much be doing with women neither, in the relationship sense. Sarah-May and I were travelling by then. It was always just the two of us really. Then we wind up in your patch, Fenby, and stayed and everything became still.'

'Fenby's like that,' Esme said. A tired yet expectant calm had descended over the camp. The smoke scratched the air and the bark of a log exploded in the fire with a crack.

'Yes, a place like Fenby, things can seem seductively permanent, but permanence is an illusion, and the only certainty is change,' Bella said. 'Suddenly, change happens all at once, and you're left thinking, how did we not see that coming? It was bound to happen.'

'Is our world falling apart?' Esme asked. Laughter broke out from a group on the other side of the fire. 'Dad says it is.'

'Well, if it is,' Bella said, 'It's up to us to rebuild it. Young folk like you really. It's people clinging to old worlds that are the problem.'

The following morning, Bella, Sarah-May, Luca, Esme and Davey were already through the remaining river channels and out onto the Great South Fen Lake before the sun burnt off the mists and frets gathered over the water. Ely Cathedral in the distance rose like the mast of a ship.

Out across the lake were islets, tiny bumps of land the lake waters lapped around with mean and parsimonious smallholdings. Close to Ely there were two hamlets connected by causeway roads when the waters were low, but when rain swelled the lake, boats were the only transport, and when the waters receded, the causeway roads were generally in poor state and left unrepaired.

As the boats, some urged on by sails, a few by small on-board motors, but many being rowed, passed islets often strung along ridges of the former landscape, people were sometimes gazing back at them. A couple stood, watching the boats from a cultivated eyot where a thin line of trees and a low hedge acted as a windbreak for a field of grain, still green, and on the lower bank of the eyot, alfalfa. They wore clothes many times mended. The woman had her hands on her hips, he was holding a pitchfork. They said nothing but watched the boats pass on toward Ely.

One of the last islets was Prickwillow, on the outskirts of Ely.

It was a scattering of houses on a spit of a cay wrapped in small fields demarcated with picket fences where people kept farmyard animals and grew vegetables, the excess they'd take to market in Ely. Esme saw a treehouse, in which two children watched them. One of the children, who was wearing a horizontally striped t-shirt, pointed a stick at them, held like a rifle.

From Prickwillow, the sandbanks started to build as damns and breakwater constructions to protect Ely when the winter rain surges came. There were wind turbines standing over the mere south of Prickwillow and East of Ely itself, which once provided all the energy Ely needed. Unfortunately, many of the rusting, creaking wind turbines did not work at all because the privatised operators went bankrupt, and the state wouldn't pick up the cost for running and maintaining them. Local efforts to maintain them were rudimentary and inefficient due to a lack of resources and expertise, so only about a third as much energy was produced as before and much less than they could if they'd been replaced by the high-tech machinery coming out of China and India.

Sun shined sparkling through the mizzle, casting rainbows spangling and glinting off the wind turbines and the water around them. In the shallows, sedge gathered around willow trees, their sinewy fingers reaching down to their submerged feet. When the savage east wind blew, stoic pigeons and cawing gulls, drawn inland, would cling to the trees and the wind turbines, their claws closed fast against the east wind, ruminating melancholy about change.

The Isle of Ely rose twenty metres above the water level, an island of Kimmeridge clay and the highest point of the south Fens. It grew around a seventh-century abbey and eleventh-century cathedral at the top of the hill. On the low, south side of Ely there was still the marina, flush with boats, so mooring posts had been extended out back along the riverbanks, opening to a second bay, below the old, disused train lines. It was the so-called football bay because the water submerged the former football pitch of a local team who no longer existed. If one dived down below the water there were rusted goalposts, their white paint flaked to reveal the rusted iron beneath, and there were the former advertising boards for local companies who also no longer existed. There, in an outer bay, they tied their rowboat down, though tying it down asserted no kind of property claim, and to leave it for any amount of time was to forsake it. In this world, if something can be used, it will be; ownership is moot, and possession is everything. They deflated the dingy, rolled it up and carried it all up Back Hill to the cathedral gardens given over as an encampment and covered with tents and other makeshift shelters. At the foot of Back Hill, a banner read, 'Welcome to the People's Republic of Ely.'

XX

The Isle of Ely was in a state of low entropy; atomised humanity from across the Fens had coalesced into a dense, jostling, bundled, tightly packed hive of trapped energy. A passing hand reached out and grabbed Luca by the forearm. A raspy voice said, 'I remember you.' There was a moment when Luca froze before easing with cautious relief upon seeing the face of the man whose hand still gripped his arm. 'You're the American with the story, ain't you?' Luca looked at him warily. 'Well, it's true enough my presence was less memorable than yours.' The man released Luca's forearm and introduced himself. 'John Wrawe. When I last saw you, I heard you were going to lie low, take some time in the Fens. So, you're on the move again, are you?' John Wrawe feigned idle curiosity.

'The Seven Stars,' Luca remembered.

'Thas right, the pub,' John Wrawe confirmed. 'A rain-lashed night, it were, not like today.' He looked up and around at a sky of encouraging blue. 'You told an epic tale, I recall.'

'You were there?'

'I was.' John Wrawe glanced across at Sarah-May, Esme, Bella and Davey Clay. 'Are these your friends?'

'Yes,' Luca said.

'I remember you from the Seven Stars,' Sarah-May interjected. John Wrawe smiled. Esme thought it was a face not suited to smiling. 'Mum and I were both there.' Sarah-May indicated Bella. 'And Esme was there also, but she didn't stay for the meeting after.'

'Ah, you've gotta stay 'till after. It's always the after-party party where the real partying happens. Ain't that so?' His question was addressed to Luca with a glance and a wink. Luca didn't answer. John Wrawe then shook each of their hands in turn, clapping Davey Clay good naturedly on the shoulder. Another figure caught John Wrawe's eye. 'Leo!' he called out. A man turned hearing his name called. 'Leo Fric!' John Wrawe called him over. 'This is the man who pretty much runs things around here now.'

Leo Fric met them as a man used to insincere flattery with a bright smile out in front of cool observance. 'I thought Mother Michael ran things around here these days,' he joked with feigned politician's charm. 'Actually, as Mr Wrawe knows, I'm only a bureaucrat.' He smiled as one who knew his power. 'I'm an administrator. I execute the will of the community; I don't decide it.'

John Wrawe laughed. 'Ha, see you with your dashing humility.' To Luca and the others he added, 'This is the organ grinder.' He indicated Leo with his thumb. 'May not own the organ, but he's your grinder nonetheless.' Leo Fric indicated his intention to move on through the crowd but John Wrawe, jocular, put a hand on Leo Fric's shoulder. The expression on Leo Fric's face suggested to Esme he didn't much care for the hand. John Wrawe said to him, 'Hang on. I'll walk with you. I've serious matters to discuss.' Before parting with Leo Fric, John Wrawe touched his cap. 'I'll be seeing you, but remember, if you need something, Mr Fric here is the one who can apply the grease to make the wheels move.' As John Wrawe and Leo Fric wove away through the crowd, Esme noticed them glance back. She thought they looked at Luca in particular.

There was a parade gathered at Cross Green, outside the cathedral, close to the encampment. Two teenagers were crowned the king and queen of eels and carried on a float before the rest of the parade to the waterside. There, both teens began the eel-throwing competition by delving their hands into buckets of the slippery creatures, pulling one free and holding it high so the crowd could cheer the sight of the wriggling fish before, to further applause, the eels were hurled back into the water. Both teenagers were then able to melt back into the anonymity and laughter of their friends – cheered on for being such sport.

In the evening Esme and the others drifted to the market square, where a wooden platform had been constructed in a corner. A succession of speakers, musicians and even a curious theatrical performance appeared. It was a satire of one of the morality tales popular of late; its crudity, foul language and casual violence mocked moral rectitude. Bella laughed and said the people who claim shock always fizz with excitement. 'You can see it in their busy eyes.'

They were sat at a long table outside a pub in the market square. Around the edge of the market square, set high on poles, were burning torches, their flames flickering against the buildings. There was a band on the stage featuring a couple playing percussion, someone with a violin, a piano, an accordion, a trumpet and a singer with a yodelling kind of voice ...

If I was young, I'd flee this town
I'd bury my dreams underground
As did I, we drink to die, we drink tonight
And it rips through the silence of our camp at night
And it rips through the silence, all that is left is all that I hide

He was beautiful, Esme thought. His voice was beautiful, and Esme thought she might have drunk too much. He wore black jeans with black hair, and he wore a white t-shirt under a white face, which the torches lit the side of in Esme's view. The square crowded in the evening, and she joined others in dancing to the music from the stage, gazing at the singer and shaking her hair so her face was obscured when she thought he looked in her direction.

After the band finished their final song, a tall man in a grey hooded cloak took to the stage. He carried a staff like a trident, at the top of which was a bronze fork cast with an entwined eel circled, its mouth swallowing the end of its own tail. The members of the band melted away behind the grey cloaked figure. Esme tried to watch where the singer went but failed. The cloaked figure banged the staff down three times on the planks of the stage, a few moments passed, and he repeated the action again, at which point Esme presumed he must have become satisfied he had the crowd's attention.

A voice spoke, not of the man in the cloak with the staff, but another. 'Ladies and gentlemen. Ladies, and gentlemen, and anyone else …' Esme traced the voice to another man dressed in rags draped in brightly coloured ribbons and bells, his back-combed hair resembled thick, dark cords of rope. 'We are all here to celebrate the eel. The children are in bed now, and that's good, because ladies and gentlemen, this is the secret story of the eel and it's one you have to be old enough to fully grasp.'

A woman's laugh, she feigned to stifle, came from the side of the man speaking. He continued, 'And as you will see, there is much to grasp.' The woman to the man's side couldn't prevent another bubble of laughter breaking free. Despite the distraction, the man in ribbons and bells continued. 'There is a story I shall tell you that hails from faraway blue Pacific waters, where there was a girl named Hina. Everyday Hina would bathe in a private pool. One day, as Hina slipped into the pool a giant eel rose up behind her.' At this point the man in the cloak released the staff (which the speaker caught), and threw off his cloak revealing a broad, muscular man, completely bereft of hair and with a giant penis. The crowd erupted into laughter. The naked man was stood; his giant penis thankfully was not. The speaker stalked the front of the stage with his staff and hands encouraging quiet so he could continue.

Sarah-May nudged Esme's elbow. 'Like he says, much to grasp.' Esme smiled as Sarah-May laughed but she also remembered like a scar.

The man stalking the stage with the staff continued. 'The eel would rub itself back and forth against Hina's nakedness.' The crowd laughed. 'And the eel would turn into a handsome young man. So, he and Hina kept a secret affair until one day he told her he had to leave her. As she cried, he told her, "Keep your tears, for there will be water everywhere soon. The water will rise and rise and rise and will wash everything into the sea. When it happens, do not run away!"' As he spoke a box was placed before the naked man, a meat cleaver placed in his hand and a large eel upon the box. '"You must wait for me, and I will come as an eel and when I do,"' the speaker continued, '"you must cut off my head!"' And he gestured with his free hand a chopping motion, and in time with his gesture, the naked man brought down the cleaver he'd been handed and severed the head from the rest of the eel's body. There was loud applause.

The speaker continued. 'Hina pushed against the rising water and took the head of the eel up to the highest ground to bury it. Eventually the rising waters ceased, and green shoots grew where the eel god's head was buried and these shoots bore fruit and, these fruits were the eel god's gift to Hina.

The speaker in front of the naked man, facing the audience, pointed at the eel at the tip of his trident, tracing his index finger around its circled form, its centre penetrated by the central prong of the trident. 'The eel has a life cycle that takes it down to the warmer waters of the Caribbean every winter to hatch the next generation. They will follow the warm gulfstream waters the following spring, eventually arriving here in the Fens, where they mate. The changes to oceans, to the water in those oceans, and the currents flowing through those oceans means the underwater highways for the eels are weaker these days. We still have eels come, but less than years ago. So too we've seen our populations here fall. Like the eel our ability to reproduce ourselves declined; the currents of human spirit diminished by the pretty poisons of the old world and the poverty and wreckage it left for the world we now inhabit.' He looked around the audience, nodding, apparently not so distracted by the naked man. 'Now, like Noah after the flood, people should go forth and multiply, recognise God's grace in the face of your own offspring. There are women here today that to bloom they need a strong man like this Vitruvian specimen, Adam, here.' The speaker stepped aside and gestured towards the naked man on the platform, and his huge penis.

'This evening of revelry,' the speaker said, 'will soon be at an end. Go back to your homes, your tents and your caravans.' Tracing his fingers around the eel on the trident he continued, 'Fill those holes in your lives. Make merry tonight for tomorrow the march begins and after we must build anew. Tonight, revel, and who knows, the children that will rebuild the next world may be conceived in the homes, tents and caravans of Ely this very night.'

XXI

Mother Michael had assumed that at her age Ely would be a good place to finally settle; the battle at Wandlebury had taken some toll on Mother Michael and so she had intended to see out her days running hermits from Ely Cathedral. However, when Mother Michael received word that Joan Ball had been imprisoned again, it was a catalyst to leave Ely. She noted the relief and quiet delight in the face of Leo Fric when she informed him.

Mother Michael, or more precisely Mazcek, had gotten hold of an old bus and it was to lead a caravan south to rendezvous with other Eastern rebels, at Basil's Hill, between Brentwood and Southend, where Wat Tyler had rallied his Kentish rebels to join them. From there, the rebels would approach London following the old A13 westward. Most heading south had no land vehicles so went by boat, following the Great Ouse, to limit the distance to be travelled by foot. Mother Michael's bus headed south-east through Newmarket and beyond where the land undulates in chalky downs.

Mazcek's bus was white and blue, seated thirty-two, and boasted wheelchair access on a faded, peeling sticker. The hydraulics of its lift mechanism were busted beyond repair though, so Mother Michael had to be lifted, in her chair, onto the bus. She glanced around those waiting. 'I'm sorry I'm such nuisance. It's such a blasted bugger having to be hauled about every time you need to get anywhere.' She adjusted her position in the seat and the lie of her clothes. 'Had lovely legs like you two when I was young.' She gestured vaguely at Sarah-May and Esme, while Mazcek slid her from chair to a front row seat. 'Bloody things don't work at all these days, most of the time they're bound in these damned bandages.' She was still chuntering as the rest settled into seats. 'I keep telling Karen, the bloody ulcer won't clear up if it doesn't get any air, but she keeps binding my legs so tight, sometimes I think she cuts the blood off.' Only then did Mother Michael realise Karen wasn't there. She was dead and no longer around to change her bandages or apply unction to her back. Mother Michael sniffed and gazed out the window.

She then found distraction giving instructions to Neddie, sat up front next to Mazcek, who was driving. 'When you're out of robes, Neddie, do try to wear something smart. Not that awful, old brown cardigan you wore last time I was out with you.'

'I'll wear a jacket,' Neddie replied.

'Good,' Mother Michael said, 'and get someone to put a crease in your trousers. People place a lot of stores in first impressions. Isn't that right?' Mother Michael asked the person next to her, who happened to be Esme, who had been listening, amused, but was unprepared to comment.

'I thought pride was a sin,' Neddie said.

'Don't be too quick, Neddie, don't be too quick or you'll cut yourself,' Mother Michael replied. 'Jacket and pressed trousers, yes Neddie?'

'Yes, dear,' Neddie confirmed.

In the driver's seat, alongside Neddie, Mazcek secured his seatbelt, adjusted the windscreen mirror, and asked, 'All ready?' There was a confirming murmur. 'Alright, let's go, go, go.'

The bus growled like a tired dog aroused from sleep and lurched forward.

Esme had no option but to listen to Mother Michael. 'I remember as a girl, your sort of age, trips to the city on Mr

Bonny's bus with Edie. I worked Saturdays with Edie in the café. Plain girl was Edie, very friendly though, if you follow. She was the only one to write to me after the abortion, aside from me sister, Meg, o' course, but she was living up the other side o' Nottingham by then anyway, so she was no use.' Mother Michael turned directly to Esme, 'You want some advice about life. Don't leave it still wondering.'

'Huh?' Esme replied.

'Of course, these ancient bones were once young and capable of play. Which is better, your youth or the years? You may well ask.' Esme wondered if Mother Michael was mad. 'Your youth if you enjoy it; its passing if you don't.'

'Did you not enjoy yours?' Esme asked.

'It passed.' Mother Michael looked out of the window again. Due to fine weather, the water lapped low the banks of the causeway road. The fen lake water gave way to marsh and beyond to fields of grass and wheat. Mother Michael told Esme of her youth, as Rose Rowett from Lincolnshire, her affair with the foreign man, a Pole called Piotr. It was around the time the troubles between those that considered themselves 'proper English' and the immigrants escalated. In the end the immigrants were driven out, but not before she became pregnant by Piotr. It was after the abortion that Rose Rowett left for the east, leaving that name behind. Mother Michael talked more about the past than she used to. The age she had reached, with the layers of life lying atop one another, 'It's been too long for things that can't be undone,' she said.

Esme asked her, 'Do you ever wonder how things might have been?'

Mother Michael looked at Mazcek driving the bus. Her eyes

softened. 'I learnt early in life there are occasions when you need to make a decision that may hurt another person. It might hurt you to make the decision, but it's a decision that has to be made because there's no other way for life to work out.' She took a pronounced breath, seemed to rise where she sat, as though drawing, once more, on her redoubtable strength. To Esme, beside her, she said, 'I venture it's a lesson you've had to learn young also, if I'm not mistaken.'

Had she? Esme supposed she had. She wanted to tell Mother Michael her story, perhaps by telling it to someone she would've passed it on, and she could return to a state of innocence. She couldn't think of what words to use though, and she could muster no air in her throat to speak.

The bus was followed by a convoy of loaded cars, tuk-tuks and a couple of flatbed trucks with people squeezed on the back starting to get rained on. Passing through Newmarket, people in the streets clapped and cheered them. They transformed Esme's selfish act of running away into something heroic. They passed a gypsy encampment, their piebald ponies tied to stakes, chewing the verge. Esme watched the traveller children's faces watching their bus pass.

At Edmundsbury they took a break. There were crowds in the market square and spilling across the abbey gardens behind the cathedral. Edmundsbury was already a rebel town. John Wrawe had organised resistance when the mayor invited bailiffs in to complete the census. They lynched half a dozen who came, along with the mayor himself, his wife and two toadying assistants. They strapped their naked bodies to old telegraph poles and trees alongside the roads into Edmundsbury, with signs hung around their necks promising threats to others who might come up from London.

A NEW DARK AGE

During the break in Edmundsbury, Esme drifted with Davey Clay. They bought some apples and sweet pastries from stalls. They ate the pastries sat on a low wall in front of the war memorial in the market square. Davey had flakes of pastry around his mouth, and it stuck in their teeth without drink, so they cupped water in their hands from a drinking water fountain. Esme splashed Davey playfully and he responded, laughing, until they both retreated, embarrassed by two people waiting to use the water fountain after them.

Raindrops gathered on the windows of the bus. Half-a-dozen hermits, sat somewhere behind Esme, were singing, 'She'll be coming around the mountain when she comes'. Those who'd spent their break in Edmundsbury drinking and continued since pressed bottles into the hands of the hermits and slung arms around their habited comrade's shoulders. A chorus of 'oohs' followed singing, 'She'll be wearing pink pyjamas when she comes'. Amidst the drinking and singing, the songs became bawdier and the laughter more raucous.

'At last, they got her on the bed, parlez-vous.

And shagged her till her cheeks were red, parlez-vous'

Esme looked at Mother Michael. She thought Mother Michael would be offended and object with the authority she wielded. Mother Michael didn't, instead she asked Esme about herself as distraction. Esme heard Luca behind her sing along with the 'parlez-vous' refrain and get slapped playfully on the shoulder by Sarah-May.

'They took her down a shady lane, parlez-vous.

And shagged her back to life again, parlez-vous'

Esme saw Davey smiling at the singing and gave him a dirty look with hardened eyes and Davey stopped smiling, confused more than rebuked. Those that didn't sing just ignored the song. Esme thought of McCain, in her bedroom back home, moving her legs apart as she stood there, hands flat on her desk. Most of the people on the march would say it was things like what happened to her that finally prompted them all to rise, to demand dignity as a minimum. And here many of them were singing a song about gang rape and laughing. Esme wiped a tear, she thought unnoticed, from her cheek.

'And then they took her to a bed, parlez-vous
And shagged her till she was nearly dead, inky-pinky parlez-
vous.'

Mother Michael placed her hand over Esme's. 'We're making a detour. There's an old friend I need to pick up on the way. You'll like her.' Mother Michael leant across Esme and said to the man in the row behind. 'Would you be a dear, Chris, and explain the situation. I'm a bit stuck here.'

Chris Cobbe rose and stood facing the passengers. He held the rails high either side. His right arm rose over Esme's head, and he had dark patches under the armpit of his shirt. The afternoon sun through the windows had matured the air on the bus, and Chris Cobbe seemed to Esme particularly ripe. He glanced at Esme, having shared a word with Mother Michael, and Esme smiled. She hadn't paid attention to what they'd said, distracted by the dark patch under his arm.

'So, we got word, Anne and me, that Joan Ball was picked up campaigning ...' Mother Michael coughed. Chris Cobbe continued, 'Sorry, preaching, bastards charged her with sedition.' The bus booed. 'She promptly escaped...' Chris Cobbe added to a cheer. 'She escaped with a couple of other inmates and two of the guards, apparently.' There was laughter Esme joined with. 'They raced across the country to meet with the resistance, only to get picked up again near Braintree, and thrown in Highpoint.'

'Braintree's a funny name for a place,' Davey said to Esme, sat under Chris Cobbe's other armpit. Esme agreed. Davey, feeling encouraged, went on, 'Makes it sound like a fruit tree, but where the fruit are brains.' And just in case Esme didn't understand, he added, 'Like apple tree but brain tree.' Esme smiled but didn't say anything because she thought she should be listening to Chris Cobbe, and besides, she'd feel foolish if other people heard their exchange.

Highpoint Prison perched amidst low hills with scatterings of tiny villages, spinneys and streams meandering to their confluence with the River Stour. Built in the 1930s, an airbase from which to launch air strikes against Nazi Germany, in the 70s it was turned into a prison, split into a large south section, for male prisoners, and a smaller north section for female prisoners.

The bus parked in a spinney, where a narrow, winding farm-access road broke from the main approach to Highpoint Prison. Some people relieved their bladders behind trees, while Chris Cobbe and Anne Hatch reconnoitred the prison perimeter of high razor-wired fences.

When they eventually returned, Anne Hatch explained, 'The whole site is low supervision. Electric fencing, doors and gates are fingerprint access and surveilled with cameras; relatively few armed guards though.'

'How many do you reckon to be relatively few?' Mother Michael asked.

Anne Hatch shrugged. 'Hard to say for sure. From experience, very few these days. Highpoint South is bigger, used to hold nearly a thousand male prisoners, now just a few hundred, most work redeveloping the site. Highpoint North, smaller than South, has maybe two hundred female prisoners.'

'So, do you and Chris have a plan?' Mother Michael asked.

'We'll need distraction, cover and somebody fairly small.' Chris Cobbe scanned around the circle, past Bella and Davey and Mother Michael to Esme, where they rested. Mother Michael looked at her.

'I'll do it,' Esme said.

'Do what?' Bella objected. 'I'm not sure ...'

'I'll do it,' Esme repeated.

'I'll do it, as well,' Davey said.

Mother Michael began explaining that wouldn't be necessary, but Chris Cobbe clapped Davey on the shoulder with, 'Excellent, lad. We'll take Davey here, as well.'

'I'm a good shot with a capatulp. Ain't that so, Essie?' Davey smiled.

'You mean catapult,' Esme corrected him.

'Catapult.' Davey pulled it from his jacket pocket to illustrate.

'It's agreed then,' Mother Michael said. 'I'll deal with the diversion, Mazcek will be ready with the bus running. Best of luck all. Right, Neddie,' she turned to the hermit, who adjusted his round, wire-framed spectacles to indicate his attention. 'Gather the hermits. It's time for a new song.'

Chris Cobbe and Anne Hatch led Esme and Davey through the spinney to a field on the south slope beneath the prison, which was full of solar panels. The low evening sun danced off their mirrored surfaces. Anne Hatch asked Esme and Davey if they could make the sound of an owl. Davey cupped his hands to his mouth to demonstrate. 'I can whistle loud,' Esme said.

'An owl hoot would be better,' Anne Cobbe suggested.

'I can't make owl hoots, but I can whistle.' With little fingers in the corners of her mouth she demonstrated.

'Okay, you can whistle,' Anne Hatch agreed and held her hand aloft for Davey to pause practicing owl hoots. 'Can you smell that?' she asked.

'It stinks,' Davey said.

'It's the stink of several hundred shits.' Chris Cobbe smiled as Davey laughed at his comment. 'Over the hedge yonder is the prison cess pit.'

Esme pulled her sweater up over her mouth and nose due to the fetid stench.

'Highpoint is self-sufficient in most things,' Anne Hatch explained, crouched behind the hedge. 'Waste is an exception. Beyond this hedge is the cess pit for the prison. Here's the thing, you can't see it from here, but there's a small field between the cess pit and Highpoint North, and the curious thing about that field is its thick, luscious grass, while the other side of Highpoint can barely scratch any grass. Now that's interesting, do you know why?'

Esme shook her head and Davey copied her.

'It's interesting,' Anne Hatch went on, 'because the reason the grass is lush is that the drainage pipes from the prison latrines to the cesspit are broken. The shit fertilizes the grass, if the drainage works, less fertilizer for the grass.'

Esme and Davey followed Anne Hatch and Chris Cobbe along the line of the hedge. Chris Cobbe said, nodding in the direction of a yard just outside the prison perimeter, 'See there. That's the poo lorry, right. Every morning it sucks waste from the latrines and takes it and flushes it into the cesspit.'

'The lorry's important,' Anne Hatch added. 'We checked it out, spoke to one of the cleaners. Amongst their other duties, they run the poo lorry.'

They walked along the path around the prison to a caretaker's hut. 'So, let's go and have another chat with these cleaners. I think they'll be keen to help our noble cause.' As Chris Cobbe said this, he drew a revolver from inside his jacket. Davey gazed at it as Chris Cobbe cocked the gun and tucked it into the back of his trousers, adjusting his jacket after. Davey looked at the back of his jacket, where there was a slight rise over the gun. Esme felt a quickening fear.

The door was open to the caretakers' hut. A man in blue overalls was in the yard. He turned to the crunch of their feet on gravel. 'Ahoy there! Must've been your colleague I spoke to earlier,' Chris Cobbe called.

'Oh, yeah?' The man looked toward the hut, eyes narrowed. 'They're over there now, cleaning.' The man, who was called Dan, thought for a moment then added, 'Summit ain't straight here. Who are you?'

'Is that a kettle?' Anne Hatch asked. She filled it while the man explained that Betty, a woman from the village, and her daughter cleaned the staff areas during the day, they start to clean the women's cells before the evening meals. Betty needed the money 'since her kids' father died last year, and her littlest is a weaken, the little boy'll do well to live past infancy, so they say.

'Mornings, I take the lorry round to clean out the latrines then work on the site, mending stuff, painting, and such.' The kettle whistled. A row of tin cups hung from hooks that transferred the heat of hot tea to holding hands.

The clock next to the door edged toward four when they heard a vehicle on the gravel outside the hut. 'Right, that'll be the ladies back,' Dan said, levering himself up with hands pushing down on his knees.

One of the women looked at Esme, 'You sure?' Betty Belcher was a square set woman with dark hair and a whiskery chin. She wore blue overalls and folding her arms under her bosom looked obdurately grounded. 'I don't know, boy,' Betty Belcher said, shaking her head slowly, unconvinced. Though standing close she never communicated with Chris Cobbe or Anne Hatch directly. 'They know we don't do linen nor clothes, prisoners do it 'emselves. We're just rubbish and giving the floors a bit of a spit and lick.'

'She'll fit though,' Chris Cobbe said to Dan, who turned to Betty to answer, not needing to repeat the question.

'Yes. She'll fit,' Betty Belcher confirmed.

'Esme!' Chris Cobbe called her over. 'Come over here a minute.' He pulled the revolver from the back of his trousers and handed it to her. 'Take this.' Esme wouldn't touch it though, so he insisted, 'Go on, take it. Just in case. You ever held a gun before?'

Esme shook her head. 'And you a country girl. Heavy, in't it?' It was, which surprised Esme, and the handle was big in her hand. She slipped her right index finger in front of the trigger. 'I don't want you to shoot or anything, but just try lining it up as if you was aiming at the top of that fence post.' Chris Cobbe was standing behind her, like McCain had. She froze. She felt Chris Cobbe's hands as he took her arm to straighten to her eyeline. She remembered McCain straightening her jittering leg.

Every muscle and sinew in her body tightened to Chris Cobbe's touch and she had to fight not to squirm away from him. He moved clear. 'Your nose is dipping,' he said. She didn't understand so he pointed at the end of the gun.

'I don't want to shoot anyone,' Esme said.

'You won't,' he encouraged her. 'You just got to look as though you could.' So, Esme stood with the gun trying to look meaner. 'Good.' Chris Cobbe laughed. 'Relax. Once you're inside, Joan Ball will take care of everything. I just need to get you inside, okay?' Esme nodded.

Chris Cobbe put his hands under Esme's armpits; she flinched. He lifted her off the ground and dropped her into the large bin of the rubbish trolley Betty Belcher would push around the prison. 'Are you okay in there?'

'Yes,' Esme answered.

'And you've got the gun safe?'

'Yes.' Esme held the revolver up for him to see.

A sheet was thrown over her and she heard the side panel door of the van slam shut. The trolley rolled about in the back of the moving van. Esme's ears reached out like eyes. Then the van stopped, and the engine was cut. The trolley wheels rattled over metal. She held her arms over her head when the trolley paused, and an unseen prisoner would throw bags of rubbish into the bin.

'You ready?' Betty Belcher said and something about the tone of her whisper meant Esme knew she was being addressed. The bin tipped, tipped further and fell over. The rubbish cushioned the fall, bags were disturbed, and split open, fetid sludge and matter tumbled all over her. She found her hand holding something soiled she let go of upon realisation. Two arms thrust down into the rubbish pulled her free.

'You!' Joan Ball said. 'I shoulda known it'd be you.'

'Quick.' Betty Belcher hissed.

'Here, slide under the bed while we sort the cart out.' Like a lizard, all elbows and feet, Esme scuttled under the bed, still gripping the gun. Under the hang of a grey blanket, she watched Joan Ball help Betty Belcher right the cart.

Joan Ball closed the cell door. Esme could only see her legs beneath the knee. 'You gonna come out from under there?'

Joan Ball pulled a simple wooden chair against the wall the door filled half of. 'Sit here, so as we can speak and make decisions.' Esme did as she was told. Prisoners didn't get uniforms, it was deemed an unnecessary cost, so Joan Ball wore her own clothes: a dress with swirling patterns of red, orange and yellow, a black cardigan and a rosary of large brown beads hung around her neck. 'So, you've come to help me break out?'

'How did you know it would be me?' Esme asked before confirming, 'Yes, I've come to help you escape. I'm here with Mother Michael and others.' Joan Ball beamed hearing Mother Michael's name. Esme asked her again, 'How do you know me? You said you should've known it would be me.'

'I have these visions.' Joan Ball smiled. 'You've seen me before also, haven't you?'

'Yes, once, back home.' Esme remembered. 'You were giving a talk at the Seven Stars ...'

Joan Ball nodded, 'Stars. Yeah. You saw me an' I saw you.'

'You saw me?' Esme asked, incredulous she had been noticed in the dark of the crowd gathered back at the Seven Stars.

'Oh, you were high above most people ...'

'Yes,' Esme remembered. 'I was sat halfway up some steps.'

'That's right,' Joan said. 'A white face framed in black hair.' She moved her hands either side of her face in vague illustration. 'Bit like a bright moon on a dark night. Not a full moon, more of a waning moon. Mind you, I'd drunk a rarver peculiar brew the previous day; the visions were powerful, but I may've still been a little here and there.'

There were footsteps in the corridor. Joan Ball held up her index finger.

She left Esme back under the bed and didn't return for a couple of hours, and when she did return, Esme heard her approach in loud conversation. 'I feel God's subtle guidance in these matters.' The people she was with sounded dubious. 'Jus' you remember. Jesus loves us all and Jesus saves.' Joan Ball closed the cell door and turned to Esme, serious. 'You can come out now, girl.' Esme gave Joan Ball the gun and sat on the bed while the evening quietened.

They waited until the sound of Davey's owl hoots reached them. Esme looked to Joan Ball. 'I'm supposed to answer,' she said. 'Only I can't do the owl sound, so I whistle.' Joan Ball nodded.

The window opened a few inches with a cage of rusted and paint-cracked bars behind. She blew shrill with little fingers in the corners of her lips; three short, three long and three more short, and waited for Davey's response. If she didn't hear, she'd try again. She waited nervously at the window.

'Try again,' Joan said, impatient, and this time the reply came, the same pattern of short and long, as Anne Hatch had instructed. Esme turned to Joan Ball and smiled; proud and relieved. 'Okay, so like I said. You get into the bed and best be ready, girl. They'll come 'round and lock up soon. We'll have to be sharp.'

XXII

The Doc set them up in an apartment of Ismail bin Salah's, on the thirteenth floor of a large building called Marathon House, just off Baker Street in Marylebone. Eben met them at Walthamstow Station with another man who had the keys: a smartly dressed associate of Mr bin Salah's called Yahya Sulieman. Walthamstow Station had been acquired by Mr bin Salah's organisation after most of the lines stopped running. With its circular, reinforced glass and steel panel front, owning it and operating from there made a statement about where power resided in the community. The ground-floor concourse was open to the public with stores and offices where bin Salah employees would deal with issues of housing, employment or poverty for the community. As elsewhere, where the state's role withered there was opportunity for ambitious people to fill the void and be made chieftains. Most of these new lords didn't last because most were obviously on the make. A few prospered better though, like Robert Kett in Norwich and Ismail bin Salah in east London.

Past a guarded barrier and down a still escalator into the dark caverns of the former underground platforms they followed Yahya Sulieman. He commented that most of the old railway services were long gone, bar a few that shuttled workers in and out of the city.

The lights of the platform and a waiting old underground train suddenly lit up. 'Fiat lux,' Eben joked, 'or perhaps these days it should be alakazam!' He laughed and waved his hands before him like a street conjurer. Yahya Sulieman briefly side-eyed him while sliding his vintage smartphone back into his jacket.

Boarding the train, Yahya Sulieman explained. 'They have regular shift patterns in the city for ferrying workers in and out. At those times it's chock-a-block. Otherwise, the lines are reserved for private use.'

The electric doors of the train slid so smoothly open Angharad felt they mocked her provinciality. The train had no driver but was operated by computer programme. The interior of the train carriage had been refitted; the surge, sway and break as the train rattled through tunnels was cushioned by deeper, well-supported seats with armrests. They passed through a dimly lit, disused station, Blackhorse Road; the name painted on the wall faded but discernible, illuminated by the little light coming from flickering fluorescent emergency service strips set along the tunnel roof. There were Japanese-styled graffiti art and street tags like a post-modern Bayeux Tapestry, recording a story of decline and despondency along discoloured white tube walls and over the remnants of display posters still advertising a bejewelled lost world. Rats scurried along the disused platforms, rising like the waters of the Fens to reclaim some lost dominium. Nobody cared though, not even the rats scratching around, they already looked to move on with twitching noses and hungry, searching eyes.

'The entire traffic system is centrally coordinated in computer algorithms,' Angharad said. She'd closely studied the package of information the academics in Cambridge had provided that included a full system breakdown and the coding she would need to input. 'It's not just the trains, but taxis and trams, traffic lights, streetlights and security gates.'

'So, disrupt the computer algorithms and protocols,' Eben said to Yahya Sulieman. 'And they disrupt the city.' Yahya Sulieman listened but did not comment.

Angharad gazed out of the window, catching flickers of reflected light and her own face reflected in the dark. Owain's face was reflected in the window also. She watched the reflection of Owain's face watch the reflection of her own. She winked at him in reflection and his reflection winked back at her.

Yahya Sulieman left them all at the Marylebone apartment, off Baker Street. It was a conversion from the final stages of the gentrification of central London: two bedrooms, a living room where Lilburne slept on a well-sprung sofa and a kitchen.

Eben took them shopping at the local grocery store. He said it was useful for their faces to become familiar in the area. He chuntered on about acquiring bergamot oranges and vetiver oil while he was in the city. He took them on a tour of the city, passed the BBC Broadcasting House, and down Regent Street and on to a busy Oxford Circus. He led them through crowds, admonishing them, 'to stop looking about so. Everyone else has a groove, you're advertising yourselves.' They followed the Tottenham Court Road until after it became Chancery Lane, passed Starbucks and the Merrill Lynch Bank of America, through to St Paul's Cathedral, still dwelling in the shadow between the London Stock Exchange and the Bank of England – God knows his place in London. They passed Goldman Sachs, the old Bank of England, through Temple and Royal Courts of Justice.

Lilburne said justice was the wrong word. 'They were rarely just.' Waxing further, 'The rule of law involves balancing the needs of justice with the need for order. Rulers are far more interested in order than justice though, so law becomes the justice that the rulers can afford without risk to their order.'

'And you're going to change all that?' Eben quipped in a sarcastic tone.

'I want to destroy it. It's the fig-leaf of legitimacy over all this; the architecture of our misery.' They walked on from the city toward Westminster, from money to power. At Trafalgar Square, they walked along Whitehall toward Parliament Square. Eben indicated government buildings, civil service buildings, and the Ministry of Defence. They paused at the top of Downing Street, where half-a-dozen armed police guarded black, wrought-iron gates.

Lilburne looked back along Whitehall, and further, past the Cenotaph toward the looming faux-Gothic nonsense of the Houses of Parliament. 'Hereward will need people along Horse Guards and St James's Park,' He commented. After Westminster Abbey, they turned right near Lambeth Bridge passing the hated Home Office building on Marsham Street, up Buckingham Gate passed Wellington Barracks and then the grand, grey east façade of Buckingham Palace.

Restaurants were scattered liberally over this area as tourists still soaked in the atmosphere of the morbidly rich feasting in the reflected glitter of bloody imperial legacy. Eben took them to The Dorchester, in Mayfair. The shoes of the doorman shined, the lobby's marble floor also, and bells seemed to regularly chime in chirping readiness, brightly alert and echoing as they waited to be seated. Waitresses, sufficiently infused with servile deference, drifted between tables set with crystal glass and silver service.

An expensively scented couple passed them in delight with their surroundings, yet, though Angharad and Owain, Willow and Lilburne were not familiar enough with The Dorchester to notice, there would be rats beneath the floorboards gnawing at the corners of skirting boards, their tiny, clawed feet scratching. The bellboys, the valets, those on reception smiled to advertise the delight guests were sure to experience in such surroundings but to the familiar they were subtle indications of change, of decline and of loss. The fixtures and fittings were refreshed a little less often than once they would, an extra year or two of service as antiquity gathered its glory in dust. Not that The Dorchester was dusty, the dead were cleared away with the understated forbearing grace of some fashion of noblesse oblige, as they dined in pearls at the well-set tables and the theatre carried on.

Eben watched a waitress withdraw, watching her far longer than needed to ensure confidentiality of his discretions. 'A word for the wise. Don't look, but there's a man, sat at a table, using a wall mirror to keep his eye on our table. He came in not so long after us. I'd noticed him before, in Trafalgar Square and again when we paused at Buck House.'

'Is he a corporate-state agent?' Angharad asked.

'No. Unless I'm mistaken, which I'm not, that man's name is Mr Samuel P Wolfenbarger.' Eben identified a tall man, with thinning hair and large ears.

'And who is Samuel P. Wolfenbarger?' Lilburne asked.

'Oh, so now you want to know about Sam P., do you, Mr Lilburne?'

'What does he want?' Owain asked.

'Not you, or we'd know by now.' Eben briefly swilled his glass of wine before emptying it. 'Mr Wolfenbarger is like me and your associate Luca, an American. He's fairly recently arrived, though he has been travelling in Wales and East Anglia from reports the Doc has had via Mr bin Salah.'

'But he's not with the Doc or the bin Salahs?' Owain asked Eben.

'Oh no. Mr Wolfenbarger's employers hail from the same land as Mr Wolfenbarger himself.' Eben then stood up. 'Come on, it's time to leave anyway. Mr Wolfenbarger won't approach us, but neither will we be able to prevent him tracking us. You know he's there, now let's move on.'

Back across London at their apartment, John Lilburne pulled at the venetian blinds in the living room, looking down on the street floors below. He wondered whether Mr Wolfenbarger was out there.

Evenings at the apartment were usually spent distracting each other in conversation. Their neighbours in the apartment block remained largely anonymous beyond passing courtesies. There was an old woman, Mrs Maples, she wore a headscarf to cover her baldness, the effects of chemotherapy. She lived alone on the same floor as them with a tabby cat. Owain and Angharad had helped with her bags and Willow helped with the intravenous application of her medication. Mrs Maples' husband had worked for one of the major banks in the old days. When they divorced, 'I cleaned the philandering old bugger out of half what he had.'

Mrs Maples' face was set for Willow's needle prick. 'Done,' Willow said, withdrawing the needle. The tip would be washed in methylated spirit to be reused.

Through the working day, Owain hid many hours in the bowels of the Whitehall library avoiding notice while Angharad was burrowed in a crypt deep beneath the Ministry of Defence. She was assigned her own little cubicle to process data. Her work was monitored, as any employee logged on the system would be. Nevertheless, she was accepted as a name and barcode. All seemed anonymous to one another. People were often being shunted from one location to another so new faces were treated with the same indifference as the old faces, and clockwork ticked on. Circumventing the security protocols was straightforward for Angharad, and so, slowly over the weeks she introduced new protocols to the systems and adjustments to the algorithms. Some were set as sleepers with timers allowing their impact to be co-ordinated.

XXIII

Esme heard footsteps. Cells checked with the sound of view panels sliding back and forth, keys rattling and doors clunking. Joan Ball covered her pursed lips with an index finger. Esme was bait, but sometimes the bait just gets eaten. The guards' footsteps were outside the cell door; the view panel slid aside. 'Barbara!' a guard said. 'Hey, Barbara, something strange here!'

The panel shifted again. 'Who is she?' A new voice said. Locks clunked and several inches of thick heavy metal door heaved open.

Esme snapped up in bed with fingers thrust forward under the sheet. 'You aren't Joan Ball,' said a spotty, brown-haired guard, no older than Esme.

'And that isn't a gun you're pointing.' Behind the first officer, a second stood, hands on her hips, a far more foreboding presence.

There was a click that both guards turned to: Joan Ball aimed a cocked revolver at them. 'Boom!' Joan Ball blew out her cheeks and emphasised the plosive letter B. 'No, she's not Joan Ball. I am. And you're both dead if you don't do exactly as I say.'

Under instruction, Esme handcuffed the guards together with wrists behind their backs. 'Grab them keys and guns and whatnot, Esme.' The silence breathed fear into Esme's fumbling fingers; crouching by the guards, her restless knee jittered. She was supposed to be marrying the mayor of Fenby's son, not breaking a radical preacher, and wanted terrorist, out of prison.

The two guards were left handcuffed to the bed behind the closed cell door; stood in the landing Joan Ball issued further instruction. Being bossed around by the person she was breaking out was not how Esme might've imagined this rescue mission. 'The end of the landing, sixth on the right, yeah? Go to that cell first. There's a woman there, Lisa, she's sharing with someone called Bobbi. They'll think you sus, so you need to say "Jesus saves". Got it?' Joan Ball clasped a hand on each of Esme's shoulders to be sure Esme was focused. 'Don't release the other prisoners yet; later but not yet. They'll just be a bloody nuisance. If anyone calls out to you from cells, tell 'em, Jesus'll save 'em too, but not till mornin'. Then come to the staff room off the main foyer.'

'Jesus saves,' Esme repeated back. She was trying to focus on where she was, but the unusual circumstances distracted her, and she kept thinking: Am I a hero or a rebel now? Am I terrorist? Would I ever be able to go home again? 'Jesus saves,' she said again to lock those words down – it struck Esme that words have meaning, and they have use, but they're not always the same. She heard her footsteps echo on the steel landing.

At the cell door, Esme fumbled through the keys. 'You having trouble there?' a voice called out with accompanying laughter from within the cell. When Esme heaved the door back there was a sarcastic cheer, followed by, 'Who are you?'

'Jesus saves,' Esme said hopefully. Sitting on a bed against a wall, a woman with close-cropped hair stopped laughing. 'Jesus saves,' Esme repeated.

Downstairs, the door to the foyer was held ajar with a wedged chair and the same from the foyer to the staffroom, inside of which a group of five guards were sat on similar, standard-issue orange-coloured plastic chairs lined up against one wall, they were stripped to their underwear and relieved of their utility belts. A radio on a windowsill chattered low beneath the crackle of interference. Joan Ball was looking over a bank of security screens.

Bobbi, with an arm slung around Esme's shoulder, thrust a glass into her hand and filled it from a bottle she gripped tightly by the neck: 'Drink?' Esme wasn't sure if it was an offer or another instruction. Nor was she told what kind of drink the clear liquid in the unmarked bottle was, but its smell could raise the dead.

Esme clutched the filled glass with Bobbi recounting the story of her family being driven out from their home and forced to roam. 'I remember lying in bed at night, Mama stroking my forehead, waiting for them to come and start banging their pans outside our window again. Eventually we left on foot. We drifted around camps after.' Bobbi closed her eyes and necked the drink.

Joan Ball turned back toward the room from the monitors she'd been studying. 'These screens are for inside the block.' She pointed at the top row, displaying dimly lit, empty corridors. The screens were partially obscured by desk detritus, suggesting the guards rarely regarded them. 'The others run off feeds from the men's block, Highpoint South, but this one ...' She identified the bottom left screen. 'This is the front gate, and here look, jus' outside ...' Lisa stepped alongside Joan Ball to look and so Bobbi and Esme followed. 'There are a bunch of hermits. Now what's a bunch o' hermits doing turnin' up here, hey?' She announced, 'It's as I been sayin' ladies. We're on a mission from fucking God.'

Joan Ball surveyed each person in the room until she came to Esme and her un-started drink. All eyes were on her. She drew the glass to her lips, closed her eyes and drank it as quickly as she could. She gasped. It felt like it was burning the back of her throat, her stomach wanted to reject it. She touched her fingertips to her lips.

'So why is you breaking us out?' Lisa asked.

'I came away to go on the march,' Esme said. 'I came with some friends. We joined the hermits in Ely.'

'Why?' Bobbi asked.

'They had a bus.' Esme accepted a second glass of moonshine.

'But why d'you come away at all?' Bobbi asked. 'You don't look like a rebel. If you don't mind me sayin', you just look like a sweet girl.'

Esme studied her drink. Joan Ball said, 'Ah but looks can be deceptive.'

Esme then admitted, though no one was pressing, but just because she wanted to say, 'Actually, I ran away because I didn't want to get married.' Her glass was re-filled. 'It didn't feel like it was my wedding. It didn't feel like it was my life. It never did.'

They all played cards through the night. They drank and talked through the night, and soon allowed the guards to drink and play, with ankles handcuffed to a table leg. A strange, drunken camaraderie emerged in those early hours. The guards came from local villages; despite the uniforms, the keys and the guns, they weren't trained and there was no career path. The governor rewarded the enthusiastic with responsibility, such as Barbara, still cuffed to the bed in Joan Ball's cell.

By the time morning light leaked through the window of the Highpoint North staffroom, only Bobbi was still awake, somewhat drunk, lighting matches off the side of the table, licking the tips of her fingers and snuffing them out. Joan Ball was snoring, Lisa slept with her head collapsed over the table in the crook of her elbow. Around her head, the table was strewn with glasses and playing cards and matchsticks they'd gambled with. There was a saucer used as an ashtray, over-spilled, and when the first early morning sun struck horizontal beams through the window, it lit clouds of smoke still hanging in the air.

Esme could feel her eyelids twitch. She heard voices drifting across the site. Birds in the trees paused to listen. 'Morning is upon us, young Esme,' Joan Ball said to her. 'We need to get on top of it before it runs away from us.' A window was opened in the hope new air might freshen the room. One of the guards rubbed her bare arm. Esme could hear the hermits' singing drifting in with the dawn chorus.

The poo lorry crept across the yard to the toilets behind the prisoners' mess building with a quiet crunch of gravel. A large hose, like a trunk of black rubber, was being unwound by Davey. The lorry's vacuum system chugged and gurgled. The poo lorry reversed from the latrines and turned in the direction of the gates. On Joan Ball's word, Esme dashed to catch it. Her foot slipped on the cab step and the door swung open, so her hand gripped the swinging door handle while her legs trailed out behind her. She grabbed at the door with desperate hands, planting a foot on the step, and as the swinging door steadied, arms reached down and hauled her up into the cabin.

With Anne Hatch driving and Chris Cobbe alongside, Davey Clay was stood on the back platform armed with the hose as the lorry crawled toward the gate, pursued by a flood of prisoners spewing out of the cell block behind Joan Ball, Lisa and Bobbi.

Guards at the gate sounded sirens across the prison. They stood uncertainly with automatic rifles held in hollow and reluctant threat. The lorry continued forward regardless. A lever was pulled switching suck to spray, and Davey began covering the armed guards in faecal matter and waste.

One was drenched in sewage from shoulder to foot, immediately dropping his gun. Two others, close but un-hit, backed away from the stench and shit-spray. Davey laughed and swept the hose in an arc behind the lorry.

Cheers from the female prisoners chasing the lorry and slipping in the shit slurry filled the air. The promise of freedom would wash clean all the shit their lives had been covered in.

On the other side of the site, alarms rang out and the cries of the almost free crashed through the songs of the hermits. Male prisoners rushed toward the fence separating the men's and women's sites. Some prisoners tried climbing the fence and so the fence collapsed, and hundreds of male prisoners poured into the women's site.

There were three dozen guards, all armed, but helpless looking. One or two shot in the air, one or two others pointed their guns at prisoners but they didn't shoot, there seemed little point and less inclination.

Some of the escaped prisoners from Highpoint scattered, some headed south to London. If there was revolution in the air, they wanted to breathe it. Some appropriated vehicles from around the prison or a nearby village, cars, vans and trucks weighed down by the numbers clambering for rides.

XXIV

Owain and Angharad left the city to meet John Wrawe, on the Forest Road, where the Coppermill Stream trims the Walthamstow reservoirs. Above the Lea Valley reservoir was a marbled sky with a low western sun dazzling from between banks of dark cloud as they crossed from Walthamstow into Tottenham. Owain lifted his hand to shield his eyes.

The road was cracked open with potholes and fallen into disrepair, and clear distinctions between pavement and road had crumbled away. There was a tumbled-down, old, grey stone wall, from which stones lay across the road where passers-by had idly thrown them around out of boredom, unspent aggression, or in searching amidst rubble for something re-usable. Beyond the wall was an old disused overland railway line, the dead catenary lines hanging lifeless and low across the gaps of missing train-line stanchions. To the right, an iron stake fence; only enough stakes remained to maintain the semblance of its structure, gaps allowed people through to the grassy banks built up for when the reservoir water was high. People walked there; two lads stood at the peak of the bank skimming stones out across the water. They laughed and pushed each other in the shoulder. Their laughter carried on the quiet away along the bank and rippled across the reservoir. There were tents and makeshift shelters made from sheets of old plastic, corrugated iron and planks of wood or fibreboard, though that rotted and disintegrated more quickly. It mattered little, if you weren't holding it, it wasn't yours to begin with. Everything was fluid. Nothing is certain in a crumbling world.

A figure was headed toward them, a man with a heavy-shouldered gait they recognised as John Wrawe. He was eating a kebab; it must have been hot from the way he was blowing over it through his chewing. 'How do?' He took another bite of his kebab, talking as he chewed. 'Not bad this. Bloody spicy though cause the meat's old so they dowse it in plenty o' chilli sauce.'

'What's new, John?' Angharad asked.

'Let's walk.' John Wrawe suggested a path which followed the Coppermill Stream between reservoirs. Occupying this part of the Lea Valley was a fretwork of banked paths lined with poplar trees threaded between ten reservoirs. There were children sitting on the edge of one of the reservoirs they were passing, bare feet dangling in the cool, sun-spangled water, holding self-made fishing rods from canes with lines threaded through slits. There were wading birds in the reeds and cormorants stalked their colonies of sticks and branches on one of the reservoir islands. 'See that?' John Wrawe indicated two long barges drifting along the Coppermill Stream. 'They're with the Woke.' Angharad watched the two barges drift on. 'You been told locals barely noticed 'em, but I talked to some locals 'round here and they says them boats been coming for weeks now, a few at a time, passing through, carrying goods and people.' They paused to look over the reservoir. Owain combed his hand through his hair, stirred by the breeze that gathered across the water.

'What else have the locals being saying, John?' Angharad asked.

'Nowt much,' John Wrawe said, completing his kebab in one mouthful, sufficiently large that he had to use his fingertips to cram it all in, chewing some moments still before he could fully respond to Angharad. 'Folks are wary of saying too much to strangers. They think there are spies everywhere.'

'Are there?' Owain asked. A kingfisher spread its wondrous

wings of blues and greens, lifted and dived, wings flapping against the water's surface.

'Nah.' John Wrawe sniffed even as he finished chewing. 'Reckon it's just paranoia, me. When you're beaten a lot, you can end up forever twitching and looking around, expecting the next beating.' He swallowed.

'True, true,' Owain reflected.

'Me father learnt me that.' With lips closed, John Wrawe licked his teeth and poked the tip of his tongue into the cracks between his teeth like a toothpick. He rolled the paper wrap to his kebab up into a ball between his hands. 'Why are the authorities gonna spy on these poor, hopeless fuckers? You get the odd drone fly over 'cause they're cheap, but even thems gonna be more about freaking the locals than actually findin' anything out.'

'Have you been downside, John?' Angharad asked.

'Oh, yeah.' John Wrawe nodded. 'It's quite a set-up he's got down there. They rotate but there must be dozens at any time. He's built quite a militia, has Hereward. They've tapped into the grid for the lecky. Some parts are lit and stocked so as you could stay down there for weeks if it weren't for the claustrophobia.' John Wrawe laughed. 'And the rats. Fucking loads of 'em, big bastards some, 'n all.'

There were piles of debris and refuse mustered at irregular intervals. John Wrawe tossed his kebab paper ball on one they passed. Angharad asked, 'Is Hereward down there?'

'At first, and he's visited since, but the Woke are mostly still making their way down from the Fens and the Midlands. Like I say, the Woke are quite a number now.' They passed a couple walking in the opposite direction, local by the clothes but not squatters or roadside dwellers. John Wrawe remained quiet until they'd passed. 'They took Peterborough and Northampton, feigned an attack on Cambridge and liberated the detention centre built on the old airfield there.'

'emlyn?' Owain asked. They'd heard nothing since leaving Cambridge.

John Wrawe shrugged. The sun was low casting shadows across the path from the poplar trees. 'I also heard rumours of outbreaks in the north.'

'The time is nigh. We know about the folks in the north. Not this weekend, but the weekend after,' Angharad said.

At a fork, John Wrawe indicated the path they should follow, alongside Dagenham Brook and past a squatters' encampment on the other side. A woman sat on a box in the opening to her shelter cradled an infant. She watched them pass her. 'Weekend of Midsummer's, the ducks'll be rowed up,' Owain said.

Angharad asked John Wrawe, 'Any news of our young American? We heard bin Salah's people drew a blank in Fenby. Seems he's moved on.'

John Wrawe cleared his throat by hacking up a gob of phlegm and spitting it into the verge before answering. 'Ah, now there again I do have news. Your American popped his head up in Ely of all places. I was there in the square meself. I look up and he's two foot from me. He's not seen me or nowt, so I approach him. He's hooked up with some folk from the marshes, hooked up with a girl there. They'd met with some others and the whole crowd were travelling south for the rally. Well, I can't lift him off the street there and then, so I figure, as he's heading this way, it'd be easier to let him come most o' the way to us.'

'You should have picked him up,' Angharad said, thinking of the mysterious American, Mr Wolfenbarger. 'If we can't produce the American, we can't be sure bin Salah won't sell us out.'

'Listen, his party had hooked up with that batshit old hermit you were with at Wandlebury. They had a bus.'

'A bus?' Owain asked.

'Yeah, a bus,' John Wrawe answered, 'blue and white.'

'Why's that bloody relevant?' Angharad snapped.

'Anne and Chris are with them,' John Wrawe reassured her. 'I'm going to meet them in Essex, not far from Brentwood, a place called Basil's Hill. It was one of those new towns of the twentieth century that grew with new industries and died in the twenty-first century when those industries died. It's where folk from the east is mustering for the march on London. Wat Tyler's bringing his Kent people to join with our East Anglian lot.'

'And you're meeting them there?' Owain asked to reassure Angharad.

'As I said.'

'We need the American,' Angharad reminded John Wrawe.

'Trust me, we'll stick to him like glue all the way,' John Wrawe then asked, 'Why does bin Salah want the American anyway?'

'I don't know,' Owain said. 'I'd been thinking about that.'

'Oh, yeah?' Wrawe's interest piqued.

'And now apparently there is some guy from America who might be interested in him.' Owain bent down, picked a stone from the bank and threw it with a low, horizontal trajectory across the reservoir they were walking alongside. The stone bounced twice and disappeared beneath the surface.

'We're too reliant on the bin Salahs,' John Wrawe said. He rubbed his chin and scratched the stubble on the side of his cheek. 'I'll see what I can do. I don't trust this bin Salah any road.' He added, 'They ain't like us.' Angharad sighed. 'I don't mean being Islamics, couldn't give a furry shite 'bout all that, me. A person can believe whatever half-arsed crap they like. I mean, they're internationalists, rootless, they'll sell us out if it prospers 'em to.'

The sun slipped behind the horizon. Fires lit up the dark around the tents and ad-hoc shelters. 'Give over with this shit, John, will you?' Angharad said. 'Anyway, get Luca to us and you won't have to deal them.'

'I hope all your clever plans don't end up doing us in,' Wrawe replied.

'Stop chatting shit,' Owain snapped testily.

'Don't vent your spleen, dear.' John Wrawe began whistling as they walked on, breaking to add, 'I'll keep my end tidy, always do. But if this all goes tits up, don't say I didn't say nowt.' Before parting from Owain and Angharad, he added, 'Oh, one further curious detail about our Luca. I might be wrong, but I think there are others interested in our American friend; itinerant folk.'

'Itinerant folk?' Angharad asked. 'What do you mean like travellers or gypsies?'

'I mean precisely that.'

XXV

Davey Clay gazed out of the window of Mazcek's bus and pointed to flurries of people tripping over the horizon line. They were early outliers for an encampment beyond the hill. Wat Tyler brought his rebels north of the river to converge with those Wrawe had mustered between Basil's Hill and the village of Fobbinge, at the end of the old A13 commuters' corridor.

At Basil's Hill there was an industrial graveyard known as Crane's Farm. The name was in recognition of an earlier time over which utilitarian grey warehouses and factories were laid out like tombstones bordered with carparks. Gone was the tobacco company, the gin company, the company who made electrical goods, and of course, the car plant. The tall coffee bean roastery that came later survived a little longer, before it became a brothel called Paradise Street. After the collapsing began, and after the golf club on the other side of Basil's Hill got vandalised for the umpteenth time, its membership dwindling concomitantly, Paradise Street, with its discreetly anonymous location, its plush furnished and fragrantly scented cocktail bar and private suites, became a preferred site for networking businessmen. Here too though, the erosion of a sustainable provincial business class led inevitably to decline and atrophy on Paradise Street. From the fittings and fixtures to the hostesses, from the businessmen to the suits they wore, it all seemed somehow like last year's show. It was an increasingly ghastly imitation that only fooled a mind eager to be fooled, never enduringly but merely for passing moments of revelry and relief. Where once it boasted its libertine delights, it cowered, ashamed, syphilitic and rancorous. Those who still visited slipped in through the shadows, like an addict in an opium den, with a waxy, pale face barely feigning distraction, let alone delight from touches that could no longer even lose themselves in play but repeated patterns like parrot phrases, bored and where arousal was only achieved with a will to completion that wouldn't be too torturously drawn out.

Outside, people like rats moved about in the shadows of warehouses and factories. The warehouses and factories became occupied by those with nowhere else to go; the abandoned people bequeathed the abandoned buildings of the old, abandoned world. Without heating and with high ceilings, they were cold and in open areas squatters would burn rubbish in metal bins. Factions would form and fights break out, so the different floors of the different factories and warehouses would become mini-fiefdoms, dwellers on each level gathering around the authority of a powerful, usually male figure. Following internal battles most of the factories coalesced into tribes identifiable by the company's brand logo that was still, however faded, widely displayed throughout their factory or warehouse; there was Ford, GE, Gordon's, and of course, Amazon.

The Amazon group dominated the Crane's Farm Industrial Estate, they benefitted from the legacy of the stock they inherited when the warehouse got 'rolled'. The Amazon Company had platoons of security and drones patrolling overhead, and the legal right to use lethal force on site, but the numbers of people that night were nevertheless overwhelming. It wasn't, despite claims, the first Amazon depot in Britain to get 'rolled', but it added to the myth of the battle of Crane's Farm. In truth, the security was breached and overrun within thirty minutes. The security troops quickly surrendered and helped override the drones. The leadership that emerged to coordinate the attack propagated they had driven Amazon from England. This mythmaking was also untrue in two respects; the rebels of Basil's Hill were only waves in a storm which swept through provincial England, and, Amazon never left entirely in any case, but withdrew to London and the other emerging city-states, such as Cambridge, Exeter, Oxford and York. As for the leaders, they formed a council, the council soon fell out and so broke the Amazon depot into a handful of smaller rival fiefdoms that became increasingly watchful and antagonistic to each other until fighting broke out. Four became three became two became one and a man called Jeff with an office at the back issued instructions while eating pizza, sitting in an inflatable orange armchair with a gold, plastic crown on his head.

The consumer riots were several years since; Jeff died and the hundreds of people who lived in and around the Amazon depot were again fragmented and disconsolate about their fate. Many of the people who dwelled across the factories and warehouses of Crane's Farm Industrial Estate sought distraction in either the alcohol made in huge stills set up in the former Gordon's Gin factory, or with the chemicals those running the moonshine stills diversified into. Many people sat around, catatonic on moonshine drawling sad resentments and struggling to remember faces like old songs. The moonshine's clear form deceptively understated its effect. There were also people hibernating, blissed out on purple ohms staring at the sky, or opioids, never fully awake nor fully asleep, gazing into space where time dilated, reality became soft and gooey, and dream figures stepped out of the imagination to dance around the visionaries' suspended smiles.

Those with the glazed, gazing eyes watched dreamily as people, often in conflict with each other, gradually met in the no-man's land between different warehouses and factories. They had for a long time tied sashes around their arms of a certain colour to denote where they were from; Ford wore blue, GE wore red, Gordon's wore green, Amazon wore orange. Following truce between these factions there was something quite hopeful as food and drink were shared and some cooked on wire meshes, over bin fires as barbeques. Acquaintances were renewed across the divisions previously defined by turf war.

When Mazcek's bus slumped to rest at Crane's Farm, John Wrawe was already waiting for them. He led them between clusters of people to the cavernous former Amazon depot where a crowd had gathered to hear Wat Tyler speak. 'Our first demand,' Tyler announced, 'is for a guaranteed living income such that no man, woman or child need starve. If there is sufficient for the rich to have luxury, then there is sufficient for all to have what is necessary.' A clattering of clapping swept across the people listening and Tyler paused, with bullhorn ready.

Esme gazed around the surreal spectacle of Crane's Farm and the Amazon warehouse. It was hard to believe that people had taken to living in such numbers in such places. As preparations were made for Mother Michael's complicated disembarkation from the bus, Joan Ball explained to Esme, 'The people here are the flotsam and jetsam of our time, abandoned, drifting, they wash up at places like Crane's Farm. The rising seas are supposed to lift all boats but those that drown are told it's their own fault for not learning to swim.'

Tyler announced, 'Our second demand is for the full restoration of voting rights.' The suppression of the vote began with ID laws and the need for fixed addresses. Then anyone with any sort of conviction, whether spent or unspent, however minor, had to pay a fee to reapply for their voting right. Most couldn't afford the fee, so they didn't vote. Then there had been a campaign paid for by the rich: 'No Representation Without Taxation'. It effectively removed the vote from anyone without a job or on low pay. The elderly were exempt provided they had assets. White women of child-bearing age were also exempt at the beginning as the government wanted to encourage white women out of competitive labour markets and to reproduce due to a belief in the Great Replacement Theory. Later, voting restrictions were extended to all women, as the authorities found men more supportive. They argued gender neutrality was against nature and besides, removing women from the workplace would mean less male unemployment.

The sky was grey, and Esme shivered with a strange sense of foreboding. Away from the listening crowd close to Tyler, many more scattered at safe, suspicious distances. With Wat Tyler were half-a-dozen people who'd come with him from the encampment. It was unclear to Esme whether they were there to help rally recruits or as security for Tyler. They all wore black and though she couldn't see any of them carrying weapons, the way they looked around as Tyler spoke, scanning the site and even the sky above, unnerved her.

The third demand Tyler cited was the repeal of the so-called Natural Laws. The Natural Laws were passed in the 30s and 40s 'to promote the functioning of the natural order.' Abortion had become prohibitively expensive for all but the daughters of the wealthy before being outlawed. Esme had believed abortion was wrong, she'd been brought up to believe abortion was wrong, that it was a type of murder. Sarah-May said the laws weren't about the life of the unborn, they were just one of the ways men sort to control women's bodies. She asked Esme, 'What did almost all the people passing anti-abortion laws have in common? Answer – they're men.'

'Yeah, but ...' Esme had said.

'And those laws that encouraged women with tax breaks and support to stay at home and have children, who passed those laws?' Sarah-May further asked Esme but answered herself: 'It's old, grey men who want to keep their wives at home while they rake in London or wherever.'

'Yeah, but we are the ones who have the children ...' Esme had said.

'And when the Women's Protection Laws were passed,' Sarah-May said, 'whose dress code and behaviour was described in law to define if the woman had protection of the state or whether she had stepped outside the protection of the state.' Esme hadn't offered a 'but ...' She'd listened instead.

Esme wanted to kill Agent McCain. She hadn't before; she'd wanted to pretend that it hadn't been real, and if she could've forgotten about it then it wouldn't be real, but she couldn't forget about it. Thrashing against ghosts she'd turned her violence against herself. The feelings that drowned her she knew were born of what McCain did, but she didn't understand them. Why did it still matter so? She wanted to scream, she imagined screaming and everyone, even Wat Tyler falling silent. She sighed and blew out her cheeks. She wished she could withdraw somewhere quiet, and she wished she'd brought Lizzie's dress-making shears with her. She'd like to cut a line across her arm. She wanted that sweet relief. She wanted to kill Agent McCain even though she didn't know if killing him would make her feel better. She wanted to kill him anyway because he deserved to be killed.

'Our fourth demand is the abolition of National Service,' Tyler roared. 'No more will poor boys die in rich men's wars, and no more will poor boys be made to patrol the neighbourhoods of other poor boys.' Tyler concluded, 'Finally, our fifth demand is the return of land and resources to common ownership.' This was the most controversial of all the demands. It struck at what the ruling class truly valued, and it threatened the unravelling of hundreds of years of enclosure acts. It struck at the very principle of capitalism and the Great Chain of Being.

The Amazon depot was a corrugated ironclad barn with an arched, convex roof that when it rained made those dwelling there feel like they were living inside a drum. In breaks of the corrugated iron roof were strips of clear, reinforced Perspex where what light there was got in. Since the electrical grid no longer operated there was no electricity so no electric lights. All on one floor, the Amazon depot had been operated largely by robots that like the towering shelves and storage cages had been stripped away, cannibalised or traded. There was only a single floor, but the area was vast and the ceiling high. People sectioned areas off with walls of unwanted goods, metal sheets and wire fences made from the old stock cages. Safety and security, such as it was in the depot, was only achieved through good relations with neighbours. To be solitary was to be isolated and to be isolated was to be vulnerable. 'It's strange,' Mother Michael commented as they passed between ad-hoc dwellings. 'Few people live alone anymore.'

All the different dwellings springing up and crowding the interior of the Amazon depot had created a maze of passageways only known through familiarity and that might reconfigure and change with the day. Sweet scents wafted through the entire place because the depot carried a massive stockpile of scented candles and tea-lights, and so it was that passing some dwellings the warming aroma of cinnamon, or summer berries, infused the air.

John Wrawe led them to a living space made from storage cages, their wheels removed and anchored with ballast made from the belongings within them. They could be opened only from inside and were covered with plastic sheeting on the outside. In a corner was a small gas burner for cooking, and a gap at the far end where a suspended sheet separated a sleeping area. In the centre of the room was a low table with half-a-dozen stubby scented candles, unlit. Around the table were cushions and crates to sit on. Esme, and the rest of Mother Michael's party took tea and waited for Wat Tyler to join them. They were to travel onto a church in Fobbinge, where Wat Tyler was leading a small group along the Thames and ahead of the main rebel army.

While they waited for Wat Tyler to free himself from the crowd and join them, they chatted about their plans. Mother Michael said she was drawn to the church at Fobbinge, and though it was a place that she had never been, it was there she would stay. 'And so will Neddie.' He smiled acknowledgement of the decision. 'I wish you well with your march. If the battle at Wandlebury taught me anything,' Mother Michael explained, 'it was that I will be of no use in London, but there will be plenty to do after. We ...' she spoke for herself and Neddie, 'shall wait at Fobbinge.'

As they waited, they all seemed to Esme drawn into their own private thoughts. Sarah-May was talking with her mam in discreet whispers. Esme smiled at Luca. Without Sarah-May, she realised how alone he was. Esme always felt pity for the lonely. For the first time Esme didn't feel crowded by her old life in Fenby. Between yesterday and today, Esme felt able to breathe.

When Wat Tyler arrived, everyone snapped to attention. He

was a big man, but Esme was surprised by how gentle his manner was. He and John Wrawe flanked Joan Ball and Mother Michael, in chair, and led the way to the village of Fobbinge, a few miles further on from Basil's Hill. It straddled a creek that wound down to a harbour. Gulls cawed in a wind that blew across the Thames Estuary and rippled along the creek. There were travellers encamped at a bend there who ceased whatever they were doing to watch the party Esme was with pass.

St Michael's Church in Fobbinge was stood on a little raised mound, its graveyard of yew and drooping, lachrymose willow behind a wall of diamond pattern red bricks. St Michael's Church had a square tower but no spire. It was visible along the creek for smugglers' boats to navigate by. Since the Collapse, there were markets thirty miles west in London, and all along the Thames ribbon towns leading into the London 'burbs where smuggled and illicit goods could be traded. There had been tunnels beneath St Michael's Church smugglers had used from the fourteenth century that were busy again with the poverty, war and climate disaster of the twenty-first century.

At the south porch to the church two nuns were stood. One was young in the face and tall, the other was older and shorter. The older nun withdrew her arms from the sleeves of her robe, lifted her right hand holding a large iron ring with suspended keys. 'Welcome ...' She passed the key ring to Mother Michael.

Mother Michael looked around the timber-framed south porch, the tiled roof, the spandrels depicting the head of a king and someone opening a dragon's mouth. As Neddie pushed her through, she lifted her palm for him to pause, her party gathered behind her. 'You know, Neddie, being here, I feel at ...'

' ... Home,' the elder of the two nuns said. 'We have been

awaiting your arrival.' There was a stone basin with cold water in that Esme saw Luca dip his fingertips into, and with slight, deferential bend of the knee, touch the water to his forehead and chest marking the points of the cross. There was a large crucifix on the wall of the church; Jesus was nailed through his hands and feet, a crown of thorns, beautifying his suffering for the sins of others. Esme was reminded of stories of the Penitents her dad had spoken of with a sardonic smile. She remembered her first impressions of Joan Ball at the Seven Stars back home and remembered thinking Joan Ball must have been a crazy cult leader. Esme wondered if she was now a part of that cult – the idea carried a curious appeal.

There were two women sat at the end of a pew Wat Tyler approached, laying his hand on the shoulder of one as she turned her head toward him. Joan Ball first met Wat Tyler when he led a small group breaking her out of Maidstone jail. She told Esme that his first wife died following the birth of a daughter from a postpartum blood infection. It was Tyler's futile pursuit of antibiotics which led to his contact with the smugglers and hermits who fed the black markets.

His daughter, Alice, was born deaf, so while she learnt to lip read and to speak, her speech was always affected from never hearing another's voice. It was with furious self-reproach he returned to find his daughter, sixteen years of age, huddled in a corner of their kitchen, sobbing, barely able to explain having been assaulted by two state agents that had been making visits in the area for census data. Alice hadn't heard them knock, the door was unlocked and she'd neither seen nor heard them enter until they were standing a few feet from her laughing at her confusion and mocking her voice. She backed toward the kitchen door, unnerved and ready to run, when one of them grabbed her by both her upper arms. She froze and was unable to mount any fight.

Esme felt she knew Alice's story as her own. Alice was sat alongside her stepmother, Wat's recent second wife, Marcy, at the aisle end of a pew. Mother Michael reached her hand out from her chair and the woman took it. 'How are you doing, Marcy? I know it's a cliché, but you do glow.'

'It's the hormones,' Marcy smiled, 'and cocoa butter.'

'Do you have what you need?' Mother Michael said.

'Yes, yes, I'm okay,' Marcy replied, resisting their fuss. She smiled; she was one of those people when they smiled everyone around them felt more like smiling also. Her black hair was braided, she may have been exhausted but Esme was struck by how beautiful she looked, a beauty that shone in expression rather than in still pose. Mother Michael looked at the young woman beside Marcy, and with careful annunciation, and with outreached hand to touch hers briefly, almost as a blessing, Mother Michael asked, 'And how are you, Alice?'

If Alice spoke in response to Mother Michael, Esme did not hear. Mother Michael said to Marcy, 'Sorry to fuss, but the world needs babies.'

Marcy joked, 'Please, you'll start patting my bump next.' Esme looked at Marcy's bump and wondered why people would want to pat it, and then she wondered what it felt like herself. Marcy continued, 'Sometimes I feel guilty bringing a child into the world, what with things as they are.'

Mother Michael took Marcy's hand between her own and stroked it. 'The earth endures, humanity will recover, and the spirit that gives hope is eternal.'

'Now, we must speak,' Wat Tyler said.

Esme, Sarah-May, Davey and Luca climbed the fifteenth-century west tower of St Michael's Church to kill time while those of greater importance met in conference. There was a door in the belfry that afforded access to the roof, the tower was seventy-foot high, from where London could be seen on a clear day. Bella stayed with Mother Michael, claiming she didn't think she could manage the tower. 'Too many steps.'

'Just mind all that batshit in the belfry,' John Wrawe rasped jokily.

'And don't ring the bells,' the old nun sharply added, 'They're only rung for special reasons, there are patterns to how they're rung people understand.'

The belfry was a crowd of ancient wood beams and fresher cobwebs amongst which great iron bells hanged, the ropes from the bell wheels were tied to the wall. There was no batshit to be seen though, as Davey observed. 'Good,' Luca said. 'No batshit, no bats.' The floorboards creaked beneath their feet. A staircase on the far wall led up to a trapdoor to the roof.

On the roof, they walked around the parapet to see the view from all sides. They could follow the Thames Estuary towards a distant sprawl that was London. They could also see the rebel encampment on the edge of the village. Down below, moving between the gravestones, were two figures. As Esme watched them, they looked up.

An unseen owl hooted from a tree. Davey responded blowing through thumb knuckles and cupped hands. Descending the tower, they passed the two people Esme had seen in the graveyard. 'How's the view?' the big man asked.

'You can see for miles,' Davey answered.

'The view I like, it's the drop I can do without,' the man said, and Davey agreed, so the man introduced himself as Eben and his companion as Yahya. 'Yahya's a strange name,' Davey said.

'Yes,' the man agreed. 'It is Middle Eastern. I am from Egypt.'

'Pyramids.' Davey nodded.

'Yes.' The man smiled and glanced at his companion.

Eben continued, 'It's the steps that worry me.' He reached out and touched Luca's shoulder. 'This church is pretty, but these are mean steps. See how they've become worn by the years.' Esme looked down at the steps between her feet. 'You need to watch your step. One slip and you can break your neck.'

The church took the name of St Michael. The churches and monasteries of the Michael Order became gathering posts for communication and trade; Mont St Michel in Brittany, St Michael's Mount in Cornwall and all along the Michael Line from Cornwall to Norfolk.

In the oldest part of the church, the Anglo–Saxon nave, there was a blocked-in window in the north wall and to the right of it an ancient door with strap hinges emboldened with curious prongs. Through this door were worn steps that led to the church's vaults. Mazcek and Luca lifted Mother Michael's chair and she floated, hovering under their strain, down the steps.

The vault was dark with two floor-standing candlesticks either side of a transi tomb dating from the early fifteenth century. The sculpture of the body on top carved to depict a corpse, the skeleton visible, parts of the body in states of decomposition. There was also a simple wooden chair in the corner of the room set aside for the possibility someone may want to sit with the stone cadaver in grief. There was a triptych tapestry on the wall above the transi tomb displaying scenes of the danse macabre. Set in a round, Norman Romanesque arch, was a small wooden door. Esme watched the older nun pull at a finger of the stone cadaver;

it came free to reveal a detachable metal key set within the stone finger. She used the key to unlock the door, and with the weight of her shoulder pressing against it, moved the resistant door back. Behind this door a passage curved as it sloped with the glow of a dim light ahead. Esme, like the rest, followed the nuns down the passage. In the dark she traced the wall with her fingertips. Its stone was cold, as though damp. There was moisture and tiny stalactites no more than a few inches long that dropped down from the edges of the convex arch of the passage roof. Droplets of water gathered at their tips and occasionally dropped, the sound bouncing between footsteps and echoing. The passage opened into a cavern with crates and boxes stacked against the walls, a desk beneath a window with a cabinet beside and its doors locked. 'This is where it all goes on,' Wat Tyler said.

The older nun elaborated. 'We can get goods and supplies from the continent and neither Richard King, nor the city get any piece of it.'

Tyler explained, 'It started off to meet need. There were places where food supplies, clothing and fabric or even just the raw materials from which to make it were needed. The church has the infrastructure, they are pretty much everywhere, and the state bothers them less for bearing a cross. The Michael hermits are the couriers, Shelley Ryman in London, John Wrawe here and I started organising groups to protect the hermits' passage.'

The old nun spoke again. 'We provide food and clothing for the poor, though not enough. Mary, would you?' The younger nun opened one of the crates she was standing by. From within she lifted out a brown pullover and held it high with fingertips pinching the shoulders. The old nun smiled, and Mary returned the pullover to the box, and opening another crate a few feet away lifted out packets of flour and rice. The old nun pointed at some sacks against the wall beyond the crates. 'There we have potatoes and onions.'

Wat Tyler said, 'The people in the provinces are struggling, the people in the townships and suburbs have almost lost the will to struggle. Many exist on handouts, if they complain the handouts stop.'

John Wrawe turned toward the large double doors at the far end of the cavern. 'Come then, Wat, complete this tour or I'll begin to wonder whether, as some say, it is only vanity that moves you.'

Wat Tyler laughed at this and led them to the bottom end of the cave where huge wood-panelled double doors, each six-foot wide, were unlocked and pulled open. Behind these were a pair of wrought-iron gates also unlocked, pushed back, revealing a tunnel beyond, narrowing to just a few feet wide with a gradual, downward incline where grooves had been ground into the Eocene clay earth floor from bearing the burden of stacked flatbed trolleys. The young nun, Mary, walked alongside Esme and Davey Clay. Davey walked with his feet in the grooves. The tunnel was a couple of hundred metres long, at the end a spot of natural light grew into the tunnel's entrance, shaded and camouflaged by surrounding foliage.

Where the track found the creek, there was a platform of wooden boards with three posts for boats to tie a rope around. The creek meandered to a quiet harbour and the Thames Estuary beyond. Mary told Esme and Davey the tunnel was known to those who used it as the 'wormhole' and the tiny quay was 'Worm-end'.

There, standing feet astride, hands on hips, every part the hero, all handsomeness and righteous masculinity, Wat Tyler gathered them. They were taking supplies upriver that evening for those marching. While they stacked barges, Sarah-May told Esme, 'Mum's not coming. She says she's gonna stay here with Mother Michael and the hermits.'

'That's the danger with these cults,' Luca joked. 'One day you're banging a tambourine and singing kumbaya, the next day you're wearing a cowl and making conversions over garden hedges.'

'She says her chest's bad.' Sarah-May held onto Luca's hand.

Bella had told Esme that Sarah-May was ready to outgrow her. She didn't mention her chest, but Esme noticed she slowed on long walks and her breathing became heavy and tiring for her. She'd said to Esme, 'I remember things Sarah-May never will, even though she was there. I remember the laughter and smiles of her infant play. I remember the tears of her childhood confusion. I remember watching the light on her face, the breeze through her hair and how it smelt when she was an infant, and none of these things will she remember or know their importance. And it is sad to me that Sarah-May doesn't remember as I do. I want to release Sarah-May into the world and be able to smile, even as my heart is in my mouth.'

Bella didn't say any of this to Sarah-May directly. Esme thought that by telling her, Bella found a way she didn't have to tell Sarah-May. 'We must not cling to the past,' Bella said. 'We need to be midwives for the future.' Then she coughed her smoky laugh and added, 'however hard a birth it may be.'

So, Bella stayed at St Michael's Church, with Mother Michael. Sarah-May waved at her as she receded from view. They took turns poking the poles deep through the water and into the bed beneath to nudge and steer the raft along a line just clear of the bank of the creek and onto the Thames, with its stronger currents.

Esme wrapped her arms around her knees, sitting at the front of the raft with Sarah-May, looking forward rather than back.

XXVI

For the nights leading up to Midsummer's Eve, the trickle of canoes crawling down the Lea River and along the Hackney Brook had become a stream. Willow Walwyn and John Lilburne acquired canoes and were taking Owain and Angharad into Hereward's subterranean lair.

Angharad was with John Lilburne, but he was delayed. When he arrived, he brought a tale of hunkering down in some waste ground to avoid a patrol. The woman he'd acquired the canoe from told him patrols were becoming more frequent. Lilburne wasn't sure in recounting the woman's report whether the patrols had increased or just people's fear of them. Even birdsong carried a nervous twitch. The woman told Lilburne there was a full moon coming on Midsummer's night; a super, blood moon, and she said that Mars was rising.

They broke from the Lea navigation channels and rowed south through Haringey and the warehouse districts. The river was quiet. The sounds from the run-down neighbourhoods bounced and echoed and reached them like ghosts. Sometimes faces were glimpsed in the darkness the river passed, or people unseen would be heard. As they crawled along the Hackney Brook, Angharad would pick out trees or other markers on the bank ahead to measure their progress, only to invariably lose the marker post in the darkness prior to reaching it.

Angharad had only met Hereward that one time, in a pub deep in the Fens, since when his myth had only grown with his raids in the Midlands and the swelling of the numbers that followed him. It was a secret widely known that Leo Fric, the glad-handing dandy with sly eyes running Ely, was Hereward's lover. Prior to his rise, Hereward had spent time in Europe and before that little was known. 'I heard he was an activist in one of the anarchist blocs during the consumer riots,' Lilburne suggested, then admitted it was only hearsay.

All along the Hackney Brook, Angharad heard the stillness watching them. The soporific draws of paddle through water, the waiting night, all lulled the senses only to be jerked like a fish hooked on a line, by the crack of a gunshot or some other sudden barking sound.

The brook arced south of the Haringey Warehouse District. In the early twentieth century it was a centre for production of furniture and pianos. Maynards made wine gums there. Radio valves and the cathode ray-tubes of early televisions were produced in the district, and engines, ink and paper plates and later, a record company. By that time, in the late twentieth century, the industrial base was already in decline.

In the early twenty-first century bourgeois bohemians began moving into the area, taking over the old warehouses. Briefly the district rallied, reinvented with bespoke and bijou dot-com businesses and YouTube celebrities living and operating from innovative and dynamic creative spaces hewn from the refitted warehouses, their interiors stripped to minimalist chic, bare brick and chrome. In tertiary shades of corduroy, pastel shades of cotton, calico and faded denim, for a few decades these people amused themselves by imagining they were building a future of sustainable harmony and enlightened purpose woven from hemp and fed on houmous and quinoa. Their long-haired children looked like angels dancing in the rain. They enjoyed their juxtaposition with the everyday savagery of supermarket clothes, intemperate toil, the glottal stop Ts and dropped initial Hs. Their children might imitate those accents for private amusement needed to affirm the difference between peasant from professional.

The rust grows from the outside in. The creative class retreated from the warehouse district into the city while many who lived in the city were driven out by an aggressive economic war around rents. The final few were forcibly evicted, there were too few left to even protest. For those safely behind city walls the clearances were an unfortunate reality discussed in a neutral tone, where acceptance was a first step to supporting coercive enforcement.

The people who were cleared out were told there would be new housing built in areas like the warehouse district; few houses ever came. People slept, huddled in the shadows of the warehouses, rats shuffling through dust.

Those warehouses loomed over the narrow canal. A bird loitered on the ledge of a broken window, the wire frame partially detached, hanging. It caught glinting moonlight, moaning out across the night. A scream rang out from the buildings, a cry of such infinite desolation, a howl and an echo and it was gone.

Just north of Clissold Park the brook met the New River. They followed it under a Victorian red-brick arch with a road running over the top that swallowed the river and took it fading underground. The river was only a couple of feet deep there. As the tunnel sloped deeper beneath the ground the roof closed in and the light from the opening shrunk behind them and was gone. The closing space disquieted. The touch of cold walls and the dim sounds that whispered through the tunnels were searched in effort to orient and navigate.

When the Woke brought supplies on rafts along these tunnels and culverts, they would be piloted by people lying, hands supporting the small of their backs, upside down, their feet along the roof to walk the rafts. There were also iron rings set in the Victorian brickwork so pilots could pull rafts along.

At the front of the canoe Lilburne pulled on a helmet with a light attached to the front as miners might once have worn, though it illuminated little of the tunnel. The rising stench indicated the subterranean river was close to the London sewage system. Angharad and Lilburne barely spoke for their voices echoed up and down the tunnels as trailing adverts of their presence.

The tunnel opened into a larger tunnel, a basin, where rogue beams of light from ventilation shafts bounced around splintering the blackness. Lilburne indicated to Angharad round openings in the walls opposite and lashed his canoe to one of the rings along the walls by a rope and pulled it close to one of those new tunnel openings. The canoe Angharad led underground she tied to another ring. The noses of the canoes nudged each other as Lilburne pulled himself free and up into a tunnel. He reached his hand down and pulled Angharad up and with a swing of her legs she scrambled after him.

Angharad's hands and knees splashed through a few inches of water pooled in the curve of the tunnel, circular like a pipe and four feet in diameter. Lilburne said, 'There are other, easier routes, but this is more direct.' He still wore the helmet with the light but all it lit was tunnel wall and shallow water. Angharad followed him climbing a ladder down a shaft and into another narrow round tunnel. Distances were hard to judge; inclines of the tunnels could be misleading though Angharad felt there was a general downward tendency. The echoey dark of those tunnels possessed a quality so devoid of feature as to unsettle the unconscious aspects of a person. It created a terror Angharad imagined as an approximation of death, forever crawling along tunnels in the dark with no idea of location or destination. From that small tunnel they climbed into a large tunnel. Here, the water didn't reach the ankle but was rich in sewage from the stench it emitted. The light from Lilburne's helmet struck the wall, where written in white paint were the words – 'sewer rats.'

'It's not a warning.' Lilburne laughed. 'It's a label. I come and go, but for the people who've been down here weeks, it's what they call themselves.' He and Angharad walked from there, Lilburne offering some commentary. 'We're into Joseph Bazalgette's sewage system that eradicated cholera from London. Nothing is more civilising than a city's sewage system. The Victorian brickwork is beautiful. It's a phenomenal feat of engineering.' Angharad remembered the open waste channels of the slums.

They walked on, splashing footsteps through the echoey tunnels. Light from Lilburne's helmet heightened a sense of vulnerable isolation. He confirmed from his own observations that many now gathered to Hereward's banner, with the spoils of raids in the east and in the Midlands. 'Many who don't join him below ground provide camouflage and support above. He makes the dispossessed believe life needn't be an empty wait.' Lilburne feigned indifference but added of Hereward's followers. 'They adore him.'

Angharad rejected the idea of heroes, she thought believing in heroes, whether half-blood princes or professional wizards, was disempowering. They were the distracting illusions of a ruling class, spells cast and myths spun that encouraged people to believe they couldn't take control of their own lives, that unless born with special blood in the veins or the recipient of fortune's favour from an elite education, life's expectations should be prosaic and unmemorable, and the poetry of life left for the few great men to be remembered in history. She remembered Joan Ball addressing a crowd, 'The greatest trick the devil ever played was to dress as an English gentleman.'

'It's different now. Here, at least,' Lilburne said. Angharad followed him down a ventilation shaft to a narrow connecting tunnel that opened out onto a long abandoned underground station. Voices greeted them from passages ahead, whispers blown along the tunnel. The station they stepped into was a quiet hive of industry. The disused lines beyond the arches to the side of the underground station concourse were dark, but the main concourse was lit from strip lighting attached high on walls run by tapping into the city's grid. The air was better than in the tunnels, there were functional toilets that fed the same sewage system as the city's drains. There was a mural scrolled along the large back wall of the station depicting people busy in tunnels below ground in shades of black, brown, red and deep burnt orange. Above ground towers rose, old fashioned banknotes, symbolic of wealth, blew, fluttering around in the air in a central area set aglow by bright yellow sunshine. Surrounding this space in the mural, the skies were darker and clouded and lasered with rain. There were echoes of the visionary William Blake in the lines, the colours, the contrasts, the pain etched into the oppressed figures, bent, dark, distorted silhouettes in chains. Bursting through the ground, in these darker areas, pushed up by those burrowed beneath, were flowers with green leaves and bright pastel petals, and they stood straight and were determined even as the figures around them were beaten by the rain.

Maybe two-dozen people were scattered across the station. At the far end two served soup or thin stew from great metal cauldrons heated over braziers. The steam drifted along the tunnel that trains hadn't whistled along since the beginning of the twentieth century when the station was decommissioned. There were chairs where clusters of people ate from bowls balanced on their knees. Elsewhere, people came and went, many shifting crates, whereto and wherefrom Lilburne couldn't say.

A woman approached them, Lilburne introduced her as Lorna; she wore black, with hair pulled back into a ponytail beneath a plain, blue baseball cap. Angharad hadn't seen her emerge from the shifting tableau of the underground station. Lorna would take them to Hereward.

Along the platform there were blankets piled up like autumn leaves against the wall where people would sleep, and passing, there were a few rolled up in blankets pulled up over the back of their heads and the lower part of their faces. 'They've been on night manoeuvres,' Lorna explained.

Lorna talked constantly as they passed the dim sleeping shadows on the platform and followed the disused track. Noises whistled through the tunnels which Lorna said some people claimed were the sounds of ghosts. She told them a story about the ghost of a missing thirteen-year-old girl, and she laughed at people's credulity and told them another story of the ghosts of the underground. 'From my experience,' she concluded, 'a heart is a muscle that pumps blood. It has no mystical qualities of love, compassion or emotion. People die, their bodies decompose, worms will wriggle through the eye sockets. There are no ghosts, just blood and bone, and a desperate daily struggle to get the bastards before they get you.'

They followed Lorna to a door with two men stood outside, leant against the wall, sharing segments of orange. In the narrow-focused light of Lorna's torch, augmented by a white fluorescent strip light above the door the men guarded, the orange they ate sparkled, its colour bright. One of them bit into a segment, a brief spout of juice escaped and dazzled the senses. The man pulled the entire segment into his mouth with his tongue and grinned with orange flesh between his teeth. His companion knocked on the door behind him. There was no response. They waited. 'Is he definitely in there?' Lilburne asked.

'Oh yeah. He's in there.' They waited. 'He's expecting you, you say.' The one with the orange between his teeth checked. Lilburne confirmed this and so the guard, while wiping his hands on the back of his trousers, opened the door. 'You might as well just go in then.'

The door drifted open, beyond which was a fog of smoke, and through the mists a figure sat behind the desk, head bowed as though studying something on his desk. Angharad and Lilburne stepped into the room. Before entering Lorna handed Angharad a can of Coke. 'As requested by Hereward.'

She closed the door behind her.

'Hereward?' Lilburne asked tentatively to no response. He repeated the name a little more loudly and roused a sleepy, 'Huh?'

Somebody coughed.

Willow Walwyn and Owain were sat to the right. 'He says he's fine and he'll, to quote, "Sort his shit, if I just give him a sec,"' Willow said. The only light in the room came from an angle-poise table lamp and served only to highlight the drifting threads of smoke between them, laced with the smell of cannabis.

'He's stoned,' Lilburne said.

'Very,' Willow Walwyn replied. 'He said he didn't intend to get so stoned, says he's missing his Leo, but there's no ventilation, so the room's hot-boxed. There's less smoke than there was. I had the door open but after a few minutes he said the open door was giving him the fear, so we had to close it.'

'Hereward!' Angharad stepped through the mists and placed before Hereward the can of Coke. 'Here. This is for you.'

Lilburne looked at Willow and Owain, watching. 'Have you told him?'

'I tried,' Willow answered, 'but he groaned and asked me if I didn't think the whole thing was a bit overkill.'

'Overkill?'

Willow shrugged. 'When I reminded him of who he was, he groaned. I told him he'd already crossed the Rubicon.'

Angharad broke the ring-pull seal and the fizz alighted Hereward's red-veined eyes. Hereward reached for the can of Coke, but Angharad withdrew it from his reach. Hereward looked up at her. 'Who are you?'

'This is Angharad, remember?' Willow answered. 'Lilburne's here too.'

Hereward nodded slowly.

'We got to get some air in here.' Lilburne opened the door. One of the two guards had by this time sat down outside and leant against the door to eat orange, and so fell back into the room at Lilburne's feet. 'Fetch a bucket of water, will you?' Lilburne told him.

'Woah there, stranger,' Hereward called out with little authority in his baked voice.

'Drink your Coke and listen,' Angharad said.

'Last night it began in the north.' Angharad was far from sure how much Hereward was taking in. 'Preston, Liverpool, Manchester, Newcastle, Sunderland, Leeds, Sheffield, Leeds, did I say Leeds? Nottingham and twenty or thirty satellite cities.

In organised and co-ordinated raids against the institutions of corporate-state authority: government agencies, police stations, court houses. They're destroying all the census records.'

Lilburne cut in, 'A lot of that shit at Tyneview Park, it's in Newcastle, I know it well.'

Angharad continued. 'They've taken control of any media up there. They're now free-casting and steaming all over the north from Salford and Newcastle. Instead of lockdown, they got everyone to come out and occupy the streets.'

'That's the secret.' Hereward nodded, sipping Coke. 'Get numbers out on the streets. Take control of the streets. They won't be able to regain power while the streets are filled.' Then he asked, 'Has the fighting been bad?'

'Opposition has been light in most places,' Lilburne said. 'Took the bastards by surprise. Manchester was bad, and in Birmingham they were still fighting when we got the call.'

'The time to move is now,' Willow asserted in attempt to re-energise Hereward.

'Time to sack Rome!' Hereward agreed. He tilted his head back and emptied the remainder of his can of Coke in one. 'Hah!' he grimaced tight faced. 'It's the fizz-shock and the sugar rush.' He pressed his hands on his desk as he stood, then holding the Coca Cola can aloft. 'This stuff's fucking magic. I tell you, when this shit's sorted, everyone should be able to get it.' He pointed at Angharad with the empty can. 'When the revolution comes, we should nationalise this.'

'You can't nationalise the Coca Cola Corporation, you stoned tool,' Willow said.

'And the revolution has come,' Angharad added.

'Did you know,' Hereward turned to address Willow's

criticism, 'assassins took their name from the hashish they smoked before a mission?'

'That's a myth,' Willow replied.

'Is it?' Hereward asked. One of the guards returned with a pail of water, which Lilburne took and threw over Hereward, and then instructed the guard to fetch another.

'And see if you can rustle up another of these Cokes,' Hereward added, shaking the water from his hair and beard like an old dog. 'Alright then, my eager young assassins: to the war room. Let's fucking do this shit.'

XXVII

A dawn sea-fret drifted in with morning. The rafts crawled along the north shore of the Thames all the way to Grays, where they banked before the Dartford Bridge, at the point the river turned past an abandoned oil storage depot.

Distant explosions cracked and echoed over Grays and Dartford. John Wrawe nodded toward towers of grey-black smoke in the distance. 'They're blowing up the road ahead.' He strode ahead with Wat Tyler and other leading rebels. Joan Ball barely said farewell as Esme stood around, awaiting direction. She, Sarah-May, Luca and Davey were amongst the crowds, grateful for the ride and abandoned to the ordinary, gathered in extraordinary numbers.

Esme looked at the spectacle. Beyond the sandbanks, flatbed trucks were loading up with people. Next to Davey on one such truck, sat against the back of the cab, she counted twenty-three, a few more hanging off the sides. Eben and his associate, Yahya Sulieman, climbed on after Esme's group. The truck crawled forward.

Grays was a grey town; its houses were grey pebble dashed. They passed the declined industrial units of the Thames ribbon townships. On the back of the truck, two men sat close to Esme and Davey spoke a language strange to Esme but for odd words of English shining out all the more curious. Davey watched their exchange, fascinated by the sound of their gibberish. 'Pavees,' an old man whispered to Davey. 'Traveller folk.' The two travellers eyed the old man suspiciously.

The convoy crossed Rainham Marshes, beyond were grain fields filling the gaps between dreary, Thames Estuary townships of petrified, grey, wind-whipped tableaus of rusted sheet metal, dog-eared chain-fencing and brutalist concrete, crumbling back into the earth with shoots of green dissent pushing through. Sometimes the demolition of sites was abandoned halfway through as the firm hired for the demolition folded before the job's completion. Some of the dead factories and industrial plants wore ragged black flags hoisted and hanging over their crumbling, graffiti-scarred shells.

Their numbers grew as they moved through the outskirts of London. Surrounded by people marching, the trucks slowed to walking pace. Horns blasted up and down the line. The road was bordered with huge, corrugated iron fences, like walls, grey but adorned with the bright primary palate of spray-can street art. Figures of resistance like Wat Tyler and Joan Ball were celebrated. The metal walls enclosed the road and trapped the noise, so it boomed and rattled. Access roads were bottlenecked and backed-up with people feeding in from the townships. Fists of marchers began beating on the iron walls, beating out a rhythm thousands of hands clapped to, beating out a heavy trochaic metre of their chant, 'This is what solidarity looks like.'

At the Northbound Circular where the peasant rebels passed through bin Salah's areas of Newham, Walthamstow and Redbridge, there were drones, black and ominous, visible overhead. Transport ended at Wanstead Flats, from where they crossed Hackney Marshes by foot and on to Victoria Park to gather before city gates that crossed Grove Road at the south end of the park.

Walking amidst the crowds on Hackney Marshes, a couple, pausing to pass the time, shared rumours circulating that Ismail bin Salah had cut a deal with the government. They were drinking from a bottle of barley wine, which they shared, along with rumours and opinions. Dave and Johanna Ferrer were from Dagenham; she had blonde hair almost as far as the roots and a figure that denied her years but was betrayed by her rope-veined hands and crow's feet. He had a shaved dome of a head with emergent stubble over his chin and cheeks pin pricked through with grey. Like many, they were suspicious of bin Salah. The protestors remained loyal to different, sometimes uncomfortably aligned factions with priorities often at variance. The rebels claimed to follow the example of the Zapatistas of Chiapas, who avoided hierarchies: they believed leaders become targets and factions inevitably compete to the point of internecine self-destruction. It was a many headed hydra. Although Wat Tyler was known more than most; he, John Wrawe and even Joan Ball were just a few of numerous significant figures.

There was a festival atmosphere across Wanstead Flats. Luca and Davey decided to try their arm at an archery range. Esme thought Luca would get a surprise when he discovered Davey was a crack-shot. There was a row of four targets at forty yards distance. It was fenced off with spectators lining the sides of the range, drinking heavily and cheering, especially when the crossbow was badly handled, and the bolt flew off into a bank of hay and straw behind.

Sarah-May and Esme followed music toward Alexandra Lake, where Esme recognised the band that she'd danced to back at Ely. The singer's mellifluous voice and sounds blown from his flugelhorn were just as sweet.

Esme and Sarah-May were hailed by a young man stood behind an upturned barrel encouraging people to lose pennies on his nimble-fingered tricks with cards or cups. Robert Scott had one eye that was lazy but the other was quick and everywhere, with a smile that sought to charm and words that at once flattered and deceived. Esme and Sarah-May obviously had little money, but being fairer than most, he spent time teasing them with his tricks for free. 'Was that your card?' he said with a smile and a wink of his good eye for Esme. Robert Scott then delighted in impressing them with the speed his hands wove three cups in and out and around with a pebble beneath one. 'Guess,' he teased.

'That one,' a voice behind Esme and Sarah-May said. An arm reached between their shoulders, lifted the cup in the middle and revealed the pebble. Robert Scott looked momentarily deflated. Sarah-May and Esme parted to allow the man through. He was broad with curly dark hair.

He introduced himself as Francie Moore. 'Let me show you a trick. If you can learn it, you can use it yourself.' Robert Scott shrugged and agreed, handing his cards to Francie Moore, relieved he didn't demand a coin for finding the pebble. His friend, introduced as Gavin, stood behind Esme and Sarah-May, watching the trick from between their shoulders. Esme didn't like him standing so close behind her, but she said nothing, she didn't even move.

After briefly shuffling the cards, Francie spread them out, face down on the upturned barrel. He said to Sarah-May, 'I want you to choose the seven o' clubs. Now I want you to really focus on choosing that card. Just focus on the deck and touch the card you imagine the seven of clubs to be.' Sarah-May touched one. Francie said, 'Is that the one? Are you sure?' Sarah-May confirmed, so Francie slid it out of the fanned cards and placed it face down to one side. He then turned to Esme. 'Now, would you choose one for me? Would you try for the five of hearts, okay? Just think about the five of hearts and touch one of these cards, here.' Esme looked at the cards for a few moments and touched a card nestled in the middle of the spread. 'This one?' Francie asked and slid the card free and placed it face down with the one Sarah-May had selected. 'That's grand. So, I'll shuffle the cards about and choose one meself. I'll go for the jack o' spades, how about that?' Francie selected his card and held it with the two Esme and Sarah-May chose. 'I asked you to find the seven o' clubs and look how well you done.' He turned a card over and sure enough it was the seven of clubs and sure enough it was followed by Francie turning over the five of hearts and the jack of spades. Esme and Sarah-May laughed; Robert Scott applauded.

Francie handed Robert Scott his cards back. To Sarah-May and Esme, he said, 'I wonder if one o' youse might be able to help me. I'm looking for a friend. A fellar I travelled wit' for a while; American by the name of Luca.' He glimpsed recognition in Sarah-May's eyes. 'You think you might know him?'

Esme looked back over her shoulder, toward the crossbow range. Francie's eyes followed Esme's. 'Luca. Yes,' Sarah-May said.

Francie watched her as the penny dropped, and drawn from the stories Luca told, she remembered his tales of the travellers. With the ease of the innocent her words followed her thoughts. 'Aye, that's us,' Francie confirmed.

Robert Scott was fiddling with his cups and his cards and beginning to wish they'd all move on as they were blocking hopes of any trade. Gavin grinned and put a hand lightly around a shoulder of Sarah-May and Esme. Esme tightened to the touch. Francie said, 'Was it jus' chance that you had acquaintance with Luca or do you know him well?'

'We're together,' Sarah-May answered.

'Well, do you mind if we walk with you a little way here,'

Francie asked. 'It'd be grand to see Luca again.' Gavin let go of their shoulders. Relieved, Esme smiled just as Sarah-May glanced at her, so they agreed. Francie and Gavin listened with interested sounds as Sarah-May recounted what Luca had told her about his time with them.

A performance poet had drawn a crowd they picked their way through on their way back toward the crossbow range.

'But time is a cycle, not a line
Comes back around you regain your mind
You be ready for the energy I channel in my rhymes
Remedy the pedigree, the jeopardy of mine
When the world's this f'ked up, lethargy's a crime'

Davey approached, he was looking all about searching for them between the heads and shoulders of strangers such that he was paying little attention to the direction he was headed. 'Essie, hello. I got second place. Everyone cheered. They said I could join the militia. I said I'd ask you.'

'Do you want to join the militia?' Esme asked.

'Dunno,' he replied, his thoughts elsewhere. 'Some people missed the target completely.' Davey laughed. 'I kept hitting bullseye though.'

'What about Luca?' Sarah-May asked.

'Luca was quite good. He could hit the target, but I was better, you can ask him. I'm not showing off.'

'Where is he?' Sarah-May tried again.

Davey looked around and back toward the range. Esme and the others scanned the field, but none could see him. 'I waved and he waved back at me. The big fellar waved as well.' Davey tried to explain a disappearance he didn't understand but suddenly, under the pressure of inquiry, he felt responsible for.

'Who was he with, Davey?' Esme asked.

'He was talking to a man. I 'membered him from the church, he was the man who didn't like heights. The big man was friendly, the other one was quiet.' Davey sensed there was a problem and Esme could see he was starting to panic, the fingers held at his side started twitching, flicking a card that he carried. He kept looking to Esme to help him. 'The big man says to find you. Luca agrees with him, so I come looking for you.'

'It's okay, Davey,' Esme said and took hold of the cuff of his sleeve.

Davey lifted his right hand where pinched between his fingers was a card he gave to Esme. 'The quiet one with the beard gave me this.'

Davey handed Esme the card he carried. It was a business card.

On the reverse, in English was written: 'The House of bin Salah'. Esme handed the card to Sarah-May who passed it to Francie. Francie briefly glanced at the card then handed it to Gavin. He looked at the card even more briefly and slipped it in his pocket. They shared a few words in their strange language, and Gavin was off. 'He's quick and keen-eyed,' Francie said. 'If he sees Luca, he'll come find us.'

Esme switched her support from Davey to Sarah-May, fearful and confused. People were passing them as crowds moved across Hackney Marshes past the huge squatters' encampment and onto Victoria Park. 'The crowd bottlenecks ahead,' Francie advised. 'It'll be a good place to spot someone.'

'Let's go there then,' Sarah-May said.

'Thing is, the fellar Luca was with is one of bin Salah's

people,' Francie suggested. 'That may complicate matters.'

'Why? Who is this bin Salah?' Sarah-May asked.

'He's a powerful bloke,' Francie said.

'Why would he know Luca? What could he possibly want with him?' Sarah-May looked across all their faces, even Davey, but none said anything as in her question was a truth betrayed. She didn't really know Luca. He'd turned up one day in Fenby with faraway tales.

Esme shrugged and offered a hopeful, clueless smile in pale support. Francie then suggested, 'A man who has run so far must be running from something. If it made him run, it might make another chase.'

'He witnessed a murder in the States,' Sarah-May ventured. 'And he smuggled out important political secrets.'

'Aye,' Francie mulled, 'it could be that. But my instinct says to me it's something more personal, to Luca or to another.'

'There!' Davey pointed beyond a sea of heads and shoulders. 'Luca!'

Although it took Sarah-May and Esme some moments to find the spot Davey indicated, Francie beamed. 'So, it is.' And pleased Davey with the compliment, 'You've some eyes on you, fella.'

Francie led their pursuit. Esme bobbed and wove between the shoulders and sharp elbows, following Davey, Sarah-May and Francie Moore, the weft threading through the warp of the crowd. Francie paused for them to catch up. 'There.' He pointed. Thirty, maybe forty feet away, heading toward the perimeter, where some of bin Salah's own people were, dressed in black with green sashes around their arms.

'Where are they going?' Sarah-May asked, on tiptoes, straining to see.

'Come on,' Francie instructed. 'If they get to the perimeter and out then we'll have lost Luca to bin Salah.' Rushing, bouncing off unseen traffic, Sarah-May tripped and started a staggered descent, only for Francie to grab her arm mid-fall and haul her up so that he was virtually carrying her for a moment as her feet regathered their rhythm. They closed the gap, but there was still a fair distance to Luca and their sight was obscured by the flow of human obstacles.

Two people appeared before Eben, Yahya and Luca – familiar to Esme and Davey from when they broke Joan Ball from Highpoint Prison. 'That's Chris and Anne. They're on our side,' Davey said of the second pair to take Luca. Esme watched them lead Luca away with them. She remembered Chris Cobbe's revolver and the feel of it in her hand.

'Even if they are on your side,' Francie urged them on through the crowd in still ferocious pursuit, 'bin Salah's people won't give up so easily, and nor should we.' Francie, pushing people aside, powered through. Esme, Sarah-May and Davey followed in the path he created behind him. And whose side are you on? Esme thought, following Francie's head and shoulders through the crowd – simultaneously grateful for the help and suspicious of its offer.

XXVIII

The afternoon rain dripped from gutters and the foliage of trees. Beneath the diffused light of a streetlamp, Owain Gruffydd waited at the outer circle of Regent's Park, across from the boating lake. Angharad waved at him through the weave of passing people. There was opera drifting across the park from the open-air theatre; it was Aida, the beginning of the fourth act, the beginning of the end, she thought. The last time she'd heard classical music had been the chained cellist in Cambridge, and prior to that she couldn't remember.

They walked around Regent's Park. 'There's hardly any rain. It's almost stopped,' Owain said. 'We'll have left the city by the time tomorrow is done. We should smell the flowers while we can.' Angharad hooked her arm through the crook of his elbow as they crossed York Bridge. Ducks and swans glided through the rippling circles from drops of rain pebbling the surface of the lake. Aida was above it, the voices of men and women in harmony.

A young couple sat on a parked scooter, kissed. She held an umbrella and laughed at the rain-soaked crown of her lover. He shook the rain from his hair. Her summer dress darkened, dampened, from teasing him with the umbrella, presenting it and pulling it clear not only of him but herself also. The smells of roasting chestnuts drew Owain and Angharad to a stall where they purchased a small paper bag they shared as they walked.

The warm summer evening in Regent's Park could fool someone into thinking talk of decline was exaggerated and nothing had really changed. The people in the city had grown used to the howling gale outside. There was something of

Constantinople in the fifteenth century about how people lived in the city, aware wolves were howling at the gates. Time and tide and gravity and the inevitability of decline and death, and the dust of epochs passed gathering against the city walls and the people inside living like characters from the surface of Keats' 'Grecian Urn', et in Arcadia ego – Poussin's rebirth came with a finger tracing a shadow on a tomb. Decomposition feeds renewal.

'What'll we do, you and I, when this is all over?' Owain asked.

'I don't know. It's been so long,' Angharad answered. 'There's nothing left to return to now really, is there?'

Owain looked at Angharad, sighed and said, 'No, I suppose there's not really.' They walked on. 'I been thinking of late, what with all the time we've had to kill, lying low here. I don't remember Hywel all that much, or Ceridwen, I mean properly remember like. And poor little Rebecca, sometimes I think that's all she is now, poor little Becky. I try to remember what things were like. I know facts and reasons for the way I feel but I can't remember the time as it was, and the faces grow unclear in my mind's eye. Sometimes I wonder for what have we committed so much of our lives.'

The rain had eased off. Angharad looked back along the path they had come. The couple with the electric scooter had gone. Owain ran his hand through his damp hair. Angharad spoke. 'Do you blame me?'

'For what?'

'I blamed myself. I never said because I feared that as I confessed people's eyes would confirm my guilt, even if their words didn't.' Angharad held on to Owain's hand.

'Why would the guilt be yours?' Owain looked at Angharad but as he turned his face toward hers, she turned her face away and gazed along the path.

'Hywel, Ceridwen, even you, Owain, if you're honest, wouldn't have gotten involved if it hadn't been for me.' She blew her cheeks out and released some pressure from her bursting balloon heart.

'The struggle came to us,' Owain answered, and he believed it and Angharad knew that was truly what he thought, and she squeezed his hand a little more as they walked. 'I had studied in Cardiff and returned to Aberafan. The world was too big for me then. Hywel never left of course, by the time I returned he was with Ceridwen and there you were, just as you'd been when we played as children with your big, wide smile. I'd found you again.'

'I found you, you mean,' Angharad said with another of those smiles tripping into a laugh. 'I used to take you all up the Gower Peninsula and bore you about how the world should be.'

'You didn't bore me,' Owain said. 'Everything seemed less small with you, Angharad. I was less small.'

'Hywel and Ceridwen were so nauseatingly in love in those days, do you remember? I'm sure we only got together because they irritated us both equally.'

'I thought maybe it was contagious,' Owain said. They paused, looked across the boating lake and listened to Verdi. 'I remember drawing pictures in the sand with sticks we found on the beach at Oxwich Bay. We'd been up all night, it was dawn, the summer sun was yet to rise.' Angharad laughed and reminded Owain how he disappeared to pick her wildflowers from the clifftop. 'And I threaded them through your hair,' he replied.

'I'm older now. The years crease around my eyes,' Angharad commented.

Facing each other, Owain said, 'When I look at you, I see in your eyes, every age you've been. I see the wide-eyed child, as real and alive today as she was way back when we were kids. And I see the passionate young woman always in a rush, pushing me to move forward. And I see the woman I have spent more years than I can remember on the road with. You used to say always look forward, never back, for it is in the past where sadness resides. So, we always moved forward because there is no sunlight in the shade of the past, you said, and you were right.' Angharad stood next to Owain and rested her head against his shoulder. In the break of his words, she turned to him. He continued as though recounting a dream. 'I see the woman who stands before me now and the old woman you will become. And each of those creases, fewer than you imagine, mind, but each of those creases is an aide-memoire for me. All the preserved moments of our lives are still happening in your dancing eyes that those creases may gather around, Angharad.'

Beyond the inner circle around the rose gardens and the open-air theatre, there was still a zoo on the far side, diminished, of course. There were still meerkats standing sentinel, penguins toddling forlornly, otters scuttering around, caged lemurs and gibbons in trees, but the polar bear, the giant panda, the orangutan, elephant and tiger were all gone. Angharad and Owain did not walk as far as the zoo but turned along a path that trimmed the boating lake.

Aida soared in the open-air theatre and swept across the park sweeping them up. 'Do you remember when you first knew you loved me?' Angharad asked. 'I don't remember the moment. I think you must have grown on me.'

'Like lichen,' Owain joked and Angharad slapped his shoulder. 'I do remember though, see. I loved you, Angharad, from the very start.'

'I talked a lot,' Angharad said.

'No,' Owain replied, 'you listened. That's what I remember. Nobody much had listened to me before.' They headed back toward York Bridge. 'Is everything set?' Owain asked.

'The viruses are embedded in the system. All we can do is wait.' As Owain listened to Angharad, even though he was still holding her hand, the two middle fingers of his other hand tapped his thigh. 'Don't worry, Owain. These viruses are like a plague, they're highly contagious. It'll work.' He nodded but worried still. Angharad asked, 'What do you make of bin Salah? Do you think he'll keep his end?'

'His material interests aren't our material interests,' Owain said. 'John Wrawe's right about that. All the same, we've had no reason to doubt his word.'

'Is it just the destabilisation he hopes to profit from?'

'Maybe.' Owain considered bin Salah's motivations, then shrugged. 'Maybe he is as steeped in the myth of the English as the English themselves, the Americans too: all studying ancient maps with London as the omphalos, hoping to find Jerusalem here.'

'And did those feet in ancient times?' Angharad sang beneath her breath to Owain's amusement.

'No. They most certainly did not,' he answered, then, changing subject, 'So, what do you reckon about our Luca?'

'Even if John Wrawe can get him to us,' Angharad said, 'what will we even do with him?'

'Trade him,' Owain answered flatly. 'Between bin Salah and this American, Wolfenbarger, he must have some value.'

'Lilburne got the Doc's man, Eben, chatting,' Angharad said.

Owain laughed. 'Stopping that man chatting would be the greater challenge.'

'Eben thinks the merchandise Luca carried with him was not the only reason they're keen to get hold of him.'

'I don't think Luca fully grasped its importance anyway,' Owain said. 'I'm not sure how much of his story was true, but I do believe that he grabbed for something he hoped to bargain for his survival with.'

'Right,' Angharad agreed. 'There's something else, something secret, something personal.' Angharad added as an afterthought. 'And Luca's no hotel bellboy.' Applause exploded behind them. The performance of Aida had ended.

'Something else John Wrawe's right about.' They turned away from the park to follow the path back to the street.

Angharad looked both ways from the curb of Ulster Terrace, searching for a gap in the passing electric cars and taxis, scooters and bicycles. Owain still held Angharad's hand as she led their dash through a gap in the traffic, their feet slapping puddles. There was a restaurant and popular bar across the road from which the sounds of conversation, chinking glasses and music spilled. They walked on, turning right down Marylebone Road toward the apartment in Marathon House. 'There is something incredibly seductive about all this,' Angharad conceded. 'It has to end.'

They took the elevator up to their apartment on the thirteenth floor. Another couple, younger and elegant in chic city styles shared their elevator. She carried a rolled umbrella. Angharad noticed her fine narrow heels, her slender calves. He wore black shoes; their shine caught the lights in the elevator. The couple left them at the ninth floor.

Angharad remembered the farm cottage where they went when they were first on the run back in Wales. They were new to

Rhodri's militia then. Many of the Cardiff cells had been hit in the weeks before. They headed back into the hills, only to scatter when they were pursued and attacked. They thought they were clear, Hywel said they could stay, and the four who had come with them, at least for a few days. Once the army passed and the way seemed clear, they would break for Rhodri's stronghold in the northwest. Owain and Angharad had been foraging in the woods when the soldiers came. Angharad never saw them. They ran back toward the cottage when they heard the gunfire, however useless it might have been. They stumbled, tripping out of the woods and into the clearing, a field on an incline and a paddock before the cottage. They knew it was army by the heavy tracks embedded in the approach. Even the police would have closed the gate to the cottage before moving on. The little girl was shot in a partially open doorway, maybe the soldiers hadn't really seen her but shot at the moving door. She'd been shot in the side of the neck and the tummy; there was so much blood from her tummy. Ceridwen was dead in the room beyond, cut down mid-movement as though she was running to pull her daughter back. Hywel laid dead outside the front. Owain and Angharad never even got the opportunity to say sorry.

Angharad turned the Yale lock key to the thirteenth-floor apartment, and as the door opened a voice beyond greeted them. 'Ah, at last, the Gruffydds are back. Or should that be Malcolm Morris and Judith Baker. Come in, come in, close the door behind you and close the cold out, as my dear old mum used to say. I can't tell you how pleased McCain and I are to catch up with you.'

XXIX

From Wanstead Flats along Harrow Road, then left down the main drag, where the shops were closed and their fronts protected with grills, awaiting the expected riots. Onto Burgess Road and Crownfield Road with more of bin Salah's men around the bridge on Temple Mills Lane, beyond which bin Salah had no reach. Davey and Francie had lost sight of Luca. Through those narrow streets the songs and chants reverberated against the crowding buildings and filled the space between.

'It's too tight here for bin Salah's people to pick him off the street,' Francie commented to himself more than Sarah-May and Esme walking alongside him. 'My guess is bin Salah will back off, leave the big guy to carry on tracking Luca, why not. He's not so conspicuous. No, I don't think Luca's their main prize. Luca was a golden egg that seemed to fall into their lap, fallen off their laps and rolled away. With him being the quarry of so many others, they'll let him roll.' Esme looked up at Francie Moore, his eyes searching around, and wondered about his interest. For all the smiles and laughs and encouragement, he seemed as much in pursuit as anyone.

The path they marched cut across the southern end of Hackney Marshes. Looking north, beyond the marchers streaming down to join them, there were tents and makeshift shelters as far as Esme could see.

Gavin reappeared. 'So, your man was with the first pair, and it's clear he doesn't want to be with them, 'cause he keeps lookin' about. They're taking him towards a gate with guards at the top of the park when this other pair appears, a man and a woman.'

'We saw them,' Francie confirmed. 'Our friends say they know the pair.' He glanced at Esme, Sarah-May and Davey to his side.

'I'm drifting about, natural like.' Gavin was enjoying his moment. His eyes danced about and were never still as he described what he'd seen. While Francie was a man of few unnecessary movements, Gavin was active, his hands always busy with descriptive fingers. 'This second pair each pull a gun on the first pair, held low, but I seen 'em. The first pair are mighty pissed when the second take your man away with them. They stand watching for a time, then they part. The Asian looking fella fades back but the big guy is following the second pair through the streets here.'

'And Luca?' Sarah-May asked, and she looked around at Esme and Davey. 'Why would Chris Cobbe and Anne Hatch want him?'

'Maybe they're saving him from the first pair,' Esme suggested.

'Then why is he still with them?' Sarah-May asked Gavin. 'Could Luca get away?'

'He looked more comfortable, I should say, than with the first pair,' Gavin replied. 'But I couldn't say as he was free to come or go.'

Francie urged them on to Victoria Park in their pursuit. The atmosphere was more tense by the time they reached the crowds there. The songs and chants that emerged from small groups threatened like brooding clouds, less of the festival camaraderie and more like battle songs. Esme saw people openly carrying weapons or bits of piping, staffs made from broken pieces of fencing and lampposts, agricultural equipment carried by those who had come further. She saw one man hauling around a propane cannister modified to function as a flame thrower. He was bare from the waste up with the rebel's demands across his back in fine script – apparently tattooed.

In the distance, at the southwest end of the park there were soldiers positioned at the top of the towers either side of the Victoria Park Gate. They fanned out along the top of the wall that ran along Grove Road. A platform had been constructed and was filling with soldiers through steel doors, three feet thick, either side of the main gate. At either end of the platform were union flags raised in full mast billowing in the morning breeze. There were speakers playing a mixture of patriotic songs and hits from the golden past: 'Rule Britannia' followed by The Beatles' 'All You Need Is Love' – the reproduction wasn't clear, and the muddied melodies were lost beneath the gathering din of people. Drones, intended to be noticed, criss-crossed overhead.

There was also a smaller People's Platform, constructed from stacks of cargo boxes with boards over the top, close to the old bandstand. Gavin scampered up a tree like a squirrel and encouraged Esme and Sarah-May to follow, 'for the view.' So, Davey cupped his hands and gave both a leg-up.

The first to speak at the People's Platform was a woman dressed in white with dark hair, introduced as Annie Besant. Esme strained to hear her voice, quiet but rippling over the growing noise of the crowd: 'The terrible lesson now being taught, the widespread suffering, the devastation by sword and fire, the poverty caused by the dislocation of trade, the tension, the bankruptcies. Through this Armageddon the world will pass into a realm of peace, of brotherhood, of co-operation, and will forget the darkness and the terrors of the night in the joy that cometh in the morning.'

Annie Besant was a frequent speaker in Victoria Park, many amongst the crowd knew her. She was embraced by Joan Ball and by another regular local speaker, the designer and poet William Morris. His hair was woolly and his beard thick and he wore a jacket of his own design bearing a motif of peacock and dragon. Morris, in a voice not loud but clear, said, 'I want a real revolution, a real change in society; society, a great organic mass of well-regulated forces used for the bringing about a happy life for all.'

Beyond where the speakers could be heard were waves and waves and further waves of protestors. Wherever Chris Cobbe and Anne Hatch were with Luca, the crowds were so vast there was precious little chance Esme would spot him from the tree. William Morris continued from the platform: 'We shall not be happy until we live like good animals, unless we enjoy the exercise of the ordinary functions of life: eating, sleeping, loving, walking, running, swimming, riding, sailing. We are living in an epoch where there is combat between commercialism, or the system of reckless waste, and communism, the system of neighbourly common sense.'

At the end of his talk, he held his right fist high and thanked those listening as brothers and sisters, some at the front copied. Next up was a man named Gerard Winstanley who argued for a return of all property to common ownership. He spoke with a northern accent, in sonorous, booming tones, 'Everyone that gets an authority into his hands tyrannizes over others. Was the earth made to preserve a few covetous, proud men to live at ease, and for them to bag and barn up the treasures of the Earth from others, that these may beg or starve in a fruitful land; or was it made to preserve all her children?'

Esme looked along the line of trees that trimmed the Hertford Canal and marvelled at how each tree had people perched like birds in the branches.

A NEW DARK AGE

There was a space between the platform where the authorities gathered around the gate at one end and the murmuring crowds still piling in from the A12 at the other end. Across this no-man's land runners were sent. Prime Minister King had been willing, keen he even claimed, to meet with the leaders of the protest, but the movement claimed to have no leadership. The prime minister and his government were increasingly wary of large numbers descending on London or rising from London slums. The risings in the north and Scotland's declaration of independence weakened the government's hand to a point where the prime minister along with the minister of homeland security, the minister of defence and other significant members of the prime minister's inner cabal were on the platform before the gate, surrounded and protected by troops but nonetheless diminished, parading their authority without power.

Gavin dropped down like a monkey between branches, pausing to point into the distance, claiming to Sarah-May and Esme, 'Seen him. Seen your man.' Then he was the rest of the way down and following words with Francie was off again. Esme, Sarah-May and Davey dropped to the ground and followed after.

Wat Tyler led a group that included Joan Ball to meet with Richard King, the prime minister. Quiet accompanied the half dozen across the no-man's land between the protestors and the government ministers and security troops. A drone hovered, no more than the height of a tree over their heads.

Many of the protestors mumbled discontent that talks would at best be useless and at worst a trick. Many though, carried the message of Wat Tyler, if they weren't willing to meet with the government there would be nothing left but to fight. The asymmetry of their resources meant the rebels would have to conduct a long, drawn-out guerrilla campaign. Tyler warned this would wreck the land from Canterbury to Carlisle.

Esme heard it said that Tyler knew his fate. He said to comrades, 'Then let this be my end. Either way I'm dead man walking. If the government don't kill me for treason, our followers will for betrayal.'

Beyond a line of trees, Esme and the others pursued their quarry along the towpath edging the Hertford Union Canal. The crowds were thinner by the canal. To see ahead, Gavin would periodically climb onto the horizontal steel tube fence that ran between a succession of bridges that led out of the park. He skipped in and out of people, stopping, turning back to those following him with a beckoning wave of the hand. They reached the bridge at Gunmaker's Gate and watched Luca, still flanked by Chris Cobbe and Anne Hatch, approach the gate on the far bank. There used to be security on the gates, but being outside the London City Walls they'd been abandoned.

It surprised Esme that neither Luca nor Chris Cobbe nor Anne Hatch looked back. Close by the gate on the far side of the canal, a white car was parked. Its doors opened. Luca, Chris Cobbe and Anne Hatch stopped as a pair of figures who emerged from the car approached them.

At the bridge, Gavin looked back toward Francie, allowing Sarah-May, Esme and Davey to pass in front of him. The voice of one who was standing before Chris Cobbe, Anne Hatch and Luca carried along the bridge. Esme heard an American accent, but not Luca. 'My, my, my. Time will pass, boy. The question is will you?' The speaker was a tall man, and wearing a hat his face was largely obscured from Esme. They were no more than ten feet from Luca when they watched Chris Cobbe and Anne Hatch step back, and Luca step through the gate with the other American man.

'Luca!' Sarah-May called out. Luca looked back over his shoulder but kept walking. The man he was with had hold of him by the arm. 'Luca!' Sarah-May called again as she watched the tall man with the hat lay his hand on Luca's head and guide him into the back seat of the car.

The car doors closed, and the car pulled away.

Sarah-May approached Chris Cobbe and Anne Hatch. 'What have you done? I thought we were on the same side.'

'We had no choice,' Anne Hatch said, but Sarah-May rushed at her, striking her in the chest and on the chin. Francie pulled her away, holding her arms tight with his massive hands gripping the sides of her shoulders. 'From my experience,' he said. 'There are almost as many sides as there are people.'

Behind Francie's shoulder another man appeared, whistling 'Knick Knack Paddywhack, Give the Dog a Bone'. Esme remembered him from the church in Fobbinge. 'That, Ladies and Gentlemen was Mr Samuel P. Wolfenbarger.' Eben arrived polishing an apple on his sleeve. 'And as far as I can see, that is that. The Americans have their man back.'

'Who are you? And what do you mean?' Sarah-May demanded.

'I'm Eben.' He put the polished apple back into one jacket pocket and pulled a pipe from the other made of blue stained glass. 'But my interests are, or have been I should say, on behalf of another, who has himself been aiding and assisting a man of some considerable reputation, a representative of whom you have seen me with.' While he said this, he removed the lid from a tiny gold tin no bigger than the size of the end of his thumb, drawing from within some cannabis that he crumbled into the bowel of his pipe as he spoke.

'The man from Egypt,' Davey said.

'Ri-ight.' Eben continued, 'The interest of his employer, who I don't need to name, was purely transactional.' He lit the pipe and sucked. With cheeks puffed out he held the smoke in, digesting it, before coughing and exhaling. He lifted his hand to indicate they should all wait a moment. 'Transactional ...' He gasped then smiled and blew smoke out between his teeth. 'Much like Mr Cobbe and Ms Hatch here.' Esme turned, along with everyone else to the pair who had relieved Eben of Luca, only to be relieved of Luca themselves. 'I assume you're working for the Welsh.'

Chris Cobbe and Anne Hatch looked at each other and made no denial. Sarah-May asked, 'What were you going to do with Luca?'

Anne Hatch looked to Davey and Esme before replying to Sarah-May. 'He would've been safer with us.'

'That's not necessarily true though,' Eben interjected, 'is it?'

'They wanted the option,' Chris Cobbe attempted, 'but, and this is the truth, once the weekend passed, they'd have no use and just cut him loose.'

'That may be true,' Eben said. He'd replaced the pipe with the apple, which he bit into with a satisfying crunch. 'I couldn't believe it when I saw him. I told the Doc, and he couldn't believe it either. Sam P. Wolfenbarger, here in old England, as we live and breathe.'

'Who is he?' Sarah-May asked. She looked sadly at Eben.

'He is a man who resolves situations. In a former life, of which I've had a number, I spent some time in the fair state of Virginia, a small place in Alleghany County, name of Clifton Forge. It was there I first came across Mr Wolfenbarger, but that's a whole nuther story.' Eben chewed some apple. 'He was a high-flier at one time, but something happened, and he had to eat a lot of crows. Since then, he's been freelancing for folk with the means and the need.'

Behind Eben's shoulder, over the bridge and back in Victoria

Park, Wat Tyler's delegation had sent runners back to the crowd to spread word that Richard King had accepted the rebel demands. Sometimes success can appear as unapproachable as the much more expected defeat, and so a nervousness and suspicion prevented all but a few cheering. The young lad who had interrupted Eben to spread the news ran on to tell others. 'Well,' Chris Cobbe said to Anne Hatch, 'what now?'

Gavin looked up at Francie, who nodded, and Gavin raced back off into the crowds to find out what was happening.

Sarah-May intoned, 'So, Luca's going back to America then.' She looked at Eben as he had presented himself as the only one who might know. 'What'll they do to him?'

'That depends which side Sam P.'s working for,' Eben answered and began refilling his pipe. 'Luca Chimera is the son of one Alessandro, or Alex Chimera, businessman, politician and fixer of the Supreme Court in America.'

'No, that's not right. He worked in a hotel,' Sarah-May said.

'His father was more likely to own the hotel.' Eben looked at Sarah-May, and taken by compassion suggested, 'He was on the run, lying low. If he lied to you, he probably thought he had to.' Esme thought there was sense in what Eben said, but Sarah-May looked sad that Luca hadn't trusted her with his truth.

Anne Hatch asked, 'So, if the Americans know the merchandise Luca had to sell had already been sold, why go to such lengths to get him back? Surely the genie's out of the bottle.'

'To make an example of him?' Chris Cobbe offered as he looked beyond them and across the park.

'There were two crimes remember,' Francie interjected. 'You forget the girl in the hotel room.'

'Ri-ight.' Eben beamed at Francie. 'A theft and a murder; the question is which was the more valuable loss of property?'

A shot from across the park reached them on Gunmaker's Gate Bridge, a crack and an echo that silenced the crowd. Gavin re-emerged, quietened on agitated shifting feet.

Sarah-May collapsed.

Esme had never seen someone faint before and assumed they fluttered to the ground like swooning damsels in old stories. Sarah-May crashed back into Esme. It was Davey who dropped to his knees by her and lifted the back of her head in his palm and stroked some strands of hair from her forehead as she started to come around. Groggy at first, she sat up and promptly vomited on Davey's trousers, his knees and feet.

Esme crouched down and stroked Sarah-May's back and repeated to her what Sarah-May's own man had said to Esme, 'Sometimes you got to throw up to purge the shit out your life.'

Gavin, surprised to see Sarah-May on the floor, paused before making his report. 'Tyler walks across the no-man's land between government troops and the crowds, brandishing sheets of paper, waving them about in the air like they're magic or some-it, he was. There are cheers from the crowds. But them sheets a paper aren't shields of invincibility. There's a shot, just one, Tyler staggers.'

'What?' Anne Hatch asked.

'Go on,' Francie calmly instructed.

'Then there's a couple more shots, quick, crack, crack and Tyler's down.'

Chris Cobbe took his handgun from the back of his trousers and looked across the crowds in the park. The crackle of interference from a PA blew chatter away, and the crowd quietened. There was a voice, not loud, but audible to those on Gunmaker's Gate Bridge as Prime Minister Richard King.

After the events of that day, some would still find excuses for the young prime minister, Richard King. Young for such a position and thin with neatly cropped dark hair and a not unattractive face, many others always saw him as a puppet, a pretty face on a debauched body. The young prime minister stepped forward. He took a megaphone from a soldier standing close by. If he trembled at all as he spoke, it wasn't obvious. 'You wretched men!' he began. 'You who seek equality with lords are not worthy to live. Serfs you were and serfs you will remain. You will remain in bondage not as before but incomparably harsher. We will strive to supress you so that the rigour of your servitude will be an example to posterity.'

He had a word with an aide, then with a wave of his hand, drones clustered into pairs and swept over the park dropping smoke grenades. They cracked open on impact and released an angry hiss of smoke. One man got hit by a falling grenade and lost an eye, another had half his right hand blown away. Panic swept screams across the park and people began fleeing. The smoke confused and at a bottleneck at the top of the park, people fell in a melee and were crushed under foot.

Davey helped Sarah-May to her feet, Esme supported her arm. Chris Cobbe and Anne Hatch brushed by, heading in the direction most were coming from. Eben touched his brow before calmly passing over the bridge and was gone.

Sarah-May, Esme and Davey were left with the travellers, Francie and Gavin. Fights broke out between rebels and the advancing corporate-state troops. Francie claimed he could keep them safe from the rioting and violence, so Esme, Sarah-May and Davey followed him.

State troopers lost all sense of order and discipline amidst the streets and narrow passages of east London. Residents in the flats which towered over those streets assailed the soldiers with missiles from above and all around. On the borders of Waltham Forest and Newham, bin Salah's militia fired on the state troopers and protestors alike causing all to be forced into a four-way killing zone of residents, militia, fleeing protestors and state troopers. The situation only eased when the state troopers, realising how stretched and dispersed they had become, getting attacked from all sides, fell back. The drones that should've been affording the troopers air cover had mysteriously withdrawn. The numbers of protestors still in the area thinned with some finding cover amongst the warehouses and slums, some getting too far away into north London and beyond.

When the fighting did finally cease, people would scavenge from the dead. The state troops were stripped of uniforms, weapons and any personal property and dumped on waste ground where rats would fight with buzzards and other animals over the corpses. Esme would hear it said that there were those who would fire weapons to clear the rats and other animals so they could harvest the carrion. The flesh would be minced up with pepper and sold cheaply from stalls across north London. People with empty bellies tended not to inquire about the providence of the meat; some would refer to it as spiced pork, with a wink for those who knew.

Esme, Sarah-May and Davey chased Francie and Gavin through streets, oblivious of where they were headed. Gavin paused as they caught up with him, and looking back at the sky over London, pointed. 'Look! London's burning!' Esme squinted into the distance where there was smoke rising from the City. 'London's burning!' Gavin repeated, laughing.

XXX

A short corridor opened into the main living area from the door to the apartment. On hooks along the wall, Angharad and Owain hung their coats, still wearing the sheen from the mizzle that had gathered again in the evening air. Next to their coats was already a gabardine trench coat, alien to the flat.

'Is it raining again?' said the man sat at the table from which the short corridor could be viewed. He tutted and made a rueful glance toward the window. Angharad noticed the blinds had been closed.

Another man, imposing like an eclipse, came through from the kitchen carrying a tray with a tea pot, four cups and saucers, and a milk carton.

The first man said, 'We made a brew for your return.'

The second man laid the tray down on the table. 'No sugar. Real milk though.' He had an Irish accent.

'They're country people, McCain, used to the real stuff. Shame about the sugar, coarser tastes in the country.' He looked at Angharad and Owain, smiled and waited. After a pause to study them in the full light of the main room, he suggested they sit together around the table. 'Like a family. Imagine we're mummy and daddy and you're the kids telling us what you've been up to.'

'I'll be mammy,' McCain said. 'I'll pour the tea.'

'Who are you?' Angharad asked.

'I'm Miller,' the first man said. 'And my associate is McCain. We're the people who were always going to come, Mr and Mrs Gruffydd. If not tomorrow, then it'd be yesterday.'

'Where are your papers?' Angharad asked, chin high but arms folded.

'We've got a car,' McCain said. 'It's a big car and it's downstairs.'

'Sit down,' Miller said. 'Sit, sit. This is your apartment. It is your apartment, isn't it?'

Owain's hands gripped the back of a chair. 'I'll stand.'

'Have a seat, hey. You know we need to discuss matters.' Miller turned to Angharad, she remained standing also. 'Come on, be a pal. There's no need to make any of this more difficult.'

'We'll stand,' Angharad confirmed.

'Sit down!' McCain growled through gritted teeth.

'You first!' Angharad snapped back.

Miller rose to his feet. 'You've made Mr Miller stand now,' McCain said. They were all standing, hands on the backs of chairs like they were holsters; to stand was to draw, and they were all drawn. Miller suggested, 'Why don't we all sit down together, we'll count three and sit.'

'On three or after three?' Angharad asked.

'On three.' Miller glanced at McCain. 'Agreed?' There was cautious agreement; Miller counted the three.

All seated, Miller beamed. 'Tea then, McCain.'

McCain started pouring, Owain watched the amber-brown ribbon and listened to its splash like the ticking of a clock in the quiet. 'Where are the others?' Miller asked.

'What others?' Angharad snapped back.

'Rhodri's dead,' Miller said.

'Who?' Miller's eyes studied her, but Angharad didn't look away.

'McCain was there, weren't you McCain?'

'Aye,' McCain said, placing the teapot back down on the tray. 'A bloody mess, so he was.' Owain lifted his face but looked toward the corner of the room. Angharad faced McCain; her jaw tightened. She commanded her eyes to say nothing. 'I'll never forget.' McCain shook his head to himself.

'Spare us your performance,' Angharad did not say.

'Monty will want to meet you both,' Miller announced. Owain looked at him. 'You know Monty, don't you, Mr Gruffydd?'

'You appear to have the wrong person. My name's Morris. Malcolm Morris. You want to see my papers?'

'You do know Monty though, don't you?' Miller persisted.

'Never heard of him,' Owain said. 'I'm the son of a bookbinder from Cardiff. I grew up above the shop. We had a piano.'

'I met your friend, Emlyn,' Miller added. Owain's eyes hid in the check of the tablecloth. 'He claimed to be you, when we met him,' Miller continued.

'He was a liar,' McCain said.

'To be begin with,' Miller corrected him. 'He told us the truth in the end.'

'Aye. That's true, so he did,' McCain agreed and to Owain and Angharad he added, 'He betrayed you though.'

'We caught him lying, you see,' Miller said. 'There was nothing else he could do then but tell us everything.'

'You caught him red-handed,' McCain congratulated Miller.

'He was nailed to the spot,' Miller agreed and returned his attention to Angharad and Owain. 'Monty's met with him.'

McCain commented sombrely, 'The man's not what he was.'

'What? Monty?' Miller asked McCain, surprised.

'No, no, no,' McCain clarified. 'Their man, Emlyn, not what he was. Broken. Pathetic. A bad smell. A stain that needed cleaning away.'

'True. He was broken, sure, but that was before.' Miller adjusted his sitting position, so he was more upright before announcing. 'He's better now. He's on his way to recovery, he'll be mended, like a new man, mostly. Everything will be put straight, and he can be the mensch. You'll see. It's like my old mum used to say, the first step's the hardest step – or was it best foot forward? – either way you get the gist.'

'We don't know who you're referring to,' Angharad insisted.

'My old mum, why would you? You've not met her. You'd like her though, and even if you didn't like her, you'd respect her. You'd have to,' Miller said.

'No, I wouldn't,' Angharad replied.

'What did you think of the falcon?' Miller asked. 'It's with Monty now.' Owain glanced at Angharad. Miller noticed.

McCain passed a cup of tea to Miller, then to Owain and to Angharad. He didn't place the cup and saucer down in front of Angharad but held it before her to take. When she reached to take the cup and saucer, he'd withdraw it and then represent it to her again like teasing a child. When Angharad finally took hold of the cup and saucer, McCain held on for a split second and glared at her. The cup rocked in its saucer, distressed by the tension between the two sets of hands gripping either side of the saucer.

'Rhodri's dead, Emlyn's reformed, and the falcon is in a cage on Monty's desk,' Miller said. 'Isn't it time to give up the game?'

'What game?' Angharad replied.

'Bin Salah betrayed you,' McCain said.

'What game?' Angharad repeated.

'The name game,' Miller said. 'Let's start with the name game.'

'Your friend Emlyn didn't like the name game,' McCain said. 'He didn't like the rules.'

'Rules are important,' Miller said. 'Children especially need rules. They can get in trouble if they don't know the rules. That don't sound fair, does it? But rules is rules. How can you know what's right from wrong if there is no rules? Your mummy and daddy are mistreating you if they don't tell you the rules. Rules are important for order and there must be order. There's a natural order, a way things are and must be, so it all works out. McCain here, McCain often tells me, private like, that he worries about the world.'

'I do,' McCain confirmed. 'I worry. We're living in strange times.'

'You hear that, Mister and Missus Gruffydd. These are strange times indeed. You know why? People have disturbed the order and the balance.' Miller stood, lifted by the momentum of his convictions.

'Queer sorts,' McCain said. 'Godless.'

Miller looked around, nobody else stood so he sat down again, pulling at the knees of his trousers as he did. 'My old mum taught me the rules. I can still hear her voice calling me. Danny, she'd say, Danny, you make sure you respect your elders, learn from them, let them impart their wisdom to you. And I did. And I remember I had this girl once, she was Mrs Harris's girl, Rachel. We'd go for walks down by the old canal of a Sunday evening, out in our best. Beautiful those summer evenings were, they lasted, not like they are these days, here one minute and gone the next. I recall even now seeing the low evening sun over the canal glint off the chrome of a shopping trolley. I never took liberties with Rachel, because of the respect my old mum taught me. I can see Rachel now, fit as a fiddle, fit for a fiddle.' Miller went quiet, lost in thought. He heaved a deep breath. 'This is a difficult job sometimes, Mrs Gruffydd.'

'My name's Judith Baker,' Angharad replied.

'Indeed, Mrs Gruffydd.' Miller sighed for effect. 'Will the

other two be coming back here?' He turned to McCain. 'Did you check their rooms?'

'A few clothes,' McCain answered. 'Nothing much.'

'Nothing you'd not be willing to leave behind, hey.' Miller noticed the cup of tea he'd not touched, taking up the cup and drinking it in one.

'They betrayed you,' McCain said, referring to Willow and Lilburne.

Miller replaced the cup and smiled broadly. 'That hit the spot. The empire is run on tea, so they say. Marvellous stuff. You know what, McCain, we should all share a fish and chip supper, a kind of last meal if you like.' Miller stood and reached into his inside jacket pocket.

'Are you sure?' McCain asked.

'Sure, I'm sure.' Miller pulled a note out of his wallet and snapped the crisp note between his fingers. 'There's a shop around the corner, McCain. You go, I'll pay. I know the man who runs it, my father knew him. Tell him I sent you and he'll see you right.' Miller handed him the note and patted the Irishman on the arm. 'Don't worry, we'll have a chat while you're gone. Relax, you worry too much, McCain.' He drew his revolver from a holster under his jacket. 'We'll be fine. Better than that, we'll have a good natter while we wait for the batter.'

'Whereabouts is this shop?' McCain asked.

'Wait,' Miller said, and he took the money back and handed McCain his gun instead. 'I'll go. You stay with these two. I need the air anyway. It's become stuffy in here. The windows need opening to let some fresh air in.' Miller stretched out his hands, puffed up his chest and took repeated deep breaths which he blew out through pursed lips.

'Do you want me to squeeze 'em while you're away?' McCain asked.

Miller dropped his hands to his side. 'Sure,' he shrugged. 'If you want, or just let 'em stew.' He stood and stretched his arms out. 'When I get back, we'll have fish and chips and hear what the Gruffydds have to say.'

'When are they arriving?' Angharad asked.

Miller laughed and walked towards the front door, pausing along the corridor to put on his gabardine trench coat and check through the pockets of the other coats hanging there. Nothing; he looked back into the living room and grinned at the watching faces.

McCain sat and watched Miller leave the apartment, framed between the shoulders of Angharad and Owain. They heard a click and turned to find McCain fiddling with the revolver Miller had handed him. 'Why are you playing with that?' Angharad said.

'It's loaded,' McCain said. 'With bullets.'

'Does it make you feel less impotent?' Angharad asked him.

McCain stretched out in his chair, then he snapped the barrel back into place and cocked the revolver.

'Behave.' Angharad didn't flinch. 'You're not going to shoot us. You've already said your Monty wants to meet us. You don't want to shoot your load too soon, do you?'

'I could say you tried to escape,' McCain countered.

'If we're not the people you're after, we could just get up and walk out.' Beneath the table Angharad's knee jittered, she folded her leg, so she didn't tap her foot on the floor. Above the table everything was determined calm.

'You're the people we've been looking for alright,' McCain asserted.

'If we were to get up now and walk toward the door, could

you take the risk?' Angharad asked. 'There'd be an inquiry. Remember when you were young, Mr McCain. Remember that time when you had to take the blame.'

'I did my duty,' McCain said.

'They didn't listen to you though, did they?' Angharad pursued.

'I followed the line. I always follow the line.' McCain's left fist clenched, his right tight around the handle of the revolver, white knuckled.

'Daddy's gone,' Angharad persisted. 'Why should you carry the sins of the father?'

'My daddy was a good man!' McCain shouted, standing and as he did slamming his fists on the table, accidentally firing the still-cocked revolver, an explosive crack and the thud of the pounding of a bullet into the corner of the room. 'Shite! Now, see what you made me do.' McCain turned to Owain. 'Can you not control your bodging bloody woman.'

'Wouldn't know how,' Owain answered.

'Did your daddy hit your mammy, Mr McCain?' Angharad persisted. 'Did you see your daddy hit your mammy? Was he a drinker, your daddy?'

McCain pointed the gun at Angharad, and to Owain he said, 'I tell you, if you can't get yer woman to shut the feck up, I'll shoot her in the nose.'

'Angharad,' Owain said, somewhere between forceful and pleading.

Angharad persisted though. 'If I was some slip of a thing, Owain, he'd force me into one of the bedrooms to relieve his repressed frustrations.'

'Oh, no, no, no, you don't!' McCain took furious offence. 'I see you. I see you now. Don't you try that one on me. That's an old lie. That's an old lie, so it is. I told you. I follow the rules. I always follow the line.'

Sat around the table nobody spoke, spaces were more distracting than faces as even Angharad and Owain avoided eye contact while the twitching McCain drummed the fingers of his left hand on the tabletop and repeatedly cocked and un-cocked the revolver held in his right hand.

The running arpeggios of fingertips broke off, he slammed all the fingers of his left hand down simultaneously, decisively and stood.

Angharad and Owain watched him.

He didn't want to look at them, so he turned away and walked toward the far end of the living room and used the barrel of his gun to create a gap to look out through the venetian blinds. Angharad and Owain continued to watch him. A faint smell from the gunshot could be detected. After several minutes of fraught silence, McCain turned toward them from the corner of the room. 'You're so damn righteous. You know your problem?' His question addressed Angharad. 'You don't think you should have to live by the rules.'

'I don't like those who set the rules,' Angharad replied.

'Well, somebody's got to set them,' McCain asserted. 'If there were no rules, everything would fall apart.'

'Everything has fallen apart,' Angharad replied.

'Which proves we need more rules and more force to make sure the rules are kept by all,' McCain explained.

'What if the rules are wrong?' Owain asked.

'What's wrong,' McCain insisted, 'is when some people get away with not having to follow the rules that everyone else has to follow.'

'You've been outside the city,' Owain said. He glanced at Angharad. 'There are those that make the rules and those that the rules apply to.'

'The rules are there for everyone's good,' McCain replied.

'How do you know?' Owain calmly asked.

'I know.'

'Who told you?' Owain said, standing.

'I didn't need anyone to tell me.'

'Then how did you know?'

McCain looked between Owain and Angharad. 'My mammy and daddy must have told me.'

'Can't you remember?' Angharad stood. 'When did you last see your family, Mr McCain?'

McCain, stood in the corner, lifted the gun and was moving it between Angharad and Owain. He felt cornered by their presence.

'You've become brutalised by all this,' Angharad said. 'That quiet voice you try to block out, Mr McCain, that's your humanity. We're going to walk out the front door and you're going to watch us leave.'

'You can't leave,' McCain said. His command pleaded.

'We're leaving now,' Angharad said.

'You can't leave already.' It was Miller's voice behind them. The front door snapped closed behind him. Angharad and Owain dropped back into their chairs. 'We've got these fish and chips to eat.' Miller dropped a parcel of food wrapped in brown paper on the table in front of Angharad and Owain. 'Doesn't that smell good, hey? He threw in a free saveloy. How about that? Simple acts of human kindness grease the wheels of life.' Miller glanced at McCain in the corner, with the gun held out before him. 'Pull up a chair and join us, McCain. Daddy's home now to straighten things out.' McCain lowered his gun and cautiously sat down next to Miller. Miller chattered merrily on, even as he took his revolver back from McCain and tucked it back in its holster under his jacket. The gabardine trench coat he'd only removed upon arriving at the table, he draped over the back of the chair where he sat. He said, 'Let's eat out of the paper, old school, not bother with the plates.' Passing each person around the table a wrapped fish and chips; the grease of the chips, stained dark patches of the paper. 'Afterall, we don't want to leave Mr bin Salah's lovely apartment with dirty crockery. I was brought up better than that. Standards Mister and Missus Gruffydd, that's what it's all about, standards and deference.'

'And morals,' McCain said.

'Yes, morals are important. Standards, deference and morals; values generally, you might say. These were the watchwords of my upbringing. I always tipped my hat to the policeman, the schoolteacher, the doctor, the postman and the dustman. There used to be respect. Mornings were greeted with the cheery whistle of the postman, pillar of the community. I'd rise to the chink of milk bottles and the whirring of paperboys' bicycle wheels. We could be naughty, sure, we were kids, but we were respectful, not feral as they are today. When we grew up, we knew how to behave, we took responsibility, and we could be trusted with responsibility. These days nobody takes responsibility, it's always someone else's fault, someone else's responsibility.' Miller affected a weary tone but powered on. 'People became entitled. It broke the economy – free meals and free sex with free prophylactics, free everything. It nearly broke the country, all those anything-goes freeloaders.' Miller munched through his chips throughout his mini lecture, the tiny wooden fork repeatedly stabbing at chips chomped and chewed with such open-mouthed relish it seemed to be all part of the theatre for his words. He paused momentarily to encourage the others to eat, grinning, food visible between his teeth, cleaned by a stroke of his tongue across their front, upper and then lower, a momentary pause to poke a crack with the corner of his wooden chip fork and on.

'It's sad what's happened to our country.' Miller's tone shifted melancholy. 'There was a time when we all knew our neighbours and would do anything for them. I remember growing up, in and out of the neighbours' houses, and if your parents heard a neighbour had given you a clip around the ear for being too big for yourself, then your mother, your father or your mother's father, or your father's mother would give you another just to make sure you took the first seriously. Everything changed though.' Miller sighed. 'There was a time when you'd know everybody in your street. You'd know you were on the same side just by looking at them. That's long ago now in London, you're from Wales though, you must know what I'm talking about.'

Angharad and Owain watched him, slowly picking at their chips.

Instead, McCain responded to Miller, 'Carrickfergus was like that.'

'It's not the same,' Miller replied.

McCain began singing, quietly to himself, his growing assurance feeding a growing volume.

'My childhood days bring back sad reflections
Of happy times spent there so long ago
My boyhood friends and my own relations
Have all past on now with the melting snow
So, I'll spend my days in this endless roving

Soft is the grass and shore, and my bed is free
Oh, to be home now in Carrickfergus
On the long road down to the salty sea.'

Miller applauded McCain's performance rapturously. 'Ah, the old songs are the best.' McCain dipped his face, coy of Miller's praise.

Miller encouraged Owain to sing a song with references to Welsh choirs, such that Owain snapped and suggested Miller himself should sing. 'Me? No, no, no, never, no, no. I've no voice at all for singing. I used to dance. My spirit is still willing but my hips and knees and once twinkling toes will have none of it. Everything was simpler then though, wasn't it? You had a brother didn't you, Mr Gruffydd?'

'I've told you. The name's Malcolm Morris, and no, I don't have a brother,' Owain said.

Miller tapped his teeth with the wooden chip fork.

Owain watched.

Miller saw and smiled at him from behind the tapping chip fork. Owain glanced at Angharad.

'His name was Hywel,' Miller said. He laid down the chip fork and pulled a notebook from an inside pocket of his jacket with a flourish. He flicked through a few pages until finding the right one. It was all performance, Angharad thought, and looked over at Owain. 'He was shot along with his wife, well, she wasn't actually his wife. I wonder if they were allowed to be buried together.' Miller looked up, as though waiting for Owain to answer. Then he shrugged, 'doesn't really matter, just curious with them living in sin, as it were. They had a little girl, a bastard I suppose.' Again, Miller looked up. Owain wasn't looking at him, Owain couldn't look at him. Miller glanced over at Angharad. 'We don't have a name. Did she have one?' Miller studied Owain, searched and found his lowered eyes, hiding. 'Your eyes look a little watery, Mr Gruffydd. These are desperate facts.' He shook his head as though in sombre reflection. 'She was shot in crossfire. Apparently, rebels had put them in danger by using them as human shields when the soldiers came.' Again, Miller paused to look at both Owain and Angharad. 'She was shot from the neck, across her abdomen. The loss of blood must have been severe. She was thought to be seven or eight years old, just imagine,' Miller said, keeping his eyes on Owain, 'What sort of person would use a child, a little girl at that, as a human shield?'

In his thick Irish brogue, McCain intoned, 'You murdered that child. If it wasn't for you two, she would be alive today.'

'My name is Malcolm Morris.' Owain struggled to hold the timbre of his voice without the trembling vibrato of his guilt betraying him. 'I don't know of what you speak.'

Owain closed his eyes and he saw her again, lying in the doorway through to the kitchen of the cottage. The soldiers had moved on by that time. Lying on the floor, her tiny form framed in blood, staining her lilac-coloured sweater. Her little left arm seemed to be stretching out, there was a soft toy just out of her reach that she was carrying and dropped when she was shot. Lying there on the cold, hard tiles, it would remain forever out of her reach, stolen from her and discarded. Angharad picked up the soft toy. Owain remembered seeing Angharad clutch it to her chest. Owain dropped to his knees, picked the child from the floor and embraced her, hoping she would come back to life in his arms. But the blood seeped through her sweater from her still warm body. Later, after they buried Hywel, Ceridwen and Rebecca, they had to clean the child's blood from the kitchen floor with a bucket of soapy water and a mop. Angharad did it; she was always stronger than Owain. Angharad told Owain she saw in the blood an impression of the child emerge as she scrubbed the stain, and so she had to keep scrubbing. Owain eventually found Angharad crouching in the corner of the kitchen, still gripping the mop, sobbing.

What can be done with such pain? It can't be reconciled; no meaning can be hewn from it. The pain turns to anger. All other possible reason to live is buried with the dead. It finds fuel in other injustices and cruel brutalities. It propelled Angharad and Owain to this point. Owain looked at Angharad and smiled. It didn't much matter now.

She smiled back. She knew. Their journey was complete. The idea of their future or fate seemed somehow irrelevant, silly even.

A telephone started ringing; the polyphonic ringtone played Elgar. Miller pulled a cell phone from the trench coat draped over the back of his chair. It continued to ring as he searched for it. He scrambled to free his hand from the coat pocket with the phone, so tangled up and anxious was the coat. Miller looked at the phone. 'It's Monty.' He held his hand over the phone. 'I'll take it in the kitchen.'

They all watched Miller close the kitchen door behind him. Only his voice could be heard, not the words, just the sound, and even that became drowned out by the sound of a boiling kettle. 'You'll be in trouble now.' McCain nodded in the direction of the kitchen. 'Monty's called. I wouldn't want to be in your place. Now, the shite will really hit the fan.' He shook his head at Angharad and Owain. 'The walls are going to get well and truly splattered, I can tell you.'

'We're not afraid of Monty,' Owain said.

'Yes, you are.' McCain said, but what he found in Owain's

countenance made him doubt that. 'Well, you should be.'

'Why?' Owain said, his voice tired. 'You can't scare the dead.'

McCain looked at Owain, he wasn't sure how to respond. He said to Angharad, 'What's up wi' him?'

'We're done here,' Angharad said and stood.

'Where are you going?' McCain snapped and glanced toward the kitchen.

Owain stood also and took Angharad's hand. 'It's over, Mr McCain, for us, sure, but for you also. You know about Scotland and the north.'

'What about it?'

'You do know, don't you?' Angharad pressed.

'Of course, I know.' There was a pause in which McCain felt Angharad's eyes on him, testing him, exposing him. 'It's no big deal.'

'You don't know.' Owain sounded genuinely surprised.

'I do know,' McCain replied.

'You don't,' Angharad echoed.

'I do so,' McCain insisted.

'The north is in full revolt, Mr McCain,' Angharad said.

'Lies,' McCain responded.

'Scotland's declared independence,' Owain continued. 'Ireland's gone.'

'You're lying.' McCain stood. 'You're damn liars. You're damn Fenian, papist, lying bastards. You're not going to scare me with talk of some old creed.'

'It was never really about religion, Mr McCain,' Owain said. 'They just told people like you it was.'

'I'm for king and country,' McCain announced.

'The question is which country?' Owain asked.

'What do you mean?' McCain asked. He wiped his palm

across his brow as he waited on their answer.

'They've used you, Mr McCain,' Angharad said. 'You were used to betray your people.'

'I did my duty!' McCain insisted.

'You sold your soul,' Angharad challenged him.

'No!' The kettle began whistling in the kitchen followed by the sound of it crashing against a kitchen wall. Miller returned through the kitchen door.

McCain looked warily at him. 'Was that Monty?'

'It was.' Miller crossed to the table, pulled out a chair and sat without commenting on the others in the room all standing.

'What did he have to say?' Angharad asked. McCain listened keenly. They all slipped quietly back into their seats.

'There is an army of the great unwashed in East London whilst most of the military is in the north putting down rebellions across more than thirty towns and cities,' Miller said. McCain glanced at Angharad and Owain. 'They're supported by the Scotch, of course.' Miller blew out his cheeks.

'Perfidious Pict bastards,' McCain said.

Angharad joked, 'You've got the falcon, at least.'

'Oh, fuck off,' Miller said, his chin collapsing into cupped hands.

'Is Monty coming over?' McCain asked.

'No, there's too much happening.' Angharad and Owain looked at each other and began to wonder if they might get through this. 'We spend weeks, weeks, criss-crossing the country after these two.'

'And their falcon,' McCain agreed.

'It was never about the falcon,' Miller said. McCain looked confused. 'Initially the falcon made Monty curious, that was all. What were Rag, Tag and their friend Bobtail doing with such an artefact. Then of course, it established the link between them and bin Salah.'

'Oh,' McCain said.

'It was bin Salah they were after when we stumbled onto this pair of dunderheads and their revolutionary plans.' Miller turned to Angharad and Owain. 'They've manually over-ridden the gates.' He laughed a short, dry laugh. 'Monty was quite impressed with all that gremlins in the machine stuff. Did you really think they'd not notice?'

Angharad shrugged and said, 'We all do our bit and hope for the best.'

'They've already got plans to meet your peasants' army when it amasses at Victoria Park, even the prime minister's going down, so I hear. Once the peasants see the city secure and un-breached, and the security troops and drones overhead, they'll scatter.'

'Either that or they'll end up buried beneath bloody Victoria Park,' McCain said. 'So, What now?'

'We'll wrap this up and then...' Miller didn't complete the sentence. He didn't know what would happen then. Instead, a different thought occurred to him. 'Monty did have one question. The American, Luca Chimera, where does he fit in?' Angharad and Owain said nothing. 'Ah, well,' Miller sighed and pressed on his knees to stand. 'It'll all come out in the wash. Let's go, hey.'

McCain stood. 'Come on. You heard Mr Miller. Time to go.'

'What if we refuse?' Angharad asked.

'We have a car,' McCain answered her. 'It's a big car and it's downstairs.'

Standing, Owain warned Miller. 'They'll bury you.'

'Maybe,' Miller replied. 'But then it'll be in the freshly turned earth over your dead bodies. Come on.'

XXXI

The crowds spilling from Victoria Park became frantic and chaotic as the drones swept overhead, dropping gas canisters and strafing the park in gunfire. Esme saw people fall as the crowds fled. She stopped and gazed back, transfixed. It was Davey that tugged her sleeve and shook her back to life as the crowds brushed by. With Sarah-May, Gavin and Francie they ran until caught between pursuing troops and crossfire on the intersection of Roman Road and St Stephen's Road. Troops were hunting rebels into the surrounding boroughs, and more troops were joining them through the gates along the wall on Grove Road.

Esme crouched behind a dumpster with bullets firing and ricocheting. In a break in the gunfire, they followed Francie along a narrow alley and over a barbed-wire trimmed wall at the end. Gavin, perched atop the wall, pulled the barbed wire away as much as he could. Esme dropped down the other side of the wall, turning her ankle as she landed but not pausing to address its cry as they raced on down another narrow road. There were scratches on Esme's hands and one across her neck where thin scab tracts traced the barbwire.

Some people were taking refuge in the Gurdwara Sikh Sangat, off Harley Grove, but there was already fighting in nearby streets and no way through. Across the grounds of an abandoned school and onto Tower Hamlets Cemetery Park, where Gavin finally paused, and Francie permitted them a breather. In a far corner of the cemetery, huddled in the hollow behind the exposed roots of an ancient tree, Francie told Esme, Sarah-May and Davey to wait. 'You can make your own way, o' course, but if you wait here, we'll come back for you.'

Evening grew dark and in that silent waiting Esme recognised how hungry she was. She rubbed her swelling ankle. The crowds of discontented barbarians passed through. Somebody stopped to piss against a tree close to where they were hiding. He didn't see them and was laughing over his shoulder with a couple of other people while his piss arced and sprayed, steaming.

Through the night the echoes of gunfights sounded more distant, breaking up in the suburbs like rainclouds hitting mountains. Sarah-May was crying, silently. She shook her head when Esme asked if she wanted to talk and hugged Esme's waist. They barely spoke for fear in the whispering silence. Bats fluttered in the trees above them and there was an occasional owl's hoot. In the darkness there was no way for Esme to measure fear and all thoughts reached their end.

Esme heard her name being called as a loud whisper along with the names of Davey and Sarah-May. Francie and Gavin had returned. 'Come on. We'll go now before light breaks. It's quiet, but morning will bring turmoil.'

Beneath an old rail bridge on Knapp Road were a couple slumped. They could've been violent, or they could just have been a pair of smacked-out bums, either way Esme followed the others in allowing plenty of space to avoid a potential lurch as she passed them. Their path would frequently be littered with thousands of fragments of glass where shop windows had been smashed in the riots. They followed Violet Road as far as the Limehouse Cut, where Francie led them down steps under a bridge by the Spratt's Patent Limited old red-brick warehouses.

At the foot of the steps was a small area of gravel-covered waste ground before the towpath of a narrow channel that connected the Thames with the River Lea. Beneath rubbish and a draped tarpaulin was an upside-down rowboat. Davey helped Francie and Gavin turn it over on a whispered heave of three. Esme looked up and down the canal; a disconsolate, single gull sat some way along the tow path.

Then there was a pattering of feet and two silhouettes appeared down the steps.

All froze, even the two new figures, and in those searching, suspicious looks, each tried to gauge the other. They were a man and a woman, she stepped forward. 'The boat.' Esme noticed she carried a crossbow in one hand. It was clear to Esme that they had both been involved in fighting.

The man behind her held his left leg tentatively and limped. He held his hands out together holding a revolver. 'We need the boat.' His accent was northern.

'Put the gun down,' Francie demanded. He strode toward them and stood, feet apart, hands on hips. 'You won't get far rowing the state you're in. Put the gun down and we'll talk.'

The woman looked back at her associate, and he lowered the gun. 'Will you take us upriver with you?' She looked back over her shoulders. 'Troops will sweep through here soon. Not just from the park. We come from the battles inside the walls.' Francie folded his arms over his vast chest as he listened. 'The city's burning, sacked by riots. The Woke have taken over.'

'The Woke?' Esme asked. Francie glanced back at her, surprised to hear her voice.

'My name's Willow Walwyn. This is John Lilburne,' The woman said. She laid her crossbow aside and they heaved the boat onto the water, and as they rowed up the Thames, the night melted into morning.

'So, what's your story?' Francie asked.

'They'd been preparing for weeks, in tunnels under the city. It was all planned to coincide with the Great March and the risings in the north,' Willow Walwyn explained. 'We had hundreds down there. They didn't see us coming. Lilburne and I went up top before it all began. We had to meet our colleagues. They'd set viruses in the administration's systems,' Willow Walwyn said. 'The electric street buses malfunctioned, the underground shuttle trains were knocked out and the traffic lights just flickered between all the colours.'

John Lilburne cut in, 'The stores and cafes were open and debit cards still worked, and there was quiet, weekend worship at the glass temples of commerce. People groaned with the technical problems like they were familiarity and the entitlement of people used to others performing the anonymous, invisible tasks of maintaining a functioning city.' As he spoke, Esme observed him remove his boot and rub his swollen ankle, crossed over his other knee. 'That dawn the garbage hadn't been collected and the streets weren't swept as municipal workers announced a wildcat strike in solidarity with those rallying at the so-called People's March.'

The boat turned from the Limehouse Cut onto the Thames. The sky was blue with a low sun. On the banks of the Thames gathered gulls cawed from a rubbish pile. Esme could hear what sounded like gunfire and explosions bursting in the distance like a storm. Behind were columns of smoke over the city. A series of explosions had caused the Shard to come crashing down, the Gherkin and Leadenhall buildings also had fires burning across many floors. Willow Walwyn said the financial district had been targeted. 'The politicians are puppets. If you want to bring the system down you've got to destroy the palaces of their pay-masters.'

Sarah-May was asleep, exhausted. Davey rowed. Esme

sat next to Francie in the rowboat listening to Willow Walwyn and John Lilburne. 'We took a small group of three dozen to take control of the BBC. Whilst its token security surrendered immediately, its labyrinthine interior meant that for hours we roamed the corridors, people scattering before us. Engineers in control rooms were forced at gun point to prepare studios, where trembling presenters, their fixed botoxed faces smiling before frightened eyes, were forced to make impromptu broadcasts declaring Hereward had seized power. The revolution would be live televised.' Willow gazed across the river. 'Our friends should have met us there.'

'Your friends?' Esme asked.

'Yes, Angharad and Owain. We'd shared an apartment with them in the city in the weeks that preceded the attack. When they weren't there to rendezvous with us at the BBC, we left our unit to take the Google and Facebook buildings and snuck back inside the apartment block, hoping to find some clue.'

'Did you find anything?' Esme asked. Willow shook her head.

'There was no point lingering at the apartment,' Lilburne added, he glanced at Willow. 'If Angharad and Owain were caught, agents would have set the apartment as a trap for any who may come looking.'

'We snuck out the maintenance stairs,' Willow explained. 'When we re-joined our unit at the Google building, fires were already engulfing it with people trapped inside.' She sighed and rubbed her brow. 'It was awful. Complete mayhem.'

'The city was laid to waste,' Lilburne confirmed. 'When the city gates were breached, more people spilled in from the suburbs, the slums and the ghettoes. The first waves of militia to rise from the tunnels were those who had been with Hereward for longer, they attacked the targets as planned. They burst into the Ministry of Defence, rounded up the ministers and generals and took control of operation rooms. Hereward was stoned out of his mind and believed a fantasy he projected onto the collapsing world around him.'

'I remember him. He came to my town in the Fens,' Esme said.

Lilburne continued as though Esme's words were just ambient sounds. 'The second waves of militants were those that had swelled their ranks in recent weeks. They almost immediately abandoned the agreed targets and began rampaging through the city. From Down Street, they attacked the hotels and shops of Mayfair and Knightsbridge. Two dozen or so burst into the Playboy Club and Crockfords on Curzon Street, commandeering for their use and pleasure the games and the whores there. Buildings throughout Knightsbridge and Mayfair burnt from Molotov cocktails and other home-made explosives. They rampaged in units of about half a dozen where four would threaten and attack while two amongst them filled trolleys with the spoils of their raids. There were loud cheers and laughter as steel shutters were stripped away. Rebels who entered in rags left in designer fashions worth more than their entire lives. The many jewellers of Mayfair were cleared out, rebels festooned in rings, necklaces, brooches, earrings and even tiaras, sparkling in the warm, wet light of summer were a garish spectacle.'

The Thames Estuary brought a morning tide that rocked their boat as it crawled along the shoreline. The rest of the travellers' party were re-grouping at Fobbinge and that was also where Bella had remained, with the hermits at St Michael's Church. Willow Walwyn and John Lilburne said that it was as good as anywhere and that they would make their way from there also.

From her sleeping, dreaming, Sarah-May stirred. Esme touched her forearm. 'I was thinking of Luca.' Esme didn't know what to say, so she just smiled. 'I guess I'll not see him again. He'll be on his way back to America with that man.' The two who'd joined them, sitting opposite, looked at each other. 'I think I should be glad he's safe.' Sarah-May furrowed her brow. 'You do think he's safe, don't you?'

'Yes.' Esme didn't know. 'I'm sure he is.'

'Luca, of course,' Lilburne said. 'I remember you now. You were at that meeting in the cellar of the pub when Luca, the American, told his story.' When Sarah-May looked up, there was a tear trail down her cheek.

'Did something happen to him?' Lilburne asked, looking around the faces on the boat. 'I heard people were after him.'

'Why did they want him?' Sarah-May asked. Lilburne was going to say more but as his eyes met Francie, he hesitated again.

Francie interjected before Lilburne had a chance. 'It seems Luca knew lots of folks for one lying low, wouldn't you say?' Then with glances at Gavin and Davey, he said. 'These boys are starting to tire. What say, as our new friends are injured, I take Gavin's oar, and you two take your man Davey's oar. You'll have time to share your stories when we reach Fobbinge.'

Esme and Sarah-May shared Davey's heavy oar. Nobody spoke for some time, and, later when odd comments did grow into quiet conversation, nobody spoke of Luca, or the burning ruins of London.

XXXII

They'd left the Thames Estuary and were creeping back along the creek to Fobbinge. 'Two crimes, you said.' Sarah-May suddenly spoke to Francie. 'That other man knew what you meant.' She referred to Eben at Gunmaker's Gate Bridge. Gavin, pulling an oar, looked at Francie, curious what he'd say.

'That's right,' Francie said. 'Everything's so political these days. Folk can get blinded to the human.'

'What do you mean?' Sarah-May asked.

Francie searched for a memory and accompanying thought in the mid-distance. 'I'd a cousin, but we're a close family so we were closer than that. Her name was Morna. I don't know if Luca mentioned her.'

Sarah-May confirmed he had.

'Morna ...' Francie's voice caught in his throat. 'I found her body.' He coughed to clear his throat.

'Why are you telling me this?' Sarah-May asked.

'Did Luca tell you about the girl in the hotel?'

'Yes,' Sarah-May said. She looked around at Esme for confirmation.

'He didn't tell us that part. Not how she died, strangled with a ribbon tied tight around her throat.' Sarah-May's face fell into her palms with Francie's next comment. 'Our Morna was also strangled. I found her body wearing nothing but a ribbon, like a lass might use to tie her hair back, wound around her neck with the bruises it made.'

Sarah-May moaned the word 'no', muffled by her hands over her mouth.

'I didn't see any other signs of violence.' Francie brooded on his thoughts, and when he spoke, he was far away, his grief washed in the tears of Sarah-May's sobbing. 'I think he must have been behind her.' Francie gazed at what he imagined in front of him, the space where another should be.

'I want you to know that I liked Luca. We all did.' Francie glanced back at Gavin, who nodded. 'One night, on our travels, we were talking. Just him and me, like.' Sarah-May looked up with sore eyes – she couldn't not listen. 'He told me something. I don't think he meant to. Sometimes he'd talk a little too much because he liked telling stories, you know, and we were drinking freely.'

Sarah-May laughed, snot bubbled from her nostril that she wiped away with her sleeve and a sniff. 'He was a good storyteller.' Francie allowed the hint of a smile, bitter but as one admitting the charms of a villain. 'He liked the way that we were a family who looked out for each other. His own parents split when he was young. He told me when he was thirteen, he walked in on his dad having sex with some girl. Luca said his father didn't see him, but the girl did. He told me how their eyes held for some moments. Luca said there was a red ribbon the girl must have used to tie her hair back that Luca's father had used to bind her wrists to the bedstead. It was a sad tale, but we all have sad tales. It was when I found Morna's body with a red ribbon around her neck that I remembered it.' Francie brushed his own neck lightly with his hand imitating the ribbon. 'I liked him,' Francie repeated. 'We all did.'

A low sun lit along the creek, bright beams striking out between trees. Somebody must have seen their boat from further up the creek, for below St Michael's Church of Fobbinge, stood on the smugglers' decking at Worm End were Mother Michael,

Neddie and Sarah-May's mam, now dressed like those with her in grey robe. Sarah-May gasped with relief upon seeing Bella, who held Sarah-May not just pleased by her return but as only a mother can know their child's pain.

Mother Michael studied Willow Walwyn and John Lilburne as they climbed out of the boat. 'Have you hurt your leg, John?'

'Foot. Yes,' he replied, smiling at her through the grimace.

'Silly boy,' Mother Michael replied. 'And are you also injured, Willow.'

'Not severely.'

'No,' Mother Michael confirmed. 'Well let's get you all inside, we'll treat your wounds, and you can tell me about those less fortunate.'

EPILOGUE

For two days they remained in Fobbinge. People fleeing London brought accounts that the fires of revolution were running out of oxygen and the state would survive. Then, many speculated, the retributions would begin.

Sarah-May and Bella remained in Fobbinge when Esme and Davey returned north with the travellers' caravan. Willow Walwyn and John Lilburne came with them though, appreciating the cover the travellers afforded them.

A few days later, they camped several miles from Fenby. In the early hours, Davey reprised his owl hoot to rouse Mrs Quickfall, with Esme looking about the quiet street. Eventually Mrs Quickfall's face appeared at an upstairs window. 'Esme,' she whispered. 'And Davey. You're back then.'

Mrs Quickfall fed them tea and slices of slices of bread and blackcurrant jam, while she listened to their adventures and tales of the sacking of London, rebels, gypsies and the fate of Luca. 'You will have to face your father,' Mrs Quickfall said to Esme. 'And young Tom Jr, the mayor's boy. You will need to speak with him.' It had been her dad Esme feared confronting on her return. Tom Jr didn't provoke the same fear. Even the fear that she would be forced to marry him had diminished; not because she had warmed to the notion but because she knew now that she couldn't be forced. 'So,' Mrs Quickfall continued with a glance including Davey in her next question, 'do you intend to take root back in the sticky ground of the Fens, or will you come and go, like the eel, returning with the seasons.'

Esme shrugged and looked at Davey. He looked back at her as

one happy to wait for instruction.

'Good,' Mrs Quickfall said lowering her cup to the saucer she held on her lap. 'Might I suggest how you could proceed next?'

'I'd be grateful,' Esme said, and so, she and Davey followed Mrs Quickfall's plan. 'First you must both go home, where there are concerns that need alleviating. Davey will then find the mayor's son and ask him to meet Esme privately. Davey will take you to rendezvous with Tom Jr." Mrs Quickfall looked them both over, dishevelled as children called in from play. 'Right, let's turn some mountains back into molehills.'

When Esme appeared inside the backdoor of the pump house, Lizzie smiled, and Esme felt more pleased to see her than she would've imagined. Her dad stared at her some moments before saying, 'Pull up a chair then girl. Lizzie, fetch Es a cuppa.'

In the morning Esme told Lizzie her story while they pegged up the washing, and when her dad returned at lunch, Lizzie acted as Esme's intermediary with him. Esme wondered if some vestige of Lizzie's own youthful adventures flavoured her willingness to support Esme. 'Blasted old Mrs Quickfall,' Esme's dad said and, 'If you don't mind out, you'll only be left with Davey bloody Clay. And you won't find it much fun a decade hence nursing his idiot children.' He looked her over, there was a smile lurking behind his severe tone. 'Well, have you nothing to say?'

Esme shrugged.

He swilled the tea in his mug. 'We'll speak of this again.' Esme nodded.

Davey was in the yard behind Esme's dad's shoulder, nervous of coming to the back door, shifting from foot to foot, hoping to catch Esme's eye through the window. Her dad had already noticed him. 'Davey seems to be waiting for you.' Esme looked but didn't smile, she felt herself wait for her dad's permission. 'Go, and we'll talk of what's to be done this evening.'

Tom Jr was waiting. He looked up at Esme's approach. 'I need to speak to Tom on my own,' Esme said to Davey. 'I'll meet you tonight, at the old car.'

Esme sat beside Tom. 'Hello,' he said, and it was clear to Esme from his tone that he carried no judgement of her. 'It's nice to see you.'

Esme explained, slowly but with barely a pause until she'd got it all out. Sat side by side, they avoided eye contact as she explained about the state agent in inferences. When she was done, they sat some moments more, neither talking. Eventually, it was Esme who asked of him, 'Did you really want to marry me? I mean really, rest of our lives and all that.'

Tom seemed to think about his answer. 'I've never felt the same need to escape as you. I've never felt quite as trapped. Maybe I lack your imagination, Miss Esme, but I can't wish for things I can't imagine.'

Esme smiled as he moved his eyes to meet hers. 'Don't call me Miss Esme, please. Just Esme.'

'Esme,' he said. 'I'd like for us to stay in touch. I have thought of you often and will continue to. I would not want you to feel trapped in marriage with me. I admire you, Esme. I admire your spirit. I hope that one day I might give you reason to admire me.' In that moment, Esme did admire Tom, and saw him with her own eyes as she never had previously.

She asked, 'What about your parents?'

'They're my parents.' He stood. Esme instinctively followed. 'I know you found them intimidating, but they are good people. They'll come to understand.'

'And you?' Esme asked. 'Will you marry another now?'

'No. Not this year, at least,' Tom replied. 'Maybe next. I'll see.' And he smiled at her, and she returned it before their timidity turned each other away.